FRIDAYS AT
ENRICO'S

FRIDAYS AT
ENRICO'S

DON CARPENTER

FINISHED AND WITH AN AFTERWORD
BY JONATHAN LETHEM

COUNTERPOINT
BERKELEY

Library of Congress Cataloging-in-Publication Data
Carpenter, Don.
Fridays at Enrico's : a novel / Don Carpenter;
[edited, with introduction, by] Jonathan Lethem.
pages cm
ISBN 978-1-61902-301-7 (hardback)
1. Beat generation—Fiction. 2. Authors, American—20th century—Fiction. 3. San Francisco (Calif.)—History—20th century—Fiction. 4. Portland (Ore.)—History—20th century—Fiction. I. Lethem, Jonathan. II. Title.
PS3553.A76F85 2014
813'.54—dc23
2013043960

COUNTERPOINT
1919 Fifth Street
Berkeley, CA 94710
www.counterpointpress.com

Printed in the United States of America
Distributed by Publishers Group West

10 9 8 7 6 5 4 3 2 1

CONTENTS

FRIDAYS AT
ENRICO'S

PART ONE

Jaime and Charlie

1.

Jaime and Charlie got married in a log chapel in South Lake Tahoe the night before their last finals. Heading back to San Francisco the next day, hung over and drinking bottles of Miller's, Charlie decided that college was a fraud, and although he was one final from a master's degree, an easy final, he was damned if he would take the damned test. Charlie wasn't driving. He didn't have the strength. Jaime was erect behind the wheel, barely able to see over it, only five feet tall, her nose up, her bloodshot blue eyes hidden behind dark glasses, the hot wind blowing her blonde, almost white hair. She was nineteen years old.

"I'm not gonna take that goddamn final," he said. He had seen through college. The time, he now realized with hungover chagrin, would have been better spent just lying around reading. He explained this to his new bride as they drove across the flat hot Sacramento Valley.

"Or I could just veer into the oncoming traffic," she said, after he finished.

Charlie rummaged around in the glove compartment, looking for something to take away the pain. Beer was not enough. He found an Alka-Seltzer in its ragged foil package. It would help, if he could find a way to get it down. He thought about crumbling it and dropping the fragments into his bottle of beer. He thought about putting the wafer on his tongue and taking a big swig. He thought about James Joyce's "Grace" and smiled.

"Are you serious?" Jaime asked him.

"About what?" he asked.

She loved Charlie, but in many ways he was a big baby. He had the nicest smile she had ever seen, wide, bland, easy, the smile of a man who had seen some life and enjoyed what he saw. Charlie was one of the Korean War veterans in the department. He was writing a long novel about his experiences in the war. He was self-educated but brilliant, and everyone thought that of them all, Charlie was the one who would probably become famous. Not that any of that mattered to Jaime. She knew herself to be a better writer than Charlie, but she lacked his life experiences. They had fallen together quite naturally. Charlie sat behind her in Walter Van Tilburg Clark's literature class. It had been Jaime's first day of classes at San Francisco State and she was nervous. Walter Clark, a big bear of a man wearing a faded old sweatshirt instead of the usual suit and tie, was telling the thirty students in front of him which books they would be reading. Jaime was trying to take notes, but she smelled liquor breath coming from behind her and for some reason it irritated her. She turned to glare at Charlie.

"Would you please not sigh so loud?" she heard herself saying to this smiling man of about thirty.

"Sorry," he said. His voice was thrillingly deep. She could not help noticing the legal-sized pad of yellow paper on which he was drawing cartoon pictures of naked women. She raised an eyebrow to let him know what she thought of his art abilities, and turned back to her note-taking. After class as she was walking out of the HSS Building into the small courtyard facing Nineteenth Avenue, Charlie caught up to her. He was dressed in an old fatigue jacket, jeans, and dirty motorcycle boots. San Francisco State in 1959 was pretty informal. Most of the students worked part- or even full-time, and a lot were vets, but Charlie really looked like a bum. His dark brown hair was too long and seemed barely combed, but when he spoke to her in his deep friendly voice, Jaime felt something.

"You read any of them books?"

At just that moment they broke out into the open sunlight and for no reason at all, Jaime felt wonderful, no longer lonely.

"You mean *Moby Dick*? Have I read *Moby Dick*?"

"Yeah, and them others. *Passenger to India*? You read that?"

Jaime stopped walking and turned toward him, holding her books up to her chest. He smiled down at her like a friendly old dog. She was about to correct him when she decided he was putting her on. Why this should thrill her she did not know. She laughed and they sat down on one of the concrete benches in the patio and shared her last cigarette. Their Clark class was the last class of the day for both of them on Tuesday and Thursday afternoons. They began meeting before class, out on the patio. After a few weeks of sitting together talking Jaime realized that Charlie did not know her name. He called her "Babe," but he probably called most women "Babe."

"My name is Jaime Froward," she said one day just as they were walking into class. She spelled it for him.

"That's great," he said. "I'm Charlie Monel." He reached out and shook her hand warmly. She could not tell if he was putting her on or not. In class Charlie never volunteered, never spoke up, just sat, head bent, drawing pictures in his notebook. By midterm she had no idea whether he was paying attention or not. The midterm exam was a single essay question, the hardest kind of test. Jaime chose to write about *Death Comes for the Archbishop*, and filled three little blue books with her precise handwriting. She had sweated freely while writing, which was a good sign. When finished she turned to see Charlie bent over his blue book, scribbling, his face an inch from the paper, pencil clutched awkwardly in his hand. He seemed to be writing furiously. The bell rang. Jaime turned in her books and walked out of the class. Charlie and a couple of the others were still writing. She went out to the patio and sat down, lighting a Pell Mell, as she liked to call them, and waited. He came out nearly twenty minutes later, his face bland, hair all over the place. He grinned at her and sat down.

"Got a smoke?"

She handed him her pack. "What did you write on?" she asked.

"*Moldy Dick*," he said. "It's mah favorite book."

When the midterms came back, Jaime was infuriated to find that she had gotten only a B+. Charlie had gotten an A and a whole column of comments from Clark, in his tiny blue pencil script. The only thing Clark had written on Jaime's book was, "You have a nice appreciation of Cather."

"Can I read your paper?" she asked Charlie. She knew her face was red with anger. Back at Drew she had been the best literature student they ever had, or so they told her.

They sat down on the bench and read each other's midterms. Charlie's was hard to read. His handwriting was messy, as if he had taught himself how to write. But once she caught on, she read his essay with fascination and some envy. Charlie's style was exuberant and his ideas sharp, she decided. Although he was pretty crude. She finished while Charlie was still concentrating on hers. He moved his lips as he read, something she had always made fun of, but now realized wasn't funny but touching, even charming. He stopped. "Yours is better," he said. He smiled painfully.

She felt a stab of pleasure. "Then how come you got the A and I got the B plus?" she asked, wishing she hadn't.

"Beats the shit outta me," he said with a shrug.

"Well, at least we didn't flunk," she said.

"You wanna come over to my place?" he asked, looking right at her, for once not smiling. This was the moment she had been waiting for all semester. The pass, at last. She'd turn him down gently. After all, he had liked her midterm.

"Well okay, sure," she heard herself saying. "Where do you live?"

2.

Charlie lived in North Beach, on Genoa Place, between Union and Green, halfway up Telegraph Hill. The apartment was small, two rooms separated by a half wall, two big windows looking out over the alley. Still, it was a nice view, with each of the apartments across the street a different pastel color and plenty of bright blue sky when it wasn't foggy. In late 1958 when Charlie moved in, the place had been a terrible mess. The former tenant had been an amphetamine dealer. The place smelled of stale Chinese cabbage and leaky plumbing. The little toilet was filthy and nobody had cleaned the walls or under the fixtures in years. The apartment was covered with tattered layers of old wallpaper, paint splatters, dried-on food, and other things Charlie couldn't recognize. The story was that the amps dealer had committed suicide by taking barbiturates. He lay down on his smelly old mattress, expecting to die, but a couple of acquaintances from the Hot Dog Palace down on Columbus came knocking and, when he didn't answer, broke in with a screwdriver. They hoped to find amphetamines but found the dealer instead, barely breathing. According to the story, they ransacked the place anyway and found the stash, outfit and all. They shot up right there, and as a humanitarian gesture, shot speed into the dealer's arm. He woke up later to find his stash gone and a long explanatory note written on a paper bag.

After getting rid of the dealer's junk, Charlie washed the floor and walls, scraped and repainted the wooden floor, and removed the paint from the woodwork and the wallpaper from the plaster. He spent three days cleaning the stove and the little refrigerator. He stained the wood and whitewashed the plaster. The place began to look and smell wonderful. He bought a cot and mattress from the army surplus store on Stockton, kitchen things from Figone Hardware on Grant, unpacked his cardboard suitcase, unrolled his sleeping bag on the mattress, unpacked his books and put them up on orange crates, and was home. The amps dealer had finally succeeded in killing himself by going out to Land's End after filling up on barbiturates, and sitting watching the ocean until he went out. When they found the body he had the phone number of the city morgue in his pocket.

Charlie's car was a 1940 De Soto sedan, pale gray and rusty, but a good old reliable car. He and Jaime spent the twenty-minute drive from State to North Beach talking about school. All very noncommittal. He parked on Union just above Grant. He wondered if he should run around the car and open the door for Jaime. She had been awfully quiet on the drive. Charlie didn't try to hustle her with a lot of bright stuff, and now that they were in North Beach he wondered why he had brought her with him at all. She was damned good-looking, that was why. He smiled as innocently as he could and said, "Well, here we are."

"I think I better go home," she said in a small voice.

Charlie felt relieved. He didn't want to seduce some poor damn nineteen-year-old girl if she didn't want to be seduced.

"Where do you live?" Charlie asked.

"On Washington, near Fillmore," she said. "I can take the bus."

"No," he said. "We're here now, come on in, have a cup of tea, and I'll drive you on home."

She said nothing so he got out and came around to open the door for her. Their eyes met as she got out. Hers were very large and blue, the color of the sky. They regarded him evenly, intelligently, even speculatively.

"Hi," he said to the eyes.

"Hi," she said back to him. He kissed her lightly.

"Come on, it's just up the alley."

"I'll leave my stuff in your car." They walked side-by-side up the narrow slanting alley.

She liked his apartment. She had expected—dreaded—a messy little place, but found herself in a monk's cell. There were no pictures on the wall, no brave posters or photographs, only a wall of books. There was the cot, with a brown army blanket under the neatly zipped sleeping bag, and a bare table and old wooden kitchen chair, obviously where he wrote, with a cardboard box underneath filled with manuscript. On the divider between the rooms, there was an old tin alarm clock ticking away and a water glass with some fresh nasturtium leaves and flowers.

"Oh, I love it," she said. "How much?"

"Forty-five a month," he said. He went through the arch into the kitchen. "Do you want tea? I have Lipton's or Japanese green tea."

"Lipton's is fine." There was no place to sit except at his little table. Or she could just undress and lie on the bed. He could come out and find her naked. Surprise! Actually, she had no intention of sleeping with him, at least not today. He didn't seem like the kind of man who would just push her down and take her. She felt safe. She went over to the books.

"You have great books," she called to him.

"Mostly junk from McDonald's," he said. "You know the place I'm talkin' about? Down on Turk Street?"

"In the Tenderloin?"

He came out with the tea things, a brass teapot and two little Japanese terra cotta cups. "It's the best used bookstore in town. They got thousands of books, and nobody down there knows the value of anything. Hemingway, fifty cents, Melville, fifty cents, Norman Vincent Peale, fifty cents. It's all fifty cents to those guys."

They drank their tea and talked about books. Charlie had a little radio in the kitchen, and he turned it on. Cool jazz quietly filled the air and Jaime relaxed. As they talked she waited for him to make a move. She wondered if he was good at seducing girls. She hoped so, because she was shy. At least she thought of herself as shy. She felt a little shy right now. Waiting. Her own boyfriend, whose name was Bill Savor, no longer appealed to her. He was a boyfriend out of default. There were no similarities between Bill Savor and Charlie Monel. Bill was a student, but not in the Language Arts program, even though he wanted to be a writer. Instead he majored in Education, so he'd have a junior college teaching certificate to fall back on. If you had something to fall back on, you certainly would fall back. To hell with that. All or nothing. More like Charlie—or was she romanticizing Charlie?

"Are you a romantic? Or a realist?" she asked him abruptly.

"About what?"

"My boyfriend's a realist."

"If you have a boyfriend, maybe you better leave," Charlie said, but he didn't look as if he wanted her to leave. He'd just called her bluff, is all.

"No, I mean, he's a writer, but, you know, he doesn't think there's any money in it, so he's studying to be a teacher." Blah blah blah. Her face was reddening, she was certain. When was he going to make a pass? Never?

"Why are you so worried about it?" he asked her. It was as if he had broken into her thoughts.

"What do you mean?"

"I ain't going to make a pass at you," he said. "If you like me then we can just get undressed and go to bed. Nobody has to seduce anybody."

He grinned and sipped his tea. She grinned back, pressing her fingers together in her lap. "That's how I feel too," she said. "Well, I guess I better be getting home. I'll take the bus, you're all home and comfortable now."

"Naw, I'll drive you."

"You don't want to lose your parking space. I know how hard it is to park in North Beach. We come over here on weekends, you know. Driving around half the night looking for some place to park . . ."

Charlie listened to her blathering and wondered why he didn't just make a grab for her. But he didn't. He stood up, took her hands into his, looked down into those big blue eyes and told her he would now drive her home. Did he see disappointment? He wasn't sure.

3.

After North Beach, Jaime's family home out on the lower lip of Pacific Heights seemed tame and middle-class, stifling. The house itself was beautiful. She loved the house. It was one of those carpenter Victorians with an ornate false front, angular bay windows showing a lot of white lace curtain, false Doric columns on either side of the little front porch at the top of a flight of false wooden steps. The house was painted a pale yellow, and all the trim, columns, and trellises on either side of the steps were painted white. Red roses grew up over the trellises, and western calla lilies crowded the border next to the house, behind a tiny ragged patch of lawn. The house was on a block of half-respectable two-story houses, some of them cut into small apartments, but all neatly kept-up behind a parking strip row of big leafy red flowering eucalyptus trees. Jaime had lived there all her life except the first year, when they lived out in the Sunset, which she didn't remember. And for most of her life she had treacherously wished the family fortunes would improve enough for them to move north, up over the ridge, into Pacific Heights proper, where the really rich lived.

But her father, her poor old drunken father, worked as a reporter for the San Francisco Chronicle, and as Jaime grew up and began to understand life, she also began to understand that her family was never going to join the rich, no matter how much she and her mother wanted them to. Her father, it turned out, was the wrong kind of writer.

Jaime dragged herself up the steps after Charlie let her off with a grin and a "See ya!" She did not get over to North Beach that often. She knew it was where most of the writers hung out, and for that reason she tried to avoid it. But there was a fascination, she had to admit. Charlie was attractive, too, but much too old for her, there were already wrinkles around the corners of his eyes. Pale eyes. Pale brown, almost green. Nice eyes. And he wrote well, though messily and with some of the worst spelling she'd ever seen. Somehow his terrible spelling made her feel good. She was one of those people who could spell.

She loved her front door. It was a thick heavy door, painted white, with a massive old brass decorated doorknob and a brass knocker just below the beveled glass windows. It was substantial, a door of respect. Jaime opened it with her Schlage key of respect. Inside, as usual, the house was cool and quiet, smelling of fresh flowers and floor wax. "Mom?" No answer. Her mother was out playing bridge. That was fine. Jaime loved having the place to herself. Her brother, now twenty-five, was living in Taipan, working for the government, and Jaime had taken his room, upstairs overlooking the backyard. She trudged up the stairs holding her books to her chest. The wallpaper showed country scenes, hunting scenes, from Victorian England, she supposed. The stairs were carpeted with a Persian runner and the hand railing was polished dark wood. All so respectable. There was even a chandelier of real crystals in the front hall. Why did Charlie's monastic little apartment make her feel jealous?

Her room was bigger than Charlie's whole apartment, with neat twin beds side by side, a little desk with her Hermes portable typewriter, an overstuffed chair covered in a flowered print, and a bridge lamp behind it where she sat and read. She had her own bookshelves, which of course couldn't compete with her parents' grand library downstairs, with the Hemingway, Faulkner, Steinbeck, and Fitzgerald first editions in their glass cabinet, and the big signed Picasso etching over the funny purple brick fireplace. Riches she found herself rejecting, in favor of Charlie's freedom.

What would she ever be able to write about? She took out her midterm blue books. B+. Maybe she wasn't as talented as she'd hoped. Walter Van Tilburg Clark ought to know. He was the most respected of the writer-teachers at State. He had written *The Ox-Bow Incident*, a classic western story Jaime didn't happen to like very much, even though it was beautifully written. She liked instead Clark's story about Hook the Hawk. She had heard around school that Clark had thrown the finished story into his wastebasket, and his wife had fished it out and sent it to the *Atlantic Monthly*, and that he had also thrown away the final draft of *Ox-Bow*, which his wife dutifully fished out of the wastebasket and sent to Random House. Clark apparently suffered from these bouts of depression, where he thought his work stank badly enough to throw away. Jaime knew the feeling. In fact, it was coming over her now.

She heard the thump of the front door and assumed her mother was home. She undressed and was walking naked down the hall to take her shower when she saw her father coming up the stairs. She shrieked and ran back into her bedroom. "Daddy!" she screamed. With the door safely shut she gathered her wits and laughed. I'm so cool, she thought. Properly dressed in her old pink chenille bathrobe she ventured out of her room again. Her father was in the master bedroom, lying on the bed, fully dressed except for his jacket. He lay on his back, looking at the ceiling. He was a short plump man with round rimmed silver glasses, blue-and-white-striped shirt, a bright red knit tie, yellow-and-green-striped suspenders, oxford gray pants, and cordovan wingtip shoes buffed to a creamy shine. Jaime loved her father, but she knew he was drunk. Otherwise, why would he be home?

"I'm sorry I screamed at you," she said.

He did not look at her. Instead he pursed his lips tightly and breathed heavily through his nose. The heavy smell of liquor floated through the room.

"Day off?" she asked brightly.

"I got fired," her father said grimly. Jaime laughed and went into the bathroom to take her shower. She had the water running and was just stepping in when she realized he was not being sarcastic. He really had been fired. In an instant she saw it all going up in smoke, the house, the family, college, her career. Her father had been fired. Probably for being a drunk, although up to now she had assumed that most reporters were drunk most of the time. But maybe her father was an especially drunken reporter. She'd never gone down to see for herself, but she had heard about the long afternoons and evenings at Hanno's, the bar in the alley behind the paper. Drunken reporters sitting around talking about sports and Hemingway. Her father right in the middle. Until now.

The fear lived in her stomach. She let the hot water hit her neck. She was nineteen. Could she get a job? Would she have to, to help support her old parents? Maybe her mother could get a job. Her mother had worked. She could work again. Jaime soaped her breasts and wondered if she could get a job as a call girl. She imagined herself walking down a hotel corridor, dressed in slut clothes, knocking at a numbered door. And having the door open to reveal a grinning Charlie Monel. No. She knew she could not work as a prostitute, not even for the experience. Not even for the money.

At dinner her father explained. He had napped, gotten up, drunk a couple of cups of coffee and then a Martini before dinner, and now he was charming and relaxed. Apparently he'd been fired in some sort of mix-up.

"Don't worry," he said. "I have a grievance I can bring up before the Guild, I have my severance, we won't be out on the street, and besides, I can always get a job at the *Examiner*. The *Examiner*'s been after me for years. Nothing to worry about. I'm sick of Abe and his goddamn nonsense anyway. It's time I moved on."

By the end of dinner he was talking about finishing his novel. This was very upsetting for Jaime, who remembered all her father's stories about the great novel he would write, which would move them over the hill and into the real Pacific Heights. As a child she had ransacked his desk and everywhere else in the house, and she never saw any novel manuscript. Perhaps he kept it in his desk at the *Chronicle*. Perhaps he hid it in a tree trunk in the backyard. Perhaps it didn't exist.

"Excuse me from the table, please," she said, and went upstairs and threw herself on her bed. She could hear her mother and father bellowing at each other. She wondered what their net worth was. Did they have enough to survive, or was her father lying again? She heard them coming up the stairs, still arguing, and then in their bedroom changing and arguing. Her parents argued a lot, usually about unimportant things, things outside their lives, politics mostly. They were left-wing Marxists, Trotskyites, believers in World Revolution Now. Although, as Jaime had noticed and commented on, they were perfectly willing to live off the blood of the peasants a little while longer, perhaps just until the revolution was complete, when they would all presumably go off and live in a commune somewhere.

Her mother, in her dark blue wool coat, stuck her head in the door and said, "We're off to the Knickerbockers' for bridge, good night, dear . . ." In a few minutes the house was quiet.

4.

She couldn't sleep. Her mind raced with thoughts, not of the future but of Charlie Monel. It was a bad sign that she couldn't completely remember what he looked like. But she could remember the purring tone of his voice, and that spare tiny clean apartment where he lived and worked. It was odd that she hadn't seen a typewriter. Maybe he wrote by hand. Even more literary. Charlie would probably write his novel about the Korean War and be a famous writer, admired, another Norman Mailer or James Jones. She had no war to write about. She thought about Stephen Crane, who had written his great war novel without ever having to go to war. He just made it up. She wondered if she could make up a war novel. Sure she could. She could be one of those upon whom nothing is lost, like Henry James's woman who walked past a barracks and wrote about army life. Or maybe he made that up. She thought about submitting her war novel to Random House, her favorite publisher. She saw the manuscript as being about three feet thick, in several ream boxes. They would open it and pass sections around the office to read excitedly, quoting passages to each other. She could see Bennett Cerf's pipe drop out of his mouth at the stunning, tear-jerking, epiphany ending. Tears stream down his face as he murmurs in that growling Harvard voice, "We want this book!"

Imagine their surprise when they discover it was written by a little girl, barely out of college, who never heard a shot fired in anger. National Book Award. Pulitzer Prize. Uh, Nobel Prize. Pearl S. Buck won it, didn't she?

But even in her fevered imaginings, she knew they wouldn't publish a war novel by an inexperienced girl, no matter how good it was. They just wouldn't. Her heart sank back down into reality. Her father had been fired. She might not even be able to finish college. She might have to go to work, although not as a prostitute.

Jaime got up to go to the bathroom. She missed her cat. Eliot had gone out the window one night and never returned. He was an unfixed cat, only because Jaime never got around to taking him in, and so was pretty scarred up. A big wide-faced orange-striped tabby, king of the neighborhood. As Jaime sat on the toilet she realized she was wide awake, too awake to go back to bed. She had two choices. She could get into her pajamas, get in between the covers and lie there all night worrying, or she could get dressed and go to North Beach. She went into her room and checked her wallet. Twelve dollars. Plenty of money.

She caught the 55 Sacramento bus. It wasn't quite eleven thirty. There were only a couple of other people on the bus, sitting alone. Jaime, dressed in her jeans, an old yellow flannel shirt and her favorite brown sweater, sat behind the driver as the bus rolled down to Van Ness and then up and down Russian Hill. There were a few people out, mostly Chinese in this part of town. She watched them coming out of a brightly-lit Chinese delicatessen with their white bags of takeout, people happy and smiling and talking to each other, boy, that food was going to taste good when they got it home . . . She was hungry herself, and wondered what was in the mystery white bags. Probably all that Chinese stuff that looked so good in the tray and then when you got it home tasted awful, bitter or even rancid. She had an image of Charlie, wearing an army helmet, his head sticking out of a foxhole. He was eating a bowl of something with chopsticks, grinning and smacking his lips as the sky lit up with explosions. She sighed. Would they starve, now that her father was out of work? I'm so middle-class, she thought. What would Charlie say? He'd make light of it. In fact, that was why she was coming down to North Beach, to get Charlie to reassure her. And there was a small tickle of excitement way down somewhere, telling her that she might let him sleep with her, if he was especially nice and reassuring.

She got off at Grant Avenue, which was still crowded with Chinese, tourists, and drunks, the sidewalks jammed, traffic stopped in the street, brilliant garish lights from the tourist stores, bars and restaurants playing over everything. Jaime hadn't been to Chinatown at night for a long time. She'd forgotten how remarkable it smelled, the smells of life and death, she decided, making a mental note to have a character looking for life come through here, not seeing the bustle of life all around him. Irony. At Grant and Broadway she turned right, walking past the open door of a nightclub from which loud Dixieland jazz blared. Jaime liked Dixieland. Her father had quite a collection of jazz records. Maybe they could sell them for money. Jaime stood listening for a while. There were plenty of people out, well-dressed men and women out for the evening, lots of Chinese going about their business, a few younger people dressed carelessly, a lot of them with beards. This really was a great part of town, she decided. I've been a snob.

Charlie wasn't home. At least he didn't answer his door. Up here on Telegraph Hill at this time of night there was little traffic and, after you got off Grant, almost nobody on the sidewalks. Jaime felt perfectly safe. Just disappointed. Where could he be? She pictured Charlie surrounded by people, raising a glass of beer in a salute. He's probably in a bar, but which one? North Beach was full of bars, and plenty of them catered to poets and writers. The trouble was, she wasn't sure which ones. She'd heard of the Co-Existence Bagel Shop, the Place, the Coffee Gallery, all on upper Grant. Only a couple of blocks away. She was sure they wouldn't let her in without ID, and she didn't have any. And she didn't want to go in one of those places, find Charlie, and have everybody know she had come looking for him. It would have been different somehow if he'd been home, alone, in bed, reading or sleeping. But how foolish of her. Charlie didn't seem to be the kind of guy who'd go to bed early with a good book. Of course he was out on the town. But instead of walking down to Grant, she walked over to Kearny and down the steep Kearny steps to Broadway. She was planning on catching a bus for home, but as she crossed Broadway, all lit up, the bars and restaurants all busy, the sidewalks busy, she saw Charlie, dressed in a long white coat, standing at the curb in front of the El Miranda supper club. When she was halfway across the street a car pulled up, Charlie opened the door, a nice-looking couple got out, and Charlie got in, driving off. So he parked cars for a nightclub. That was his job. For some reason, this made Jaime feel wonderful, protected, on the right path. She waited only a few minutes and Charlie was back, walking toward her through the crowd of merrymakers, grinning as if he had expected her and she was right on time.

"Hey, Jaime," he said.

"Hi, Charlie," she said.

"Well, you caught me at work."

"Is the pay good?" she heard herself saying. How stupid. She wrapped her arms around her body.

"Are you cold? You only got a sweater. It gets real cold around here. The goddamn wind, you know. All these trucks. Wait a sec." He was gone, a ticket in his hand. The customers were a well-dressed pair who looked at Jaime with what appeared to be contempt. She was the girlfriend of the guy who parked their car. Trash. Not even wearing a skirt. What a whore.

Charlie drove up in the customer's car, a nice Cadillac, and came back to her. She was a little cold now.

"Fucker didn't tip much," he said. "Sorry about the dirty word."

"Oh, I don't mind," she said. He hadn't asked her what she was doing out so late at night. He hadn't asked where her boyfriend was, he just acted natural. "I swear a lot myself," she said. She smiled up at him. "Shit fuck hell," she said, and he laughed a beautiful laugh.

"Hey, I'm off in a little while. How about waiting for me? We could have a drink." She started to say yes but he interrupted, a sudden look of concern on his face. "Hey, you're pretty cold. You better wait inside."

"Here?"

"Naw, this's a real expensive joint, they wouldn't even let you in. Go around the corner to the Tosca Cafe. It's a great place. Go in, sit at the bar, tell Mario that you're waiting for me."

Then customers came, and with a wink Charlie was gone. She waited, really chilly now, for him to come back. "When do you get off work?" she asked. "I really have to get home soon."

"I'll drive you home," he said. "Hey, we could stop at the Hippo for burgers! We only got three cars left. It shouldn't be more than an hour."

"Okay," she said. She didn't mention she was underage, and all the way down Broadway she worried about being asked. Tosca was a few doors down on Columbus. She opened the big glass doors to be greeted by warmth, a wonderful smell of anise and the most stunning aria in the world, Cho-Cho San's from *Madame Butterfly*. The place was jammed with well-dressed, good-looking people. The long bar was two deep, and the booths and tables in back were all full, people standing around the end of the bar talking and laughing against the music. Jaime felt as if she had found a home. There was a little red leather bench by the front door, and so she sat down, not even trying to approach the bar, and waited. Unfortunately, she had to go to the bathroom. She wondered where it was. She got up and walked down the bar, as casually as she could make herself look, so that no one would notice that a poorly dressed nineteen-year-old girl was passing through. No one stopped her. The old table waiter smiled and pointed to the women's room.

"Thank you," she said, and saw her mother and father, sitting in a red leather booth, staring at her through the smoke.

5.

Walking toward them, her stomach suddenly tight, she noticed again how much her parents looked alike. They both had round red faces, her father's decorated with glasses and his small moustache. Jaime was afraid that she would some day look just like them, plump and fastidious. They were supposed to be playing bridge.

"Hi, folks," she said. "What a surprise."

"How did you find us?" her father demanded. The ashtray in front of him was full of Kool butts, smoked down about two inches and then smashed and broken into the ashtray. Not knowing what else to do, Jaime sat down next to her mother, who made room for her and smiled, saying, "She wasn't looking for us, were you, dear?"

"No, Mom," Jaime said. "But now that we're on the subject . . ."

The old waiter came up to them and looked inquiringly at Jaime's father, who ordered two more cappuccinos.

"And for the young lady?" the waiter asked.

"I'll have the same," Jaime said, and the waiter went away. The three of them sat uncomfortably looking around at the other people in the room. Jaime noticed the chandeliers, with their fake candlesticks and little red lampshades. Charming, like everything else in this place except her parents. The waiter came and placed their drinks before them, with a glass holding what looked like ice cream cones, except that they were rolled round instead of into a cone. Her mother took one and bit into it with a crunch, and Jaime smelled the anise smell that had made her feel so at home when first came in. She now knew why. She'd been smelling that smell on her parents' clothes for years. Years and years. She'd never known what it was.

"Look," her father said finally, "we felt pretty bad about my job, we came down here for a few drinks . . ."

"Oh, Farley," his wife said a little crossly. "We have to tell her." She sipped at her cappuccino, and Jaime sipped at hers. It tasted like hot chocolate with brandy in it. "This is good," she said, and took another sip.

"All these years," her mother began. "We've been telling you we were going out to play bridge."

"I understand," Jaime said.

"I don't think you do," her father said.

"You didn't want me to know you were just going out and getting drunk," Jaime said. "I understand perfectly."

"That isn't it at all," her father snapped.

"Yes, it is," her mother said.

"I forgive you," Jaime said. Her stomach was still tight. She took another sip of the warming drink. The structures of her life were falling apart. Her illusions about her parents shattering left and right. They were not after all middle class people, respectable people. They were instead frauds, drunken unemployed frauds. And she was sitting drinking with them.

"By the way," her mother said.

"I'm here to meet someone." Maybe it was the brandy.

"Good, you can introduce us," her father said.

"We didn't want you to learn any bad habits," her mother said. She and Jaime sipped their drinks and looked at each other. "Like drinking . . ."

"Or lying," Jaime said. Which seemed to destroy any bridge of friendship she and her parents might have been building. The three sat quietly while opera music, loud talk, and laughter filled the room. Eventually Charlie came in. Jaime spotted him standing by the espresso machine at the end of the bar, talking and laughing, now dressed in jeans and a brown sports jacket. Jaime wanted to jump up, run over, grab him by the arm and leave. But she didn't. She seemed nailed into the booth. All she could do was pretend she hadn't seen him, light her last Pell Mell, sip the last of her drink, and wait for Charlie to discover her. Just at that moment her mother said, "Where's this boyfriend of yours?"

"He's not my boyfriend," she snapped, and Charlie walked up to them, a speculative look on his face.

"Farley, Edna," he said to Jaime's parents. Of course he knew them. His favorite bar, their favorite bar.

"I'm their daughter, hello," Jaime said.

"Move over," Charlie said, and sat beside her, the four of them crowding the booth. "Hey Speedy!" he yelled at the old waiter. "Three cappuccinos and a Monica Bianca!" He grinned at Farley. "So you're Jaime's dad? That's great!"

"Uh, how do you know my daughter?" Farley asked.

"Is this the man you were going to meet?" Edna asked Jaime with some alarm in her voice.

"Yes, Mother," Jaime said like a dutiful daughter. Yes, this hulking parker of cars is my date. But it was amazing how well they got along after the initial awkwardness. Maybe it was the atmosphere, all adults out having a good time, or maybe it was just the brandy. Charlie's drink turned out to be hot milk, Kahlua and brandy, and Jaime switched over to that for her second drink. By then her father and Charlie were talking about war. Farley and Charlie go to war, she thought sarcastically, but then felt ashamed and listened to them. Her father had been in the army during World War II. There was a picture of him in his study, in uniform with two other young men. They had their arms on each other's shoulders and smirked at the camera drunkenly, their hats askew. When Jaime had been little it made her proud that her father had more stripes on his sleeve than the other two. That was basically all she knew about his army career. He never spoke of it. She wondered with a start if his so-called novel manuscript was About The War, as Charlie's was.

"So, what kind of outfit were you in?" Farley asked Charlie.

"Infantry," Charlie said, and winked at Jaime.

"Infantry," her father said musingly, mashing another half-smoked cigarette into the ashtray. "Were you in during the war?"

"Oh, yeah," Charlie said. "Sure as shit, excuse me. I enlisted to get out of small town Montana—you know, enlist, beat the draft. Remember that one? Well, they got me good. I enlisted May 10, 1950. He grinned at Edna, who smiled back, quite a nice smile, Jaime thought. My God, my mother's flirting with him.

Charlie went on. "You know the rest. They ran us through basic at Fort Lewis and ran our asses right over to Korea. Excuse me," he said again to Edna, who beamed at him.

"I used to work for the *Chronicle*," she said. "I've heard it all."

"Well, good," Charlie said. "We can all speak openly then."

"Seen any combat?" Farley asked doggedly.

"Well, sure," Charlie said. "Quite a bit." He didn't go on, so Farley asked if he'd ever been wounded.

"Actually," Jaime said, just to break up the interrogation, "he was killed in the war."

"I never got shot or caught any metal," he said to Farley, ignoring the interruption. "But I was a POW for a while and fucking near lost my right foot. Frostbite, you know. I did lose a couple toes. Purple Heart, ha ha."

"You have the Purple Heart?" her father said, the agonizing envy obvious in his voice. Charlie nodded and her father went on, needing to know the whole terrible truth. "Any other medals?"

"Well, yeah," Charlie said. "Good Conduct Medal. Pacific Theater Ribbon. Korean Service Medal. Bronze Star."

Farley finished his drink and looked around for Speedy. He seemed stricken. The Bronze Star. She didn't know exactly what it was, but she knew it was something her father desperately envied. His face was redder and stricter than ever. Maybe he thought Charlie was lying. Maybe Charlie *was* lying.

"You have a Bronze Star?" her father finally said, after Speedy had taken orders and left.

Charlie sighed. "Well, yes I do. But not for anything much. Two or three of us got 'em." He seemed to want to change the subject. "What about you?" he asked Farley. "What branch were you in?"

"Oh, I was in the army too, but I have no medals," Farley said tightly.

"See any combat?" So Charlie wasn't going to let him off. Jaime waited for her father's answer.

Farley weighed his words carefully. "Only with my superiors," he said, and Charlie let out a huge laugh. "Well, didn't we all have to do that!" he said, and the tension evaporated.

"Okay, no more war stories," Edna said, and put her hand on top of Farley's. Jaime admitted to herself that through all the commonplace teenage animosity, she liked her mother.

"Mom, you're a good woman," she said. She put her arm around her mother, who kissed her wetly on the cheek.

"What a nice family," Charlie said. "Well, we're going out for hamburgers now. Care to join us?" He finished his drink and stood up. Jaime kissed her mother on the cheek and slid from the booth.

"Thank you, no," Farley said. To Jaime he said, "How will you get home?"

"I'll bring her, safe and sound," Charlie said cheerfully. "Come on, Jaime. I'm hungry enough to eat the ass—well, I'm pretty hungry."

"You were going to say, 'eat the ass out of a dead mule,' weren't you?" Farley said with a loose grin. "We said the same thing in my time."

Jaime and Charlie made their way up the bar to the front door, Charlie patting people on the back, saying hello to this one and that one, obviously he came in here a lot. And nobody had asked for ID. Of course she'd been with her parents, but Jaime made a mental note about the Tosca Cafe.

6.

The wind blew cold as they walked up Columbus to Broadway. Quite naturally Charlie put his arm around her shoulder to warm her, and she moved in next to him just as naturally.

"Listen," he said, "we can keep going up to where my car is parked, get the car started, drive all the way over to Van Ness, or we could turn right and get our burgers at the pool hall. You ever eat one of Mike's hamburgers?"

"Who's Mike?" It was almost two, and the street was nearly empty. They turned the corner and walked half a block to a crowded pool hall with a busy restaurant counter.

"People come here after the bars close," Charlie said. Flames and hissing came from the long stove behind the counter, where three cooks in white fried hamburgers and flipped what looked like scrambled eggs in little frying pans. Charlie pushed them up to the counter, and after a few minutes they were seated, watching the cooks. Charlie ordered for them both. "No mayo, no mustard, no lettuce or tomatoes, just fried meat and fried onions on these hollowed-out French rolls," Charlie said, his eyes full of appetite. Jaime felt warm and entirely safe. She was also slightly drunk. She hoped she wouldn't eat and then suddenly throw up. When the hamburgers came, on a sheet of waxed paper, there were little shriveled green peppers as a garnish, and Jaime picked one up and put it into her mouth. Tears came to her eyes. "Delicious!" she said.

"Eat up," Charlie said cheerfully, and took a huge bite, the juices running down his face and onto his hands as he ate. She bit into her big clumsy unadorned hamburger. It was the best she'd ever tasted. She wolfed it, getting juice all over herself, then ate her other little pepper and both of Charlie's. Charlie ordered them little glasses of a strong, almost bitter red house wine, and they turned to watch the pool playing. The place was filling, with bartenders, barmaids, strippers, parking lot attendants, Italian men in blue suits and gray hats. Jaime was the only tourist in the crowd, but she didn't feel like one. People kept coming up and saying hello. She wasn't a stranger here, not with Charlie.

The table in front of them wasn't a pool table but a snooker table. Jaime had never seen one before. As they watched a slim young man named Tommy playing against a thickset older man named Whitey, Charlie explained the game.

"Tommy's better than Whitey, isn't he?" she asked after watching a while.

Charlie laughed. "Tommy's a girl," he said. "Watch how Whitey limps a little more as he falls behind. Tommy parks cars across the street, next to Enrico's. Good snooker player."

And a lesbian, Jaime thought with a thrill of shock. The girl Tommy had been flirting with her. Grinning at her after good shots, shrugging after a miss. It was unmistakable. Tommy wore a men's Hickory shirt, khaki pants, and little men's Oxfords. She was obviously one of the better players, because a crowd was watching the game, generating a lot of bitter-smelling cigar smoke. Everyone was so cosmopolitan. She'd led such a sheltered life. With a shock she remembered that her father had lost his job. Middle class no more. Thrown into the street. But Charlie was here to protect her.

"Don't you love this dump?" he yelled at her. She smiled.

"Let's have another glass of wine," she said. Maybe nobody in North Beach checked ID. Maybe that was why the place was a popular tourist attraction.

"No more wine," Charlie said. "It's damn near three."

"Oh!" Jaime said. "I have to get home!"

"I wanted to shoot some snooker, but okay, I told you I'd take you home, so off we go." He slid off his barstool, holding out his hands to catch her. They were warm and dry. She loved his hands.

Outside was cold, the street bare. "We could walk up Grant or climb the steps," Charlie said.

They climbed the Kearny steps, Charlie slogging along, Jaime taking three at a time. She got to the top ahead of him and perched herself on the low wall blocking the street, watching Charlie huff and puff his way up the hill.

"You better quit smoking," she said to him when he got to her, panting and holding his chest. He leaned against the wall beside her, almost sobbing for breath. Then he laughed. "You're so young," he said. "Come on." He pulled her gently down off the wall and folded her into his arms. They kissed. Jaime had accepted that she'd sleep with him instead of going home. It seemed perfectly natural. She was probably more relaxed about it than Charlie. They walked up Kearny toward his apartment. When they got to his car he pushed her up against it and kissed her again. This was a lingering kiss, but gentle. When they broke she put her cheek against his and whispered, "Take me to your place."

"Don't you want to go home?"

"I want to be with you," she said. She'd come down here hoping to find him, but not to sleep with him, just to talk, tell him about her life falling apart, ask his advice. All that seemed unimportant now.

She stood in the middle of Charlie's living room–bedroom while he went into the kitchen and turned on a light. The place looked eerie in this light. It wasn't going to be a monk's cell tonight. She no longer felt like sleeping with him, of course, but here she was, she had asked for this, and so poor Charlie was going to have to go ahead and seduce her.

"Don't you use a typewriter?" she asked as he came back into the half-light.

"Sure I do," he said, and pulled her to him. She let herself get pulled.

"Uh-oh," Charlie said, and let her go.

He was too sensitive. She moved toward him and put her hands and cheek against his chest. "You have to do all the work," she said. "I'm pretty scared."

"You sure you want to do this?" he asked.

"Yes," she said. "But I guess you don't. That's all right."

"Do you want me to take you home?"

"No, damn it, I want you to take me to bed."

"Then why'd you go cold?"

"I don't think you like me," Jaime said. She was angry. All the liquor warmth was gone. She felt empty and stupid.

"Well, putting it that way, I better take you home," he said, with bitterness in his voice.

"If I could just have a glass of water first," she said in her smallest voice. She sat at his desk while he went into the kitchen and came back with a little cheese glass of water. He sat on the bed and watched her sip.

"You okay?" he asked.

"I'm fine," she said. "I've had a bad time today. I'll be all right in a minute."

"I really do like you," he said. "Are you a virgin?"

"I don't see what that has to do with anything."

"Thank you," he said. "It explains everything . . . our *reluctance . . .*"

Jaime stood up, her heart pounding. "I'm not reluctant," she said, and came over and took his head in her hands and tilted it up and kissed him, pushing her tongue into his mouth. In a moment they were both on the bed, holding each other tightly, kissing and moaning.

"Do it to me!" she cried out.

7.

Jaime's father had been keeping a mistress, and he died at her apartment, actually in her bed. But Jaime didn't discover any of this until the night before her father's funeral. All she knew was that he'd died out of the house somewhere, of a stroke.

It would have been exaggerating to say that Jaime and her father had been estranged at the time of his death, but they'd certainly been arguing. About Charlie, of course. After their first night together Charlie had brought her home around eight in the morning, a bright clear morning full of promise. She was already completely in love with him, but didn't realize it yet. In fact she thought everybody must have felt this way after making love all night. She looked forward to feeling like this on many mornings of her life. She couldn't understand why she'd waited this long.

"This is it, huh?" Charlie said, squinting up at the house. "Looks like a real mansion." Jaime kissed him and got out of the car.

"See you in class," she grinned at him.

"You sure will," he grinned back at her.

She was surprised to see her father in the dining room in his bathrobe. She'd forgotten he had been fired, or hadn't realized that of course this meant he'd be home all the time now. Unless he got another job. He looked awful, sitting there in his blue satin bathrobe with its pale red satin lapels. He wasn't wearing his glasses and his eyes were red and somehow monkey-looking, like those of the primates in the zoo. Sad mad old eyes, she thought, and tried to bull her way through the situation.

"Morning, Dad," she said, and sat at the table in her usual spot.

"What the hell do you mean coming in here at eight o'clock in the morning?"

"I'm hungry," she said, just as her mother came in from the kitchen, hung over, in her pink wrapper and her old pink mobcap that made her look like Martha Washington. Mom carried the coffee pot, and as her father began his harangue Jaime held out her cup to be filled. Charlie was too old for her, of course. And he parked cars, never mind his ambitions to be a writer. Everybody wanted to be a writer. Meanwhile he was just a parker of cars and a rapist, or practically, since he must have seduced or somehow forced Jaime. She wondered what her father would have said if he'd known that Charlie had been the first. She didn't tell him. She took her lecture with her head erect, sipping coffee. She was damned if she'd look penitent. She didn't feel the least bit penitent. Her father insisted she not go out with Charlie anymore, but her mother saved her.

"Dear," she said to him. "We can't ask her not to date."

"We can ask her to stay away from men twice her age!" he said angrily, red face getting redder.

"No, we can't," her mother said quietly. And it was over. But her father must have died feeling bad about his daughter.

Jaime's brother, Bill, flew in from Taipan, tanned and stricken. There was a kind of wake at their house that afternoon before the funeral, with a bunch of newspaper reporters in their best blue suits, standing around the living room getting drunk and talking about the good old times. After the last drunken reporter had been poured down the front steps, Jaime and Bill sat cross-legged on her twin beds in what had been Bill's bedroom and talked. Jaime didn't quite know how she felt about Bill. He'd always hated their father, and now his guilt and sadness were hard to bear. He was her brother, of course, and that must have meant something, but she felt remarkably cool toward him, even after such a long absence. Bill had been overseas for two years, and he was six years older than she, a mature young man who'd chosen a life in civil service. Bill had a thin face, thin body, and was the tallest member of the family at five eight. His only attractive feature was a pair of blue eyes even harder and darker than hers.

"You know where Dad died, don't you?" he said to her finally. He told Jaime about the mistress, and explained that their entire life had been a sham, the happy family a lie. Her father had been screwing around for years. This one particular girlfriend he actually paid the rent for.

"Where did he get the money?" she heard herself asking, from the depths of her numbness.

Bill knew nothing about money. But he knew their father had died during intercourse and gone immediately into rigor, and that it had been difficult to get the body out of the apartment on Pine Street, the cops and ambulance attendants laughing and joking because they'd known old Farley Froward, everybody knew him, and everybody knew old Fairly Farley would have been just as callous and cracked just as many jokes.

"Where did you hear all this?" Jaime asked Bill. He grinned his mean little grin and said, "Weren't you listening downstairs?"

"I wasn't eavesdropping," she said meanly. This all made her feel as if she was somebody else, hovering in a corner of the room, looking down at the foolish humans. Including her, who hadn't thought it was possible that her own father was unfaithful. Or that any woman would have him. Was her mother a fraud too?

"What about Mom?" she asked.

"Mom's been putting up with it for years," he said. "Why do you think she drinks so goddamn much?"

"I never thought about it." Their father was dead, his ashes to be scattered into the Pacific in two days. She'd apparently known nothing about him.

"Do you have any other family secrets to tell me, before you fly away?"

He looked at her oddly. "What do you mean?"

"Is Mom dating other men? Is the house really rented? Is our name really Froward? Anything else I ought to know about myself?"

Her brother stood, his face reddening. "You don't have to get shitty about it," he said mysteriously, and left the room.

She had seen Charlie several times at school since their night of love and they'd even made love again, in the back of his De Soto, parked down by Lake Merced. This second episode had clarified things a bit, since she hadn't known whether she meant anything to Charlie or was just a nice pretty young piece of ass. After some comical maneuvers they had an extremely passionate coupling, and at the end of it Charlie told her he loved her.

"Oh, don't, Charlie," she said, not really able to believe it. "You don't have to say that."

"I know it," he said. "But I do."

"I like you, Charlie," she heard herself saying, "but I'm not ready for love." It was like dialogue from a bad movie. Charlie laughed and said, "You don't have to be ready for anything," and drove her back to school.

Then her father died. She refused to withdraw from school. When she saw Charlie before their Clark class, he already knew about her father and held his hands out to her without saying anything. She put her head against his chest. One of the other boys in the class grinned at them and said, "It figures."

"Never mind," Charlie said to him, and put his arms around her. "Maybe you shouldn't be here," he said.

"I need this," she said, not knowing whether she meant the class or his arms. But she didn't see Charlie over the holidays. She managed to get through the break by throwing herself into her schoolwork and writing, and she found herself spending a lot of time with her mother. She didn't go to North Beach, and quite frankly thought about never seeing any of those people again, just drifting away from San Francisco. She could work at little jobs, observe life, write short stories to teach herself, and then move on to the novel.

They'd have to sell the house. They had Farley's severance but they were deeply in debt. The good furnishings, the family car, a '57 Buick, would also have to go. They'd end up broke and stripped. Edna had worked at the *Chronicle* a long time ago, but now she hated the paper and blamed its editors for Farley's death. "They gave him high blood pressure and then they blew him out," she said grimly to her daughter as they sat in what was still for the time being their living room. Both had glasses of wine. Edna didn't seem to mind Jaime's new habit of drinking. It made them closer.

"What are we going to do for money?" Jaime asked.

"I just don't know," Edna said. "I'm forty-four years old. I don't think I can slim down and meet a breadwinner at this point in my life." She chuckled and looked puckish. "I guess you'll have to do it."

"Marry a breadwinner?"

"Breadwinners are great," her mother said. "Ooh! Bread! Did we win?"

Jaime laughed and laughed. But their problem was real. Her mother had said that if they sold the house and moved to a less expensive neighborhood, there would be enough money for Jaime to finish college. Neither spoke of about Edna's lifelong desire to move the other way, into Pacific Heights proper. Her mother was never going to get what she wanted. Life was not going to give her anything more. For Edna, it was over.

"Oh, Mom," she said sadly.

8.

Kenny Goss slept very little. His small wiry body didn't seem to need it and his brain was always seething with thoughts. He had tried living with a girl once, but they had lasted only a few days. "You're too intense," she told him and left. Now he lived in a very small apartment on Jackson Street, near Larkin. It was on the second floor over a Chinese laundry, and all day when he was home he could hear the rumble of the machines and the voices of the family who ran the laundry, reassuring voices for Kenny. He had been raised to believe that the Chinese were filthy awful people, and every time a Chinese person proved his mother wrong he felt happy. He loved his mother, but he knew better now than to believe her. She didn't just have it in for the Chinese: she hated Jews, Germans, Japanese, etc. and etc., professing to love only those countries that were primarily Catholic. Kenny had been raised a Catholic. He had even spent a few days in a Catholic orphanage over in Berkeley while his mother found them a place to live. But the minute he was old enough to think, he freed his mind of the overwhelming smothering craziness that was to him Catholicism. Whenever he saw his mother these days she'd remind him that he was bound for hell, and he would remind her that all he had to do was repent, confess, commune, and that was that. All in his most sarcastic voice.

On this particular morning Kenny was sitting in his car at 6:00 a.m., outside a house on Washington Street, waiting for the right time to run up to the front door and see if the people were awake yet. As was his usual habit, the night before he had picked up a copy of the bulldog edition of the *Chronicle* and read the ads, looking for anything that might be fruitful. This ad said, "Household furnishings for sale. Many good things," and the address close enough to the high rent district to make Kenny interested. Not that he cared about furniture. Kenny was a book scout. He spent most of his spare time running around the

Bay Area looking for underpriced used books. One of his tricks was to answer ads like this morning's, looking around at the furniture but actually keeping his eye out for books. Often the people holding home furniture sales were in bad shape and didn't know what they were doing. Sometimes the person who collected the books had died, and the widow wouldn't know their value. He'd picked up quite a few good bargains this way, including a copy of *Hike and the Aeroplane*, a children's book which had been Sinclair Lewis's first published work. Kenny sold the copy he found, not mint, not even excellent, but very good, for one hundred and fifty dollars. He had paid fifty cents for it.

He sat in his old maroon '49 Ford sipping coffee from his thermos cup and reading the morning *Examiner* by flashlight. This time of year the sun wouldn't be up for another hour. It was cold, but Kenny was comfortable. Last night had been good. He sat up writing for several hours, the laundry below closed, the apartment building almost silent except for the usual quiet domestic sounds, and he had been able to churn out three whole pages. He was writing an insane little story about an old Chinese man who worked in a laundry every day and then went home to work on his invention, which was made of a lot of tiny moving parts, gears, wheels, pins, shafts, etc. No one was sure what the old man was making, but everyone was very respectful. Kenny wasn't sure what the old man was making either, but he hoped his imagination would come to his rescue. He seemed to be coming near to the end of the story, and he still didn't have any idea what the story was about. He had to trust himself, he knew. Writing blindly, following only impulse, was the secret to finding out what lay in the deepest parts of his mind. What his mother would call his soul, but which he preferred to call his essence.

He looked at his watch. Five to seven. He knew from experience that a lot of people would answer this ad and it was best to be early. Oddly, none of the other book scouts he knew had caught on to his trick of answering furniture ads. Usually he was the only one even slightly interested in the books. He got out of the car and saw his breath. It was a nice cold morning. He went up the steps and rang the doorbell. He hoped they wouldn't be angry with him, but they usually weren't. They wanted that sale to begin.

After a while a plump little woman in a gray sweatshirt and green slacks opened the door and looked out at him without saying anything.

"I'm here for the sale?" he said.

"Oh," she said. She seemed a little strange, but she widened the opening and let him in. He could see right away that the furnishings were good. Persian rugs everywhere, Tiffany lamps, at least three of them in the living room, good-looking and well-cared-for antique furniture. He walked around the living room pretending to look at the furniture.

"I'm Mrs. Froward," the woman said and gave him a moist hand. He realized she was drunk. At least she had booze on her breath.

"This is all such nice stuff," he said, walking around. He looked at the pieces in the dining room. Still no books. This was actually a good sign. If a household like this had only a few books, usually they would be displayed in the living room. Of course they might have no books at all.

"Do you have any bookshelves for sale?" he asked her. "That's what I'm looking for mostly."

"This way." She led him down the hall to their library. For Kenny, it was like walking into King Solomon's mine. Everywhere he looked he saw beautiful books in their original dust wrappers. Names leaped out: Joyce, Faulkner, Fitzgerald, Steinbeck, Hemingway . . . He reached for a copy of *The Sun Also Rises*, in its original dust wrapper. The book was in excellent condition. He opened it to the copyright page and saw the letter A where he hoped to find it. First edition. He checked a Fitzgerald. First edition. He hoped his hand wasn't trembling as he slid the Fitzgerald back into place. He turned and smiled at Mrs. Froward.

"Nice books," he said. "Are you a collector?"

"My husband collected the books," she said. "He's gone now."

Just exactly what Kenny hoped to hear. But something was bothering him. "I could buy all these books," he heard himself saying. "If it's cheap enough."

"What do you think?" she asked. She sat down in a nice-looking leather chair, well-worn, probably where the dead guy sat and read over his collection. He looked around. Approximately two hundred books.

"I could give you fifty cents apiece," he said. "A hundred dollars for the whole bunch. I could haul 'em out of here this morning."

She looked up at him, and this time he saw the pain in her eyes, for only a second, but it was there. "I don't know," she said. "You'd be getting a lot of valuable books. I wasn't actually thinking of selling the books, but we need the money."

"Look," he heard himself saying, "you're gonna have a lot of furniture dealers here pretty soon. They'll be trying to screw you, excuse me, but they'll want to get all this really valuable stuff cheap. You have to be ready to bargain . . ." His heart sank as he listened to himself. But he couldn't steal from an old drunk woman. It just wasn't in him.

"You don't know the value of any of this stuff, do you?" he asked her. He sat down on the little love seat, and noticed for the first time with a shock that the small painting on the wall in front of him was a Matisse. Or it looked like a Matisse. "Matisse?" he asked her and she nodded absently. She must have been up all night drinking. Her husband dies and she's helpless. And then the scavengers arrive. Kenny sighed. If he had been a real businessman he would have made her an offer for everything in the house, screwed her blind and made a fortune. Instead, because he was a writer, because he needed to be a man of honor more than he needed the money, Kenny told Mrs. Froward the facts of life.

"Lady, you're not in shape to sell your stuff, pardon me."

"That's true," she said. "But sell it I must."

He sighed again. Last chance to be a vulture. "Let me call you a reputable dealer," he said. "Somebody who can take over and auction off your things for the right prices. It will take a while, but otherwise they'd take you to the cleaners."

He telephoned Butterfield's and told them what was going on. They were sending a man over, and meanwhile, Kenny would stop people at the door and tell them the sale was over.

"Why are you doing this?" she asked him.

"I don't know, lady," he said. He couldn't tell her he was a man of honor, could he?

9.

Jaime thought her period had stopped because of the death of her father. But no, she was pregnant, and had obviously gotten pregnant on her first night of love. And to top that off, when she told her mother, Edna snapped, "Fine. Then you're his responsibility. You can go live with him."

"Oh, fine," Jaime snapped back, thinking about Charlie's luxurious apartment. On that first night Charlie had unzipped his sleeping bag and laid it on the floor next to the cot, and they made love on that. Later when she felt sleepy she just pulled some clothes over her and slept. But she could not imagine living like that. She was a middle-class girl. She was not used to poverty. And anyway she didn't think Charlie was going to be happy about being a father. There was really no other choice. Abortions cost money.

She and her mother were living in the house while the realtors tried to sell it, and there were strangers in the house all the time. Most of the good stuff was gone, sold at auction, and the house was strange, full of odd echoes. It seemed as if her father were merely on vacation, and had gone off without them. She missed him, but she also felt a little resentful about his absence. Why didn't he take us with him? She expected to see him coming in the front door, black topcoat collar up, wet gray felt hat pulled down to his eyes, specks of rain on his glasses and moustache. Her mother was busy selling things and looking for an apartment they could afford that wasn't in a slum, and Jaime tried to do her schoolwork, pay attention in classes, and write. She'd been working on a short story about a girl much like herself. It wasn't going very well and now seemed to have no point. Too much had happened to her since beginning the story. She threw the pages into her wastebasket. None of her personal furniture had been sold. Her room was intact, the only intact room in the house. The only one with a rug, though not a Persian. She hadn't told Charlie she was pregnant yet. He'd pulled back after her father's death, out of common decency, or because he found her too easy. When they ran into each other he always seemed friendly and concerned, but she made herself aloof, as if the death of her father had affected her deeply, as deeply as it might have affected a character in a Russian novel, although Jaime had read only one, *Anna Karenina*.

Then finally one day in class when Professor Clark was looking something up in a book, Charlie tapped her on the shoulder and she turned. His eyes seemed gold that day. "Hi," he said to her.

"I'm pregnant," she said, and turned back. Numbly she listened to Professor Clark reading from the Upanishads (they were reading *A Passage to India*) and waited for Charlie's reaction, although he could hardly interrupt the lecture. Then he touched her on the shoulder, and she knew, just from that single touch, that everything was going to be all right. She started to cry. At that moment Clark looked at her and must have seen the shine of the tears. His blue eyes widened, and he went back to reading. It's not the lecture, Walt, she wanted to tell him. She got a Kleenex from her bag and blew her nose noisily.

"Gesundheit!" Charlie whispered and she felt his hand at the back of her neck. Clark grinned and kept on reading. When the bell rang Jaime stood up and turned to face Charlie. She knew her eyes looked terrible, but Charlie just pulled her in to him and she cried against his field jacket.

Of course his place would be no good for them. The family house had been snapped up, probably at bargain prices, and Jaime and her mother had to move out within a month. Edna seemed distracted and was drinking too much. Jaime couldn't talk to her. She did not know whether this was the happiest time of her life, or the worst. Only when she was with Charlie did she feel good. Only with Charlie did she feel safe. And this was insane. What did she know about him? He was from a small town in Montana, Wain, Montana. His mother was dead and his father worked in a lumber yard. He'd been a soldier and had won a medal her father envied. She knew he was an enthusiastic writer with few literary skills, and finally, she knew everybody around State thought he was their most promising student. Probably because he was big and strong and had a nice smile.

They went outside to smoke a cigarette under the trees in the courtyard between HSS and the administration building. It was raining a little.

"I thought you might be," he said.

"Be what?"

"Pregnant."

"What made you think so?"

He smiled. "Because I wanted you to be," he said. He put his hand against her cheek, his cigarette dangling romantically from his lips. "You know how I feel about you," he said.

"How?" She had gone over the line. She should never have asked him that.

"I love you," he said.

"Oho," said another student in passing. Charlie threw him an ironic smile and turned back to Jaime. "I'm nuts about you. I want to marry you. I want you to have our babies. Et cetera."

"I don't want that," she heard herself saying. "I have to finish college."

"I can wait," Charlie said. Suddenly his face contorted with doubt. She wanted to laugh at his comical expression, as he realized she might turn him down. "Wait a sec."

"I do love you," she said.

"You're not planning on an abortion or anything like that, are you?" There was anxiety in his voice. His hands were on her arms, his cigarette in his mouth.

"I don't know," she said, feeling the power. "I don't know what I'm going to do."

"Please don't." He spat away his cigarette and kissed her urgently. "Don't you get it? We're perfect for each other."

Now she was in control. "Let's walk down and have a nice cup of poisonous coffee," she said. Quietly talking, they walked arm-in-arm across the gently sloping lawns to the cafeteria, where they found a group of young writers sitting around having coffee. Jaime and Charlie joined their colleagues, their secret warm between them. They'd live together and have their child. Charlie, after he got his degree, would look for a teaching job. Jaime would have the baby and then come back to school. They'd share everything. If they still loved each other a few years down the line, they could marry. She'd be twenty-one by then, and able to decide.

She looked at her fellow students. There was nothing but men at the table. Of the handful of women in the program, none were considered potentially great writers. Really, most of the creative writing students were headed for teaching careers. Few would become writers. Right now they were talking about money. Some had applied for the Eugene F. Saxon Award, ten grand from the MacMillan Company for the most promising partial manuscript. Jaime would have applied herself, except she had no novel.

10.

When Charlie got the Saxon he was more surprised than anybody. He hadn't even wanted to apply. His thesis advisor had cheerfully told him that Part One could not only get him a Saxon, but if submitted with the proper recommendations, could get him a scholarship to Iowa's writing program, the most prestigious in the country. "Paul Engel will love it," Dr. Wilner said. Charlie knew that Part One wasn't ready. It had all the people and all the stuff, but it was crude as hell and irritated Charlie every time he read it over. Part One had taken him years to get on paper, even in its roughest form, and now, after all his teachers and friends had worked it over, it still irritated him. It was *not good*.

But a long time ago, when he had first decided to become a writer, he sat down and thought about the various ways to go. He could just start writing. Put down his experiences and what he thought about them. That was what had gotten him into this in the first place: the things he had seen. The way they made him feel. Or another way to go would be to sit down and doggedly read through all the war novels and see what had already been done. The drawback being that he might end up imitating the other war writers, and that was not what he wanted to do. Hell, he wanted to write the *Moby Dick* of war. Or at least try. The third option was to get a college degree, though he had not graduated from high school. Just learn what they could teach. He did have a GED certificate, given him by the army when they thought they were going to make him into an officer, so he could get into some college that didn't have too high standards. He ended up doing all three.

Funny how things happen, though. Here was this ten-thousand-dollar gift, the same amount the army would have paid his father if he'd been killed. All he had to do for it was finish his novel, which he intended to do anyway. But here he was, unexpectedly in love with a girl who was unexpectedly pregnant. Just at the exact moment in history when he could afford to get married. He could even afford to quit parking for El Miranda and settle down to full-time writing and reading.

He had read all the war novels he could stand, just to find out what was left for him to say, from *The Gallery*, by John Horne Burns, and *Guard of Honor*, by James Gould Cozzens, all the way to *War and Peace*, by Guess Who. He read Hemingway and Dos Passos and Mailer and Jones. He read *The Red Badge of Courage*. They all had two things in common. They were great books and great writers, all far beyond anything Charlie Monel could do even if he spent the rest of his life writing. Two lives. Especially that fucking Tolstoy, who almost made it worth Charlie's while to commit suicide. You want to talk about your *Moby Dick* of war, Jesus . . .

The only thing left for Charlie, should he decide to continue his meaning-less career, was to say what went on in Korea and Japan while he had been there. What had happened in Kim Song. What his fellow POWs had been like. What he had been like. That stuff was left to him. Otherwise he would have quit long ago.

Now the only problem he faced was talking Jaime into getting married. He'd fallen in love a fraction of a second after he first saw her, he decided. It wasn't quite love at first sight. But she was acting skittish, one minute ready to spend her life with Charlie, the next minute wanting to go off somewhere by herself. She was perfect for him. She was much better looking than he had any right to expect, and she was smarter, funnier, and a far better writer than Charlie. They could live together and raise their children and she could teach him to write as well as she did, while he taught her to jump out there a little more in her writing. And he could protect her from the harsher forms of reality. She shouldn't work. Work, being a waitress or something, would break her down. She'd been talking about running off to a small town and getting a menial job, so that her writing would take on more reality. Charlie doubted it. There was nothing wonderful about working at a menial job. The wonderful part of his working day, like any working stiff's, was getting off work. She romanticized work the same way she romanticized writing. Of course so did he, but in a different way.

When Charlie told Jaime about the Saxon Award she seemed to take it well, not getting too excited, giving him a nice kiss and telling him that he of all of them deserved it.

"Really?" he asked. "Why?" He wanted to know.

"Because you have such promise."

They were side by side in The Coffee Gallery, drinking beer. It was a Saturday afternoon and the place was filling with tourists, not ordinary tourists but low-lifes, motorcycle types, bad-guy types. He didn't like these new people who were jamming North Beach. They drove up the rents and filled all the good bars.

"How long could we live on ten thousand dollars?" Jaime asked.

"Oh, two, three years," he said.

"You're such a monk," she said. "But you're going to Iowa, aren't you?"

That was the question. Should he go ahead and apply for that greased-up scholarship? Did he want to arrive in Iowa City with a pregnant wife? Did Jaime want to transfer to Iowa? Could she get into their undergraduate program? Was he willing to leave her behind? He imagined sitting in a snowbound dorm in the middle of nowhere, getting a letter from Jaime where she tells him about going to Tijuana for an abortion. It made him shiver. If she'd do that, she didn't really love him. He didn't know why he felt this way, but he did.

"You wouldn't get a fucking abortion, would you?" he asked her. There was a table of guys next to her. A big black character in a sleeveless tee with a big chromed length of chain over his shoulder was grinning at his remark. Every time he and Jaime had a private moment, some asshole interfered. He glared at the guy, who smirked insolently. They could have been out in the street in about twelve seconds, but instead Charlie smiled and said, "Have a beer!" He signed the waiter for rounds for both tables.

"No," said Jaime.

"No what?"

"No, I won't get an abortion."

He moved his head down closer to hers. "Then let's get fucking married."

"*Let's get fucking married,*" she mocked. He didn't like her swearing, but since it was him that taught her, what could he say?

"If we get married, I won't go to Iowa," he said. "We can get a place here in North Beach and live on my grant and write."

"Sounds like heaven," she said. Something was wrong. She loved him. He knew it. Or hoped he knew it. But she was holding back. She had him by the nuts, of course. She knew he'd do anything she asked. So, what the hell.

"What's bothering you?" he asked. He inwardly cringed, waiting for something awful. But after draining her glass of beer she burped gently, excused herself and said, "My mom. If I move in with you, she's all alone." She squeezed his hand. "I could keep living with my mom and have the baby while you went to Iowa."

"Fuck that noise," he said. "Your mother can live with us."

"No, she can't," Jaime said sadly. "My mother's a drunk."

11.

The last big event before finals was Charlie's master's oral. He had to sit in a little room with three educated men and tell them, in his own words, some great truth from literature that they presumably didn't already know. He had to commit an act of scholarship right in front of them. He'd known all along that this event was coming up, but he hadn't let it worry him. Not until the night before.

"Jesus Christ, what am I going to say to those people?" They were in his apartment, which had changed dramatically in the last few weeks. Instead of Charlie's old war surplus cot, they now slept on one of Jaime's twin beds, which she and Charlie had brought over from Washington Street. And there were lots of Jaime's things around the place, clothes, books, a noisy fruit grinder Jaime used to make her "Tiger's milk cocktail," which Charlie had tried once. Actually, he preferred the stuff they had given him in prison camp. Jaime was in the kitchen now, dressed only in her underpants and one of Charlie's tee shirts. Her blonde hair stuck out all over the place. She did the dishes while Charlie straightened the sheets. After dinner they had jumped into bed, of course. They were always jumping into bed these days. She'd go home soon to her mother's new apartment, and Charlie was feeling the panic.

"Just tell them you're big and strong and that you promise to write beautifully, if only they give you this master's degree. Beg them," she said over the clatter of washing dishes. "Ask them to consider that you've fought bravely for your country, and now you would like a master's. They'll be sure to feel sorry for you."

"God damn it," he said, and sat down on the freshly made bed. Jaime's bedding. And there was a big box of bedding and stuff over in the corner, taking up precious room. First she filled him with love, then she filled his apartment with stuff.

"If you swear at them, they'll probably be frightened," she said, and came into the room. She looked at him fondly. "You're getting stage fright, aren't you?"

"Is that what it is?" He'd felt this way in Korea, but in Korea he'd expected to. Here and now it felt bizarre that he should fear meeting three men he knew perfectly well liked him and had every intention of passing him through. These were the same guys who were pushing him toward Iowa, so that he could be like them, respectable writers who also taught college. Ray West, Utah man, author of a book about the Mormons and a great short story called "The Last of the Grizzlies," which is exactly how Charlie was feeling tonight; Herb Wilner, author of brilliant stories published in places like *Esquire;* and old Walter Clark. Charlie rubbed his stomach, hoping to ease the discomfort.

"I have to go home and study," Jaime said. "You're getting your master's, but I'm probably going to flunk out." She and Edna had moved to a big apartment on Sacramento Street, between Leavenworth and Jones. Charlie had helped them move in. It was kind of pathetic. All their good furniture was gone, and what was left didn't halfway fill the place. They had beautiful hardwood floors, which Charlie washed, waxed, and buffed for them with a rental buffer, but nothing to go on them except for some little rag rugs. Edna had obviously rented the wrong place. She should have rented a small furnished apartment and saved herself some money, instead of this ghost apartment, full of echoes. Charlie could tell Jaime hated to go home to it. But she was the only company her mother had. Edna didn't like her old friends anymore. Most of them were connected to the *Chronicle*, killer of Farley, and the rest were socialists, Marxists, communists, etc., and as far as she was concerned, a pack of fools. She wouldn't even go to Tosca anymore, not that it was a Marxist hangout, but the memories must have troubled her. Charlie hadn't known Farley very well, just one of the reporters who drank around North Beach, but he'd seemed like a nice guy, maybe a little tense about world affairs. He could imagine how Edna might miss him. But she just sat home in her expensive, under-decorated, ghostly apartment, swilling red wine.

"We should all move in together," he said again. Though he didn't particularly want to, it was better than this. But Jaime wouldn't have it.

"I don't want to become a cliché," she said to him mysteriously.

The actual master's oral was comical, he decided, well after it was over. He was fine in the morning, attending classes, taking some books back to the library, eating a stuffed pepper in the cafeteria, but when he showed up at Wilner's office the stuffed pepper exploded or something and he had a terrible need to shit. Instead he knocked bravely on Wilner's door and clenched his buttocks.

Wilner opened the door and came out. He was a small mild-looking Jewish man who had been All-American in 1944. He smiled nervously at Charlie and said, "Let's go for coffee." As they were crossing the campus Wilner said, "I threw up a couple of times before my master's oral." They sat in the cafeteria, and while Charlie sipped nervously at his bitter coffee Wilner told him stories of how the biggest bravest guys sometimes collapsed into terror at the thought of orals. "It's really mysterious," he said. "How these big bruisers will turn white at the thought of exposing their minds."

"Yes," said Charlie. It was too late to kill him.

Wilner stood up abruptly. "Well, time to go," he said. The oral lasted forty minutes, from the time he walked into the tiny office where Clark and West stood grinning and shook his hand until the point when he walked out of the room, his knees weak, his stomach tense, his buttocks still clenched. He had no idea how he had done. He leaned against the wall and waited for Wilner to come out. He'd chosen to speak on *Moby Dick*, even though he had been warned that *Moby Dick* was a very demanding subject, and perhaps larger than he needed. But he loved the book and knew it better than any other, and so he opened his mouth and started blathering, word tumbling after word, no sense being made, until he didn't have any words left in him and shut up.

Wilner came out and silently they walked down the long empty corridor toward Wilner's office. At the door he turned and shook Charlie's hand.

"Call me Herb," he said. He had a nice strong handshake. Charlie was a Master of the Arts. All but for the formality of his last final, four days away. And then the application to Iowa.

"Honey bear," he said to Jaime over the phone. "I gotta get out of town. Let's drive up to the mountains, just overnight or so, get some air, do a little gambling, get drunk, have fun, and then come back for our finals."

"You're the boss," she said. Charlie had to laugh.

PART TWO

The Portland Group

12.

The Portland group formed itself around Dick Dubonet, after he sold a short story to *Playboy* for three thousand dollars. *Playboy* usually paid fifteen hundred for a story, but, Dick discovered, if they wanted to run your story in the front of the magazine they paid double. Dick's rent was thirty dollars a month and he spent about the same for food. Utilities ran about four dollars, telephone another four. By far his largest monthly outlays were for his car, beer, and cigarettes, with an occasional wildcat expenditure for coffee at the Caffe Espresso. Dick was a bachelor and needed these apparently needless expenses in order to catch girls. Since he was not willing to really spend money on them.

He was in fact in bed with a girl when his agent called to tell him the news. A beautiful creature he'd met at a tavern near the college. She'd come home with him because he already had a reputation as one of the few successful writers in Portland, or in the whole state of Oregon, so far as he knew. He had been publishing short stories for two years, in magazines like *Nugget*, *Caper*, and *Fantasy & Science Fiction*. At twenty-five he had sold his first story for eighty dollars to *Ellery Queen's Mystery Magazine*, about a writer who gets revenge on editors by poisoning the flap glue on his return envelopes. Which were of course returned to him, leaving no evidence. It was a cute little story, and the editor wrote him a nice letter as well as the eighty-dollar check. A few months later the editor, Robert P. Mills, wrote to Dick that he was resigning to become an independent agent. Would Dick like to be his first client? Getting an agent was half the battle. Since then Bob Mills had been selling a story a month for Dick, and his career was launched.

"Who was that?" the girl asked. She looked at him slyly from under his covers. He didn't mind her looking at him naked except for jockey shorts. He had a good although small and wiry body, and a pretty good tan. His skin was dark to begin with, his eyes almost black, his hair curly and dark. He knew he was good-looking but it didn't make him conceited.

"Just business," he said coolly. He tried to remember her name. He thought about getting back into the warm bed and making love to her again. They'd done it twice during the night. This would make it three times, just about the minimum if he wanted her to think of him as a lover. Did he? She was cute, but he couldn't recall anything about her. And there was another problem. He wondered if this sudden good news, amazingly good news, might render him impotent for a time. He would be thinking feverishly about *Playboy* and the possibilities of the future, instead of concentrating on his lovemaking. It was too great a risk.

"Okay, honey, up and at 'em," he said instead, wearing his Smilin' Jack smile. It took nearly an hour to get her out. She wanted to shower, she wanted coffee and a cigarette, she wanted to talk, but all Dick could think about was his growing relationship with Hugh Hefner. He couldn't get over the fact that the very first story he'd sold to the best-paying magazine in the country had actually gone for double. That was like Herbert Gold or Nelson Algren or somebody. From a small-time hack barely making a living he had become, in one telephone call, a literary figure. With the girl safely gone and the events of the night entered in his journal, Dick got out his carbon of The Story. He needed to know what made this one different from his other stories. They were all pretty much alike as far as he could tell.

Dick's apartment was a large studio on the second floor of an old wooden building near downtown, on SW Fourth Street. There were windows on two sides and plenty of light, important in Portland because of the weather. His bed was a mattress on the floor with a nice crazy quilt his mother had given him. There were a couple of old overstuffed chairs and a kitchen area with a small old refrigerator and stove. His desk in the corner overlooked the back garden, and now he sat at it, in jeans and white tee, trying to figure out how he'd hit the daily double. The story was about a man tricking a woman into bed by pretending he didn't want to, surely nothing original, just an excuse for humor, he'd believed when he sent it to Bob. He'd hoped maybe Caper would buy it for two fifty. Instead, *Playboy*, king of the girlie books, had paid Three Thousand Dollars!

By the end of the week everybody in Portland knew about it. Dick hardly had to pay for a beer or an espresso, people were so eager to hear about the sale. There were only a handful of writers or artists of any kind in Portland, and they all tended to know each other. Now they all knew that Dick Dubonet, not the most hopeful of the bunch, in fact often looked down on because he was willing to start at the bottom, had hit the jackpot. Even the most egregious Reed College aesthete would have to acknowledge that three thousand dollars was a lot of money for couple of hours of work. Well, five or six hours.

The best part had been telling his friendly competition, Martin Greenberg. Marty was a wonderful guy, tall and thin, with sunken hungry eyes and a small delicate almost female mouth. Marty was contemptuous of Dick's girlie book sales, having himself much higher ambitions. Meanwhile he lived off his girlfriend and if he was writing anything Dick hadn't seen any evidence. He talked a good game, though, and was fun to argue with. And it could not be denied that Marty had a way with girls, especially intellectual girls. Hanging around with Marty had often gotten Dick laid.

They ran into each other in the middle of the Park Blocks, Dick walking to Meier & Frank to buy some new jeans, Marty heading up to Portland State to spend the afternoon in the library.

"Hello," said Dick in his deepest voice. Marty was wearing his topcoat, and his somewhat thinning brown hair was blowing around. Rain fell lightly, but neither of them paid any attention. They shook hands formally and Dick wondered if Marty had already heard.

"Let me buy you a cup of coffee," he heard himself saying. Marty's eyebrows went up. He knew Dick didn't throw money around.

"What happened, did you sell something big?" Smart bastard.

"What makes you think that?"

Marty just grinned, hands in his pockets, and so Dick told him the news. "Three grand?" Marty said.

"Minus commission," Dick said. Marty did not have an agent.

Suddenly Marty looked serious. "Is this true?" he asked.

"Yes," Dick said. It was a little infuriating that Marty didn't ask about the story itself. Like most people, he seemed interested only in the money.

"Listen," Marty said. "I need to borrow some dough."

"You do?" Dick had walked into this one.

"Fifty bucks," Marty said, with a little of the New York guttural in his voice.

Dick sighed. He'd lend his friend the fifty dollars. The price of success. Or, to be more accurate, the price of braggadocio.

13.

Too late. He'd boasted too much. When he walked into Jerry's Tavern every head turned, or so it seemed. He showed his teeth in a smile. He even went up and ordered a beer, which he hadn't intended doing unless there was somebody, preferably female, he wanted to sit with.

"On the house," said Nick the bartender, sliding the fifteen-cent glass of Blitz-Weinhard over to him. The first taste was delicious, as always. When he lowered his glass and licked the beer off his upper lip he found himself looking into a pair of eyes almost as dark as his own.

"I'm Linda McNeill," she said. Her skin was incredibly white, her hair black, cut in a pageboy bob. "I'm a friend of Marty Greenberg's," she said and smiled, showing deep dimples of amusement.

How did you recognize me? he wanted to ask, but didn't. Marty had been seeing a girl who played in the Portland Symphony.

Dick signaled for two beers and escorted Linda McNeill to a booth. She seemed to have a nice figure under her winter clothes.

"I'm glad I ran into you," she said. "I'm leaving for San Francisco in a couple days, just to see some friends, you know, and here you are?"

"How did you recognize me?" he asked.

"I've seen you around. Here, the old Lompoc House, Caffe Espresso, you know, the regular places." She went on to explain that while she wasn't much of a writer herself, she knew a lot of writers, and was going to see them, a lot of them, when she went to San Francisco. In twenty minutes or so she mentioned Jack Kerouac, Lawrence Ferlinghetti, Allen Ginsberg, Gary Snyder, William Burroughs, and Gregory Corso. Apparently she knew them all, was one of the supporting figures of the Beat movement, which she discussed eagerly and incessantly, while Dick bought her round after round of beer. She'd removed her scarves and hat and dark blue coat, revealing a promising figure. Talking with great enthusiasm, she also from time to time lifted her hair in the back, showing a beautiful slim neck and also pushing her breasts toward him invitingly. She was taking a sheaf of her poetry down to give to Don Allen, San Francisco editor of *Evergreen Review*, and the reason she'd wanted to run into Dick was to see if he had any stories she could carry to Don Allen. Apparently she and Allen were close friends and he willingly took her advice on what to publish.

Which Dick didn't exactly believe. But Linda was such a vivacious talker and was so pretty and seemed to be flirting with him, though not in an obvious way, that he played along. Not that he wanted to be published in *Evergreen Review*. They paid almost nothing, he knew from reading *Writer's Digest*. And though the Beat writers were getting a lot of attention, they were not his kind of people.

"I went to high school with Gary Snyder's sister," he said at one point.

"I'll tell him hello for you," she said.

"I do have one story that might fit in," he said later, when they were both a little soused and he'd gone through three dollars. "Would you like to read it?"

"Sure," she said. "I'm a good judge of material."

"I'd love to read some of your poetry," he remembered to say. "I'll take you home, if you like, and on the way we can stop at my place and pick up the story." She agreed and they drained their glasses and went out of the tavern into a wet cold night. They drove the few blocks to his apartment in his little yellow MG, his pride and joy, and she was properly appreciative. "What a cute little car! I can't get over how cute it is!"

"Would you like to come up for a minute, get warm?" he asked as he parked outside the building.

"I could wait right here," she said. "Will you be long?"

"Well, I'm not exactly sure where the story is."

He helped her out of the car. Her hand was warm and dry. Which meant she wasn't at all nervous. A good sign, because Dick had every intention of making a pass. He was getting excited. He loved the chase. He followed her up the dark stairs not touching her. He did not want to make any mistakes now, no stupid moves. You had to herd them carefully into place, not spook them, then let the natural consequences of proximity do their work.

"I love your apartment," she said, when he turned on the light. "This is a real writer's pad."

"Would you like to use the bathroom?" he asked politely. "I'll start looking for that story." She went into his bathroom, which he kept neat for just such occasions, and he looked into his refrigerator. One quart of beer. He hoped it would be enough. "Would you like a glass of beer?" he called out.

"Do you have any coffee?" she asked through the door.

"Good, I'd rather have coffee too," he said, to put them both on the same side. He started boiling water, got out two cups and saucers, and spooned a heaping amount of Folger's Instant into each cup. He wondered about all those famous poets she claimed to know. And Kerouac. She talked about Kerouac as if she had lived with him. He wondered what she was doing in Portland. Of course a lot of the Beat movement came out of Reed College, but that was all over with.

She came out of the bathroom and stood in the middle of the apartment, her hands at the back of her neck, lifting her silky black hair. "I've been thinking about wearing my hair up," she said. "What do you think?"

"I think you're the most beautiful woman in Portland."

She laughed. "No, really. Up or down."

"I like both." He moved toward her and she did not tense up but smiled shyly and lowered her eyes, raising them again as their lips touched. He didn't push it, just a nice gentle kiss, but as he was about to pull away he felt her hand on his cheek. That was the sign he'd been waiting for. He put his tongue into her mouth and she put her arms around him and pressed her pelvis into his, causing his penis to begin swelling immediately.

"Oh, you feel good," she said.

It is so great being an adult, he thought, as they easily and happily went to bed. But while he might have gotten into bed with Linda McNeill feeling adult, by morning, after hours of lovemaking, he felt like a child. A happy child. The sex exceeded anything Dick had experienced, and Dick had been a ski instructor in Aspen, Colorado, and considered himself fairly sophisticated. But this girl was something else. It wasn't the moves. He knew the moves. It was the passion, the spirit. All he could think of was the Kama Sutra, the Thread of Passion. She had lazily, sensually, humorously, lovingly, joyfully wrapped him in the silk threads of her passion, and made of him a cocoon.

14.

Dick Dubonet's father had been a lawyer with a small personal practice. He died of a heart attack when Dick was seventeen, leaving trust funds for Dick and his mother. Dick's became available to him on his twenty-first birthday, just in time to save him from law school. He finished his B.A. at Lewis & Clark and spent a couple of years skiing, first at Timberline, then on to Aspen and the ski patrol, where he was also a member of the Torch

Team, holding a flaming torch as he and the other patrollers performed their nightly ceremonial, the Descent of Fire. He took a lot of notes for a novel about the ski patrol. He'd known for years he wanted to be a writer, and he made sure to do a little writing every morning. His trust fund gave him a little over a hundred dollars per month. It wasn't great but it was a base. It took the major worry out of life, left him free to travel, to look around, to meet girls, to make friends.

But instead of being a happy ski bum, Dick was miserable. It was a capacity of his, to be unhappy for no reason. Maybe that was why he saw himself as a writer. There was a famous novelist living in Aspen, Leo Norris, who'd written three best-sellers, big fat books Dick could hardly work his way through, but they'd made old Norris rich and famous, and Dick would always pay attention when Norris came around. He had a big spread outside town with a steady stream of glamorous visitors. When he came to town to party he was always surrounded by beautiful people, although he himself was a little gnome with fierce red eyebrows and voice that could slice bacon. The first thing Dick noticed about Leo Norris was how unhappy he seemed, how unsatisfied with all the things that should have made him happy. Dick once ran into Norris at the little grocery next to the Aspen Lodge. They were both buying instant coffee, and both wanted the last jar of Folger's. Dick actually had it in his hand when Leo Norris pushed his angry face into his and all but snarled, "I was just about to reach for that."

Dick's first thought was *tough titty*, but he didn't say it. The man's rudeness was shocking, even to a member of the ski patrol. He clearly wanted Dick to give him the jar and take some lesser brand for himself. He probably knew that Dick knew who he was, and was hoping his fame and wealth would entitle him to the Folger's. But it was a cold morning, Dick had a slight hangover, and there was a nice girl waiting in his bed.

"Better luck next time," he said to Leo Norris, and was amused to see the famous writer actually bite his lip in frustration. "Oh, hell, take it," Dick said, and handed over the jar. He made a mental note not to become an asshole.

Eventually Dick grew tired of ski bum talk. He burned his notes for a novel and returned to Portland, found the perfect bachelor's pad, and settled into learning to write. He was an orderly person, and knew that the best way to succeed was to work hard and be thorough. He kept records of his expenditures, which were few. Being a writer cost almost nothing: typewriter, twenty-five dollars, a nice little used Smith Corona portable; paper, a dollar a ream, plus carbon paper and newsprint for second sheets; manila envelopes and stamps; and that was about it. He was in business.

Of course there were all kinds of writing. He wanted to try them all, but the important thing was to get some short stories written, to break through the publication barrier, to get paid for his work. Then branch out. He read all kinds of magazines, looking for ideas. Read mystery stories, science fiction, romance, straight fiction, everything from the *Saturday Evening Post* to *Rogue*. When he found a story that appealed to him, he'd sit down and doggedly retype it, learning the construction, learning the tricks. And every morning he'd get up, drink two cups of coffee, read the *Daily Oregonian*, then sit down at his shiny black typewriter, crack his knuckles, and write at least a thousand words. Seven days a week, no matter who stayed overnight, or how he felt, or whether it was a holiday. If there was a girl in the apartment, he'd explain to her carefully that he had this obligation to write. Most took it in good grace and found their way out. Some he had to indulge, even take home or sit over coffee with, but eventually they'd be gone and he could sit down at the machine.

Tap tap tap, out came the stories, usually ten to twelve pages. Dick typed his first and second drafts single-spaced, with narrow margins, on both sides of the paper. The third and final draft he typed on fresh bond, double-spaced, formatted as he'd seen in *Writer's Digest*. He kept a record of every story he mailed out. When the ten by twelve manila envelopes came back he slit them open without any hope in his heart, removed the story and the rejection slip, read the slip, and then put the story into a fresh envelope and sent it to the next magazine on his list, which started at *Playboy* and ended down among the pulps. There were magazines that kept your material forever, and others that would print you without paying. He avoided these, and carefully read the

Writer's Digest reports. He didn't send his stories to the *New Yorker, Esquire, Atlantic Monthly,* or *Harper's.* He didn't consider himself good enough yet. He stuck to girlie books, mystery books, and sci fi books. Now that he was a pro he no longer thought of them as magazines.

He could maintain this existence on his small inheritance because he was a careful spender. Much as he loved women, he'd resolved not to marry or even get serious until he had at least fifty thousand dollars in the bank. That was a comfortable distance and so he was shocked to find himself in love with Linda McNeill.

After that first night together, Dick did not want to let her go. He wanted her here, in his apartment, where could look at her, touch her, talk to her. It was like suddenly discovering you needed heroin, and lots of it. He knew it would be an awful mistake to let her know how he felt, but after only a little while he knew he could hide nothing from her.

"I love you," he blurted. He'd been looking at her skin, her incredibly white skin, just going over her body an inch at a time, stroking her, brushing his lips against her, while she lay back in his bed smiling.

"You do, huh?" She touched him on the shoulder.

"I say that to all the girls," he said, trying desperately to recover himself, but she laughed.

"I don't believe you."

"Which don't you believe?"

She put her hands into his hair and turned him so their eyes met. Hers were calm enough, even amused. "I love you too," she said. "But we aren't going to get married, are we?"

"Gee, I hope not," he joked.

"That's good." She pulled him gently up to be kissed. Her lips actually seemed to burn him, he was so sensitive.

They stayed together for three days. On that first morning Dick had at one point said, "Well, here's my routine. I gotta write for a couple of hours. You'll have to leave, but we can get together this afternoon, unless you have something to do . . ."

She was still in bed, covers pulled up against the cold room. "Why?"

"Why what?"

"I can stay here while you write," she said. "I've been with writers before, you know."

Kerouac. He'd forgotten about her adventures with the Beat writers. But he didn't know if he could write with her there. He had to bluff it out. He made coffee and brought her hers in bed, then went to his typewriter. He was in the middle of a story, for *Playboy* he hoped, so it was relatively easy to start working. Habit took over. She made no noise, and soon he had all but forgotten her. He turned in his chair, an old wooden folding bridge chair. She was lying in his bed, black hair against the white pillow, her hands grasping her shoulders. Dick had never seen anything more beautiful in his life.

"You're good, aren't you?" she said. "I can tell from the way you type."

Somehow he believed her.

15.

His perfect bachelor pad was now too small. It was fine that she had experience with writers and knew how to keep quiet, but apart from that first time it bugged Dick to have her in the room while he tried to write. On the other hand, he hated it when she was gone. The dilemma could be solved only by moving. He got no work done for a month, while he and Linda honeymooned, took side trips around the northern part of the state, and looked for a place where they could live together. Linda wouldn't tell Dick where she had been staying or who with, if anybody. "It's not right," was her only explanation. She wouldn't let him drive her home, asking to be let off at the intersection of NW Twenty-First and Johnson, a shabby industrial neighborhood. Dick understood, just as he understood that Linda would never explain why she'd left exciting bop neon San Francisco for dull wet Portland.

She'd come north with some guy, of course. And was living with the sap at NW Twenty-First. And was going to leave him for Dick Dubonet.

Dick was never satisfied. Either the places they found were too expensive, too small, too big, or too far from downtown. Dick couldn't see himself living east of the Willamette River, though prices were higher on the west side. Then they found a treasure. His friend Karl Metzenberg, who owned the Caffe Espresso, told him about a block of hillside houses that had been condemned for a freeway interchange, a big chunk of Old Portland being wiped out to allow north–south traffic to cruise through without stopping. But the project had been delayed, leaving a whole block available at unbelievably low prices.

SW Cable Street had twelve houses on the hill side, each with long flights of wooden steps rising through old green-stained concrete retaining walls and lush overgrown gardens. The houses on the down side were all rented to artists. The hillside houses were harder to rent because of the steps. Dick and Linda had their choice at forty-five dollars a month. The landlord was a bank and didn't care. Eventually all the houses would be torn down. It was perfect. They took the house at 33 Cable, big living room, big kitchen and dining room, two bedrooms. For his office Dick took the front bedroom overlooking Cable Street, with a view on good days of Mount Hood, sixty miles east.

They spent a week buying things at St. Vincent and the Goodwill. Dick calculated that the move and the addition of Linda was going to cost him dearly, running his nut up to two hundred dollars a month. Good luck that among the traits they shared was the trait of thrift. She was as careful as he was. They found bargains to cackle over and take home, so though Dick spent money like water he worried about it only in the early morning, when he'd wake up in a cold sweat. She was so beautiful it made him paranoid. What did she want with him? Could it really be love? Or was she being clever? She still thought of him as the kind of writer who could command huge sums from magazines. She didn't know the truth. Had the money attracted her? She could be pretending to go along with his cheapness to lull him into security. Then, when he can't live without her, she becomes a spendthrift.

He hated such thoughts, but early in the mornings, when he was wide awake and she slept, they came to him. For the ten thousandth time he concluded he had an inferiority complex. She was attracted to him because he was a success, yes, but also for other qualities. Handsome. He had to admit that. Nice car. Money. Talent. Although he was not quite sure about the talent. He hoped he had talent. If he didn't, he'd make up for the lack by working hard. Another good talent. No wonder she fell for him. What a prince. He knew why he'd fallen for her. She was too good for him. Too beautiful, too attractive to other men. More inferiority complex. When he walked into a tavern or party with Linda it made him glow with conceit. As if he needed her to prove what a hot guy he was. The sale to *Playboy* had done a lot for his ego, but Linda had done more.

The writing suffered for a month, but he had fourteen stories in circulation. Fortunately for his sanity, Linda found a job as a secretary downtown, and was gone all day. Thank god. But it wasn't until she handed him her first paycheck, eighty-seven fifty-eight after deductions, that he began to believe that she really did love him. And he needed the assurance, because Linda was having trouble liking what he wrote.

First he laughed. "You're not supposed to like it." She'd been less than wildly enthusiastic about his new story, which he hadn't sent to anybody yet. "It's for men. It's a man's story."

"I like it," she lied, making it clear by her innocent expression that she was lying. "Have you read 'October in the Railroad Earth'?" And there it was, the inevitable comparison. The odious comparison. "Yeah," he said. "I admit I'm no Kerouac," he added gruffly.

"Oh, I wasn't—"

"Sure you weren't." His feelings weren't hurt long. He was used to people complimenting him on a story and then taking it back with a cutting remark. A lot of people secretly wanted to be writers, and they were jealous. He was used to people saying, "I read your story," and then waiting for him to ask them how they liked it. Falling into the trap. So they could say, "Oh, it was okay," or some other critical remark. He hoped he would not react every time Linda snubbed his work, and told himself it shouldn't matter that she didn't gushingly love every word he wrote. But it did. He told himself that if she loved his work after a while he probably would have grown tired of her. This way, there was a constant excitement, a constant need for him to improve. She would be his goad, his shining ideal.

They gave a party when the *Playboy* story appeared. It was the lead, as promised, and had a wonderful illustration. There was a picture of Dick in the front of the magazine with the other contributors, and Dick entertained everyone telling them about the photo session, which had lasted three hours for a tiny little head shot. Everybody on the block was invited, and Dick's friends from Portland State and Reed. Painters, sculptors, musicians, lots of musicians with their guitars and banjos, a few would-be writers, some teachers and social workers, and after the party got going everybody who was not playing an instrument got up and danced, the new Portland-style dance, where you put your hands on your hips and kicked up high. It was a great party, and people talked about it for months. Portland finally had a group.

16.

Stan Winger started writing down his various thoughts and ideas in the Multnomah County jail up at Rocky Butte. There was nothing to do anyway but sit on the benches and play cards, and Stan was broke and looking at sixty days. At first it seemed stupid, just scrawling down whatever he felt like writing, but Marty Greenberg had been very enthusiastic about Stan's brain and had talked about intellectual freedom and the power of ideas. Of course they had both been full of coffee, sitting around half the night at Jolly Joan's on Broadway. Jolly Joan's was open all night, a big room full of night people and insomniacs, one of Stan's regular hangouts when he was on the bricks. The regulars pretty much all knew each other, at least by sight, and

Stan and Marty had got to talking one night until 4:00 a.m. sitting next to one each other at the long counter. There were only a few people in the place at the time, and Marty was flirting with the waitress in her pink and white uniform.

"Let me take you away from here," he kidded.

"I'll bring your order, then we can fly to Mexico," she said. She was plump and cute. Stan could never have kidded her easily like that. It was a quality he admired. He'd seen Marty a few times, and figured him for one of those intellectuals, which turned out to be true.

"You're buying the tickets," Marty said, and winked at Stan.

Stan smiled and picked up his coffee to cover his shyness. He wished he had the gift of talking to people. Fortunately for him, Marty Greenberg had the gift, and opened Stan up like a can of peas. Over a month or so they became buddies, at least late-night buddies, and Stan went into JJ's now hoping to run into Marty for one of their deep conversations. Stan had never realized how bottled up he was.

"You're a shy man, you don't like to talk about things," Marty told him. "So you should become a writer."

"I can't write," Stan said. "I didn't even graduate from high school."

"All the better," Marty said, and they started talking about the educational system and how fucked up it was. It was Stan's opinion that what had happened to American education was that the students had learned to beat the system. "It used to be if you fucked up you were punished, but kids finally learned that the teachers were scared of the kids, and scared to punish them. You know, 'Flunk me and die.'"

"You're a fairly clear thinker," Marty told him another time. Was Marty a student? Stan wasn't sure. Stan didn't tell Marty he was a thief.

Writing down his thoughts was hard at first. Though his mind was bursting with ideas, when he actually sat down on the narrow wooden bench in the dayroom, men all around him playing cards or dominoes, and opened the stenographer's pad he had hustled, just seeing that blank page of little blue lines emptied his brain. He sat clicking his ballpoint pen until somebody

said, "Hey, asshole, what the fuck you doin'?" Embarrassed, he bent forward
and started writing. He couldn't think of anything else, so he wrote about the
room. It was something to do. He did not get along easily with other men,
in jail or out, and he was far too shy to get along with women. The great
thing about being a thief was that it didn't take up all that much of your
time. The bad thing was that you had a lot of time on your hands. Especially
if the stealing wasn't going that well, which was often. Stan had never made
a really big score. Actually, he wasn't much of a thief. He really didn't have
any control over himself, that was all, and when he would go a little crazy he
would do the stealing. It was like an aura coming over him, a light feeling,
an empty feeling, but not unpleasant. His mind would just get silly, and he'd
feel as if no one could stop him. Nothing was real. He'd be walking down a
street and see a house and know that it was empty and he could penetrate. By
this time he'd be really excited, still feeling invulnerable, and he'd find himself
walking around to the back, as if he owned the place, casual, just this small
ordinary-looking guy, walking up to the kitchen door or down the outdoor
staircase or lifting open the window and slipping inside, that exact moment
of penetration giving him a feeling he could not describe, taking over the
entire center of his body, so intense sometimes that he had to stop halfway
and get control over himself.

Then inside, in the silence of the house, the good feeling would take over.
He was powerful and in control. The house was his. Once he was sure he was
alone, he would just walk through the silence, enjoying the way every house
was different inside. He usually broke into homes that were well kept up.
They were the ones that made him feel good. There was something incredibly intimate about being in somebody's house, as if he and the people of
the house were very close. And yet he would do these things. Things having
nothing to do with making a living. Things he didn't like to think about.
Most of the time he was neat and careful, just going to the places where
he knew people kept their valuables. But then, their jewelry or cash in his
pockets, an even stranger feeling would overtake him. He might find himself
pissing on the bed or into bureau drawers full of women's underthings. What

the hell was that all about? Often he would take a crap on the dining room table, or somewhere else just as bad. Or sit down and have a meal out of the refrigerator, with this intense sexual feeling passing through him, making him brave beyond sanity. When, in fact, he was a complete coward.

He read over what he'd written. He was disgusted by it. Real bad. Pointless clumsy shit. But when the deputies took his notebook from him, he realized the power of the writing. There'd been nothing in those few pages to bother anybody, just descriptions of things and people, lousy descriptions at that, and the guards had to tear it up. To show their power. But what they showed him was their lack of power.

Another guy might have grinned at the deputy and said something like, "Go ahead. It's all right here," and tap his head. Hinting at an exposé. But of course Stan Winger was not that type of guy. He just bent over and picked up the pieces from where the deputy had dropped them, and moved along.

He lived on SW Fourth Street at the Mark Hotel, where his room cost him seven dollars a week. He did all his stealing in the daytime, and suffered insomnia at night, so the writing was good for him. Under his bed were stacks of paperbacks and pulps, which used to be his only form of home entertainment. Now he could sit on the bed with his notebook on his lap and write. His dream was to develop his writing skills to the point where he could make a living at it. He'd write the kind of stories he liked, pulp, only without all the bullshit he hated. He didn't take himself all that seriously, but after a while he found he was writing every night. He'd long since stopped writing mere impressions, and had moved onto actual stories by the time he showed any of his work to Marty Greenberg.

"You wrote this?" They were at Jolly Joan's, it was about four in the morning and snowing hard against the big front windows. Marty's face was lit up as he read through the notebook, stopping once in a while to laugh or consider Stan with amazement. "This stuff is great!" he said finally, slapping the notebook shut and handing it back to Stan.

"Gee," was all he could say.

"No," Marty said, waving his hand. "Not really great, but great for what you're doing. I've never read any detective stories, but you seem to have a real grasp of the medium."

By this time Marty knew he was a thief. As Stan had imagined, the knowledge made Marty even more interested in him.

"You know what you ought to do? You ought to write about stealing. From the inside. That could be a real contribution."

Stan had not been thinking about a contribution. The idea of writing about stealing terrified him. "You want me put away?" he joked, and Marty laughed.

"I want you to do your best."

17.

Marty took Stan Winger for coffee at Karl Metzenberg's Caffe Espresso one rainy night, explaining that the place was the hangout of a lot of Portland's artists and writers. "Many are girls," Marty pointed out as they walked up the hill from Jolly Joan's. Stan envied Marty's way with girls. At twenty-four he'd never dated or kissed a girl. He'd been robbing houses since he was thirteen. No time for girls. You could put it that way. One reason he'd dropped out was that the only reason for going to school was meeting girls, and none of the girls at Parkrose Junior High or David Douglas High were interested enough to speak to him. And of course he couldn't speak to them first. The words wouldn't come. This is part of what drove him to a life of crime. He needed money, and as a foster kid he never had any. With money he could buy love.

Now, coming in through the tall white double doors of the Caffe Espresso, he felt on the edge of a new adventure. He'd never been taken seriously before, except as a thief, and then only by the cops. But Marty Greenberg took him seriously as a beginning writer and seemed to like him as a person. The place was about half full, a middle-sized room with two high wooden ceiling fans lazily moving smoke around. Marty introduced Stan to Metzenberg, a chunky young guy wearing a dress shirt, bow tie, and a big white apron, bowed and scraped like a maître d' in a movie, but with an ironic grin that meant he was half-kidding. Metzenberg escorted them to a table in the back corner. All the tables had white tablecloths. Marty ordered espressos. Stan had never had one, but was willing to try. Some of the girls in the room were pretty terrific looking, college girls or graduate students, according to Marty.

"Stan's a writer," Marty said to Metzenberg, just loud enough to be heard by the two girls at the next table.

"Dick Dubonet just left," Metzenberg said. The girls at the next table were really paying attention now. Stan knew who Dick Dubonet was, though until Marty told him, Stan hadn't realized that in a city the size of Portland there would be published writers.

The guy wrote for *Playboy*. One of Stan's favorite magazines, although he suspected they airbrushed their nudes. But he didn't much like the stories. They seemed soft to him, too much about romance, an element lacking in Stan's life. He much preferred stories that had more at stake, life and death. Sometimes *Playboy* had stories like that, but not often enough. He wondered which kind Dick Dubonet wrote. But he didn't ask. He didn't know how to phrase his question. He wouldn't ask Marty, not in this intellectual stronghold. Stan never felt anxious about robbing houses until afterward, but the prospect of girls put a cold hand on his chest.

Marty was already talking to the girls at the table. Stan tried to look keen instead of nervous. Both girls had taken glancing looks at him, and as far as he could tell had looked away without interest. If Marty actually did pick them up, he'd have to take care of them himself. Stan had already decided he wasn't going to make any passes tonight. He was just too tense.

But the girls got up and left. Stan felt better immediately, but he also felt a little disappointed. The day was going to have to come when he slept with a girl he hadn't paid for. He thought about getting a whore tonight. Not as easy as it used to be, not in Portland. When Stan first started visiting whorehouses there had been several downtown, all protected by the cops, in upstairs hotels over businesses. The price had been five dollars short and sweet or ten dollars long and sweet, easily worth the money as far as Stan was concerned. Then Portland had elected a woman mayor, Dorothy McCullough Lee, and after taking office the first thing she did was call the head of the local mob, Francis Feeney, and tell him she knew the address of every whorehouse in Portland and wanted them closed that night. They were closed that night. Stan was forced to go north, to Vancouver, Washington, just across the Columbia River, to get laid. That was okay, because Vancouver had a couple of pretty good card clubs and Stan loved to play cards. In fact, he sometimes told people he made his living as a gambler. Ha ha. But people would believe it was a romantic way to earn a living. He'd explained this to Marty, who assured him he wouldn't tell anybody he was a thief, instead stick to the story that he was a gambling man.

So now there were no girls in Portland who'd make love to Stan. Of course there would be girls for rich men in the big hotels like the Benson or the Multnomah, but they weren't for Stan. Anyway, he liked the cheap hookers in Vancouver. He could talk to them easily. They were like him, born criminals, no excuses.

"I'm sorry to see them go," Marty said when the girls were gone. "I was kind of hoping to get laid tonight. Or at least introduce you to Dick Dubonet."

"I thought you had a girlfriend," Stan said. People at other tables were playing chess. He'd played a little jailhouse chess. He wondered how he'd do against these intellectuals. Probably not too well.

"You're right," Marty said. "But my girl is home. We're here." He explained that he and his girl, a waitress at Jolly Joan's, lived together only as a convenience. They'd known each other at Reed College, and when they both dropped out before Junior Quals they ended up living together in a little place on SW Second. "But we're not in love," Marty said. "I'm ashamed, but there you are."

They discussed love for a while, and then Dick Dubonet came in, dripping wet, slapping his big safari hat on his jeans and waving with a big grin. "Marty!"

Stan stood up to shake hands with the writer. He was a good-looking little guy, about an inch shorter than Stan, who was only five seven himself. He had a good hard handshake, though. Stan was ashamed of his own, his palm wet most of the time, so that he was unwilling to really squeeze a guy's hand.

"Sorry, my hand's wet," he said, and wished he hadn't.

"All of Oregon's wet tonight," Dick Dubonet said rather loudly, as if he was talking to all the people at the nearby tables. He sat, tilting back in his chair, very much at home. Obviously, the local kingpin.

"We were just talking about love," Marty said, loudly himself. "Stan's a writer too."

Dick's eyebrow went up. "Really? What's your name again?"

"I haven't published anything." Stan grinned down at the tablecloth.

"Ah," Dick said. "Would-be writer."

"That's it," said Stan, hating Dubonet fiercely.

Marty put a hand on Stan's wrist and smiled. "Don't hate him," he said.

"Huh?" Was it written all over his face? "I don't hate anybody," he said.

"How often do you write?" Dick asked, in a friendly way.

"What do you mean?"

"Every day? Once a week? Two hours a month?"

"None of your fucking business." He looked Dick right in the eye. His stomach hurt. He was no fighter, but he didn't have to take this shit. They all sat and listened to the room for a while. Some kind of classical music tinkled in the background.

"Okay," Marty said. "My fault. Let's start over."

Stan looked at Dick, waiting for his comment. Dick looked upset, no longer in charge. Maybe he's a pussy inside, just like me, Stan thought, and his heart warmed. He made himself smile. "I'm sorry," he said. "I'm too touchy. I'm not a writer, just fooling around. I like pulp stories, you know, mysteries, stuff like that."

"I've published in *Ellery Queen's Mystery Magazine*," Dick said. He wasn't smiling but he wasn't angry either.

"That's a great magazine," Stan said.

"I'm sorry." Dick held out his hand. "I'm an asshole."

"Me too," Stan agreed. This time their handshake was warm and firm.

"Then it's agreed," Marty said, holding up his little espresso cup in salute. "*Tres assholes!*"

18.

He wasn't breaking into houses at this particular time. Instead he made his money boosting clothes for a guy. The guy had a regular list of businessmen customers he stole for. The customer told the guy what he wanted and the guy told Stan and Stan went into the store wearing old stuff from the Salvation Army and walked out wearing the items requested. It was easy but took nerve. It wasn't like house penetration but it was fun, exciting. You had to be careful you didn't get all heady and start boosting everything in sight. "Never grift on the way out," was good old con advice.

One day he walked into Sichel's, the best men's store in Portland, to pick up a camel's hair coat, size forty-two, when he ran into Marty Greenberg, standing in front of the triple mirrors admiring himself in a new topcoat. Marty smiled slyly and modeled the coat. "How do you like it?"

"Uh, fine," Stan said. He wondered how Marty could afford a hundred-dollar coat, but didn't ask. He couldn't steal anything now. He felt the energy he'd worked up flushing away, leaving him empty and depressed. He watched Marty trying on stuff, realizing that the guy was just having some fun. Stan pretended he too had come in just to look around.

"Best store in Portland," Marty said.

"So I've heard."

They were around the corner from Jolly Joan's. "Let's go say hello to my girlfriend," Marty said. It was sunny out, a nice spring day except for the cold wind. They walked together, hands in their pockets, heads bent into the wind. For some reason just seeing Marty made Stan feel like a different man. He could always go back and get the jacket later, although he didn't want to try Sichel's again so soon. Fahey-Brockman across Broadway had good jackets.

"How's the writing going?" Marty asked him. He held open the glass door to Jolly Joan's and Stan moved into the billowing warmth and clatter.

"It's going great," he said.

Meeting all these new people had made Stan self-conscious about sitting up all night scrawling in his notebooks. Before, he'd just been fucking around. Now he was *writing*. And these other guys had their own women, they were easy around women. In fact, unless he had things wrong, both Marty Greenberg and the famous Dick Dubonet had women who worked, and Marty didn't even have the excuse that he was writing. Marty was a philosopher, and when he did decide to write down his thoughts, it would be a huge work the whole world would have to pay attention to. But meanwhile he let his girlfriend or roommate or whoever she was do the working and pay the rent. Stan knew a couple of pimps from jail. They were funny entertaining guys, like Marty. When they weren't in jail they hung out at the Desert Room and talked about their big plans. Just like Marty, only Marty's big plans were philosophical rather than entrepreneurial, if that was the right word.

Stan didn't stop writing. He made sure he wrote two hours a night, recalling Dick's scornful inquiry. But he got tired of bending his short stubby fingers around a ballpoint and writing with his pad on his knee. If he was serious about this, he'd have to teach himself to type. He thought about stealing a typewriter and immediately backed away from the idea. The stealing was one part of his life. He wanted the writing to be different. All right, pure. Not part of his sickness, which he admitted ruled his life. The sick sexual desire that came over him on stealing days. The thing that was going to put him away. Bizarre, sick, unspeakable. Marty thought he was a hero for robbing houses, although he didn't know any details, only that Stan had "done a little stealing now and then." Said with a sly grin, as if Stan was Jesse James.

So he went down to the typewriter store across from Gill's, the big bookstore, and bought himself a used Underwood portable. He didn't tell Marty. He went up to Cameron's used bookstore and bought a typing book for a quarter and took it back to his room. Typing wasn't hard, once he got the trick of balancing the little machine on his knees. He picked up a used music stand to hold the exercise book. After he got tired of the exercises he struck on the idea of retyping stories he particularly liked. This would give him practice and teach him a little bit about how other writers, real writers, did it.

Marty's girl worked the counter at Jolly Joan's. She was beautiful, with big wide dark Jewish eyes, olive skin and high cheekbones, a real beauty, a girl who could be a movie star. She grinned across the counter at Marty and wiped the space in front of him with her wet rag.

"Hello, Marty," she said, then smiled at Stan. He could not recall ever having a woman this good-looking smile at him directly. It was like a shot of morphine. "Is this your friend Stan?" He shook her hand. Thank God his own happened to be dry. "I've heard so much about you," she said. She took their coffee orders and left. Great figure too, Stan noticed. He turned to Marty, who grinned at him.

"Yeah," Marty said. "Her name's Alexandra Plotkin."

"She's beautiful," Stan said stupidly.

"Shockingly beautiful. It's actually a problem. You know, big stalkers coming up to you and telling you how lucky you are to have such a girl. Of course she's not really my girl, but I don't tell them that."

Late that night Stan tried to write, but he couldn't get Alexandra's face out of his mind. Smiling at him. He gave up, put his typewriter in its cardboard box under the bed and tried to sleep. Sleep would not come for a long time, and he lay quietly, seeing her face hovering over him. Finally he must have slept, because he found himself in this big dark gloomy but beautifully furnished house, walking through the place in his stocking feet when he sees Alexandra standing in the middle of the floor, her arms at her sides. When he woke up he felt warm and pleasant, remembering how she looked in the dream. She was not Marty's girl. She had smiled at him. Maybe she could become his girl. Oh, Jesus. What a fool. He had to chuckle to himself, laying there like a jerk daydreaming. He held onto his prick for dear life, why didn't he just jerk off? A mystery. Maybe he respected her too much. Maybe, though, some day, he might really have the chance to—he refused even to use bad language about her in his mind—sleep with her, make love to her.

Even if he was willing, he wouldn't know how. Whores teach you nothing about romance. He had an idea for a story. About a burglar who meets a girl. A silly story, because burglars weren't the heroes of stories, but it was writing itself in his head while he lay there, and so he let it. Four days later he had the story down on paper, typed and everything. Reading it over he decided it was as good as a lot of the stories he had read. All it really needed was some educated person to help him fix up the grammar and spelling. He was a terrible speller, he knew. He'd have to get it typed by a professional. His own typing was too messy. He wondered how much he could get for the story from *Ellery Queen* or some other magazine. At the moment, sitting on the edge of the bed with his eleven pages in his hands, he recognized a great similarity between stealing and writing. Both were intensely private matters.

The thought of showing his story to Marty frightened him. And he knew he had to ask Dick Dubonet to read it. Marty didn't really know anything about this kind of writing. Sneering Dick Dubonet. Stan's stomach tightened at the thought of Dubonet looking up from his pages with that expression of contempt. Stan didn't think he could handle it. He would lose these new friends, and all that their friendship seemed to promise. On the other hand, if he didn't at least try to get them to read his story, he was a pussy.

19.

Marty's girl was quiet, with long straight blonde hair, not terribly good-looking from Dick's point of view, but with a nice little body concealed under layers of clothing. Her name was Mary Bergendaal and she played French horn for the symphony. She sat leaning against Marty as they sat and talked. Dick wasn't sure how he liked being sold somebody else's story.

"I'll read it," he'd told Marty over the phone, "if you buy me a Jerry's hamburger."

So here they were, with their hamburgers and fries in a basket, talking about American literature as it related to the pulps. Mary hadn't wanted to eat, and even refused the French fries Marty offered before putting them into his own mouth.

"Thing is, he's not really a writer," Marty said between bites.

"Then why should I read his story?"

"Out of human kindness," Marty said. "No, wait. Really. Don't you want to help others?"

Dick laughed. "Sure, if you put it that way." He felt good. The burgers were excellent, and he decided he enjoyed being the expert. He only wished Mary Bergendaal was better looking or more animated. He liked playing to pretty girls. She wasn't homely, she just didn't have much animation in her face. Maybe she put it all into the French horn.

"You have to understand," Marty said. "I've been encouraging this guy. He's practically illiterate, working-class kind of guy, and he has this deep urge to write stories. This is the first one he's had the guts to show to anybody."

Marty pulled the manila envelope from under his topcoat dramatically, fanned himself with it, and said, "It's hot stuff. I like it." He handed it to Dick, who hefted it in his hand and then put it on the seat beside him.

"I can't promise to get to it right away," he said. What bullshit. But he continued. "I'll try to have an answer for you in a week." Ugh. Arrant showing off. He looked at Mary. She looked at her cigarette.

"The point is to encourage him," Marty said. "Not put him down."

"Oh, don't worry, I'll be kind."

He read the story the minute he got home. Linda wasn't back from work yet, so he had the place to himself. He had expected crapola, and was pleasantly surprised to see that the guy knew how to put together a simple sentence. He found himself sucked right in, but didn't really much like what he found. A cute idea, burglar comes into a house he thinks is empty to find a beautiful girl sleeping in her bed. The burglar tries to talk his way out of it, but the girl sees through him. The twist: she likes him. The irony comes when they find him sleeping in bed with the girl. Cute. But the characters and dialogue were crude and the ending not as surprising as the author hoped. Not very original, either. In fact, a piece of shit. But Dick had promised to be kind to this guy, this insomniac buddy of Marty's from downtown. Marty was always going on and on about the characters you meet "on the street." Now here was this character who wanted to pull himself up into the middle class by writing. It seemed sad, pathetic. All over America, he imagined, working class people who read only crap aspired to try to write this same crap. The guy needed a typist. And a college education. Dick wondered what Stan did for a living. Marty said he was a professional gambler, but Marty romantically exaggerated everything. Dick figured the guy had some menial job.

Did he have the strength of character to look Stan Winger in the eye and tell him to forget writing? Trouble was, people thought just because they knew how to read and write, they could *write*. He sighed. If he told the guy the story was okay but rough, he might take it back, write like hell, then come back to Dick for another reading, for advice, maybe even for the name of his agent. He wondered what Bob Mills would say about a story like this. Maybe that was the easy way out of this social dilemma. Tell the guy he loves the story and send it to Mills, let him reject it. Then Dick would be off the hook. But he'd also look like a putz. Dick wished Marty had minded his own business.

Linda came home and Dick forgot about the story, leaving it out on the coffee table while he and Linda went into the bedroom. After dinner he came out into the living room while drying one of the dishes to find Linda reading Stan's little story. For some reason this made him angry, but he kept it to himself.

"How do you like it?" he asked, nonchalant, his stomach hard as a rock.

"This is your best story," she said, looking over at him seriously. She went back to reading as if she couldn't tear herself away. Dick exploded.

"My best story? Can't you tell I didn't even type it? And it's not my style, and it's a piece of shit." He stood trembling. She calmly kept reading. Linda didn't react to his tantrums anymore. He breathed deeply to relieve the strain, waiting for her to finish. To his disgust she gave a little exclamation, as if the end had surprised her, and then smiled up at Dick.

"Who wrote it?" she asked.

"Some asshole," he snapped. He grabbed the story from her hands and took it into his office. *Tres Assholes*, he remembered, and his mood softened. He was acting like a jealous idiot. And in front of Linda. He rubbed his face hard, to break up the nasty expression, stretching his facial muscles into a big smile. It hurt. What the hell did she know? He went out into the living room. Linda sat looking at him.

"I was just kidding," he said. "I think it's a great little story. For a pulp story."

Linda picked up a copy of *Esquire* and began thumbing through it. Dick wandered into his office. *Your best story.*

They met to discuss the story at Caffe Espresso on Saturday afternoon.

"First," Dick said to the pathetically tense face of Stan Winger, "I liked the story a lot. It needs work, don't get me wrong, but hell, I was expecting some piece of *crap*, not a story as smooth as this." Stan's face stayed tense. His knuckles, folded on the white tablecloth, white with strain. Dick handed him the manila envelope. He felt warm, even paternal. "I'd say run it through your typewriter one more time, then it's time to look for a typist and a possible submission."

"That's really great," Marty said. Stan said nothing.

"In fact," Dick said in his deepest voice, calmly, nicely, "I think I could send this to my agent. Then you'd have a professional opinion."

"Thanks," said Stan tightly. He wasn't very good-looking. Really, no threat to Dick. Dick would have to learn to control his jealousy. This was actually a very pleasant experience, being the teacher, being the expert.

"See?" Marty said to Stan. "I told you he'd be helpful."

"I really appreciate it," Stan said to Dick. "Your time and everything."

"Think nothing of it," Dick said expansively. "Some day we'll be colleagues. You'll be helping me." He hoped he wasn't piling it too deep. But people never seemed to tire of flattery.

"One little thing," Dick said. "I'd work on the character of the burglar a little bit. Doesn't quite ring true."

Marty snorted and gave Stan a look.

"What's funny?" Dick asked.

"Nothing," Marty said. He looked at Stan. "Can I tell him? He's very cool."

Stan smiled shyly. "I used to be a burglar," he said. "You know, little stuff. I based the story sort of on that."

"You're a criminal?" Dick said.

"A professional criminal," Marty said smoothly.

"Used to be," Stan said. There was a light in his eye Dick had not seen before. "Need anything?" he asked Dick, wickedly.

20.

"You liked the story so much," Dick said to Linda, "why don't you type it up for him?" They were at Buttermilk Corner, the upstairs cafeteria where Linda liked to have her lunch. She was buying. Dick had the cheeseburger and a baked apple, while Linda ate two chicken pot pies. She worked in a law office and sometimes had empty hours to fill. She'd offered to type Dick's clean copies for him, but he saw a trap in it. He felt more comfortable typing his own stuff, thank you, especially because it gave him another run at the material.

"I wouldn't mind," she said. "He's fascinating anyway."

"You mean because he's a second-story man?" Dick had been unable to keep the secret.

Linda smiled. She had a peasant face, he decided. As she got older her features would thicken, likely her body would thicken, and she'd become one of those solid women in cloth coats and babushkas you used to see in *Life* magazine. "Why don't we have a party?" she said. "You could bring your criminal friends and I could decide if I liked him enough to do his typing."

It was another guitar and banjo party, with a lot of dancing. Brownie McGee and Sonny Terry had been in Portland the week before and played in a garage over on the East side. The place had been packed, a memorable night, and everybody was still running around singing the blues. Dick invited Stan Winger, but Stan just sat in a corner nursing a beer and listening. He didn't even tap his foot while everybody else was stomping and screaming. It was a great party, lasting until five in the morning, and Stan was one of the last to leave. He seemed drunk but able to hold it.

He'd liked the party. It was the first he'd been to, or just about, and it made his stomach tense at first, but the people seemed so open-hearted and willing to accept him among them that he relaxed and spent the evening sneaking looks at the pretty girls. The beautiful girls. He couldn't get over how good-looking the girls were at this level of society. And Marty Greenberg's girl, more beautiful than anybody, wasn't here. Marty was with a tall redhead he introduced as Cybella. Whoever she was, a great dancer, with wonderful long legs that she kicked up into the air not caring what she showed, panties and all. All the women were like that, openly getting drunk and kissing guys and showing their bodies. Half had on low-cut dresses or blouses and there were tits everywhere.

As he was leaving, Dick and Linda, arm-in-arm, thanked him for coming and then Linda, with a sparkle in her eyes, took him aside on the front porch. The clouds to the east were getting light underneath. She put her hands on his arms and looked him in the eyes very seriously. Of course they were both drunk, and Dick was only a few feet away, talking to others who were going down the stairs, falling down, whooping, etc.

"I love your story," she said. "Here's your reward," and kissed him gently on the mouth. After the kiss was over he just stared at her, feeling her fingers on his arms. "I'll type it for you, if you like," she said. "So Dick can send it to his agent."

"Gee," Stan said like an idiot.

Linda laughed and pulled him to her. "Such a fine writer," she said into his ear.

He walked home filled with Linda, and hating himself for it. Not love, but certainly passion. She was Dick's girl and just being kind to Stan, but he couldn't help wanting her. This was how he repaid Dick for going out of his way to help. It was evil of him to think about Linda's kiss and how her breasts felt against him, how warmly he felt them now, remembering. But before he completely vanished into a daydream about Linda, he told himself severely that even if the opportunity arose, he wouldn't make a pass at Linda. He'd never made a pass at anybody anyway. Though maybe Linda would be different. She'd kissed him, hadn't she? And said that nice thing about his story. Maybe she'd make all the moves. The thought warmed him.

But the business of getting the story typed and sent to Robert P. Mills was not the pleasure Stan had hoped. He finally met Linda late on a Tuesday night at Jolly Joan's with his latest revision, now fourteen pages long. They sat in a booth and Stan sipped coffee while Linda read over the new pages. His buttocks sweated while he waited for her verdict. Not that it was going to be a verdict, but that was how he felt. Finally she looked up, her eyes soft. "You're a good writer."

"Sorry about the bad typing," he said. "And the grammar and spelling and all that stuff."

"I can help you with that if you want. I can clean it up."

They spent an hour drinking cup after cup of coffee and going over the story. By the end of it, Stan wondered what she'd meant by "good writer." She'd sweetly and quietly taken apart just about every sentence in the thing. She didn't like his choice of words and she didn't like the way he used exclamation points and she didn't like the characters, or at least she wanted to change them into entirely different people. By now Stan wasn't sure he even recognized the story. He didn't feel like a writer anymore. She was the writer. All he'd done was put down some crude stuff that she turned into a real story. She stacked the pages, squared the edges, and put them back into the envelope.

"What a night, huh?" she said with a grin. He didn't have the strength to speak, so just sat with his mouth open, gasping like a fish out of water. "I'd better drive you home," she said. "Dick will think we've run off."

"I can walk," he said. He'd been daydreaming that after they cleaned up the story she'd make a pass at him and he'd easily take her into his arms. But now he felt empty and sexless. "Give it back to me," he said. "It's not ready to type." He held out his hand for the envelope, but Linda put it in her lap with her purse.

"No. Let me type it and we'll see. If you don't like it, then we'll change it." She smiled as if everything was fine.

When they got to his part of town he suddenly panicked at the thought that she might, just might, ask to come up. He couldn't let her do that. He lived in a hole in the wall. "Let me out anywhere," he said.

At the corner of Jefferson and Second she stopped the car. There was no traffic. It was nearly three. Was he supposed to lean over and kiss her? He remembered from the party that these people kissed at the drop of a hat. She wouldn't be upset if he gave her a little kiss. He tried to smile, but grimaced instead. They were side by side in Dick's little yellow MG and he could smell her.

"I'll have this typed in a day or two," she said. "It depends on the workload."

"I appreciate this," he said. She leaned over and kissed him. When they broke she looked at him inquiringly. He could think of nothing to say except, finally, "G'bye!" and he was out of the car. He watched it drive away. Exactly the kind of car he wanted for himself some day. But he couldn't keep his mind on the car. He knew he'd failed. She'd given him the go-ahead to make a pass, and he'd been tongue-tied.

As he undressed in his tacky little room where they never could have come, he realized she hadn't been inviting him at all. The inquiring look had to do with something entirely different, like maybe he had bad breath and didn't know it. As he walked down the empty hall naked carrying his white towel, he decided to get a bottle of Listerine. You never knew.

21.

After Dick read the rewritten, edited, and cleanly typed version of Stan Winger's story he had to admit it was pretty good. His agent might not reject it. Maybe Dick had discovered an important new talent. Maybe he'd given a helping hand to somebody who was now going to kick him in the face. Could he turn his back on Stan? Just tell him coldly that the story wasn't good enough? No. He sent it to Bob Mills and sat back waiting, hoping, to hear bad news. He might be ashamed of himself, but he wasn't a perfect human being or anything close to it. He felt jealous. Being a thief gave Stan an unholy fascination, especially to Linda, who spoke of him constantly and enthusiastically. She'd say, "This guy would get along so well with Corso," or "Jack would love Stan." She'd never offered to introduce Dick to any of her Beat friends. In fact, every time he suggested they might take a trip down to San Francisco she put him off. "I'm not ready to go back," was all she would tell him.

Linda was getting letters from her Beat friend John Montgomery, full of gossip about Jack and Gary, Phil and Michael, etc., driving Dick crazy. Montgomery was in *The Dharma Bums*, and Linda would tell people she'd gotten a letter from her dharma bum. Then she'd call Dick her ski bum. "From dharma bums to ski bums," she joked once. "What a *schuss!*"

Dick's agent seldom wrote to him. Mills was content to scrawl a penciled note across the bottom of letters of rejection or acceptance, and he did so on the matter of Stan Winger. "Winger story like O. Henry," he scrawled across the bottom of a rejection slip, "but I'll send it around." The slip was from the *New Yorker*, cold flat rejection. Mills had been sending Dick's stuff to better and better magazines since the *Playboy* publication, but getting nowhere. Yet Dick's stories were getting too good for the regular girlie magazines, and *Playboy* was curiously reluctant to repeat.

Dick thought about writing a story about Stan Winger. Good revenge, if Stan's very first submission got accepted somewhere. A story about a thief who steals his mentor's girlfriend. Of course that hadn't happened, but the elements were there. The fiction would exaggerate reality into something entertaining. What kept him from writing the story was that Linda would read it. Not that it would give her ideas, but one never knew. It might even make her mad. "Don't you trust me?" in that indignant righteous voice. So a good story didn't get written, and everybody in West Portland sat around waiting for Stan Winger's story to be accepted or rejected.

Stan himself wasn't in suspense. He'd been astonished that the agent had taken the story, although Dick pointed out that Stan was not yet a client. "He's just sending it around," he told Stan. Stan was embarrassed, but there was nothing he could do about it. Linda had pushed him into this, sending a really bad piece of writing to a legitimate literary agent, ruining Stan's reputation in advance. He knew what he had to do if he was going to impress Linda. He had to learn how to write. He talked to Dick and his friends about taking night classes in writing, but they discouraged him. Portland State had a night class, but he couldn't get in without a high school diploma. Downtown there was Multnomah College, a kind of business school for working people, which advertised in the *Oregonian* and the *Yellow Pages*. He went down to an office building of SW Alder and found that they taught composition and had one section of Creative Writing, and, yes, they admitted anybody who'd pay the fee. Stan signed up for Comp and Creative, and paid his fees.

To Dick's great relief the story was rejected by the first magazine Mills sent it to. Unfortunately it wasn't a cold rejection but a hot one. "Send us more!!!" some idiot had written on the slip, below which Mills added in pencil "???" Dick decided it was time to get Stan Winger off his back. He'd helped him to an agent, an editor (Linda) and entry into Portland literary society, such as it was. Let him get his own mail. Dick walked down Broadway to Jolly Joan's and left the rejection slip with Marty's girl Alexandra, who'd passed it along to Marty, who'd find Stan. Crooks were so devious. Stan obviously didn't even want his agent to know where he lived.

Stan shyly showed his very first rejection slip to his teacher, Mr. Monel. He liked Mr. Monel from the first. A big man, no more than about thirty, with a big happy face and a mop of hair. He stood in front of the creative writing class, six females and Stan, and announced that he didn't know a damned thing about creative writing, but when the boss learned he was writing "this big ol' novel" in his spare time he got the class. "You can't teach creative writing," he said blandly, "and you can't even learn it. I guess you have to be born with it. What we can do here in this class is write a lot, read the stuff to each other, and try to help." Exactly what Stan wanted, and this was the guy he wanted it from. Stan couldn't help going up to Mr. Monel after class and asking him out for a beer.

"Sure," Charlie said with a big grin.

22.

Charlie loved Oregon. Just crossing the border had been great, California hot and dry, the sky blue, and right across the border big black and white clouds pouring rain down onto deeply green forested mountains. Mountains, but not like the sawtooth ranges of his native Montana. Green, but not like the green of anyplace he'd ever seen, every tone and shade of green imaginable, hot greens and cold greens and deep dark greens and almost white greens. Charlie had never seen so much green in his life. And the rain, as if to tell Charlie what he and his family were in for, fell in great splattery drops all the way from the border to Portland. Charlie stayed behind the wheel of their brand new 1961 Volkswagen, which by an astonishing coincidence was also green, a gold green. He had meant to switch off driving chores with Jaime, but the rain poured down so continuously Charlie kept the wheel. Also, there were these huge logging trucks on the road, a whole lane wide and loaded with tree trunks fifty and sixty feet long, roaring down the Oregon roads as if they owned them. Charlie more than once had to hold the wheel hard to keep from being run off the road by the rush of wind and wet when one of these logging trucks blew past. It was like entering a whole new world, just exactly what Charlie and Jaime wanted. Crammed into the tiny backseat were Edna and the baby Kira. The Lyons Moving Van Company had their books and goods, and Charlie only hoped the movers wouldn't run into the loggers.

A couple of days later the rain lifted for an hour, just to show Charlie and Jaime the beauties of the country around their new city. They were in the Council Crest neighborhood, up in the west hills of SW Portland, being shown a house that was far too expensive at eighty dollars a month. It wasn't raining, although everything was wet, and they looked through the big picture windows regretfully, because they had to say no. The view was downtown Portland, charming through the mist. Then the clouds lifted, and they could see, for what must have been hundreds of miles, rolling forested hills surrounding the city, and in the distance no less than four snow-covered volcano mountains sticking up over everything. Mount Hood, Mount Adams, Mount Jefferson and Mount St. Helens, Charlie learned.

"Oh God, how beautiful," Jaime murmured, and moved in close to Charlie. He put his arm around her.

"We're Oregonians now," he said ponderously, and squeezed her shoulder. Kira and Edna were back at the Sunrise Motel, also Oregonians now. Thank

God for Edna, Charlie thought for the hundredth time. Not only their built-in babysitter, she'd helped Charlie convince Jaime that leaving San Francisco wasn't going to destroy their lives. Jaime had been adamant when Charlie's only job offer had been Multnomah College.

"I guess I'm not a first-round draft pick," he said with a grin, but she chose not to understand him.

"It's not any kind of pick," she said mysteriously.

"Better'n Iowa," he said. What wasn't? Iowa had accepted Charlie, after he ate his pride and went in for his last final. Yet Charlie couldn't accept exile from his family. Jaime had convinced him that the Saxon money was needed for the baby, and so went the idea of them lying around for a year or two finishing novels. Charlie couldn't understand why Jaime wasn't writing. She was good, so much better than Charlie. Her immediate creative task, if you like, was the baby, whom she had insisted on naming after the sound bald eagles make. According to Jaime. *Kiiir*, that was the sound of eagles Charlie recalled from Montana. Kira was a good name, though, and fitted the baby, who was already uniquely feminine and mysterious to Charlie. It was here, too, that Edna showed her true colors. As soon as she found out her daughter was pregnant she made a face and said, "I guess I'll have to stop drinking," and she did. She had bad dreams for a few nights, but then was all right.

The first obvious effect to Charlie was that he discovered in his mother-in-law a gifted conversationalist and a friend. Edna was all right. At first they hesitated to drink even beer in front of her, but she laughed. "Oh, go ahead. I've had my share." She lost weight right away and turned out to be an attractive woman, still round-cheeked and round-hipped, but looking a lot like her daughter.

Edna liked the idea of moving to Oregon, though it was a move to a low-paying job with no security, just a business college, not much better than a racket. "We all need to start over," she said.

They found a perfect rental in Lake Grove, eight miles south of the city, near Lake Oswego. The house had been built right after World War II on an acre of woods, with a small clearing back of the house for growing vegetables.

There was a small mother-in-law apartment built onto the garage, tiny but perfect for Edna, a graveled circular drive up to the front, a low wooden fence, and greenery everywhere. Inside, the house was dark and cozy, with a big fireplace, a big kitchen, and three bedrooms. They spent a couple of weeks buying used furniture and considered themselves home when Edna put her signed Picasso print up over the fireplace.

Everything should have been perfect. He had a job, money in the bank, an office to work in. He was having trouble with his novel, a bit of trouble, not much, just that the fucking thing was no good. It was, he'd begun to realize, very difficult to say anything new about war. The ground had been thoroughly gone over, from Homer to James Jones. Even Charlie's POW experience had been touched on in a little book called *The Enormous Room*, by e.e. cummings. Charlie had been awfully depressed reading it. It described cummings's experiences in a World War I French hospital, and when he finished it, tears streaming down his face, Charlie knew that cummings had said everything about being a prisoner. cummings immediately became one of his favorite writers. Of course nobody, not even e.e. cummings had said *everything* about *anything*. So Charlie wasn't relieved of his obligation to finish his horribly long, terribly boring, totally unnecessary war novel. Which he was never going to show to anybody again unless it was at least halfway decent. This was part of the reason for coming to Portland. To get away from the intense literary competition. To a place where he could write in peace and begin to accept the realities of married life.

His teaching job was absurd but wonderful, and he decided he was glad no respectable school would hire him. Multnomah College was a practical, no-nonsense place for people who wanted to get ahead. Most of the students were young adults who'd presumably already been out into real life and didn't like it. They wanted to learn from Charlie how to write competently, and he was damned well going to teach them. It took only a couple of classes to realize that because the school had no admission standards, his job was really very important. Charlie could teach his students how to succeed in all their other classes. He could see right away that most of them had never had any breaks. They were here to make their own, and Charlie meant to help.

So the job was great. The house was great. Everything was great except Jaime.

23.

She hated it all, from the rain at the border to their ranch style house buried in the woods. It was the first ranch style house she'd ever been inside. It seemed incredibly shabby and mean-spirited, with its boxlike rooms, low ceiling, tacky iron fixtures, and linoleum everywhere in the place of tile. Jaime was used to the California all-tile bathroom, and the hell with anything less. The only advantage to the house that she could see was that it was eight miles from Portland, a city almost as deliberately ugly as Oakland.

She was twenty years old with an infant daughter, living in the middle of nowhere with her crazy mother and a husband who taught at a third-rate business college. No wonder she was depressed. Just yesterday she'd been living in a dreamworld of wealth and social position, only she hadn't realized it. Life on Washington Street had been unbelievably refined and secure, and San Francisco unbelievably sophisticated and full of life and variety. All gone now. Jaime lived among people who did not seem to know they were in Rain Hell. She felt like an exile.

She was astonished nonetheless by her mother. Edna had gone from an incomprehensible drunk to a bright active person in less than a year. Jaime liked it that her mother wasn't stupid drunk all the time, but unsure how she liked having Edna live with them. She was meant to be there to care for Kira, but Jaime actually did that while Edna just criticized. Nice for Edna, living in her own apartment behind the garage, with its own tiny fireplace and upstairs sleeping loft, but she spent all day at Jaime's kitchen table, drinking endless cups of tea and talking while Jaime took care of the house and the baby. Outside, rain. Charlie bought a cord of wood somewhere. He'd spent a whole afternoon outside with a couple of Oregonians in checked mackinaws and bill caps, stacking the wood in the covered area between the house and garage, and now just about the only time Jaime went outside was to retrieve wood from the stack. Every time she did she smelled winter Oregon, a heavy woody wet smell that she hated as badly as she hated the rain itself.

Then Edna shocked her by saying she felt useless and wanted a job.

"Good luck, Mom," Jaime said.

Edna quickly bought herself a used Mercury out of her mystery horde of money, drove off to Portland and landed herself a job at the *Oregonian*, the state's biggest newspaper. She worked proofreading classified ads, as she'd done at the *Chronicle* years before. This gave Jaime some relief, but not enough. When Charlie was home, which was rarely, he was either asleep or in his office writing. Jaime didn't inquire how the writing was going, and he didn't ask her, either. She'd never read Charlie's entire manuscript. It filled two cardboard boxes and must have weighed forty pounds by now. She was frankly afraid of his novel-in-progress. She wasn't sure why. The thing would change their lives no matter how it came out. If it was what they hoped, Charlie would move up into the world of letters, and that could be destructive. But if the book was a failure it would kill him, eviscerate the Charlie she loved, turn him into one of those bitter old teachers with a failed novel in their desk drawer.

As for her, she'd given up. Kira took all her energy. Even when she had Kira asleep, her mother off at work and Charlie gone, she still had no mind to write. It was enough to sit quietly at her kitchen table with a cup of tea in front of her and the radio playing insipid pop music. She thought of the girls she'd known with ambitions to be artists, the trombone players, the poets, the painters and actresses, those who like Jaime had dreamed of novels. What happened to them all? Was it the same as for Jaime? Their ambitions buried under marriage?

Jaime's experience with snow was limited to trips to the mountains as a girl, and she'd never been in an actual blizzard. Her first was in many ways her best. It started on a Sunday morning, all of them at the kitchen table.

"It's snowing," Charlie said, looking out the window. Jaime was feeding Kira and didn't turn to look.

"Great," she said, but secretly she was a little excited. When she got the chance, after Kira was snoozing in her playpen, she went out on the back porch, where the overhang protected her from the snow, which came straight down. She watched it fall, wondering why it made her feel so good. The flakes were big ones, clumps really, and the ground covered fast. There was an incredible silence, too, *the silence of falling snow,* she tried in her mind. It hung on the trees and shrubs, altering the appearance of everything, and for the first time Jaime began to think she might enjoy Oregon. Then Charlie came out and like a little boy had to make snowballs and throw them at her.

"Come on!" he yelled. "This is your first snowstorm!"

She played along, getting wet and cold, running around in the snow. They watched it pile up all day, making comments like, "Boy, it's really getting deep!" Charlie explained to Jaime and Edna that this wasn't a real blizzard, you had to go to Montana to experience that. "I've seen the temperature drop from seventy to ten below in about forty minutes," he told them as the snow blew silently against the windows.

"Oh, put it in your book," Jaime said. There was something bizarre in her reaction to the snowfall. She wanted it to go on, to cover everything up to fifty feet, and then see what would happen. It was an anarchistic feeling, a don't-give-a-damn feeling. Let the traffic go to hell, let the snow fall, let business and schools close, let everything stop while the snow covers everything.

"Remember 'The Dead'?" Charlie said, interrupting her thoughts.

"Yes," she said. The Joyce story, where the snow fell all over Ireland.

He grinned. "You want me to go out and stand in the snow, to prove I love you?"

"No, but thanks."

The next day when they got up the snow was still there, and had developed a nasty icy crust. Charlie had to shovel out their circular drive and wait for the snowplow to find their road.

"What makes you think there's a snowplow?" she asked him. She was standing on the front porch watching him shovel.

Charlie blew happy clouds of steam. "Of course there's a snowplow." An hour later the snowplow did pass, and Charlie and her mother went to work. It was eerie the way the cars sounded, just the engine thrumming as the wheels moved over the silent snow. After they were gone she sat at her kitchen table. Kira slept in the corner. Snowflakes started coming down outside. Jaime thought about killing herself.

She considered keeping this random existential temblor to herself, but that night in bed she told Charlie. He lay on his back, and touched his leg without looking at her. "You got to get used to these winters."

"You think that's what it is?"

He turned to her and after a moment smiled. "It's just the winters," he said. "Let's face it. Snow country is suicide country."

"Have you ever thought about it?"

"Sure. Everybody in Montana all winter long thinks about nothing else. If the guns didn't freeze up they'd all be dead." He chuckled. "Joke."

She'd touched something in him, she knew. His experiences as a prisoner of war, maybe? He never talked about those. "It's all for the book," he told her. "I don't even think about it unless I'm working." Had he considered suicide in the prison camp? Had it been horrible? Probably very cold. She wondered if the snow reminded Charlie of being a prisoner.

"Let's make love," he said, and put his warm hand on her belly.

"No," she said.

24.

It wasn't long before Charlie knew Stan was a thief. They'd drink beer at one of the downtown taverns and talk about writing, but after a while Stan was telling Charlie about his adventures in county jail. "You ought to write about it," Charlie said. Stan was an enthusiastic writer of pulp stories, but Charlie thought he could do better. He didn't criticize the pulp, he just kept urging Stan to write more about internal stuff.

"You don't always have to have a surprise at the end," he told Stan one night as they sat drinking beer at the Broadway Inn.

"That's what they buy," Stan said.

"You ought to read more classical stories," Charlie said. He mentioned Maupassant, Chekhov, Hemingway, Steinbeck, and John O'Hara. Stan got out his little steno notepad and dutifully wrote down the names. A week later he came up to Charlie after composition class and said he was deep into Maupassant. "Boy, this guy can write," he said with a big grin, and Charlie felt a burst of pleasure.

"You fuckin' ay," he said in a low voice so the other students wouldn't hear. Stan winked, as if they had a conspiracy going. Sure enough, Stan's writing improved at once. He wasn't writing great stuff, but his dialogue was getting real.

One night Stan had news. A story he'd written, one he'd not shown to Charlie, had actually been bought, by *Raymond Chandler's Mystery Magazine*. For fifty dollars.

"You just passed me by, son," Charlie said ruefully. "I've never sold a thing." Stan admitted he had a lot of help on the story, and asked Charlie to a party, to celebrate the sale.

"Bring your wife," Stan said.

"I'll try," Charlie said.

The winter had been a long one, with snowstorm after snowstorm, melting and freezing, raining for long dull weeks on end, then snowing again. Charlie didn't mind. His new Volkswagen loved the snow, and he could drive around in it when people with big cars and power steering were sliding off into snowbanks. He taught Jaime how to drive in snow but she was always tense behind the wheel and he ended up doing most of the shopping, and anything else that required leaving the house. He worried about Jaime. She stayed in all day, not writing, and while she usually seemed in good spirits, Charlie sensed a time bomb ticking away somewhere. He'd been invited to parties and evenings of beer-drinking by his students and even the college administrator, but Jaime always had some reason not to go. "You go ahead," she said. "I'll be fine."

"I hate to leave you alone."

"I've been alone all my life."

Of course she had the baby twenty-four hours a day, and her mother at night, but Charlie knew what she meant. He tried to come home right after night classes, but the trouble was that after two hours of teaching he was always so jacked up. If he did come home Jaime would either be asleep or he would bore her to death talking about what happened in class. If he didn't come home he'd go out beer drinking with Stan Winger, then come home drunk.

"Come this time," he said. "Stan's an interesting guy." He paused. "He's a thief."

She didn't get it right away. "He steals other people's stories?"

"He breaks into houses."

The party was on SW Cable, in the hills just west of downtown. The roads were clear of snow but it rained a very cold rain, and Jaime didn't speak the whole eight miles into town. She'd been reluctant to spend an evening among Oregon hicks, especially a bunch of literary hicks. Charlie wasn't worried, though. Jaime was so pretty she could act any way she wanted and people wouldn't mind. He hoped she wouldn't call anybody a hick, though. Californians were resented in Oregon as it was.

"They aren't hicks," he said over the sound of the windshield wipers. She made a little noise.

Walking up the slippery steps to the house, Jaime took Charlie's hand and said, "I'm pregnant again."

"That's great," Charlie said after too many steps. "Watch your feet." They were at the front door, which opened wide, and Charlie felt the heat from the house against his frozen face. There was a bright-eyed little guy in front of him.

"I'm Dick Dubonet, welcome to my chalet," the guy said.

Jaime smiled and held out her hand. "Hi, I'm Jaime Monel." She walked into the party as if she owned the place.

"Ooh, what a beautiful wife!" Dick Dubonet said, and Charlie liked him at once. Not for calling Jaime beautiful, but for being such an enthusiastic asshole. Charlie had been prepared to dislike Dick Dubonet ever since he heard Stan's hero-worshipful description of the guy. And he was everything Charlie expected, too loud, too literary, too short. What Charlie hadn't expected was this openness, this lack of sophistication, even though the guy was obviously trying to act sophisticated.

"And this is my wife, Linda," Dick said.

"I'm not your wife," Linda said, smiling up at Charlie.

"I don't see why we need the state to approve our relationship," Dick said.

There were about twenty people at the party, and over by the couch several musicians with guitars and banjos. The music was loud and energetic, but nobody was dancing. On the dining room table, food and drink, mostly quarts of Blitz-Weinhard beer, and Charlie went to the food, trying to get his mind to work again. Another child, right now. Was that what he wanted? Was that why Jaime had been acting so strangely? He put potato salad and salami and olives on a paper plate and poured himself a glass of beer. Behind him people were starting to dance. Stan was beside him, filling a plate.

"The literary crowd," Stan said. Proudly, Charlie thought. Well, why not? He turned around, prepared to enjoy himself, prepared for another child.

What he was not prepared for was Linda McNeill, into whose eyes he found himself looking, as the five-string banjos hit their stride.

25.

Stan saw the look that passed between Charlie Monel and Linda, and it spoiled his evening. He knew what it meant, and being the all-observant one, he also saw that Dick Dubonet also saw the look, brief as it was, and if Stan was any judge, Dick didn't like it any more than he did. The look was simple. The best-looking female in the room signaled to the best looking-man, "I'm yours." And the banjos played on.

"*Wake up, wake up, darlin' Corey!*" everybody yelled over the banjos, while Stan as usual sat in a corner not even tapping his foot. He'd been building up this gigantic fantasy of himself and Linda. All based on a look she'd given him, not that long ago, and based on her giving so much time to him, helping with his story. He'd made himself believe that getting the story published would change his life, and now he saw that what he'd meant was getting together with Linda. He had automatically assumed. He had forgotten himself. He had forgotten reality. Women like that were not for men like him. They were for men like Charles W. Monel.

But the kitty came back, the very next day,
The kitty came back, 'cause she couldn't stay away . . ."

Of course Charlie's wife had to be young and beautiful herself, with flaming red hair cut like a boy's and her thin boyish body. She was dancing now with Jeffrey Lyman, a happy-go-lucky kid Stan figured was a homosexual, but a nice guy. Charlie would collect his due from Linda, Stan was sure. Why wouldn't he? These people were artists, they probably swapped wives and girlfriends all the time. The couple kissing on the couch hadn't come in together. Stan thought about getting laid, but Vancouver was a long way off through cold rain, and Stan didn't feel like sitting on a bus. One of the things that made him stew in corners at parties was his own sexual inadequacy. Probably why he broke into houses, too. It explained his whole life. Including why, at this party in his honor, he felt so shitty. Get published had only highlighted his inadequacy as a human being. Take the matter of Linda.

She'd been the one to tell him his story had been bought. She did it by inviting him to lunch at the Buttermilk Corner. Then, when his mouth was full of roast beef, she said, "Bob Mills called. Guess what?"

"What?" he asked, after grinding up his food and swallowing. His heart was in his mouth anyway. He had hoped she invited him to lunch because she was falling in love with him. Now, his mouth hanging open, he listened to her tell him the good news. It was quite a letdown.

She reached out and touched his hand. "You don't look happy. Cheer up, you're a published author."

"I'm not an author," he said through a red flush of embarrassment.

"Yes you are." Linda gave him that beautiful smile. "Not only that, you're one of the best writers in Portland. With just one story."

She probably knew he had an inferiority complex.

Now at the party she came over and sat beside him on the floor. The musicians had put away their instruments and the phonograph was playing loud jazz. Stan was a little drunk, and when she put an arm around his shoulders he turned his face away to keep her from smelling his breath. But it didn't work. She took him by the chin and turned his face toward hers. She was about an inch from him.

"I want a kiss from the guest of honor," she said, and kissed him. For the second time. It emptied his mind. When he came back to reality she was smiling at him, her eyes filled with the affection he'd never experienced in his life. Why shouldn't he fall in love?

But it was a love he'd keep to himself. For all the depressing reasons you can think of. She was Dick Dubonet's girl. She'd helped him, out of the goodness of her heart. And she was going to sleep with Charles Monel.

Whom (possibly who) he had brought to the party. Proudly. His teacher. Oddly, he didn't hate Charlie for this. It wasn't his fault.

Five weeks later they got the news that *Raymond Chandler's Mystery Magazine* had folded. So Stan wasn't paid and wasn't published. Stan talked to his new agent on the phone and Mills told him in his deep dry voice that the story was a good one, and he would very likely place it soon. And keep writing. Stan hung up to see a grinning Dick and a sad-looking Linda.

"Good thing you didn't spend the money," Dick said.

"I knew something would happen," Stan said. Not bitterly.

"Let's all go down to Jerry's for a burger," Dick said. "My treat."

"Well in that case," Linda said, with a rueful smile at Stan. It was quite a ride, with Linda on his lap in the little MG. Jerry's was only half full. Marty Greenberg was there with his French horn player, and they sat together. Marty had too many women, Stan thought. This one wasn't even pretty, in any regular sense, her chin small, her cheeks round, her eyes downcast most of the time. She had beautiful hair, though. And beautiful skin. Before their food came, the two women went to the toilet together, and the three men relaxed.

"She's going through some problems," Marty said of Mary Bergendaal.

"I'll bet she really blows that horn," said Dick Dubonet. They all laughed.

Stan remembered the conversation only because a few weeks later he came into Jolly Joan's at around three in the morning, after a couple of hours writing, and found Marty sitting alone at the counter over a cup of coffee. Stan sat next to him, glad to see a friendly face. But Marty was glum.

"How's the coffee this morning?" Stan said.

"Do you remember Mary Bergendaal?" Marty's eyes looked haunted and Stan knew in a flash what he was going to say. My God, it had been written on her face.

"She's dead, isn't she?" He felt a chill enter his stomach.

Marty frowned. "Yes. How did you know?" He didn't wait for an answer, but started talking about Mary Bergendaal. She'd been so self-contained, just a quiet little girl, spending most of her day practicing or playing. Marty was her only friend outside the Portland Symphony, and he had not been much of a friend. "I let her do it," he said, his usual amused expression replaced with, well, anguish. She was twenty-four years old and had killed herself with a shotgun. Marty had spotted the gun under her bed several times.

For some reason Mary Bergendaal's death affected Stan more strongly than it should have. He didn't really know her. They sat across from each other once, at Jerry's. What could he have said. "Don't kill yourself." Sure. Maybe the reason he felt such compassion for this girl was that she represented himself. A loner, dedicated to her art. Finally the moment comes when you realize. It's all so fucking useless. Without love.

Stan's next story was about Mary. He didn't have the time or the inventiveness to fake it up, he just wrote about a lonely girl who got tired of jokes about blowing her French horn. He called it "The Last Straw," and sent it to Mills without showing it to anybody, not even Charlie. Mills sent it right back. "Nice story, but not comm." Stan agreed. He didn't even know why he had sent the damn thing in. He just wrote it because he wanted to. Reading it over, he decided that it was badly written, but his best story. He put it away, with his experimental stuff.

26.

Her first Oregon winter ended in miscarriage. The pain was awful. She sat on the toilet holding her stomach for hours, not really thinking, hearing the endless rain pelt the roof. Charlie hadn't come home from class yet. Her mother was in her own apartment, Kira asleep in her room. One of the beauties of Kira was that she slept well. The pain came and went like a finger probing her belly, then in a black flush of pain her unborn child fell from her. Her name would have been Isis.

Jaime blamed herself. She hadn't wanted to be pregnant, and when she told Charlie it was obvious he didn't want another child so soon either. To be a wife and the mother of two at her age seemed like burial. But when the child died inside her she went into a blackness that made earlier depressions seem shallow. This was so black it didn't even seem black. She was perfectly rational, she just didn't feel anything. She was below feeling, below suicide. Sitting at the kitchen table, bleeding into a Kotex and waiting for Charlie, she thought about a simple ordinary death for herself. They had no pills in the house, nor any guns. She'd have to cut herself to death. She remembered the Jack London story about the man who hadn't done it right. She thought of her girlfriend in San Francisco who'd nicked her arms with a razor blade, sixty-four shallow little cuts, because she'd gotten only one birthday card. Hesitation marks, they were called. Jaime didn't want Charlie to come in and find her sitting there with a razor blade in her hand, blood everywhere, tiny cuts up and down her inner arm. "I couldn't do it . . ." No. Her mother's car was out in the garage. She could take the vacuum cleaner hose, attach it to the exhaust pipe, run it into the car through the window, stuff the window with newspaper to make it airtight, and turn on the gas. Thum thum thum death.

Her depression dropped below suicide quickly as she thought about the effects on her daughter, her living daughter, Kira. Asleep now in the next room. What would she learn from her mother's death? To kill herself. Down Jaime dropped, a speck in the cosmos, ha ha ha, below that to the atomic level of organization, and then down, down, below the atomic, past the sub-atomic, into the nothing of reality. Emptiness. Not even a reason to die.

Charlie came in drunk. "Oh, you're up," he said. "You okay?"

"I'm fine."

He leered at her glassily. "Then let's do it," he said in a deep purr, and bent down, kissing her on the back of her neck. She could smell beer and potato chips on his breath.

"I can't," she said. "I just had a miscarriage."

"Huh?" Charlie let her go and she could not see him. The rain hit the roof.

"It's all right," she said.

"Oh, Jesus." Charlie put his hands on her shoulders, and she could feel his energy pouring into her, filling her with a terrible sweet sad love. "You must feel so bad," he said.

"I love you," she said dryly. After they went to bed he held her until she finally fell asleep. The rain had gone all night, of course, and the next day, but then it stopped, and the Oregon sky turned bright blue. As if to say, a child lost, a world gained. No, thought Jaime. I will not love the spring. But the air was dry and sweet, the sky blue, everything in sight green and growing. She found herself wandering through the woods in back of their house, looking at the little trilliums that came up and put out their white three-petaled flowers. The ferns were rising out of the almost black ground, and birds sang in the trees. Jaime couldn't help feeling alive. Then she heard a baby cry.

She was a hundred yards from any house, in the middle of the trees, and the sound was close. Who could leave a baby out in the woods, even on a warm spring day? She heard no other voices as she moved toward the crying, her heart beating rapidly. It wasn't a baby, but a Siamese kitten. Who, when it saw Jaime, let out a very loud meow that sounded just like a baby's cry.

Jaime laughed and picked up the kitten, who had bright blue eyes. It couldn't have been more than six weeks old. What was it doing in the woods? Jaime never found out. They asked their neighbors, but the answer they got was, "People throw cats away sometimes."

"I'll call you Isis," she told it, and held the kitten to her cheek. Yet the cat did not replace the child. Jaime's depression didn't lift, in spite of spring. Instead it got so bad she turned to writing. She didn't know exactly what. The miscarriage had reminded her that she'd lost her father unacceptably early, and had never gotten used to the loss. Just to invoke him, just to try to understand him, she started writing about her father, and their life on Washington Street. After a few days of writing while the baby slept, she hungered for the times when by writing she'd take herself from this cabin in the woods, back to a civilized place and time. It was heaven walking the streets of San Francisco again, even if only in her mind.

"What are you writing about?" Charlie asked, once he found out.

"Just some notes. About my dad."

"That's great," he said warmly. "You ought to write a book about him."

"Maybe," she said.

27.

Charlie felt sorry for his best student and invited him out to Lake Grove for a backyard picnic. It was May, the whole Willamette Valley buzzing with life, hot blue skies, thick humid air rising off the river filled with insects and birds, and of course loving couples everywhere. Stan Winger didn't seem to have any luck with girls. He wasn't bad looking, in Charlie's view, just sort of indistinct, too shy, the kind of guy whose appearance you can't quite remember. A highly forgettable guy, Charlie thought with irony. Raised in foster homes, juvenile hall, jail, raised with the ethics of the street, which were surely better than no ethics at all. Charlie remembered the four New York street guys who were in Kim Song. They held together. Them and the Christians. They had been a pain in the ass, but they hadn't fallen apart. The way Charlie and near everyone else had. Well, he'd have to fix Stan up with a girl.

"How come you don't have a car?" Charlie asked Stan. They drove south out of Portland, along the banks of the river.

"I don't drive," Stan said. He had on black pants and an old white dress shirt. His picnic clothes, Charlie thought.

"I'll teach you how, if you want." He tried to imagine an American kid growing up without being taught to drive.

"That would be great," Stan said, without enthusiasm. He was a little tense. This was not his first picnic, he'd been on a couple of hell-raising parties outdoors with kids from the Broadway Gang, once up at Rooster Rock State Park on the Columbia River, screaming drunken runaround sunburn antics, and once here on the banks of the Willamette, beer and girls and nude swimming in the night, only Stan didn't have one of the girls, didn't go nude swimming, only got drunk and arrested with the others at the end. Some of them had been middle-class kids, and the cops let them go home. Stan and a couple of the others were sent to Woodburn. Six months on that beef, and he hadn't even gotten laid. Maybe that was why he was anxious, or maybe he was just a hopeless asshole, and would never have a good time, no matter what. Or it could be that Dick and Linda would be there.

They drove up the circular gravel drive in front of the house and parked. There were no other cars in the drive. The patch of front lawn was ragged and overgrown, and the front door stood open, with a little cat sitting in the doorway in the sunlight washing itself. The cat looked up at Stan but didn't move, so Stan had to step over it, into his teacher's house. It was better than he'd hoped, warm and inviting. Jaime came out of the kitchen smiling, holding out her hand.

"Stan, it's so good to see you." She wore a man's tee shirt and Stan could see the outlines of her nipples, which made his face heat up. She obviously wore no brassiere, and her hands were wet. "I'm glad you're early," she said, leading him into the kitchen by hand. "I need you to help me cut up potatoes."

Charlie drove off to buy beer and Stan was left alone with Jaime and the child, in her playpen in the corner of the kitchen. Jaime's red hair was growing out, the blonde roots showing. After he finished cutting up potatoes Stan sat with a cup of coffee and listened to Jaime talk about everything under the sun, charming witty conversation that he could only grunt at from time to time, as if he was following. He realized after a while that she was "entertaining" him. No wonder Charlie loved her. Bright, funny, beautiful, graceful, a good hostess, and Charlie said she was one of the best young writers he had ever read. Of course he was talking about his own wife, but even so. Charlie always tried to be nice, but he didn't lie. And Stan now realized, he wouldn't commit adultery, either, not with Linda or anybody else. It was dishonorable.

"Would you like to hold Kira?" Jaime asked. She handed the little girl to Stan. Kira didn't seem to notice him at first, but then looked up into his eyes and smiled. He'd never been so flattered in his life. He didn't dare examine the feeling he discovered, holding this priceless object. This human child. This vulnerability. Then, still looking into his eyes, Kira opened her mouth and began to yell, not a loud yell, just a child's.

"Lunch coming up," Jaime said, and took the child.

"How old is she?" Stan asked.

"Sixteen months," Jaime said. She sat Kira in her high chair and started feeding her. Stan sat sipping his coffee, feeling as comfortable as he had ever felt inside a home. Jaime's mother came in from the back somewhere and sat down with her cup of coffee. Jaime introduced them and said, "Stan's one of Charlie's best students."

Edna winked at him and grinned. "You don't look like a student to me."

"I'm really a burglar," Stan said, and grinned at her.

Edna laughed. "You ever go to the dog track?" It turned out they had something in common. Edna and her friends at work bet on the dogs. In fact, all day long while they were proofreading ad copy they were also discussing which dogs to bet on that night. Stan had been out to the dogs a few times. It seemed stupid to bet on these animals, when at the first turn they nearly always ended up in a pile and nobody on God's earth could predict which would win.

Dick and Linda showed up in the little yellow MG, followed by a couple of other cars full of friends, including Marty Greenberg and his waitress girl, Alexandra. The kitchen crowded with people talking and drinking beer, and Stan was one of them, relaxed, comfortable, knowing nearly everybody, not the stranger in the group for once. Marty came up and bummed a cigarette. "Let's go out into the jungle," he said, and Stan followed Marty into the sunlight. Charlie had an old picnic table and a couple of benches, and they sat down. The babble from the kitchen was loud through the open windows, and smoke poured out into the air. Everything smelled of wet wood out here.

"I was raised in Brownsville, Brooklyn," Marty said. "This is heaven."

"What brought you out here?" Stan asked.

"Reed College."

Charlie came out, carrying a can of beer. "Come on, you guys," he said, and led them down a trail between the trees. In a couple of minutes they were out of range of the house, and all Stan could hear were the birds in the trees and the sounds of their feet on the soggy ground.

"Watch out for large furry animals," Marty said.

It was hot and muggy in the forest, the green undergrowth up to their knees and the ground mushy underfoot. Charlie led them to a clearing. In it stood a few scraggly rows of small yellow-green plants. Charlie pointed proudly. "Marijuana," he said. "The crop of the future."

"My goodness," Marty said, grinning. "Isn't it illegal to grow this stuff?"

"It's not mine," Charlie said blandly. "Although I plan to smoke it."

"Whose is it?" Marty said stupidly.

"Hey," Stan said to him. "Cool it."

"Should be ready for plucking in about a month," Charlie said.

"Keep me informed," Stan said with a sly smile. He had smoked a little reefer. He loved it.

"If they catch you smoking this stuff," Marty said, "they make you go to Lexington, Kentucky, to be cured."

"Don't be afraid," Stan said. He winked at Charlie, who winked back. "Don't be afraid" was one of their favorite lines from *The Enormous Room,* which Charlie had loaned Stan a month ago. The walked back to the house and Stan was emboldened to say to Marty, "You know not to say anything, don't you?"

Marty looked at him. "I keep forgetting you're a criminal." But he smiled as he said it.

28.

"You have no character," Linda told Stan. They squatted down next to Charlie's marijuana plants. She reached out to touch his cheek. "No lines of character. Nobody ever told you how to be. You're fresh clay, Stan. All you need is molding."

He blushed angrily, caught out. Of course he didn't have any character. But why bring it up now? Because he'd shown her Charlie's marijuana? He hadn't meant to.

"Where did you boys go?" she had asked. She took his hand and they walked off into the trees. She seemed to be leading, but they ended up at the clearing. "God, how great," she said, squatting down.

"I didn't mean to bring you out here." Her touch burned his cheek.

"You need a mentor," she said. "Somebody to guide you. And Charlie's the one."

"He's my teacher," he said stupidly.

"Charlie's a great man," she said, and took back her hand, sitting on the ground. Stan sat and immediately felt the wet seeping through his pants. She was beautiful. She had on a light blue men's workshirt tied at the waist, and cutoff jeans, showing a lot of white skin. She kept on about Charlie, what a great writer he was going to be, and what a good man he already was. She was making Charlie sound like Jesus Christ.

"Did you know he was a war hero?" she asked.

Stan shook his head. He was beginning to wonder if Charlie and Linda weren't lovers after all. She seemed to know a lot about him.

"I guess you wish he was here instead of me," he said, and immediately regretted it. The words just slid out of his mouth, and he watched her to see the curl of contempt. But she smiled at him sadly and put her hand on the back of his neck and pulled him in for a kiss, her tongue sliding into his mouth, the smell of her filling his mind so that he couldn't think, only feel. He took hold of her unthinking and pushed her to the ground. They kissed passionately, and then she was lying on top of him and he could feel her breasts. She moaned heavily, kissing his face. His cock was hard and getting harder as she pushed her pelvis into his, and with a feeling of complete freedom he realized they were going to make love, right here in the woods, under the sky, Stan and Linda.

But no. She pulled back, panting, and sat up. "Oh God," she said. Stan sat up. His pants and shirt were wet and dirty, and he started brushing himself off. He panted a little himself, and could hardly believe that she'd pulled away just at the moment he was certain she wouldn't. She had sticks and wet leaves stuck to her, and he helped brush her off, too.

"Uh-oh." She gestured and Stan saw they'd rolled on some of the little marijuana plants. Linda laughed, and tried to upright the plants, but some were crushed flat. "Good thing we didn't fuck," she said. "Or the whole crop would have gone." She laughed again, a bright sharp laugh, and held out her hand. He scrambled to his feet and pulled her up.

"Just one of those passionate moments," she said to him as if it hadn't meant much, but then she took his hands and kissed them. All his mixed-up emotions calmed at once. "Thank you for not taking advantage," she said, and they walked back to the house. Charlie was going to know somebody had been rolling around on his marijuana, but Stan hoped he wouldn't find out who. Actually, he didn't give a damn. Caught rolling around with Linda? Guilty.

The party went late. Stan had been going to catch a ride back to town, but Charlie said, "Hell, spend the night. I'll take you back tomorrow." And so Stan spent a quiet Sunday with the family. He slept in Charlie's office, sleeping bag on a cot, but comfortable, and at some point during the night the little kitty jumped up and slept on him, purring loudly at first and then falling asleep pushed up against his legs. Stan was afraid to move. He didn't want to irritate the cat. In the morning he was the first up, but after sitting at the kitchen table by himself for twenty minutes, afraid to make coffee for fear of waking anyone, Edna came to the door wrapped in a pink bathrobe. "I'll make coffee," she said, and started right in. Soon they all sat around the table, drinking coffee and smoking cigarettes. The radio was playing classical music and Jaime was feeding the baby in her high chair. Stan and Charlie both admitted having headaches from drinking all that beer. But Charlie didn't have to write that day. They didn't write on Sundays. "You have to take one day off a week," Charlie said. "Or you go crazy." Charlie wrote every morning for at least an hour, and Jaime wrote at least an hour during the day. What discipline, Stan thought. None of that "inspiration" crap, just turn it out, scribble scribble, every day but Sunday.

They really did nothing. Picked up the house and put all the beer and wine bottles in the garbage. For lunch Jaime cooked fried chicken, and they sat out in back at the picnic table and talked about what vegetables they would grow this summer. It was time to plow and plant. Stan immediately volunteered to help with the truck garden. "If you need somebody to pull weeds," he said. Maybe he'd gone too far, but no, Charlie grinned and said, "You can come out here any goddamn time you want to pull some weeds," and Jaime said, "You're welcome anytime anyway," and Charlie said "Of course," and they all smiled at each other. Stan felt like a member of the family. He napped in the afternoon like everybody else (he imagined Charlie and Jaime were making love, because Edna had the baby back in her apartment behind the garage). The kitty came and slept on Stan again, helping along that family-member feeling.

Charlie drove him home, and by ten that night they were sitting in the Volkswagen outside Stan's apartment building, a slum building in a slum neighborhood after a day in Lake Grove. The two sat side by side, smoking. Charlie had turned the motor off, so Stan knew he wanted to talk. Stan waited.

"Are you still stealing?"

They'd never discussed it before.

Stan nodded. "I know, I oughta quit."

"I'm not going to get moral on you," Charlie said. "But I'd hate to see you end up in jail."

"Well," Stan said. He had nothing to say. He knew perfectly well he shouldn't be a thief. Except he was.

"I know it's stupid to tell you to get some job somewhere. Hell, I don't like hard work any more than you do." Charlie explained about all the shitty jobs he'd held over the years. "Hateful shit, but God, man, better than jail."

"I don't know," Stan said. "Jail's not bad." He tried to make a joke of it. "Jail's just jail, man."

"I've been in jail," Charlie said. "I was a POW for fourteen months."

"Jesus," Stan said.

"I just wanted to say, if you need my help getting a straight job, just let me know. You're my best student."

"I mostly make it gambling these days," Stan lied, to let Charlie off the hook. "I play the card rooms up in Vancouver, you know?"

"You must be a great poker player," Charlie said in a flat voice, and dropped the subject.

29.

Sneaking through the woods was something Dick Dubonet was very good at. Like an Indian he did not step on the snapping twig, nor brush the random branch. Silently he tracked Stan and Linda through the trees, his heart still, his mind alert. Then he watched them in the clearing, just out of earshot. He didn't want to move any closer, and various birds were making a lot of noise, so he could only watch. When they started kissing and rolling around on the ground, Dick got so excited he almost cried out, and he urgently wanted to jack off. He was in an anguish of jealousy and so turned on he wanted to shriek. He'd come out to Lake Grove expecting to be jealous, but not of Stan Winger. Winger wasn't handsome, he wasn't muscular, he owned nothing, and at heart he was a cheap criminal. What's to be jealous of?

Yet here he watched Linda and Stan like a voyeur through a window. To his relief and disappointment they didn't strip and make love right before his eyes. He heard Linda's peals of laughter, and when she and Stan started back for the picnic Dick froze and let them pass within ten feet of him. He waited until they were beyond hearing, then moved toward the clearing. It was as he had thought. Marijuana, about half the plants squashed into the ground. Without thinking, Dick squatted down and tried to restore the plants. They'd probably straighten up by themselves. Dick had never smoked marijuana, but he was willing to try, so he plucked a few of the bigger leaves and stuck them in his pocket. It was very hot in the clearing, and sweat popped out all over his body. He'd smoked some opium once, in Naples, while in the army. The opium had made him vomit, but then provided the sweetest dreams he could remember. He wondered how the marijuana would compare. All he knew was that Negroes and musicians used it a lot. So it must be great.

Nobody had noticed his absence, certainly not Linda, who was in the house when he returned. Dick sat at the picnic table with Jaime and the little girl. He'd been prepared to dislike Jaime, since she was even better-looking than Linda and belonged to Charlie. She looked funny with her hair half red and half blonde, but it was also sexy, and Dick wondered if there was a chance. Not that he wanted a chance. But he was so afraid of losing Linda to Charlie that he thought about deliberately trying to seduce Jaime. A revenge seduction. Trouble was, he liked her. She'd been a lot of fun at the party at his house, and now at her own she was gracious, sweet, very nice to Dick, telling him how much she'd enjoyed reading his *Playboy* story, which quite frankly not many of his friends had done. Marty Greenberg had almost sneered, since the story was no competition for Dostoevsky, but this lovely sophis-ticated San Francisco girl had made a point of mentioning that she liked it, and as far as Dick could tell there wasn't a hint of patronage. Of course, maybe she and Charlie sat alone together and laughed and slapped their knees at his stupid little commercial story. But he didn't think so.

There was a big quilt on the back lawn at their feet, with a tarp beneath it to keep the damp out, and Jaime and the little girl sat on the quilt, Jaime holding her daughter's hands up as she tried to walk.

"She's never taken a step," Jaime said to Dick. A burst of rude laughter came from the house, where Charlie was holding court.

"Is she supposed to? She seems awfully little."

"Any time now," Jaime said.

Dick lowered himself to the quilt and sat cross-legged a few feet from little Kira. He drank from his beer bottle and then dangled it before the girl. She smiled at the bottle and started walking toward it. Jaime let go of her hands and Kira toddled—that was the right word—over to Dick and fell on her butt. She laughed up at Dick and his heart broke. He picked her up and cuddled her in his arms and when she squealed with delight he felt like the King of England.

"You're magic," Jaime said. Her eyes glowed. Dick passed the wiggling child over to her mother. "What a nice child," he said softly. He'd been so touched. He had no idea. Jaime grinned at him, bouncing Kira. "It's something, isn't it?"

"Yeah."

"When are you and Linda going to have a baby?"

"If this is what they're like, soon."

"Will you watch her? I want to tell Charlie his daughter took a few steps and he missed it."

"I'll be careful," Dick said. Jaime handed Kira over and the child immediately started yelling, her face red and angry. Smiling, Jaime took her back and went into the house, leaving Dick to himself.

An emotional day. It got no better driving home later than night. Linda talked all the way about Charlie's novel, which she had taken a peek at.

"He showed you his manuscript?" Dick said, seething with envy.

"Oh no, I sneaked a peek. He keeps it in boxes, all this hand-written stuff and really badly typed stuff, tons of it. I just read a few typed pages. But this is the real thing." Charlie's dialogue. Charlie's experience. Charlie's thundering prose. Charlie's awful handwriting, Charlie's terrible spelling,

Charlie's clumsiness. "It's raw," she said, as if rawness was the highest quality in literature.

Dick's own military experiences were not the kind you put into a war novel. He'd been a reporter in the army, working on *Stars and Stripes* in Naples. While Charlie and a lot of other guys were in Korea, fighting, freezing, being captured and brainwashed, he weekended on Capri and sat around drinking with his *S and S* buddies talking about art. No fucking novel there. Dick's military experience had been a bust, so far as writing was concerned. And Charlie had the Bronze Star. Give me a fucking break. Dick wondered how he'd gotten it, envisioning Charlie rushing through the smoke with his rifle at port arms, mouth open in a defiant scream. All Charlie had said about it, when pressed, was that he had been the best-looking man in his platoon, and so they'd given the decoration to him. Dick knew enough about the military to suspect there was more than a little truth to what Charlie said. But brave *and* modest? Charlie was getting to be a real pain in the ass.

Even so, Dick liked him a lot. He didn't really believe Charlie and Linda would do anything behind his back. In fact, he trusted Charlie more than he did Linda. And he was sure in his heart that Charlie was going to be a famous writer. Dick's own work wasn't going that well. He and Charlie even talked about it. Charlie had been very respectful of the *Playboy* sale, saying, "Their money spends real good, don't it?"

But the only other money he'd seen from his pal Hefner was at Christmas, when he'd received a check for one hundred dollars, a gift from the magazine. His stories they rejected, and so did everybody else. He'd sold only two little pieces since then, and none of the stuff he'd written after *Playboy*. The pay was meager, eighty-nine dollars for one story and one hundred fifty for another. No way to get rich. Everybody was right, you had to publish a novel. Then editors would remember your name. Trouble was, Dick was afraid to write a novel. It chilled his heart to think about working on something for that long and then having it rejected. Maybe he didn't have a novel to write. No war or air strike, never killed anybody. Nothing to write about. His life? A laugh. Sure, most novelists just made up their plots. He could do that. He did it with stories. It was too many eggs in one basket, and so while day-dreaming of his novel to come, Dick did nothing about it and kept at stories with a *Playboy* slant. If he could just sell one more, even at fifteen hundred instead of the big three thousand, he'd feel ready to embark on larger work. He could see it in the front of *Playboy*, under his picture. "Dubonet is hard at work on his first novel."

Meanwhile his friendship with Charlie needed attention. Dick tried to think of some adventure where he could show Charlie the beauties of living in Oregon. And show himself, too, because he was getting ready to move on. Could San Francisco be a destination? Linda was always full of San Francisco, North Beach, and all the rich cultural experiences of living in a truly creative environment. Likely Charlie and Jaime wouldn't be in Oregon long. Charlie already spoke of jumping back to San Francisco right after he finished his novel.

"Oregon's a great place to write," he said with a beaming smile. "But I wouldn't want to die here."

30.

Nothing is as pure as you thought it would be as a kid. Take writing. Take love. Take friendship. These had all been pure things to Dick Dubonet when he had been young and innocent. He still thought of himself as an idealist, but his ideals had come under a lot of attack recently and he was wondering. Just wonder, that's all. When he and Linda had fallen in love they'd been able to talk to each other, and Dick felt he could say anything to her and she wouldn't laugh or be offended. They'd lie in bed in the darkness and he would tell her his dreams of the future, of making good money as a writer, giving him in turn the freedom to expand himself into the world, to travel, to see the world as it is, and to write about what he saw. But first he'd have to build up his reputation with the magazines, then write the novel he hoped would get him the money and attention to carry out his life plans. Which now included Linda, in fact were meaningless without Linda.

And suddenly he felt Linda slipping away. He wanted to bring it up but found he couldn't. What if he said something like, "You seem awfully interested in Charlie"? She might reply. He didn't know if he could handle any of the possible replies. "Yes, I am." That would kill him. "No, I'm not." He wouldn't believe it. "Mind your own business." Meaning, if the end came, it would be his fault for hounding her about Charlie. "Oh, baby, I just love you too much to fool around, and I apologize." Sure.

She wasn't really fooling around, she was just making it look to everybody as if she was. Dick had walked into the Caffe Espresso one night when he thought Linda was home to find her sitting with Charlie and Stan and some tall homely girl he didn't know. He joined them for an espresso and pretended he wasn't at all surprised to see Linda. She made no explanation. Dick had come in hoping to find Charlie, who'd made the habit of dropping in every once in a while after his night classes. Dick hoped to engage him in a game of chess. He hoped Charlie knew how to play. Dick considered himself half-good, which, he felt, made him one of the best coffeehouse players in Portland. It would be fun whipping Charlie Monel at something, even only chess. But when he brought it up (there was a chess game going on at the next table, two Reedies in glasses, bent over their board) Charlie just laughed and waved his hand in surrender.

"You'd whip my ass," he said, and refused to be cajoled into a game.

So writing, friendship, and love were all tangled in his heart. He couldn't help thinking Linda had come to him because of his potential as a writer. It hadn't bothered him before, in fact he thought it part of his due. But then Charlie moved to town and everybody began talking about him as the hottest thing since Kerouac. So naturally Linda was attracted. Live by the sword, die cut to ribbons. Fair enough, except he was fond of Charlie himself, and could see what Linda saw in him. Here was a real writer, a big man, a strong man, a guy with combat experience, a killer and yet one of the slain, POW in hell. How could Dick fight that? He wanted Charlie for his best friend. He wanted to help Charlie with his writing, which Dick had heard was pretty rough, and he wanted Charlie to help him with his, which lacked passion, or lacked something, a something Charlie might be able to help him with. So Dick buried his feelings, but that was okay, because maybe buried feelings came out in the writing. Maybe this was how Charlie was meant to help him!

The spring had been a hot wet one, and now the summer was promising to be a Portland Special, low clouds heavy over the city most of the time, rain falling, temp in the eighties, so that when the sun did break through the clouds the heat and humidity made you want to grab your throat and die. Dick and Linda often drove out to the Monels', and beyond, to a place on Lake Oswego called Latourette's where you could swim free. They all went down for long afternoons of swimming, drinking beer, and talking, and if it rained they didn't care. Latourette's was a big empty lot on the lake's south shore, a mile from Charlie's place, the lot steeply falling away from the road, with an old dock, and otherwise only wild greenery and some rocks along the shore. Usually Stan Winger would be with them. He'd been spending a lot of weekends at the Monels', and was apparently part of the family now, or at least acted it, making his way down the cliff holding Kira and her baby bag as easily as if she were his own kid. Dick had to admit he was a little jealous of Stan's closeness to Kira, when after all Dick had seen her take her first steps. He felt this made him part of the family too.

Dick didn't mind a bit when there were others at Latourette's. High school boys came by, and it gave Dick a secret pleasure to see the way these kids covertly stared at Linda and Jaime in their bathing suits, these beautiful women, the kind most men never get to talk to, much less touch. Dick was with them, talking to them, and as the boys would soon find out, touching them intimately. Although Linda hated it when he was too affectionate in public. "Stop kissing me," she said to him crossly one afternoon when they sat in Charlie's kitchen listening to the rain. Thank God Charlie had been out of the room, but Stan, sitting right there, had a hard time keeping his face straight.

Then something extraordinary happened. Dick wonder if reality existed at all, or if he was living in a dream. One night as they were eating dinner in their own home on Cable Linda said, as if asking him to pass the potatoes, "My son's going to be with me for six weeks. If you don't want him here, I'll get a place of my own."

"What?" he said. "What?"

Her son was nine. Which mean that she must have been only about fifteen when he had been born.

"Of course he can live with us," Dick said. "What's his name?"

Linda smiled. "His name is Louis. After his father."

His father! Who turned out to be just exactly who Dick didn't want him to be, a big, muscular, tattooed man with a mop of dirty brown hair like Charlie's and wide intense psychopathic eyes. He brought the boy over one Sunday afternoon. Louis the father drove a really noisy old Ford that had been chopped and channeled, painted with red and gray primer, and looked like the dream car of a high school boy. He came up the steps carrying the boy on his shoulder, looking like Paul Bunyan, all he needed was an axe over the other shoulder, really. But he wasn't a logger. Dick got no satisfactory explanation of what he did or what had happened between him and Linda. All she'd say after her ex-husband left was that she'd met him sailing, and that they'd been divorced in Mexico.

Little Louis was a different matter. An ordinary-looking nine-year-old except for his eyes, which were hard. Dick saw instantly that here was a kid who trusted no one. A kid with a lot of bad experience under his belt already. Like Stan, raised in foster homes. Sometimes Stan got that same hard-eyed look. It wasn't going to be much fun, having this damaged kid for six weeks. But on the other hand, what better way to bind Linda to him, than to befriend her son?

The three sat very formally at dinner that night, the boy barely eating his food, Linda obviously nervous. Dick's heart went out to her. She was probably more scared of having a kid around than Dick was.

"Listen," Dick said as brightly as he could. "I have a great idea. Let's get a cat!"

"Oh, that sounds wonderful," Linda said, looking at her son. Louis's eyes didn't soften.

31.

Linda's job was too valuable for her to just quit, so it fell on Dick to oversee Louis. It wasn't easy. On their first morning alone together Dick explained that he had to sit quietly and write all morning, and Louis would have to entertain himself.

"Will you be okay?" he asked finally. He didn't know what else to say. Louis nodded without meeting his eyes, and Dick went into his office and shut the door. He sat at his typewriter and cracked his knuckles, took the little glass paperweight off the manuscript and inserted the top page in the machine. He sighed. He was in the middle of a story about two men who fight over a woman, and now, staring at the page, he wondered why he bothered. He worried about the boy in the next room, who made no noise at all. He was nine. He should have been a Cub Scout, with a lot of Cub Scout friends to play with, as Dick had been. Dick had had all the amenities of a middle-class neighborhood, Cub Scouts, Boy Scouts, neighborhood friends, a mother who didn't work. While the poor kid in the next room had nothing. He wondered what life must be like living with his father. Linda didn't seem to know what the man did or where he lived or anything about him. "How come he got custody?" was one of Dick's first questions, but Linda only said, "He wanted it." Meaning, of course, that she hadn't. What kind of woman was she?

Poor Linda, her incompetence uncovered. A perfect woman except for this tragic flaw. She did not love her child. Dick thought maybe she was confusing the child with his father. Dick supposed he was a brute, a woman-beater, probably a child-beater as well, although Dick didn't see any bruising on Louis. Or maybe Dick was just jealous, because big Louis was so big, with all the romantic energy of a motorcycle outlaw, although Linda insisted he wasn't one. She'd met him sailing. "He doesn't look like any of the yachtsmen I've ever met," Dick said ironically.

Linda threw him a look. "He was crewing," she said. "He never owned anything." She, too, had been crew. In fact, Linda had been around boats a lot, had lived in Newport, on the Oregon coast, for a couple of years.

"Blowjobs for boat rides," she said to him once, when they were drunk and talking about the past. He'd been shocked but laughed to show he wasn't. "I love to sail," she said wistfully. "When we get rich let's get a boat of our own." There were so many things they were going to get, when they were rich. A cabin in the mountains, where he'd teach her to ski. Trips to exotic places. Weekends in India. Life at the top. He looked at the page in his typewriter. No words had written themselves. He wondered what Louis was doing. He had to trust Louis. He couldn't keep checking up on him, or the boy would feel oppressed. He went to the door, opening it. Louis sat in the middle of the living-room, cross-legged, staring at nothing.

"You okay?" Dick asked. He felt pain just looking at the poor kid.

"I'm okay," Louis said. His eyes said, "Fuck you."

Dick looked out the window. The clouds hung low, but it wasn't raining. The air was muggy, and it was going to be an oppressive day. "You know what?" Dick said. "I don't feel like working. Let's get out of here and go for a ride."

Once in the car and moving, Dick thought desperately about where to go. He found himself on the road south, toward Lake Grove. He didn't know if he'd be welcome at Charlie and Jaime's at nine on a weekday morning. They'd both be writing, if not otherwise busy. But Dick had nowhere else to go, and the kid was driving him crazy with his silence. "Isn't this a great car?" Dick said, and Louis nodded, looking out the window at the trees. "In good weather we can take the top down," Dick finished lamely.

They pulled into the circular drive. There were no cars in the garage. Maybe nobody home. "We might have made a long trip for nothing," Dick said. But Jaime opened the front door, looked out at them blankly, and then smiled and said, "Come in." Now Dick was even more anxious. Jaime would see clearly that he was in over his head with the child.

"Just cruising around with my pal," he said brightly. They entered the house. "This is Linda's son, Louis, who's come to stay with us for a while."

"Hello, Louis." Jaime didn't wait for an answer, but took Louis by the hand and led him to the kitchen table. In a few minutes they were all having toast, and he and Jaime were having coffee. The little girl, Kira, was asleep. Jaime had been writing but was glad for the interruption, or so she said. "Charlie's out at the air base today, teaching GED," she said. Louis was looking at her hair, about half red and half blonde by now. She smiled. "I made a serious stylistic error, but I'm letting it grow out." When the boy didn't reply, she looked at Dick inquiringly.

"He doesn't talk much," Dick said. He wanted to tell Jaime what was going on, but not in front of Louis. At that moment Isis the cat walked in and the whole day changed. The cat meowed and jumped up onto the table, and Louis's eyes lit up. The cat walked right up to him, sniffed his toast, and meowed at Louis, as if to say, "Toast? Only toast?" Louis smiled for the first time, at least in front of Dick.

"Cats are diplomats," Jaime said.

"Can I hold him?" Louis asked. Jaime smiled and nodded and Louis picked up the cat under the front legs and held her up in front of his face. The cat meowed, but didn't squirm or try to get away. The hardness was gone from Louis's eyes, and Dick felt the urgent need to keep it from coming back. Although he knew it would come back. Soon the boy and the cat were gone from the table and were playing on the living room rug, just out of sight.

"What's up?" Jaime asked, and Dick told her.

"Do you know where I can get a good cat cheap?" he asked. The boy was walking around the house with the cat on his shoulder. Outside, the rain started up. Jaime smiled. "I'll ask the neighbors," she said.

"A dog would be too much trouble."

She laughed and then said some very funny insulting things about dogs, the way they eat, slobbering over everything, the way they want to sleep in the middle, the way they need constant reassurance. Dick laughed his head off, having a fine time on this day that had begun so badly. He was really starting to like this girl. Then the little girl woke up and Jaime brought her out, looking sleepy and out of sorts. Jaime let Dick hold her while she fixed some baby food.

"You're going to have to buy a lot of games and puzzles and stuff," Jaime said. "How did Linda lose custody, do you know?"

"I think she just gave him up," he said in a low voice. In the next room, Louis talked to the cat. The child in Dick's arms was starting to blubber, and he thought he smelled something. "You better take her," he said, and Jaime rescued him.

Soon it was time to leave, no getting around it, and he had to separate Louis and the cat. "You'll have one of your own soon," he said, but Louis's eyes hardened again. "Yeah," he said, and got into the car. Jaime held Isis. Dick felt like crying.

"Wait," Jaime said. Dick stood holding the car door. "You can have Isis."

"You're not serious."

"Sure I am." Jaime handed the cat to the boy. The cat immediately started to purr, and Louis stroked her, his eyes softening at once. "You need her more than I do." Jaime softly touched Dick on the arm.

"Under these conditions, I accept." He wanted to kiss her.

Jaime bent down to speak to Louis. "If she gives you any trouble, just give her a swift kick in the pants." The boy smiled happily. "Thank you," he said.

"See what a polite kid he is?" Dick said proudly.

32.

The three spent a lot of time together, Dick, Louis, and Isis the cat. Dick worked for two hours each morning, and it was a great relief to learn that Louis could not only take care of himself, he was such a quiet kid Dick could leave his office door open, keeping one ear cocked for sounds of trouble. Sometimes little Isis would come in and jump on his lap, purring loudly and then falling asleep, her claws lightly hooked into Dick's jeans. Louis, after he made up the couch where he slept, folding the sheets and blankets into a cardboard box, spent mornings reading comic books from Dick's collection, or drawing on the big pad of paper his mother bought him.

He was good, too. He didn't make childish pictures, but drawings of birds, usually hawks, and usually eating a mouse, or pinning a mouse beneath its claws. Dick watched from his doorway as Louis sharpened his crayons carefully, using a little red plastic pencil sharpener Dick had lent him. He sharpened the crayons slowly, watching the waxy material curl and break off, picking it up from the rug and putting it into his mouth. Then he'd get on his belly and begin to draw, spending a long time over the feathers, filling them in carefully and stopping to resharpen his crayons to the smallest point.

"Where'd you learn how to do this?" Dick asked one day, looking at an osprey with a dying trout under its claws.

"Out of a book." Roger Tory Peterson's *Field Guide to Western Birds.* Dick dug out his own copy and handed it to Louis, who grabbed it and said, "Oh boy!" But when Dick proudly showed Louis's best drawings to Linda she said, "Why can't he draw something nicer?" She saw only the predatory aspect. "Why can't he draw houses or cows, like anybody else?" she said. Friend of Kerouac.

In the afternoons Dick made sure they went out. Ordinarily he spent afternoons rewriting, reading, or napping, but now this was good, it got him out of himself, out of the house, into the world. He and Louis drove all over Portland, up into the West Hills to the zoo, way out to NE Marine Drive, along the Columbia River, up the Columbia to Rooster Rock and Multnomah Falls, once all the way to the fish hatchery, where they stood looking down into ponds filled with millions of baby salmon and the long pools where they kept the old sturgeons, six feet long and more, fish that looked ancient as dinosaurs. And they often drove out to Lake Grove to visit the Monels.

Dick always thought he'd be a poor father. Now he was amazed at himself, and at the way it felt. The way Louis automatically reached for his hand when they were about to go anywhere. The way the hand felt in his. The way he and Louis shared jokes. And especially the way the little guy seemed to realize how serious Dick was about his writing, the respect, almost religious, with which Louis kept quiet during writing time. This so touched Dick that tears came to his eyes when he thought about it. One night in bed with Linda, after making love in what seemed an unusually tender way, he said, "Let's have kids."

"I really don't think so," Linda said sleepily. She turned from him, indicating by her stillness that she didn't want to talk, but he went on.

"Isn't there some way we could keep Louis with us? I mean, if you don't want to get pregnant again."

She turned back toward him. He couldn't make out her expression. "Leave things the way they are, okay?"

"I don't like the idea of sending him back with his father," Dick said. There. It was out. "In fact, I don't trust the father at all."

"Neither do I. But we can't keep Louis."

"Why not?" Dick persisted.

Linda sat up and looked him right in the eye. "I don't want him." Her voice wanted no response. It broke Dick's heart to know that the woman he loved was so cold. On the other hand, if she hadn't been, he probably would never have met her. This gave him no consolation. He was going to have to break with her. Just as soon as he could build up the courage.

The hard look was gone from Louis's eyes. Dick dreaded its return. He could envision it, when the father came back to take Louis away. Louis crying and holding onto his legs, the kitty crying, Linda strangely dry-eyed. He dreaded the day. Yet when it came it was nothing like Dick's expectations. Louis was packed and ready to go at 6:00 a.m. though his father wasn't expected until ten. Dick had, in a moment of love, given Louis his collection of DC comics from the forties and fifties, and it was like tearing out part of his heart now, to see the comics actually leaving the house. To say nothing of Louis. Dick feared crying or making a scene in front of the outlaw father, but he didn't, and Dick had to reevaluate his opinion of Big Louis, who had tears streaming down his face as he came into the house. Little Louis grabbed his own father around the legs, not Dick, and cried happily to see him.

"Daddy, can I take my cat?"

Big Louis smiled inquiringly at Dick. "Cat?"

Dick wanted to tell the man to dry his tears, but didn't. "There's a cat, yes."

"Please, Daddy? I'll take care of her. Her name's Isis—"

At this, Isis walked into the room and gave a loud meow.

"You can take her as far as I'm concerned," Linda said. She wouldn't look at Big Louis.

"Well, sure," Big Louis said. Off they went, the three of them, with Louis's pitiful box of things.

"I was wrong about him," Dick said to Linda after they had gone.

"No, you weren't." Dick was left with the disquieting feeling that he'd been conned by the McNeills, father and son. This was reinforced when at about two in the morning Isis came into the house and into their bedroom and woke them by jumping on Dick's legs, letting out a single cry and settling there to sleep.

"What's the matter?" Linda asked sleepily.

"The kitty came back," Dick said. He stroked Isis's ears and she began to purr.

The kitty came back, the very next day
The kitty came back, 'cause she couldn't stay away . . .

"This worries me," Dick said to no one.

"The cat probably jumped out of the car," Linda said, and went back to sleep.

<h1 style="text-align:center">33.</h1>

Jaime finished her novel in the hottest part of August, after three days of clear blue sky and rising temperature. Naked except for white cotton underpants, she sat at her desk with Kira sleeping fitfully beside the desk in her crib. She typed the final words, hesitated a moment, looked at her watch, then typed the end. 4:23 a.m., August 21, 1962. She put the fresh pages with the older ones and hefted the whole manuscript. It couldn't be finished. But it was. Sweat ran down her sides. She considered waking Charlie and decided against it. She wasn't sleepy. The humidity had been what got her working nights, and now the humidity seemed to have finished her book for her. All that was left was to title it, add a dedication, and send it off.

She went out into the kitchen. At least she could celebrate with a morning cup of tea. Isis sprawled sleeping on the kitchen table, such a little cat, even stretched out. Jaime stroked the cat's belly and Isis woke, yawned and stretched even more. Dick Dubonet brought her back because he said the cat reminded him of Louis. Poor Dick Dubonet. And poor Charlie. Poor all of them, she'd been the one to write a book. It sat in the next room innocently, like a time bomb. The current title, the working title, was *Memories of My Father*. By Jaime Froward. But it wasn't just about her father, it hadn't been for a long time. It was about her whole family and their life on Washington Street. It was a memory, a love poem, a recognition. She tried to think of a better title. *Song of My Father*. No. Sounded used. *A Family Memory*. Yes, but. The kettle whistled and she poured hot water into her mug. Charlie came into the kitchen, sleepy-eyed, wearing nothing.

"Got enough water?" he asked.

"It's awfully early," she said.

"I can't sleep either." He threw a teabag into his big green mug and went to the stove. Jaime watched his back. Charlie had a beautiful behind, she decided for the hundredth time. For a guy. Nice big square butt, not too big, not too square, just a good solid working butt. "I finished my novel," she said to his butt.

Charlie turned easily, holding his mug, the Lipton's tag hanging out, steam rising from the surface. "Great," he said easily. "What's it called?" He sat opposite her. The cat got up and arched her back in a yawn, then dropped off the table and walked out the open back door, tail high.

"I don't know yet." They had a rule never to talk about each other's work. This conversation was ground-breaking. Of course she was done, it was all right.

"What's it about?" He rubbed his face and grinned at her. "I'm taking it awfully well, aren't I? Really. What's it about?"

She told him. Just scenes from their life on Washington Street. An affectionate family portrait. Nothing literary, nothing for the ages, just a little book about some ordinary people whose life was gone now.

"Why don't you call it *Washington Street?*"

"Perfect," Jaime said, and it was. She went into her office and typed the words on a blank sheet. It looked just fine.

Charlie came in and picked up the manuscript, 309 pages, and weighed it in his hand. "Yep, it's a novel," he said, still curiously detached. "When can I read it?"

"Let me get it retyped first." She typed well enough, but not perfectly, and she wanted the manuscript to be perfect when she sent it to New York.

Back out in the kitchen they sat at the table and sipped their tea as the sun came up, promising another smothering heat. What would she do with her day? Or at night, when she couldn't sleep? Her novel had been her anchor, and now it was gone. All the pleasure of finishing, of knowing she was capable of writing a whole book, was submerged under this sense of loss. And she'd been working on the novel, let's see, only three months and some days. Charlie had been working on his novel for years, she didn't know exactly how many, but years and years. It seemed unfair. Charlie sat there, pretending to listen to the music on the radio, nodding his head, playing with his teabag, probably stabbed through the heart.

They should celebrate by making love, she knew. But it was so hot, and Charlie probably didn't feel much like it.

"I'm going to shower," she said, and stood up. Charlie just winked at her and said, "Go ahead and use all the hot water," feeble joke, but he didn't follow her into the bedroom or the shower. Getting cold and wet was some relief. What was she to do with the manuscript? Submit it cold, over the transom? Submit it cold to agents? Call Walter Van Tilburg Clark and ask his help? She decided against it. Time to get out of the bush leagues and into the majors. She didn't want help, she was going to do this all on her own. At this moment Charlie came into the bathroom and pulled open the glass door, a big lewd grin on his face as he stepped in and joined her under the chilling water.

After breakfast that morning they both worked in the garden while Kira played in her playpen on the back porch out of the sun. They had rows of sweet peas, carrots, beets, zucchini squash, a melon patch, and two rows of corn five feet tall and growing. The marijuana crop hadn't worked out. That which hadn't been crushed was eaten by forest animals. Not deer. Jaime had to ask one of the neighbors why there were no deer in the area. It seemed perfect for deer. The neighbor laughed. "Up here," he said, "we eat deer." So maybe the rabbits were eating the marijuana. They certainly acted strangely enough. Almost every night at dusk, if it wasn't raining too hard, the little rabbits would come out of the woods to play at the far end of the clearing behind their house. A rabbit would be sitting there hunched up nibbling a bit of clover, then for no reason suddenly jump straight up in the air, somersaulting and landing on its feet, still chewing as if nothing had happened. Kira would scream with pleasure, but it didn't seem to scare the rabbits.

Jaime had to admit, even as the sweat stuck her tee shirt to her body, she was falling in love with Oregon. So was her mother, who'd found a boyfriend at the *Oregonian*, a sportswriter. If she married this guy, then Charlie and Jaime could rent out the little apartment behind the garage to Stan Winger, and get him out of that tenement. She worried about Stan. He seemed happy only when he was here, being part of the family. The look in his eyes when he had to go home broke Jaime's heart. Poor guy, writing away at his pulp stories. Trying to better himself after a life of nothing good. Better to have him here. Maybe he could get a job. Jaime knew he made his living in some way nobody would talk about. She feared that one day he would be arrested and just disappear into prison. Horrible. Strange and silent as he was, Jaime liked Stan a lot. And he obviously worshiped her, though he was even more obviously in love with Linda McNeill. But it was a poet's love, an unrequited love. She wasn't sure Stan would always be satisfied with love from afar, but then Dick and Linda's relationship seemed under a strain after Linda's son left. Dick was getting autocratic, issuing orders to Linda in a tone nobody liked. Linda, instead of being defiant or funny about it, just obeyed, looking sullen. They were doomed, Jaime decided. Maybe little Stan had a shot.

She pulled off her cotton gloves and wiped her face. She and Charlie had been on their knees digging weeds. She glanced at the porch to see if Kira was all right and saw Dick Dubonet in the shade in a white tee and jeans. He waved and she waved back, even though she didn't really want company. She was still waiting for Charlie to explode.

"Wanna do some weeding?" she cried out to Dick.

"No thanks," he said in his deep sexy voice. He pulled his nose and said, "I've come for my cat."

Jaime came up on the porch. Charlie kept weeding.

"I made a mistake, bringing Isis back. I miss her. Linda misses her. Can we please have her back?"

Isis was in the woods somewhere. Dick grimly walked through the trees, calling out, "Isis . . . *Isis* . . ." Jaime watched him from the porch. She didn't want him to have the cat. The cat had been given to the child. But she couldn't refuse Dick. He was too pathetic. He'd lost his child, given away his cat, and now he was about to lose his woman. As far as Jaime knew he hadn't published anything in a long time, and according to Marty Greenberg he was desperate. "He keeps writing these shitty *Playboy*-type stories. No wonder nobody will print him. The stories have *Playboy* written all over them. Which of course *Playboy* would hate. So the man's in a hole."

Jaime fixed lunch and set a place for Dick but he didn't show up. It wasn't until three in the afternoon that he emerged from the woods, defeated. "Something's happened to her," he said, and sat at the table. Charlie had gone to the store, taking Kira with him, and Jaime had nothing to do. Normally she'd spend this precious time writing. Dick sat opposite her, sweat and dirt on his face. He looked bad. An emotional man, despite his macho pose.

"She'll be fine," Jaime said. She got two beers from the refrigerator. "She spends half her life in that jungle back there. And every time we let Kira loose she starts for the woods."

"How's your book coming?"

"I finished it," she said. Into his blank stare she added, "I still have to go over it, you know, get it typed."

"How long is it?"

"Oh, it's short," she said, to appease him. "Only about three hundred pages."

"Well, I think that's great news," he said, although his voice cracked slightly on the word great.

Jaime laughed. She hadn't felt this good in weeks. "It's probably a piece of shit," she said.

"Oh, no," Dick said. "I'm sure it's a wonderful little book."

34.

The only way Dick could recover from the blow Jaime had dealt him was to be generous. "I don't know what you plan," he said in his deepest voice, "but if you need the name of a good agent . . ." Jaime looked surprised. Good. He went on, praising Robert P. Mills as a kind and generous man who would, because he was one of the little guys, give his clients a lot of personal attention. "He's best for mystery and sci-fi, but he knows his way around ordinary regular fiction."

"I'm flattered that you would offer him," Jaime said.

Dick laughed. "Well, all I can do is recommend. After that you're on your own." They both laughed.

Dick grew even more generous when Charlie came in with a bag of groceries and sleeping Kira in his arms and Jaime told him about Dick's offer.

"That's great!" Charlie said.

"If you want a really good typist," Dick said, "Linda has plenty of time at work."

"Oh, I couldn't ask her to do that," Jaime said. "I'm willing to pay."

"She'll take the money," Dick said, and grinned at the others, who grinned back.

Linda typed the manuscript for thirty bucks, one original and two carbons. Dick hadn't read it, and hadn't been at the meeting between Jaime and Linda when the manuscript changed hands. "What's it like?" he asked Linda one night.

"It's good." She sat on the living room couch reading a magazine.

"How good?" he joked.

She looked over. "It's very female. People aren't going to buy it."

"You can't possibly know that," he said happily. Later when she brought the completed job home in a cardboard box he sneaked a peek, pretending he was examining the typing. "It's beautiful," he said to Linda.

"You mean the typing," she said.

But he was reading now. Very simple stuff. Sentimental. Mawkish, he'd have to say. He turned to another page. The same. Lightweight sentimental reminiscence. No competition. Dick felt happy, then was ashamed of himself. The time, the effort. He himself had never managed it, and Jaime deserved all possible praise, just for writing the damn thing. Even if it was only three-hundred-odd pages and she'd ripped through it in less than a year. Much less, if Dick remembered when she'd started it. But, he had to tell himself, she'd bulled her way through. Good for her.

"Great typing," he said to Linda later, "but I wouldn't count on a quick sale. If I were Jaime."

"You aren't," she said.

Jaime's novel was not his greatest problem. It could be months before that issue resolved itself. Right now he had to worry about his own work. Was it time to start his novel? Had he set an artificial goal, by waiting for another big sale? Maybe the suspense was killing him, and it was time to stop watching *Playboy*. Maybe starting a novel would break his bad luck streak. He'd been thinking that writing a novel would take a year or two, maybe even more, if Charlie's was any example. And he quailed at the thought. But Jaime had done it in months. He'd do the same. With his life experiences he'd write a far more interesting book.

He could hear Linda's contempt if she found out. "Monkey see, monkey do." Uh-huh. If he did start a novel he'd have to keep it a secret from Linda and everybody else. That would mean eating up the rest of his bank account without sending any stories into the marketplace. He had nineteen stories out now, ten with Mills, and nine he was sending around to little magazines himself. What yield could he expect from these nineteen stories? He took out the carbons and looked them over one at a time. It was raining hard and he had the doors open to let in the fresh air. Usually an afternoon spent looking over his pile of work could be wonderfully pleasant, but not today. He realized with a sinking heart that most of the stuff, maybe even all of it, was, well, not as good as he remembered. Not good, and not very commercial. As the rain poured down Dick's spirits slowly went through the floor. By the time Linda got home he felt exhausted and grubby.

"Where's dinner?" she asked. He'd totally forgotten to make any. He hadn't even thawed the lamb chops.

"Sorry." He didn't explain, just sat stiffly on the couch, feet straight in front of him, hands jammed in his pockets.

"I'm hungry, damn it." She went into the bedroom and he heard her undressing. He wondered if he had the manhood to go in there and just grab her, throw her to the floor, and make love to her. That would do it. But it would also kill him. And what if she just shrugged him off? "Oh, stop that!" He'd feel like an idiot. Besides, his groin felt cold, not warm.

"I was working," he said.

She came to the bedroom door, bare to the waist. "Let's just go out."

"In this rain?"

"Well, fuck you," she said and went back into the bedroom. It was too late to say "Fuck you!" back. Anyway he was afraid to. When she came out of the bedroom again she was dressed to go out, in cutoff jeans, men's blue work shirt, Dick's brown fedora, and her dark green raincoat. She looked wonderful.

"Where are you going?"

"I'm going out to eat."

"We can't eat out every night."

"That's too bad," she said, and left through the open front door. Outside the rain pissed down angrily. She'd gone off in the rain. He might never see her again. In his present mood he couldn't do a damn thing about it. After a while he went into the kitchen, took the package of lamb chops out and opened it. No sense starving.

Linda came home at nine, wet, and not speaking to Dick. He was just frying the chops. "Got room for a lamb chop?" he called out. No answer. Maybe she was getting her period.

35.

At first he'd been too stiff, sitting in his office *scrutinizing* the book instead of just reading it as he would any other damned book. He could hear Jaime and Kira out in the kitchen. She knew he was reading it. She went on about her housework pretending it didn't matter to her, and half Charlie's reading problem was that he was simultaneously trying to think up what to say after he finished. If he could. What excuse could he give, however, for not finishing it in one mammoth read? "So far, so good." "Gee, it's great. What's for dinner?"

He forgot himself and just read. He started giggling, then laughing out loud uncontrollably as he read his wife's book. He knew Jaime could hear him, so he didn't try to restrain it. The stuff was really funny. And touching, though so far from Charlie's own early life that it seemed to be from another planet. Instead of having to make excuses, he finished it easily by five that evening. He sat at his desk, curiously empty. He had nothing to say to Jaime. He'd been sitting there laughing his ass off for three or four hours. She'd figured out by now that he thought the book was funny. Something his own book was not. And finished. And, as far as Charlie was concerned, literature. Which his book was decidedly not.

The only question before Charlie was how to let Jaime know how much he loved her book without getting into the business of his own. He got to his feet and went to the door, placing his hand on the cold knob. Shitty old iron fixture, rusty and ratty like all the fixtures in this house. He turned the knob, put a big smile on his face and pushed open the door.

Jaime sat feeding Kira. The kitchen smelled of spaghetti sauce, which simmered on the stove. Charlie looked around, conscious of Jaime's eyes on him. He liked this kitchen. He'd been happy here, they all had. This had been a wonderful part of their lives.

"Your book is everything you hoped," he said.

"What do you mean?" He heard anxiety in her voice, and it made him feel good. What was that? He'd have to get over that.

"I always said, you're twice the writer I'll ever be," Charlie heard himself saying, damn it. Just what he didn't want to say, but here was Jaime coming into his arms.

"Is it good?" she begged him.

"Better than good," he improvised. Was this to be his life? "I need a beer and some dinner," he added lamely. What was he supposed to do, dance around the room?

But dinner put things into perspective. As good as her book was, it at least had a chance of getting published, could even make money. It if got through the agent barrier, the editor barrier, the publisher barrier, the critical barrier, then at last the public barrier. Wasn't that the point? To make one's living as a writer? And now his wife had proved, at least to him, that she was going to do exactly that. Never mind his feelings about his own book. Work In Progress. He was after a lot. He wanted to get it all in. Etc. He could not get away from the absurd feeling that if Jaime had been sent to Korea, captured, left to rot in a prison camp and then stuck in an army TB ward for over a year, she'd have come out of it with a great novel.

"Well, you gonna send it to Mills?" he asked her the next morning.

"Why don't we go to New York? We could fly there, take a room at the Algonquin Hotel, and walk around introducing ourselves to agents."

"I have to teach," Charlie heard himself saying. "But you could go." It would be fun for her to see New York. He remembered Frankie Pippello from Kim Song. He wondered what Frankie was doing. He could look him up.

"It wouldn't be any fun without you," she said, pretending to pout.

"It's so impractical."

"Expensive and foolish. I crave doing it."

Charlie had to remember that Jaime was a beautiful twenty-one-year-old girl, which wouldn't hurt. Not that she needed it, but maybe she did, maybe everybody did. It was a tough game, just ask anybody they knew. Ask Dick Dubonet, fighting his lonely war against *Playboy*. There were things to be said in favor of not being published, Charlie realized.

"Let's do it," he said. "Fuck 'em."

She laughed. "Let's think about it."

Just before Charlie left for work the phone rang. "It's for you," Jaime said to him. She handed him the phone and then walked out onto the back porch where Kira played in her pen.

"Hello?" he said.

"Charlie," said Linda. "I hate to interrupt your writing—"

"I'm just on my way to the air base," he said. "I teach typing today."

"Oh, I was hoping you'd be downtown . . ."

"What's up?"

"I just feel like talking to you, is all. Nothing important."

"I can be late," Charlie said. "I'll call the base."

He got dressed for work. They were casual at the air base, so he wore comfortable clothes, jeans, boots, old dress shirt. It was a nice day for a change, sunny and cool. He stepped out on the back porch to kiss Jaime and the baby good-bye, but they weren't there. He could see Jaime, holding Kira, out among the trees. "Bye!" he yelled, and Jaime waved. He went back into the house and into his office. He didn't need his briefcase today. He looked around. His manuscript, neat in its cardboard boxes. He picked them up. Heavy. He carried them out the front door and down the graveled drive. He set the two cartons next to the trash cans beside the mailbox and went back and got into his car, started it, and drove off.

He met Linda at the corner of SW Fifth and Alder. She was dressed for work in a black suit with a red blouse open at the throat. She smiled up at him. "Coffee?"

"Sure."

She led him into a little café and they sat at the counter. They were the only people in the place apart from the old man in a dirty apron behind the counter. They ordered coffee and sat quietly waiting until the old man brought it and went back to his corner. Then Linda said, without looking up, "I'm leaving Dick."

"Oh?"

"I'm going sailing." She turned to him. "I'm tired of Portland."

"When do you leave?"

"In a few days. The boat's in Astoria."

"Where you headed?"

She smiled. "Greater Polynesia. Around the world. I don't know. Hawaii first."

"Sounds great," Charlie said.

"I just wanted you to know. I always thought there was something between us, you know?"

"Yeah," Charlie admitted. "Does Dick know you're leaving?"

"He should, but he doesn't. It's just that I'm up to here." She held her hand to her neck. "I could leave today, in fact." She sipped her coffee. "You're my only regret."

"Where's Astoria?" he asked. She told him and he said, "Let's go."

She looked at him. "I'll cut class," he said.

They got into his green Volkswagen. "Are you sure about this?" she asked him.

He looked at her blankly. He felt nothing. Had felt nothing all day. Whatever held him together all these years had dissolved, at least for now, and he felt pleasantly empty.

"I've always wanted to fuck you," he said to Linda. He started the car.

"Now's your chance." They drove west, out of Portland.

36.

When Jaime took out the garbage she found Charlie's book and right away she knew. She picked up the two cartons and carried them back into the house, trying not to think. Kira was asleep in her playpen, lying on her stomach holding her teddy bear. She'd lost her old teddy bear and Stan Winger had given her this new one, a cinnamon bear with a white vest. "Every kid should have a first-class bear," he'd said when he handed it to Kira. Jaime thought about calling Stan. But he had no phone. She could call the air base, but she knew Charlie hadn't gone there. A man doesn't throw away ten years of work and probably his wife and child, and then go off to teach typing. She knew what that phone call had meant. Charlie and Linda were together. Jaime sat at the kitchen table, stomach hard as a rock. She knew Charlie was with

Linda because that's what she'd have done under the same circumstances, with some man. She didn't want to think Charlie might be gone for good. She assumed an insane wild romantic running off, followed by a sheepish return. The question was, how would Jaime make him pay? Or would she?

Charlie wasn't even really missing yet. He'd gone to teach typing. That left him free at four in the afternoon. His next class was Comp at six forty-five, and he usually went downtown to the Portland library or his office at Multnomah to correct papers. Sometimes to movies, or to hang out in a pool hall. Sometimes Jerry's or the Caffe Espresso. He wasn't due home until after night class, and even then sometimes he'd go out drinking beer. Charlie wasn't officially missing until well after 1:00 a.m. tomorrow morning. She wouldn't worry until then.

Shortly after dinner, while Kira made noise in the background and her mother sat at the kitchen table looking at her, Dick Dubonet called and said that Linda hadn't gone to work and was missing. "I hoped maybe she was out there," Dick said. "Can I talk to Charlie?"

"He's at work." Just then Kira let out a shriek. After some meaningless words, she hung up. Her mother stared at her.

"Where's Charlie?" she asked.

"I don't know."

"Oh God."

Jaime pulled Kira out of her chair and held her, patting her back as if she were an infant. "Tell me, Mom," she said, a hard edge in her voice. "How did you deal with it?"

"With what, honey?"

"Am I supposed to take him back? He's obviously out fucking Linda."

Edna looked unsurprised. "Are you sure, dear?" Edna was fine, Edna was getting married again, to a man whose entire life was devoted to box scores. Edna hadn't read the manuscript, didn't know what it was about. Jaime wondered if she'd ever have the courage to tell her. "It's about you swallowing Dad's adultery, about our life of sham and deceit on Washington Street, and how wonderful it all was." Yeah. In the book she'd forgiven her father. Was that what sent Charlie running to Linda?

But lying in bed that night, stomach tight, she considered the devastating effect her novel must have had on him. Such a good man probably couldn't face the swelling of jealousy, the envy, the rage at her for doing what he himself could not. Couldn't face such a mass of ugliness coming up out of himself. So, recognizing his inherent evil, he flees to a woman. Not just any woman. The one Jaime herself might have run to, if she'd been a lesbian. A woman with a beautiful ancient face. Just the opposite of Jaime's modern mug. The same with their bodies. Jaime's was slender, small, perfectly proportioned, unless Charlie was a liar as well as an adulterer, while Linda's was spectacular, her breasts a little too big, her waist a little too narrow, her behind smaller than you'd expect, yet still voluptuous. No wonder Charlie sought to bury his suffering in her voluptuosity, if there were such a word.

Jaime awakened at three, thinking she heard something. Going into the kitchen all she saw was Isis. "Where's Charlie?" she asked the cat. She got a glass of water and then checked Kira. Looking down at her child she knew she'd forgive him. It was that or wreck everything. She wasn't going to do that.

Charlie rarely spoke of his time in the prison camp, but once Marty Greenberg had asked him how many of the POWs had cooperated with the Chinese. "We heard a lot about brainwashing," Marty said. He smirked. "Does it really work?"

Charlie laughed. They were sitting around a booth at Jerry's eating burgers. "Brainwashing? Hell no, anything they asked, we told 'em. There wasn't any fucking resistance. Two guys escaped and made it back to our lines and got court-martialed for their trouble. They're still doing twenty in Leavenworth." Charlie had been drinking. He pointed a finger at Marty. "Brainwashing is something the government made up to cover the fact that everybody cooperated. Good clean American boys wouldn't tell the Chinese shit, right? So there better be some weird oriental method of making us talk. Brainwashing my ass!"

Lying in bed waiting for the noise that meant he was home, she wondered now if Charlie had been brainwashed. Maybe that was why he couldn't finish his book. Simple as that. Or Charlie's book might be so big, so important, that it was simply going to take years and years to write, and she'd have to help Charlie stay on track. Certainly forgiving a little adultery was part of the deal. Even the way it made her feel. Betrayed. Abandoned. Down below the hurt, rage, hate, revenge. When she got him back she'd make him pay. No, that was terrible. Either let him go or keep him. And if you keep him, forgive him.

She awakened to Kira's cry. She looked at the clock. It was after 6:00 a.m. Charlie was not beside her. She rose and tended her child and then made herself a cup of tea. Her mother came in dressed for work and sat down. Edna's eyes were sympathetic.

"Do you want some tea?" she asked her mother. Why did she feel so humiliated?

"I'll get something at the drug store," Edna said. "Have you decided what to do?"

"No," Jaime admitted. The phone rang. Dick Dubonet. He was hysterical, and Jaime had to be superior to him and ease his mind, telling him not to jump to conclusions, Charlie and Linda were probably somewhere drinking coffee and talking. "They are friends, you know," she snapped at Dick, and got off the phone.

"Is that a possibility?" her mother asked.

"No." Jaime began crying for the first time. She sat at the table and cried while her mother stood behind her holding her shoulders and murmuring in her ear. Jaime felt about fourteen. Fourteen and jilted.

"I can stay if you want," Edna said.

"No."

Then the house was quiet, her mother gone to work, Kira asleep and the cat off in the trees.

37.

After three days, when Charlie hadn't come home crestfallen and sheepish, Jaime lost her temper. He'd left her without a car, not that she ever went any-place. The thoughtlessness infuriated her. What if Kira got sick in the middle of the night and her mother wasn't there? Edna volunteered to leave her car at home for Jaime and take the bus to work, but Jaime wouldn't have it. She'd leave Oregon first. She called Southern Pacific and found out what time the Shasta Daylight left for California. She called their landlord, Mrs. Baker, and asked if they could get out of the lease and discovered Charlie had never signed the lease. Jaime gave thirty days notice and asked Mrs. Baker if she knew anybody who wanted a small chocolate-point Siamese with a crook in the tip of her tail. Mrs. Baker did not, so Jaime called Dick Dubonet, though she hated the idea of talking to him. What if he started crying?

Dick was fine. "I'll come right out," he said cheerfully. She heard his little MG in the drive less than an hour later. They sat on kitchen chairs back in the shade of the porch while Kira ran around like an expert. The garden was gone except for a few dry cornstalks, and most of the greenery under the trees had died back. Dick spoke forgivingly of Linda, and obviously expected her back any day. They'd run off to have an affair, that was all. In the old days that would have meant the end of everything, but not anymore.

"What are you getting at?" Jaime sat tilted back in her chair, a cold bottle of Miller between her legs.

"Just that maybe you shouldn't be so drastic," he said. "Why move? Are you really going to leave Charlie over this?"

"You make it sound like nothing. It's not nothing."

He smiled appreciatively. He had beautiful teeth. He was in fact a very handsome man. It was a gorgeous fall day again. Oregon at its most beau-tiful, and Dick in the backyard in tee shirt and jeans. It would serve them right, wouldn't it? Come back to find Dick and Jaime happily entwined? But Dick made no pass. In fact he was everything you could ask of a friend.

"You've never strayed, have you," he said.

"I've never slept with anybody but Charlie," she heard herself admitting. Dick's eyebrows went up, but he brought himself under control by taking a big slug of beer.

"That makes it different."

"Yes," she said. "Why does that make it different?"

"Well," Dick started, then stopped.

"I want to move because it's time to move. It really doesn't have anything to do with Charlie."

"You finished your book, now it's time to go. I'd love to read it sometime. But don't show it to me. Send me a copy, a free copy. Autographed."

"Is everybody mad at me for finishing my book?" she asked him. He laughed instead of answering, and she said, "Anyway, you can have Isis. I can't take her on the train, and I won't put her in a box in a baggage car somewhere."

Isis wandered in from the trees and Kira ran to her. "Key! Key!" she cried. Kira picked up the cat and walked around the yard holding her. The cat was limp, obviously enjoying herself. "Kira's gonna miss her," Dick said. "Maybe after you get settled you can come up and visit us."

"That would be nice." Suddenly she knew she was really leaving Oregon. Charlie or no Charlie.

He came home the next day. Jaime happened to be sitting on the toilet when she heard the familiar rattle of the family VW. It was around three in the afternoon, Kira sleeping in her playpen on the porch. Another perfect day. Beautiful Oregon, she thought helplessly, as Charlie came into the house and called her name. Was Linda with him? Of course not.

Jaime came out of the bathroom numb and frightened. Charlie stood in the middle of the kitchen, staring at her. His hair was getting too long, she noticed, and he had a slight sunburn. Fucking out in the sun?

"School called," she said to him coolly.

"I'm sorry." For once, Charlie wasn't grinning. "I just went nuts."

"All right," she said. "Why are you back?"

Charlie got a beer out of the refrigerator. "You want one?" She nodded and they sat at the table, drinking beer like a couple of college chums. "You want to know what happened?" he asked her.

"Sure." He wasn't acting guilty. Still, she couldn't let herself feel anything.

"Linda's gone," he said. "She's not coming back. She's going sailing with some friends, down the coast to Mexico, then across to Hawaii."

"Why didn't you go with them?"

"I damn near did," Charlie said. "I told you, I went nuts. She told me she was leaving Dick, and I offered to drive her to Astoria. That's down the coast, beautiful little town. But we stayed in Seaside. It's a resort town, deserted now with the kids in school. Amazing place. Most of the businesses shut, big wide beach with nobody on it. We both wanted to get away, see? So I drove her to the coast. But I wasn't ready to come home. We talked day and night, I mean we really talked. Linda is terrific."

"Is she a good fuck?"

Charlie looked her right in the eye and said, "We didn't. We slept in the same room, but different beds."

"Are you asking me to believe that?"

"I'm telling you what happened. I love you. I'm not that crazy. We didn't sleep together. We talked about it, but we didn't do it. I think we were both too numb. We walked along the boardwalk, we played some pinball, and sat and got drunk in this little club that plays nothing but cool jazz, and we sat up at night and talked. I talked about you, she talked about her life, Dick, her kid, everything under the sun. You want to know something? She's a fine person. I wish her all the best."

He said this last with such honesty, such conviction, that she began to believe him. Her stomach started to unknot. They drank more beer and smoked more cigarettes. Charlie kept talking, now about how her novel had temporarily deranged him because of its obvious excellence. "In Kim Song you had to be a psychopath just to survive," he said. It was getting dark out, and Jaime fed Kira. She'd been very happy to see her daddy, and now sat on his lap while Jaime spooned food at her. "After I read your book I think I just kinda fell back into that, you know, the old look-out-for-yourself mode. It's not much of an excuse for running out on you, but there it is."

Jaime fed Kira her banana. They hadn't slept together. She believed him. She had to. She concentrated only on what would happen next. They'd go to bed, after dealing with Kira, and if they made love, it would finish the event. It would be all over, and all forgotten. She'd have to call Carol Baker and tell her they were going to stay after all. She'd have to get the kitty back. But no. Linda wasn't coming back. Dick would need the cat. Charlie stared at her.

"What?"

"You have a look in your eye," he said. "All I can do is apologize. Do I live here or not?"

38.

Charlie wanted to be honest, but he couldn't. The practical truth was, he wanted to keep his marriage even though he didn't deserve to. He'd taken marriage lightly enough up to now. Easy to be married and play by the rules because he had no reason not to. He was in love with Jaime and didn't want or need other women. Everything on a high moral plane of love. He'd even wondered why other men strayed. He'd never been tempted. He hadn't even been tempted by Linda.

When he read Jaime's manuscript he knew at last why he could not finish his own book. He wasn't a writer. Jaime was. It wasn't the words, it was the organization. Jaime knew instinctively how to put things so they flowed from one scene to the next. Charlie's work was all over the place, great long sections of dialogue followed by great long sections of description or action, but nothing flowed. It was maddening. Ten fucking years to learn the ropes. Like everything else he had tried. Automobile mechanics. He'd been all thumbs at first, but then he got it. Same with football, same with drill, same with shooting, hunting, fishing. Even academic stuff. Charlie could organize, research, outline and write a term paper with the best of them. But off on his own, trying to write honestly about his experiences, he couldn't. A built-in barrier. One he'd hoped, expected, would eventually fall away if he did everything right, followed the rules. But no. As he read Jaime's work he saw clearly that she had a natural gift he didn't have. Call it talent.

Charlie had no talent. He had the tools. He knew the rules. But he couldn't play. Sitting in his office sweating over Jaime's writing, he recalled the little guys who never got picked for football until last. Charlie had always been picked first. Or done the picking. He'd been bland enough about it, picking only the guys with talent. Leaving the little guys, the guys with no talent, standing there with their fingers up their asses. Now Charlie found himself one of that group. Talentless unpicked asshole. Embarrassingly eager, humiliatingly gung ho, and yet unavoidably and eternally untalented. He'd been given a Eugene F. Saxon Award, not because he was talented, which he wasn't, but for some other reason which he didn't even want to think about.

But had to think about, with Jaime's novel in front of him. The same fucking reason he'd been awarded the Bronze Star. Not that he didn't deserve it, every asshole who got off the boat in Korea deserved at least a Bronze Star, and if it had been up to Charlie, the Congressional Medal of Honor. But he'd gotten the medal because they didn't want the American People thinking all their POWs had been such cowards. They hadn't been cowards, of course, it just looked that way. And to the American military, appearances were everything. So the best-looking guys coming out in Operation Little Switch were given medals. There had been brave guys, of course. But the Chinese killed them right away. Charlie heard they made the condemned guys dig their own graves. He didn't particularly believe this because the ground was too hard for anybody to dig in, much less men condemned for their defiance.

Charlie defied nobody. All he did was lie there and cough up blood. When the guy next to him shit near his face it was three days before one of the Christers cleaned it up. Lots of school spirit in Kim Song. Everybody thought Charlie would die any day, so they pretty much left him alone. He saw things from where he lay. He saw a man getting raped while four other guys played pinochle a few feet away. He watched guys eat shit. Crazy guys, of course. Charlie never ate any shit. But he swallowed his own lung blood, to keep alive. For the nutritional value, don't you see? The Vampire of Kim Song.

He'd numbed over, to save his ass. It worked. He got out on Little Switch because he had TB. Nobody had said good-bye but Pippello, tall skinny fucker with gaunt hungry eyes, grinning and waving. Pippello had given him some free marijuana once. Usually they sold it, but Pippello had a little compassion in him somewhere, and came up to Charlie, squatted down and offered him the roach. "Fuck it," was all he said when Charlie thanked him. The marijuana had been good. Two good hours in fourteen months.

It was lying there in Kim Song, later in Tokyo Army Hospital's TB ward, that Charlie had decided to become a writer. There seemed to be so much he wanted to say. Now he knew he would not say these things. Most had been said already. The rest didn't need saying. If he quit, the world would lose nothing. Jaime would lose nothing. He'd been valuable as a potential novelist, but now he had no value, not even the Saxon Award value. He'd have to save up and give that back, because of course it wasn't an award at all, but an advance on royalties disguised as an award. A returnable advance, he learned, reading the fine print. Which hadn't meant anything at the time, since he was going to finish his novel and MacMillan would be paid back a thousandfold. That's why he ran off with Linda, and that's why he couldn't possibly explain about the fucking. So he left it out. Confessing would only hurt Jaime anyhow, and he wanted his family. It was now all he had.

39.

Being rejected didn't bother Stan Winger anymore. He had four stories with Mills circulating around the magazines, and while none of them had been accepted he kept getting all kinds of encouragement. It made him feel good, but it didn't change anything. He still had to steal for a living. He wasn't boosting rags these days, because the guy he worked for left town. So he was back breaking into houses, but the thrill was gone. Every time he went into a place the fear would start mounting as soon as he turned off the sidewalk, and would not end sometimes for a couple of days. No more sexual pleasure. He knew that was what it had been. Going through a window gave him a hard-on. But it was over. Now only fear. The only redeeming factor he could see was that he didn't feel the urge to do terrible things, like crap on the dining room table or piss on the bed. He'd graduated from sexual punk amateur to professional thief. He was actually a jewel thief, though he'd take cash if he found it. His fences liked gold and stones, and even took Stan around to a couple of jewelry stores to explain to him the differences between costume jewelry and real jewelry. Stan learned how to judge the karat level of gold by heft. He learned how to tell the real stones from the fakes by looking at the edges of the facets for signs of wear.

But it was taking a lot out of him. He was averaging only a few hundred a month, most of which he blew in Vancouver. Lots of houses didn't pay out and he'd have risked his freedom for eight dollars worth of shit. He'd get home from a job with cold sweat sticking his clothes to his body and have to lie down for an hour before he could even shower. His writing suffered. He wasn't putting in near enough time. Whatever progress he'd seemed to be making all disappeared. He'd type a page, taking an hour to do it, and the pull it from the little machine and wad it up, throwing it against the door in frustration. If he didn't sell something soon he was going to quit or get thrown in jail.

The Monels had generously taken him into their lives, treating him like a member of the family. Something nobody had ever done, not even the people who'd been paid to. Stan's only regret was the need to keep his two lives apart. Charlie and Jaime knew he was a crook, he just didn't want them finding out he was a lowlife too, who spent most of his time and money on poker, pinball, or girls. Working girls, of course. They were so much easier to deal with. They always gave you a smile, were always glad to see you, and there was never any nagging after-effect. Unless you caught the clap or something, which thank God Stan never had.

But Charlie hadn't been the big stable guy Stan had thought. The night Charlie failed to show up for Comp class Stan went down to Jolly Joan's for coffee and found Marty Greenberg, looking more gaunt and Jewish than usual.

"What's the matter?" Stan asked, sliding onto the next stool.

Marty looked at him blankly. His hair was thinning rapidly, even though he wasn't yet thirty. He ran a hand over his scalp and smiled, not a good smile. "She left me," he said. "Alexandra. She moved to San Francisco yesterday."

Stan thought a moment. "Remind me. Which one was Alexandra?"

"She worked here days. Remember? I lived with her."

Stan remembered. The most beautiful of Marty's women. The one who let Marty live with her without contributing anything but his good looks, such as they were. "She left you, huh?" Stan spoke with little compassion.

Marty laughed. "Your reaction is similar to everyone's," he said. "Everybody is glad she left me and now I have to find a job. Well, fuck everybody, I've already found a job."

Marty had signed onto a ship, a gigantic U.S. government dredge, and would be leaving in a few days, to stand off the Astoria bar, sucking sand from the sandbar and moving it elsewhere. His friend Lev Lieberman had gotten the job a year ago when he flunked out of Reed, and now had passed it along to Marty. Lev himself was going to Israel to work on a kibbutz. Lev was a philosopher, like Marty. "Any job that connects you to humanity is a good job," Marty insisted to Stan. "I don't think of this as a shit job. It's an opportunity to work among working men."

"Yeah," said Stan, not convinced. Things fell into place, when Marty explained that the ship, the USS *Breckenridge*, had its home port in Sausalito. Which, by the strangest of coincidences, was just miles north of where Alexandra Plotkin had moved. After dredging the bar for a while, the *Breckenridge* would steam south for San Francisco, and spend some months off the Golden Gate. "Charlie didn't show up for class tonight," he said at last, to change the subject.

"Didn't you hear?" This time Marty's smile was not so painful. "Charlie and Linda." Apparently Dick Dubonet had been all over town looking for Linda and had discovered Charlie was missing too. "Wherever they are, I envy them both."

"Yeah," said Stan, but his heart sank. Of course they were together, hadn't Stan spotted that right away? This was the real world, not the fantasy world. And wasn't he glad? No, he wasn't. And not for himself. He was thinking about Jaime. Who'd been so kind to him. Charlie had done this to her, and she was going to be badly hurt. Stan felt terribly angry at Charlie, then had to stop himself. He was *moralizing*. How dumb. He was mad at Charlie because Charlie was doing something Stan didn't have the guts to do. That was all there was to it. Any compassion he felt for Jaime, or even for fucking Dick Dubonet, was incidental to his own cowardice. The truth was, he felt betrayed. Why had they done this to him? He had to laugh. Charlie and Linda weren't thinking about him, but themselves. Which was how Stan had learned to get through life too. Yet it was disappointing to find that his idealist friends weren't so ideal after all.

"I hate to leave Portland," Marty said. He laughed. "I never thought I'd say that."

Stan went home that night, thinking about Linda. Lying in bed after an hour of unrewarding effort at the typewriter, he felt an awful regret. That he had not been able to tell her how he felt. If only he had been able to tell her.

Three days later he was walking down Alder Street, trying to decide whether to go up to the Blue Mouse and watch old black-and-white movies or drop into the Roundup and watch old westerns, when a pair of large men who were obviously cops came up to him. He knew what was going on before they opened their mouths.

"Stanley Winger?" one of the cops asked.

"That's right," Stan said.

One of the cops smiled. "We have you for a lot of B and E."

"We're clearin' up a crime wave here," said the other.

"I'm afraid you're it, Stanley," said the first cop.

"Don't be afraid," Stan said. He held out his hands for the cuffs, but the cop must have thought he was resisting, and knocked him down.

40.

A week after she ran away, Dick Dubonet got a postcard from Linda asking that her things be boxed and sent to her care of Whitney White, P.O. Box 139, Sausalito, California. Paranoid alarm bells went off at the mention of Sausalito, also the eventual destination of Marty Greenberg. But Dick had to convince himself that it was a simple coincidence. Everyone was going to California, that was all. The postcard ended, "I wish you well, love, Linda." So final. He hadn't even known there was a problem. Now he hated his own house because it reminded him of her. Everything did. He wouldn't be able to go to the Caffe Espresso, Jerry's, or even the Buttermilk Corner, without thinking of her and losing control.

He knew why she'd run off with Charlie. Very simple. As a final, terrible insult to Dick. Like a wolverine, shitting on everything it could not eat. He'd never known such love or such hatred in his life. She could just sit him down over coffee and quietly tell him she was tired of their relationship, like a civilized woman. No, if she'd done that she would have had to listen to him begging and pleading for her stay, telling her how in his heart they were married, and he had always thought in her heart too. He could see her sitting there drumming her fingers, always impatient with his careful explanations. No wonder he had to order her around and make demands. She created the environment she hated, and then she left.

Dick went onto the porch to look down at his little MG. He'd owned the car a long time. It wouldn't reflect Linda, he hoped. Ironic if he couldn't even drive around in his own fucking car without his heart breaking. But looking down he knew. The car would subtly smell of her. There would be little things of hers tucked away here and there, handkerchiefs, little wads of tissue, an old crumpled Camel pack, endless bobby pins. As he stood there, Isis came out and jumped onto the wooden rail, her tail up. She rubbed against Dick's arm and purred loudly. Oddly, the cat did not make him suffer. He stroked her behind the ears. It was the middle of the morning. Dick should have been at his typewriter, but he'd made the classic mistake of going down to get the mail the second it arrived, an old writer's habit. And look what it gave him. A nice fat morning kick in the balls. The air was clear and crisp and Mount Hood gleamed white in the distance. He thought about just packing his stuff and going to Aspen, getting on the ski patrol again, spend the winter among people blissfully free of ambitions, except of course sexual and sporting ambitions. He could just rent the house furnished and leave.

No. The idea of spending another winter on the slopes offended him. He wasn't a child anymore. Most of the skiers he knew were also surfers, going from one sport to the other without ever passing through reality. Boys and girls with tanned bland faces and empty minds. No. Dick was a grown-up now, time to face responsibilities. Go clean out all of Linda's stuff, box it and mail it like a good little boy, then get to work on his novel. He wouldn't even have to hide the fact that he was starting a novel. There was no one around to hide it from. Marty was out on the sandbar, working as a deck hand, an astonishing transition to everyone but Marty. Dick didn't know Stan Winger that well, he'd been actually more Linda's friend, and of course Dick wasn't speaking to Charlie or Jaime. Out of embarrassment more than anything else. He could understand Linda running away, but

Charlie's sudden change into a bastard mystified Dick. To treat his wife so badly. He'd had to find out about Charlie's return from Marty, who seemed to know every fucking thing that was going on around Portland. What was Dick going to do for information, now that Marty was afloat? He didn't know. He knew only that everything had been great, and now everything was shitty.

He lifted Isis and stroked her, looking out over Portland. He loved this place. Tears came to his eyes at the beauty of Oregon, the city below, the endless rolling forests and mountains. The great hunting and fishing. He and Charlie had talked of taking a hunting trip, getting enough meat for everybody, big venison feasts. Tears rolled down his face now as he thought about the time they all went crawdad hunting on the Tualatin River, the big drunken crawdad feast afterward. Just standing there, Dick was so filled with emotion about the beauties of the past that he wanted to raise his fists in the air and scream, a high endless scream of love and despair. But he didn't. After a while he went into the house, washed his face, blew his nose, and sat back down to work.

PART THREE

The Golden Gate

41.

Charlie sat on the first stool in the corner, looking out the big open window of the no name bar at the people walking on Bridgeway. A warm day, lots of people out. Sausalito was getting popular. Charlie preferred it to Mill Valley, where he lived. Downtown Mill Valley was dull, just stores, but Sausalito had its waterfront, boat yards, yacht harbors, bars, restaurants, incredible views of the bay and San Francisco, everything you could ask for if you had your afternoons off. It had been a Portuguese fishing village before they built the Golden Gate, and there were still a few commercial salmon boats harbored just north of town. Charlie liked to buy his salmon right off the boat, pick up a whole fish for a few dollars, gut it, split it and grill it on his backyard barbecue. He was hungry just thinking about it. Charlie liked to eat.

His mood was strange. He'd gotten another manic phone call from Bill Ratto, begging for some new material. Charlie dreaded the thought of putting himself back in Kim Song, just to come up with even more "transition material" for his editor. Easier to sit here in beautiful Sausalito and drink beer, dreaming of walking down to the fisherman's dock and picking up a nice little salmon. Kim Song was far away and long ago. Almost fifteen years.

Charlie spotted two men he knew, walking down Bridgeway together. He hadn't seen either for years, and he'd never seen them together. Kenny Goss, an intense young writer he'd known in North Beach years ago, when they'd both hung out mornings at Caffe Trieste, drinking espresso with the

Sicilian scavengers. And walking along with him, dressed in a blue workshirt and faded black workboots, Marty Greenberg, the Jewish intellectual from Portland, looking tanned, balding, and competent.

"Gentlemen," he said as they passed the window. They stopped and stared. Charlie grinned and ran his fingers through his beard. "It's me, Charlie Monel. I grew a beard."

"I knew it was you," Marty said with a grin. "I was just trying to think if I owed you any money."

The two entered the bar and Charlie joined them at the front window table. "I didn't know you guys knew each other," Charlie said. Kazuko the barmaid came up and took an order for three beers.

"Nice-looking girl," Marty said.

"Don't waste your time," Charlie said. "Her old man's a junkie. She's devoted to him. All her time and money go right into his bloodstream."

"Obviously, you're a regular here," Marty said. He explained that he and Kenny were shipmates, deckhands on the *Breck*, home-ported about a mile up the road. They were fresh in off the sandbar, pay in their pockets.

"Like Dobbs and Curtin in *Sierra Madre*," Charlie joked. He was delighted to run into them. The hardest part about being a successful writer was how to fill the time. Successful in the sense that he had a book in the works.

"Charlie's been working on this huge novel for years," Marty explained to Kenny, who hadn't said much up to now.

"I know," Kenny said.

"Kenny and I go way back," Charlie said. "We're fifties beatniks, aren't we?" He lifted his bottle at Kenny, who gave a brief smile. He'd always been such a serious guy. "How's the writing going?" Charlie asked him, just to be polite.

"Okay." Kenny was obviously embarrassed by the question.

"You still married?" Marty asked him.

"You bet," Charlie said. He'd assumed they knew all about Jaime, but after a few minutes realized they didn't. Such was fame. Of course these guys spent most of their time out dredging sand. "Jaime's book was on the *New York Times* best-seller list for two weeks," Charlie said. Proudly.

"Only two weeks?" Marty said.

Charlie told them all the happy news. Jaime's book had been bought by the second publisher who saw it, Harcourt Brace & World, for a thousand dollars, and then like lightning she sold parts of it to several magazines, made a gigantic paperback sale, and then another big sale, to Paramount.

"Clearly, you're rolling in money." Marty seemed impressed.

"Jaime is."

"What about your book?" Marty asked. "I know it's a cruel question."

"Not cruel at all." Charlie told them that Jaime's editor had asked about his book and had looked at a couple hundred pages, hadn't had much enthusiasm for them but had passed them to a younger editor, Bill Ratto. Ratto had gone mad over the pages, flown west to read "absolutely everything" Charlie had written, spent a frantic three days in San Francisco, never leaving his hotel room, being visited by dozens of writers, boxes and sheaves of manuscript all over his room. Ratto had seen a lot of potential in Charlie's stuff. "You could have another *Catch-22* in here, or *Thin Red Line*," he said, sitting on his bed with Charlie's pages all around him. Ratto was a white-faced New Yorker whose Harvard accent slipped into New York Jewish. Ratto was not a Harvard man or a New York Jew, however. He was from Denver, but he was a committed editor. "We shall blow the lid off American Literature!" he told Charlie. Of course they were smoking marijuana at the time.

So Harcourt bought Charlie's novel for a five-thousand-dollar advance, and Bill Ratto assured him over the telephone, "Just send the whole manuscript to me. Let me put it together. You just sit out there in California and write your next book." Visions of Maxwell Perkins slaving over manuscripts. The famous editor who saved Thomas Wolfe, Hemingway, Fitzgerald, and more lately, James Jones. Charlie wasn't so sure all those great writers actually needed saving. "He cut *From Here to Eternity* in half," Ratto said with great enthusiasm on one of the hour-long phone conversations.

"I'd like to see the half he cut."

"Don't worry, we'll make you a star," Ratto said. He'd been fooling with Charlie's manuscript for a year and a half, and they weren't even close to a book. Bill kept wanting more material. When Charlie forced himself to write it and send it in, Bill wouldn't be happy with it. "I don't know," he'd say, never exact as to what he didn't like. "I'm no writer," he'd say, if Charlie insisted on specific information.

"So you're just sitting around waiting," Marty said.

Charlie had to laugh. "I like sitting around."

"You've gained weight." Marty poked Charlie gently where his stomach bulged out above his jeans. Marty was fine. He wasn't back with Alexandra Plotkin, but he was relatively happy. "She's working at David's Delicatessen in San Francisco," Marty said. "She won't even give me free food."

"I have to go," Kenny Goss said. Practically the only thing he said. They were on their way to the city, where Kenny kept a room. A change of clothes, then out on the town.

"Wanna come along?" Marty said. "North Beach, liquor, women, magic . . ."

Jaime was in North Beach. She'd been there four days, staying in their Genoa Place apartment. She wrote eight hours a day and had no time for Charlie or Kira, who was in Mill Valley with her au pair. Did he want to go to North Beach and risk running into Jaime?

"Yeah," he said, scratching his beard. "I'd love to."

"Why don't you meet us at City Lights at around nine?" Marty said. "Bring Jaime."

42.

Their Mill Valley house was on a cul-de-sac off Panoramic, high up on Mount Tamalpais, surrounded on three sides by redwoods and eucalyptus. On the other side a low hedge allowed a view of the bay almost as good as the view from the Sausalito waterfront. The place had cost them thirty thousand dollars, though it was only a little ranch-style house with three bedrooms and a bath and a half. Randy Wilde sold it to them. Randy was a waiter at the Trident restaurant in Sausalito who was dabbling in Marin County real estate. A big handsome Englishman, Randy was also an actor and a writer, and had played cricket for the Queen. Like all the English Charlie had met in the United States, Randy was eccentric. Real estate salesmen in Marin wore coats and ties, but Randy ran around in cutoff jeans and Hawaiian shirts, showing off his biceps and muscular legs.

Jaime had wanted to pay cash for the house, that literary money burning a hole in her pocket, but Randy laughed and said, "That would be a mistake."

"Isn't cash any good?" Jaime asked. They sat on the deck of the Trident, watching the boats on the bay.

"Tax matters," Charlie said, and Randy nodded. Jaime was hopeless about money, now that she had a lot of it. She'd even wanted her advance money to come in all at once, until Charlie explained about taxes. So she limited the amount she could get from sales of *Washington Street* to fifteen thousand dollars a year. But she also had the thirty thousand from Paramount, and at least twenty-five thousand from foreign sales. The money did not take Charlie's breath away. It was heady at first, to know you weren't going to have to worry about money for a while, unlike most of the human race, and Charlie didn't have any problems with guilt. This money wasn't the blood of the poor, in any way he could see. But he was careful to keep their bank accounts separate.

Driving home Charlie thought again about stopping in at the salmon dock and buying a fish, but decided against it. A hundred to one that Jaime wouldn't be home for dinner. She hadn't been home for days. He didn't want to cook salmon just for himself, the au pair and Kira, although Kira loved salmon. He still drove his golden green Volkswagen, but Jaime had picked up a 1961 Porsche in perfect condition for twenty-three hundred dollars. Charlie puttered up along the mountain ridge to Echo, their little cu-de-sac. He parked on the gravel drive and went into the house, holding down his disappointment at not seeing the Porsche. Kira was starting school in a few days. He wanted Jaime home for that. It was more important than writing.

Charlie had been raised by his father and grandfather, and neither of them had been very good at it. He'd grown up thinking his mother was dead. That's what he'd been told by his idealistic liar of a father. Died in childbirth, wonderful woman, would have made a great mother, etc. Charlie finally found out that his mother had dumped him and run. She was probably still alive somewhere. Charlie had an image of her, a big fat blonde with a happy laugh and missing teeth. He had sympathy for her. He wouldn't have stayed with his father either, given a choice. Not that his father was a bad man, just incompetent. He worked in a lumber yard as a salesman and would never be anything else. His whole life was devoted to his belief that it was still possible in America to have your own piece of land, live on it, grow everything you needed, and shut out the world. His father's version of true freedom.

Charlie wasn't so sure. He saw his father spend his life sitting at the kitchen table with a yellow scratch pad, trying to figure his way into freedom. Any money he saved would eventually end up spent on foolishness, as the old man would realize that at five dollars a week it would take forever to get the kind of property he needed. The realization made him brood and drink. He never hit Charlie except to cuff him now and again, but he was terrible on himself, and once in a drunken rage cut himself badly with the breadknife, dramatically demonstrating how he would cut his throat. God damn it, if things got any worse, and waved the knife and ripped a cut in the side of his neck that sent a big spurt of blood halfway across their tiny kitchen. "Let me die!" the old man cried as they carried him down the stairs to the ambulance.

Kira and Cynthia sat in the living room watching television. The au pair wasn't the usual girl from Europe. Cynthia was from Grosse Pointe, Michigan, a tall thin girl with long straight blonde hair and a long straight nose, cold blue eyes, and a murmuring way of speaking that irritated Charlie. Jaime found Cynthia and Jaime paid her.

"How's my girl today?" Charlie said to Kira, who came over and hugged his legs, then went back to sitting in front of the television. They watched *Popeye* cartoons. His daughter was so beautiful he wanted to die. That was how she made him feel sometimes. That to live would be to watch her beauty diminished by the realities of life. Other times, more realistic times, he saw she was a tough little cookie, like her mother.

"Are you going out tonight?" Cynthia asked him.

"Yeah. You?"

"I have to go out for a while, but Debbie's coming." Cynthia brushed back her hair and smiled up at Charlie. Debbie was the babysitter, as opposed to the au pair. Both, Charlie knew, were call girls. They never spoke of it, but Jaime had gotten them from her friend Tanya Devereaux, a notorious San Francisco madam. Charlie had known her in North Beach years earlier, when her place of business had been on Upper Grant. Now she was out on Twin Peaks, running a call house. Jaime had met her at a cocktail party and now they were fast friends. The ever-deepening mystery of women. Charlie didn't pry. Charlie didn't make a fuss. Cynthia was a damned good au pair, Kira loved her, she was neat and clean and quiet, and she was a talented girl who wanted eventually to be a commercial artist. She and Kira spent hours drawing together, sprawled on the living room rug, a nice thick peach-colored rug that Charlie very much enjoyed walking on. In fact, he enjoyed having money quite a lot. He only wished it had come in the traditional way, through the husband. But times were changing. He didn't mind. Times had been shitty.

For the first time since getting out of the military Charlie had a closet full of clothes to pick from. He chose jeans, white tee, green cashmere sweater, a present from his rich wife, and his hacking jacket, also a present from his wealthy famous wife. His new brown boots were Justins, good thirty-dollar boots, a present from himself. Fully washed, dressed, and looking at himself in the mirror, Charlie had a moment of real pleasure. Not at his reflection, displaying a thirty-five-year-old man with too much belly, but at the sight of a rich man. He only hoped it wouldn't kill him.

43.

North Beach had changed. You could drive around lower Telegraph and Columbus for hours without finding a place to park. Jaime rented a garage on Union. But there was room for only one car. Charlie parked near Chestnut and walked toward City Lights. He was twenty minutes early, so he stopped in at Gino and Carlo's for a beer. The place was empty except for three longshoremen playing pool. Charlie sat at the end of the bar next to the pool table and watched. Aldino bought him a bottle of Miller's. He poured the beer into his pilsner glass slowly, wondering how many bottles of beer he'd drunk in his life. A lot. He wondered why a really great beer like Blitz-Weinhard wasn't sold outside Oregon. He hadn't tasted any of that creamy Blitz in years. Maybe he'd go into the beer business, import Blitz-Weinhard into California, make a fortune. Charlie Monel the Beer King. Fat Charlie the Beer Boy. Barley Charlie the Beer Queer.

A couple of house painters, Stuart and Bob, came into the bar in their paint-stained white overalls and white caps, said hello to Charlie, and sat at the table next to the pinball machines. This was a comfortable bar, but a strange bar. It opened at six for longshoremen on their way to work, then around midmorning the place was held by Italian men, usually wearing blue suits and gray hats, smoking poisonous little twisted Italian cigars. At three thirty in the afternoon the longshoremen started filing in again, and by six the place would be full of Italians, longshoremen, and one or two local women. Then came a lull, such as right now, when the Italians and the working men went home for dinner. Then, Charlie knew, the poets would start coming in.

Poets drank at Vesuvio and across Columbus at Twelve Adler Place and Tosca, but the only real poet's bar was Gino and Carlo's. Charlie and Jaime rarely came in before midnight, when things were just getting started. They'd seen Ginsberg, Orlovsky, Whalen, Spicer, Snyder, Welch, and Brautigan, all drinking and laughing and encouraging Spicer as he endlessly tried to beat the pinball machine. The poets had great minds and a lot of courage, and they drank like animals.

Charlie finished his beer. Did he want another beer? He'd hoped to see Jaime in here. She'd sometimes come in at this hour to get some dinner at the USA Café or the Caffe Sport, and might stop in at G and C's for a drink or two. Jaime always got up in the morning and wrote, no matter how bad her hangover. He thought about trudging up the hill to the apartment. She might be asleep. She wouldn't work this late at night. Far more likely she was out somewhere, at a cocktail party, a book party, a dinner party, or just dinner and drinking with friends. She had a lot of friends who weren't Charlie's. Charlie had decided long ago not to attach himself to his wife's coattails, and seldom went to the literary events she seemed to like so much. Why shouldn't she? Everyone fawned, kissed her ass. Which she took as her due. Which it was.

Shig Murao worked the bookstore's tiny counter and hailed Charlie as he came in. "Your friends are downstairs," he said.

"Thanks." Charlie went down the narrow stair to the basement. Marty and Kenny sat at a table near the avant garde–poetry magazine rack. There were a few other people in the basement, a convenient place to hang out if you lacked money. They'd let you sit around all day reading. Not even a clerk down here. You could stuff all the magazines and paperbacks your wanted down your pants and walk past Shig, no one the wiser. Apparently nobody did that, or not enough to make Ferlinghetti change the policy.

They went next door to Vesuvio, which was already crowded and noisy. Jaime wasn't there. At a table in the middle of the room they got down to some serious drinking.

"I'll have a lemon-orange," Charlie decided. Lemon Hart 151-proof rum and orange juice. No reason not to get entirely drunk. At worst, he'd have the Telegraph Hill apartment to sleep in, should he find himself too drunk to drive. It was one of the reasons they rented the place.

"Where's Jaime?" Marty said at last, when they were drinking their drinks.

"I have no idea." He smiled to show it didn't matter. "She's just finishing her second book. Keeps her busy."

"Who are you talking about?" Kenny asked. He drank a glass of beer.

"Jaime Froward," Marty said. "*Washington Street?*"

"Jaime Froward is your wife?" Kenny asked.

"Yes, I am Mr. Jaime Froward," Charlie said modestly.

Kenny smiled for the first time that night. "She's good," he said.

"Thank you," Charlie said modestly.

"Kenny is a rare book scout," Marty said. "When he's not sucking sand."

"What do you guys do on board when you're not working?"

"We read," Marty said. "The ship's library is extensive. There are, I believe, six Max Brand novels, paperbacks of course, and two Rex Stout mysteries."

"We take books out," Kenny explained, as if Charlie might misunderstand. A literal, serious person, Charlie remembered.

"You scout books?"

Kenny explained the difference between good books and valuable books. "Value has only a slight relationship to quality," he said, with a quick grin. "You know what I mean."

"Yeah," said Charlie. To Marty he said, "Have you heard anything from the old gang in Portland?"

Marty shook his head. "What about Linda?" he asked Charlie.

Charlie shook his head. "She's probably in the South Seas. What about Stan Winger? Anybody ever heard from Stan? He just vanished one day. Jaime thinks he's in prison somewhere."

"That's probably true," Marty said. He told Kenny about Stan Winger, the young criminal who wanted to write pulp stories. Charlie pictured Stan sitting alone in a cell. No reason not to believe it was true. He thought about trying to write to him, cheer him up. It was none of his business.

They had one more round at Vesuvio's, then walked across to Twelve Adler Place, a tiny bar that had been a lesbian haunt for years, but was now just a bar. Charlie had gone in for the first time in the mid-fifties. He'd been drinking with somebody and talking about women when the guy said, "You wanna see a bar that's all women, from one end to the other? Right around the corner!" and brought him in. You knew at once that these women weren't waiting for two men to walk through the door.

Tonight the place was empty. Jaime wasn't there, and Charlie wanted to turn and walk out. Instead they sat and ordered drinks, another Lemon Hart for Charlie, and talked about James Joyce. Kenny was reading *Ulysses* for the third time and thought it was the greatest novel in the English language. Marty had read only parts of it and felt it was bizarre, an Irishman trying to write about a Jew from the inside. "It's just not possible," he maintained. Charlie had read the book and enjoyed what he could understand. He thought about the incredible life of James Joyce. The blindness. The pain. The exile. The suffering.

"James Joyce is dead," he said finally, and hot tears ran down his cheeks.

44.

Through the mist he saw some guy at the bar, not a familiar face, grinning at Charlie's tears. Without wiping his face Charlie got up and went over. "I'm sorry. I didn't mean to burst into tears." The man had a broad red homely face. Charlie hoped the guy would stand up and give him some shit, but all he did was hold out a hand.

"Sorry," he said. They shook. The guy had a good handshake. Charlie went back and sat down, frustrated but pleased with humanity. "Not a bad guy," he said to Marty and Kenny. They'd begun discussing Hobbes, whom Charlie had only heard about. Apparently Hobbes thought mankind was just a bunch of animals, and Marty disagreed.

"Do you believe in the supernatural?" Kenny asked. Charlie wondered what nights were like in the forecastle of the *Breckenridge*.

"You mean above the natural? More than natural? Of course I do." Marty gestured at the crowd around them. "You can't possibly believe this is all there is. I'd kill myself if I thought that."

"I used to believe in God," Kenny said.

"I don't believe in God exactly," Marty said. "But I certainly believe in some kind of agency of creation. And some kind of power beyond human power."

"That's because you're a Jew," Kenny said.

"No," Marty said. "Being a Jew doesn't mean you have to believe in God. You just have to try." He laughed. "So I try. But it's easier to believe in man." He turned his large serious eyes on Charlie. "It's all between us, as humans."

"What's between us?" The conversation was getting too drunk for Charlie.

"Godhood," Marty said.

"I'll be right back." Charlie drained his glass and stood. My goodness. Three Lemon Harts equaled at least six shots of whiskey. He walked carefully down the bar toward the entrance. The man who'd laughed at him was hunched over his drink and Charlie didn't disturb him. Obviously a good man, a real human, the kind of salt-of-the-earth person Charlie had tried to avoid becoming all his life. Hard worker. Provider. Charlie had read that before the Battle of Somme in July 1915, whole villages of young men had signed up to go to war, and over they went in a body, up and out of the trenches side-by-side, all the boys from the village, and in five seconds all of them were dead, machine-gunned. Five seconds in combat. The hometown paper would print a list of the casualties, and the villagers would realize that every single one of their sons had died.

Compared to that, what happened to Charlie had been a stroll down Park Avenue. The air outside the bar was cold, wind blowing down Columbus. It made him feel awake. He wanted to find Jaime. He was tired of philosophy. Tosca was right there, Jaime probably inside, sitting at a corner booth, holding court. They went there often. But it was still early. Charlie stood, letting the cold air sober him. Into Tosca, or up the hill to their apartment? Or both? What kept him from just pushing open the door to Tosca and going in? Was it the fear that she'd be there? Or that she'd not be? Anyway, fear. Fear was an old friend. Well, old friend, let's go to Tosca.

The bar was noisy, opera music playing on the juke box, both brass-eagle-topped espresso machines hissing steam into the air, the babble of conversation, the smell of cigarette and cigar smoke, a wonderful place. Before he went into the back, among the booths and tables where she'd most likely be, Charlie pushed up to the bar and ordered a cappuccino from Mario. He felt the need for some hot chocolate and coffee, to hold down all the liquor. The cappuccino tasted great. The woman sitting in front of Charlie smiled up at him. She was nice-looking, about thirty, well-dressed, obviously with the guy in tweed sitting next to her.

"Hi, Charlie," she said.

He smiled politely. Or was it leered obscenely? He wasn't sure. She talked as if they knew one another. They probably did, from one drunken evening or another. She'd just come from the symphony, that's why they were dressed up. It had been wonderful, lots of nice Stravinsky. "Now we're getting drunk," she pointed out.

"Me too."

"Where's Jaime Froward tonight?" the woman asked.

"Be back in a sec." Charlie made his way through the people to the back, to survey the tables and booths. He didn't see his wife and was intensely disappointed. He wanted to see her. He hadn't in days. He wanted to hold her hand. He loved her little hands, so delicate. The sweetest pair of hands in the world. But she wasn't here, and she wouldn't be at Enrico's, or the Jazz Workshop, or El Matador, or Frank's, or even the Coffee Gallery, all places he'd intended looking, all places they both liked. He wondered who was playing at the Workshop. Last time had been the Jazz Crusaders, real hard-driving bop from four feet away. Great. Charlie himself had no particular musical tastes, but Jaime was a music fan, especially jazz, and had a great collection of records. If Charlie couldn't find her, and he knew he couldn't, he'd just run up to the Workshop and have a drink at the bar.

Charlie drained his cappuccino and left Tosca's for Twelve Adler. Kenny and Marty sat with two girls, and Marty saw him come in and waved for him to come over, but Charlie just backed out and left the dredgers to their pickups. He'd been wrong from the beginning, Jaime wasn't out on the town. She was up in their apartment either writing or sleeping. She wasn't in town to play around, he reminded himself as he trudged up Broadway, but to finish her book. Her second book. Charlie knew only that it was about a young woman.

Jaime wrote what she wrote and kept it to herself, as did Charlie. That way they didn't drive each other crazy. Charlie showed her his manuscript years ago, and her suggestions had been very good, but they argued hotly over every sentence, and Charlie finally had to take it back from her. He walked down Broadway to Enrico's, past the all-night dirty bookstore and cigar stand. He thought about stopping in to pick up a mystery to take home and read himself to sleep, as he did on so many nights. A nice Perry Mason or something. But he didn't, and he didn't stop at Enrico's, only looking past the outdoor tables as he went by, not seeing Jaime of course, since he was certain she was at their apartment. He trudged up the Kearny steps. The first night they'd gone out together she'd run up these steps like a monkey, and he'd followed with his worthless lungs, then as now making him pant like a fish. Sweat popped on his forehead. She'd better be home.

She sat at her desk, the gooseneck lamp on, her manuscript in front of her, a red pencil in her hand. She looked up at him, her face breaking into a beautiful smile. She was so beautiful. And she was glad to see him.

He went to her and pulled her to her feet, kissing her with all the feeling he could muster. He felt her fingers on his arms, her tongue in his mouth. His love for her was like a great white light. The long kiss ended.

"I finished my book," she said.

45.

She hadn't meant to say it, but the words just tumbled right out. Charlie's reaction last time she had finished a book was to take it well at first. The rest she didn't want to think about. She'd expected that by now he'd have finished his own novel. She'd dreamed of them both riding high on the *New York Times'* best-seller list, money pouring in, their pictures in the papers every day, articles in all the magazines about the fabulous literary couple. Invitations to Hollywood, what the heck, invitations to meet the Queen of England, who was, Jaime knew from listening to her mother, the queen of American high society as well. It was too late for an invitation to the White House, though. The only president she'd ever wanted to meet had been killed in Dallas. But Charlie couldn't finish his novel.

They made love in their little Telegraph Hill apartment and Charlie seemed fine, passionate as always, tender and kind. She herself was too exhausted to be much good, and had to pretend a little bit, so he wouldn't feel let down. When they finished they lay side by side quietly for a long time. She knew he hadn't fallen asleep because as soon as he did his mouth would come open and he'd begin to make a slight whistling sound. This lasted all night, unless he had his nightmares. Then he would begin to moan and sometimes even cry. But when he woke up he would tell her he didn't remember. "As far as I know," he told her once with his big bland smile, "I sleep like a log."

Now he'd be doing the same as she, lying there thinking about her book. How would he react? Her first book had been easy to write. She hadn't known what she was doing, of course, which made it easier somehow, and she'd been writing about people she'd known all her life. The only really creative thing she'd done was make up new names. The stuff had just come out of her. All she had to do was polish it up. This new book was different.

Maybe she'd bitten off too much. This time she'd made the whole thing up, instead of writing what everybody told her to write, e.g., the first book all over again only with all new people. She'd written a very internal story about a teenage girl raised in poverty in the thirties. She knew nothing about poverty except from her parents' conversations at the dinner table. And she knew nothing about the Great Depression. She was half-sure that when she sent it in to Bob Mills he'd telephone and say, "Jaime, this just won't do." Deep in her heart she knew the book was good, for all the trouble it had caused her in coming out, the terrible hours of doubt, the passages that had to be rewritten dozens of times, while the cold sweat ran down her body telling her she was a fraud, this was shitty, she should quit, give up, go back and write another sweet little story about people with no problems. That was what one stupid reviewer had called her book, although most liked it.

She felt a little gas, and was about to sneak it out when she remembered Charlie's hilarious discussion of farting at the no name bar one night. He said that women sneaked their farts not to be polite, as everyone assumed, but to take people unawares. "A man lets a fart, wham, and you know to cover your nose, or light a match. An honest warning, like a rattlesnake's rattle." Charlie kept a straight face while everybody at several tables around were laughing and falling off their chairs. Of course everybody was drunk.

"I'm about to fart," she warned Charlie.

He gave a little yell and jumped up and ran into the bathroom. Jaime laughed and farted simultaneously. "Is it over?" he called through the door. "Is it safe yet?" he asked her, looking frightened, like a little boy.

"I'm afraid to light a match," Jaime said between giggles.

"The explosion that destroyed Telegraph Hill," Charlie said in a normal voice, and sat on the bed next to her. They'd been lucky to get Charlie's old apartment, but Jaime had furnished it herself. No more Zen literary purity, now the place had a real bed, a real easy chair, a rug, and, on the walls, a couple of the woodblock prints Charlie had brought back from Japan. On the desk next to Jaime's typewriter, a single pale yellow rose in a blue glass vase.

"What time is it?" Charlie asked. Jaime went in to the stove to look, drawing herself a little water in a cheese glass. It was almost one. "Early," she said. She came back into the front room. Charlie stood looking at her completed manuscript. Charlie looked bigger naked than dressed.

"Let's go down to G and C's," he said. "My throat's dry."

"I'll get dressed," she said. "You look fine as is."

"When do I get to read this?"

His words put panic in her heart. If Charlie didn't respond perfectly, she wasn't sure she'd have the courage to send it in. He could say all the right things, but there might be the smallest amount of condescension or amusement or even nervousness, and she'd know the book was trash. Two years' hard word destroyed in the lift of an eyebrow. Well, not two years' hard work, more like six months' hard work over a period of two years. Still. Could she say, No darling, I don't want you reading it at all, not until it's in print. Then you may, but only if you control your face and restrict your comments to extreme praise.

"Can we go home instead?" Jaime said. "We can stop at the no name for a nightcap. I just don't feel like facing all those drunks at Gino and Carlo's."

"Leave the book here?" Charlie asked. "Let's take it with us. I want to read it."

"Okay."

It was three days before he actually finished the book. Jaime was only a little surprised to feel the resentment building up. Why hadn't he just sat down and gone at it? Only 226 pages, he could read it in a couple of hours. He didn't. He told her he was "savoring" the book. She knew this meant he was having trouble plowing through it. On the third day he came out of his office carrying the manuscript, his face composed. He really looked very funny, his hair all up and sticking out. Obviously he'd been running his fingers through his hair as he read. He looked like a bomb-thrower, but sweet.

"It's a lot better than your first," he said pedantically. "There were some passages of real emotion. A superior piece of work."

"Do you like it at all?" Tears welled up. He must have seen the effect his clowning was having, because he put the manuscript down on the dining room table and came to her and put his arms around her, consoling her for having written such a waste of time book.

"I loved it," he said into her hair. But it took about ten minutes of him describing in detail what he'd liked, and how much, how well it compared not only to her first book but to all books, before she believed him. "Shall I send it in?" she asked. He laughed.

Before she actually did put a professionally typed copy of the manuscript in the mail to Mills, she wanted a woman's view of it. She took the carbon over to her friend Tanya Devereaux. Tanya ran her call girl service from a flat on Alpine Terrace, a couple of blocks above Castro. It was owned by a couple of gay guys, who lived upstairs. Tanya read everything, and had strong opinions. Jaime parked her Porsche in front of the respectable-looking building and rang Tanya's doorbell. Tanya answered naked.

"Oh, I thought you were somebody else."

Jaime followed her down the carpeted corridor into her living room. Tanya had a long narrow Indian peasant face. If the Indians had peasants. Jaime knew Tanya was part Indian, but she didn't know which tribe or anything. Tanya had taken on the whole police force and beaten them at their own game. Not that they didn't arrest her every once in a while, but never on anything that would stick, and she'd walk out of the Hall of Justice thumbing her nose at them. "All it takes is an IQ over seventy," she had said. "Don't get me wrong. Most cops are good guys. But some are sadistic little bastards, and you can't give 'em an inch."

"Am I going to be in the way?" Jaime asked her.

"No. I have a fifty-dollar john coming in a few minutes, but you can wait here in the living room." She arched her eyebrow in amusement at Jaime. "I fuck them downstairs. I only do my own tricks here. Special people."

"What do you have to do for fifty dollars?"

A grin. "The same thing I'd do for twenty-five. Only the john offered fifty his first time, so he always pays fifty."

"I've heard of two-hundred-dollar girls, in places like Las Vegas, Hollywood, you know."

"A two-hundred-dollar hooker is a twenty-five-dollar hooker with a two-hundred-dollar john," Tanya said, showing pink gums.

"Ah." The door chimed.

"Relax," said Tanya, and went to answer the door. She came back with a man in a dark blue suit. He had a round face and thinning hair. He looked very well cared for, his shoes shined to perfection, his suit obviously cut by a tailor, his pudgy fingers beautifully manicured, his jewelry gold. He looked surprised to see Jaime.

"I didn't ask for a three-way."

"She's a friend." Tanya led the man by the hand down the staircase. Twenty minutes later they returned. This time Tanya wore an old kimono open down the front. She escorted the customer out the door. Jaime could hear them whispering. When Tanya came back she said, "He couldn't get it up." She went into the kitchen for a Coke, and coming out, added, "He wanted you. He asked me how much."

"What did you tell him?"

"I told him I'd ask you. You ever think about turning a trick? I could book you solid. Too bad you can write." Tanya loved *Washington Street*.

"Maybe I'll end up turning tricks, I don't know." Jaime said it to be light, then worried she'd insulted Tanya.

"I finished my book," she blurted. "I've got a copy of the manuscript outside in my car."

Tanya's face lit up. "Oh God, I'm so excited!" she said. "Can I read it? Please?"

That was more like it.

46.

Why did she do these things to herself? When Jaime handed her the typing paper box with the carbon copy inside, Tanya had just put it aside on the kitchen counter and said, "I'll read it right away." Jaime had somehow expected to drive away from Alpine Terrace with Tanya's opinion. Instead she drove away depressed. She'd forgotten how depressing the whole business was. She'd been living in her own secret world with people she'd made up herself, doing things she made up and turning out the way she intended. Now she was back in the real world, where everything was out of control. Charlie's reaction had been horrible. He hated the book but didn't want to give up his cushy life as her husband. It was certainly possible. It was possible he'd never loved her, but always seen her as a meal ticket. He was clever about it, too, always being so careful not to use her money.

Driving down Divisadero she shook her head. Paranoid thoughts kept hounding her. That Charlie wasn't what he obviously was. That she was unworthy of her success. It wasn't really success, anyway, it was a lucky event, and she'd better be prepared to have her second novel treated the way most people's first novels were—no reviews, no money, no big paperback or movie sales, and so on. She'd be prepared for this book to fall through the cracks. The critics laid for you if your first book was, in their estimation, given too much attention.

She drove north over the Golden Gate. Her movie deal had seemed so fabulous a couple of years ago. Joseph E. Levine, the big shot producer, famous for importing from Europe the shittiest movies he could find, had bought her novel sight unseen, based on something he'd heard at a cocktail party. Paramount Pictures. How flattering. He'd bought the book outright, the contract eighteen pages of dense boilerplate, which Mills blandly explained as "Pure slavery. He owns your book forever, in all media and all versions. He owns the characters, and if you wrote a sequel he'd have first right to buy it, and you couldn't sell to anyone else with the same character names. Slavery, as I say." Mills was for holding out. Jaime wanted that thirty grand. You could live three years high wide and handsome on that kind of money. But the thirty turned out to be twenty with ten to come when the picture was actually made. Which was apparently never. Joseph E. Levine finally read the book, and exploded. "These people are Communists!" he was reported to have said, and buried the project. No use explaining that they weren't really communists, more like idealists. Try explaining that subtlety to the man who got rich importing "Hercules" starring Steve Reeves.

In the process, Jaime had become fascinated. Movies were where the real money was, and Jaime wanted a lot of money. It was where the big audience was, too. She daydreamed about moving to Hollywood and breaking in as a writer, then moving on to director. Charlie was pretty cold about it. "There aren't any women directors that I know of," he said.

"Ida Lupino," she said, but Charlie went on about how terrible Hollywood was to writers. "Look what they did to *The Naked and the Dead*," he said.

"I didn't see that."

"Did you see *From Here to Eternity*?"

"I thought you liked *From Here to Eternity*."

"I loved it," he said. "But it was a real mess. They never went into the stockade scenes, and they had the army bust Captain Holmes instead of promoting him to major, as in the book." Charlie was adamant about Hollywood. "It's a whorehouse," he insisted.

Having just left a real whorehouse, Jaime wasn't sure that was necessarily a bad thing. Noticing a police car behind her on the bridge, she looked at her speed. Fifty-two in a forty-five zone. She slowed to forty-eight. Surely that would mollify the CHP guy behind her, but no. He pulled her over on the Marin side of the bridge, then walked up to the car, a little guy, blond hair, tight mouth. He looked down at her grimly.

"Hello, Officer," she said, smiling what she hoped was a friendly smile.

"Tell me something," he said. "How come you didn't slow down to forty-five when you saw me?" So she was going to get a ticket after all.

"Conditions didn't seem to warrant absolute conformity," she said. She pulled her driver's license from her wallet and handed it to him. He frowned at her. Did he recognize the name? Had he read her book?

No. He just looked at her and wrote her a ticket. She had to laugh at her insane expectation. When the cop drove on, she decided not to follow him, but to take the Sausalito exit, drop down to the no name bar, and have a drink. Talking to the policeman had made her feel slightly soiled.

The no name bar was almost empty, just a few afternoon alcoholics widely spaced at the bar, gazing down into their drinks. Neil Davis, the owner, was behind the bar, KJAZ playing over the sound system. Jaime sat in her husband's favorite seat at the end of the bar, where she could look out the open front window at the people. "See Charlie?" she asked Neil.

"Not today." But he would have said that if Charlie had just walked out the door. Good old Neil. He ran the best bar Jaime had ever drunk in. Even better than Tosca. Tosca was a big-city bar, but the no name was a world bar. People from everywhere stopped in, and not just people, famous people, people who were doing things. Interesting people. Although none of them were here today.

"What can I get you?" Neil asked.

"Ramos Fizz," Jaime decided. A candy-ass drink, according to her husband, but they made them so well here. The telephone behind the bar rang, but Neil continued making the Ramos Fizz. Only when the drink was perfect, sitting in front of Jaime on its napkin, did Neil turn to the telephone.

"Jaime?" he said politely, his hand over the mouthpiece. "Are you here?"

"Ah," Jaime said, and slid off her chair, going to the telephone by the front doors. It was Tanya.

"Where the hell have you been? I've been calling your house, your apartment, Charlie said you were at my place, then I thought about the no name. I'm only about a third of the way through, but I just had to call you. I love your book! You must have been following me around when I was a kid. Where did you *learn* all this stuff?"

"So you liked it?" Jaime said. "You're not just putting me on?"

"Are you kidding? I want the first copy!"

Jaime finally got off the telephone and went back to the bar. Her clothes were sticking to her. Praise, especially such wide open praise, made her sweat.

47.

Mills was infuriating. "I read the manuscript," he told Jaime over the telephone. It was three in the afternoon, six in New York, and Bob sounded a little drunk. Maybe he always sounded like that. Jaime waited patiently. "I liked it. I'll messenger it over to Harcourt in the morning." The line crackled for a while, then he added, "Congratulations."

His first comment on *Washington Street* had been, "I don't think I've ever read a better first novel manuscript." A far cry from "I liked it." Maybe Mills was tired. Maybe he didn't think Jaime needed flattering anymore. Maybe he was treating her properly, when what she wanted was babying.

"What's the matter, Mommy?" Kira asked her.

"Mommy's ego has been stripped bare," Mommy said. Kira was on her lap, dressed in her black and yellow sunsuit, a really horrible-looking outfit that had been bought by her adoring but distant grandmother in Portland. Kira was a beautiful child anyway, with her father's large dark eyes and her mother's pouting mouth. She wiggled down off Jaime's lap and ran out through the French doors onto the lawn. She had acted remarkably adult on her first day of kindergarten at Old Mill School. Jaime remembered her own tearful separation from her mother on the same occasion, and was ready for crying and begging, but Kira merely looked up at her as if to say, "Are you leaving me here, in this *mess?*" Charlie and Jaime walked out into the sunshine afterward, and Charlie said, "Oppressive, isn't it?"

"It's just that everything is so small." But Jaime had felt it too. Now Kira loved school, and Cynthia drove her down in the morning, leaving Jaime to write. But of course Jaime had no writing to do. Her manuscript was being pawed over by the editors at Harcourt, who'd bound her to a two-book contract. Now they had to decide how much, if anything, to offer for the book. Mills had been vague. "It might be pretty good," he said.

"If they want it at all," she said.

Charlie hadn't exploded or run off, but then his own book might be ready to publish fairly soon. He got long letters from Bill Ratto, whose enthusiasm was catching. Jaime liked talking to Bill on the telephone. His energy seemed to pour over the wire. "Let me talk to my novelist," he might say. "I think we've got a breakthrough." Ratto had the manuscript down to seven hundred pages or so, and wanted to present a novel of about five hundred. "I can't just slash and burn," he explained. "I have to make it integrate." He wasn't after more writing from Charlie. From here on it was a matter of "judicious pruning."

Charlie? He was tired of his book. If they were both home they'd sit out on their redwood garden furniture and have a civilized drink at sundown. The view from their lawn was wonderful, the bay, the East Bay hills, Angel Island, Alcatraz, the Bay Bridge. They'd sit side-by-side and watch the natural light fade and the sparkling artificial lights come on. One evening Charlie said to the declining light, "You know, there must be hundreds of guys out there who thought just because they were in combat, they had a big novel to write." He laughed. Jaime hated the sound of it.

"You have to keep fighting," she said weakly.

"Haven't I done enough for my country?" Charlie said quietly to the pale sky. And then, oddly, "Don't you wish we had some rabbits? This is the time of night they would come out."

Charlie was adrift. He showed nothing, but Jaime knew his heart was broken. Then she caught herself. She'd fallen into the same trap as Charlie, fighting off the possibility of good news. Charlie's book hadn't failed yet. Maybe it wouldn't. But a brooding sense of gloom hung over the entire project. Ratto had been so enthusiastic, but Jaime wasn't sure he actually belonged in editing. Her own editor, Dan Wickenden, was more like it. A novelist himself, he had a soft smooth Harvard voice and a real concern for literature. A gentleman. Ratto was a cheerleader. Maybe she was being harsh.

Then Gentleman Dan offered her only a ten-thousand-dollar advance. He called to apologize, pointing out that Harcourt was going through a lot of stress, but now Jaime found his voice egregious and effete instead of gentlemanly. "You'd make twice that on the paperback," she snapped at him. She hung up, making the excuse that Kira was calling her. Her body was covered in cold sweat. It was before eight in the morning. Kira and Cynthia were watching *Captain Kangaroo* and eating breakfast in the living room. Jaime came out of the bedroom. Kira let out a squeal of laughter. Jaime looked around her. All this depended on her making money, a lot of money. It could all dissolve. The ten-thousand-dollar offer meant Harcourt didn't think this book would sell. They didn't expect a paperback sale, or a movie sale, or foreign sales. They thought the book was terrible. And why wouldn't they? What did she know about poverty or anything else? She was a child.

She went to find Charlie, wanting his comfort. Charlie got up every morning around six and went into his office whether he had any writing to do or not. She wondered what he did in there. She never interrupted and she never went in. Her own office was in their bedroom. They'd argued and she'd won, taking the bedroom for her own and giving him the tiny half-bedroom. The roomier attic was for Cynthia, who'd not been in the plan when they bought the house, but instantly they'd seen that if they wanted to keep their schedules they'd have to have live-in help. With Jaime's riches they could afford to, and even had Randy Wilde looking for another house with more room. Now, with the dreadful news from Harcourt, they'd be lucky to keep even this little house.

She pushed open Charlie's door. He sat at his desk in jeans, shirtless and barefoot. He was sweating, and had a pencil in his hand, a stack of manuscript before him. He stared at her. She'd never interrupted before. Then his eyes brightened. "You heard something," he said.

"Bad news." She told him. He didn't seem upset. "Ten grand is a lot of money," he said. "And it's only an advance. It's your money."

"They must hate the book."

Charlie smiled and took her hand. His were warm, hot almost. "If they hated it," he said softly, looking into her eyes, "they wouldn't have offered you anything."

He couldn't console her. She was insulted by the offer. She'd made money for these people, and now they were being cautious. It was infuriating. She called Mills after a few days of this and told him to refuse the offer and find her another publisher.

"Are you sure?" he asked.

"Yes."

A month went by, only silence from the East. The Mysterious East. Jaime was now certain that she'd made a mistake turning down the Harcourt offer. They were her friends at Harcourt, they'd offered the most they honestly could. She recalled the sound of Dan Wickenden's voice, the reassuring Harvard tones. He'd been a good editor, sending page after page of careful notes and suggestions, always respectful, treating her as an artist. Now she had, in effect, shit in his hat. Nobody would offer so much as a dime for her stupid book. Why should they?

Charlie laughed at her. When that didn't work, he became sympathetic. "Look, it takes time. A few weeks is nothing. Relax, your book is just fine." She remembered his own less-than-perfect response. Was he hoping her book would fail? Or would she be carted off to the asylum for all this paranoia?

She put some things in cardboard boxes, threw them into the back of the Porsche, and went to live in their little apartment on Telegraph Hill. Too hard pretending to be a suburban housewife, especially with Charlie around the house all the time. If she went out for a drink there would be Charlie at the no name. Her life was crushing her, so she got out for a while. Every few days Charlie would visit her in the city, sometimes bringing Kira with him. But Jaime wasn't glad to see Kira. It broke her heart. She knew she was no mother. She didn't have enough love in her. Kira had been a terrible mistake, though it was unthinkable that she not be alive.

She tried short stories. A few stories in the *New Yorker* or the *Atlantic Monthly* would do her career some good. But she hated writing short stories. She hated the characters she made up, and she hated her attempts to write about real people. She wasn't really a good writer, that was the problem. She'd fake it well enough for one book. One of those, you know, reminiscences, *Cheaper by the Dozen, Life with Father, Washington Street,* they were all alike. Except *Life with Father* was a pretty good book.

Abandoning the stories, Jaime was filled with an anger no amount of standing in the shower could cure. She hated her life as a housewife. She ought to get a job. She could become a call girl, working for Tanya. Bringing in the money. What was the matter with that? Call girls weren't evil, they were just working women. Tanya had strong ideas on the subject, and Jaime, considering this at one after another of the bars of North Beach, drinking heavily, had to agree. People thought of her as a successful novelist whose life wasn't only under control but actually enviable. Everybody thought she was writing her new book. Nobody knew she was a fraud. Nobody knew she just lay around reading when she was supposed to be at work. Nobody knew she was waiting for the telephone to ring.

48.

Charlie began taking Kira for long afternoon walks along Bridgeway in Sausalito while he waited Jaime out. They'd park at the north end of town and walk the long boardwalk past all the sailboats and big power yachts. Sometimes they'd walk to the end of Pier Three where Neil Davis kept his little boat, a converted Monterey purse seiner. If the boat was there they might step aboard and pretend they were out on the bay. Or they'd sit on the end of the dock and watch the other boats navigating the flat calm harbor. Fish nibbled at the algae on the pilings, and Kira love to lie on the boards and stare down into the water, watching. Charlie sat next to her, dangling his feet, daydreaming in the sunshine. In Kim Song and later at Tokyo Army Hospital, Charlie learned the trick of savoring moments of peace, entering those moments and making them last. Letting his mind leave when his body couldn't. There was nothing he could do about his wife's suffering. He knew she was. She didn't pull a long face, but he knew. And he would wait her out.

Meanwhile, he spent a lot of time with Kira. Once he'd even taken her out on Neil's boat, along with Captain Neil and two of his barmaids, Kazuko and tall skinny Rachel, who was called "The Praying Mantis" behind her back, because of the way she chewed on her boyfriends. Both barmaids had bad boyfriends, and Neil was taking them on a bay cruise as therapy. Charlie and Kira walked up just as they were casting off.

"Glad to see you," Neil said cheerfully. "Come aboard!"

"Really?" asked Charlie. "Where to?"

"Out there." Neil pointed generally toward Alcatraz. He smiled down at Kira. She had on jeans and a striped polo shirt. "I have something warm for her, if it gets cold." He held out his hand, and Kira took it, and with a glance at her father stepped aboard. Charlie had a sudden vision of Linda McNeill. Blowjobs for boat rides. What if Kira fell in love with boats?

"What if she—?" Charlie completed the thought with a gesture from his gut. Neil smiled. "We'll come back in," he said. But Kira didn't get sick or anything like it. She loved going out on the water, and with Charlie holding her up even took a turn at the wheel as they puttered past the Trident, with its deckload of late lunchers and early drinkers, several of whom waved. When they passed the point and got out on the bay proper Charlie kept watch on Kira, but her eyes were bright, her cheeks ruddy. Sure-footed, she walked bravely all over the boat, her hands lifted for balance, seldom grabbing the rail as Charlie had to do.

"She's a natural," Neil said. The men smiled. The little Japanese barmaid had the wheel, with the Mantis beside her. The boat rocked in the waves and San Francisco popped white against the sky. As they moved toward the Golden Gate, Neil went into the little pilot house and took the wheel, heading straight out to sea.

"Where are we going?" Kira asked. They stood out in the wind on the fantail.

"Under the bridge," Charlie said. "You cold?"

"No." Her face was so clean, so eager. Charlie wanted to cry, he loved her so much. Together they watched the bridge pass overhead, as the waves grew deeper and the wind blew colder. Neil gave the wheel back to Kazuko and brought out an old brown sweater. Charlie wrapped Kira in it, holding her in his arms to keep warm himself. He only wished Jaime could have been there. It was getting really cold. Her carried Kira into the pilot house, almost falling and grabbing Rachel. "Oops," he said.

"Give me that child," said Rachel, and Charlie gratefully handed Kira over.

"I guess we better turn back," Neil said. Kazuko turned the wheel sharply left.

"Jesus Christ!" Neil said, his face white. The boat turned broadside to the incoming waves and all but swamped, but Kazuko held the wheel sharply down and the boat made it crashing through the waves onto the reverse course. In seconds they coursed smoothly, as though nothing had happened.

"What was that?" Charlie asked Neil. Kazuko could barely see over the wheel, her face set in determination. She showed no hint of concern, in fact none of the females were upset. Only Neil and, by contagion, Charlie. What horrible risk had he put his daughter through?

"Nothing." The color came back to Neil's face. "Normally you don't turn broadside to the wind, that's all. We could have been swamped."

"If we sank would the sharks eat us?" Kira asked.

Most of the time Charlie and Kira walked through town, window-shopping and people-watching. There was a little park, with a couple of pale brown stone elephants, palm trees, and a sunny patch of lawn, but they'd lost the privilege of sitting on the grass in the sunshine. Charlie heard the story at the no name. Ginsberg and Orlovsky and Ferlinghetti had been in

Sausalito for some reason, and had found themselves in the park. They were clowning around, maybe Peter kissed Allen, there were people watching, and that night, that very night, the police came and put a fence around the lawn. No playing on the grass from now on. The first time in history that a park had been closed due to an infestation of poets.

Now, the park closed, the hippies and other undesirables sat on the broad steps in front of the park or across the street on the steps up to Bulkley Avenue. "Look at the clowns," Kira said loudly one day, meaning some colorfully dressed hippies.

"Yes, dear," Charlie said.

The official end to their walk was always the bronze sea lion, which sat on a rock on the edge of the bay, down the long breakwater past the Trident. Charlie and Kira would sit on the bench there, side by side, looking at the sea lion and the boats on the bay. Kira usually fell asleep on his lap, and he'd carry her back through town to their car. Would this be one of Kira's childhood memories? Charlie hoped so.

Home was awkward without being tense. Cynthia took care of everything. Call girl or not, Cynthia was a fine au pair, and Kira loved her deeply. The two were always whispering together, leaving Charlie out of it. Which was fine. That wasn't the problem. It was just that living in the house with an extremely good-looking young woman who was a prostitute on the side induced certain unworthy thoughts, which demanded of Charlie constant suppression. He wondered if Jaime had stuck him with Cynthia deliberately, to tempt him. In response to Linda, years ago. Whether she did or not, he wasn't going to make any mistakes. If he made a pass at Cynthia she'd surely tell Tanya, who'd tell Jaime, and there you are. Not that Cynthia flirted; or walked around half-dressed, or anything like that. It seemed to Charlie that she was very careful not to. Which was also tremendously sexy.

His life was insane, but calm. When Jaime finally decided what to do about her book, things would settle back to normal, except of course that Charlie had nothing to do. His long-time obsession was over. No point in starting another writing project. He was no writer. The thing was to find another obsession.

49.

Then Bill Ratto called, saying he'd finished reshaping Charlie's manuscript. "I think we have a novel." He seemed bright and brash over the telephone, but that's how he always sounded. "We got you cheap at five grand," he said with a bubbling laugh. He'd be coming to the West Coast to talk to writers and wanted to have dinner with Charlie and Jaime. Charlie hung up the telephone and rolled over on his back. It was seven in the morning, ten in New York. He'd not heard from Jaime in days. Now he called Bob Mills to share the news about Ratto's call and the impending visit. He wanted to ask if Mills had word of either Jaime or her book, but found he couldn't let Bob Mills learn he didn't know where his own wife was.

Listening to the sounds of Kira and Cynthia out in the house, Charlie got up and showered and dressed. His poor old war novel. The damnable stack of pages that was his oldest friend. Why was that, Charlie? Can't you keep your human friends? Maybe the novel was done. Maybe Ratto had actually worked some kind of magic.

Cynthia and Kira sat eating in front of the television set. Charlie got himself a mug of coffee and walked out into the garden. A linnet was singing its incredibly complex song. Charlie finally spotted the little bird at the highest point on his television antenna. Shouldn't Charlie be doing the same thing? Crowing with all his might? He sipped at his coffee, hoping the caffeine would cut through his depression. He sat on one of the redwood lounge chairs, staring out at the misty bay, then felt wet seeping through his jeans. He stood, brushing at his wet seat, and went back into the house.

Three days later Bill Ratto called again, this time from the Mark Hopkins.

He was ensconced and receiving. Charlie's anger at Jaime was growing. Not for being out of touch, but because with Bill here, frankly, Charlie needed the moral support. He'd geared up to dislike what Ratto had done with his stuff, but he hated arguing about writing, especially his own, and dreaded having to do it without Jaime at his side. She had the diplomatic gifts, unless she lost her temper. Charlie was blunt. Now, at last, his manhood was offended by her failure to be where he could find her. Especially since he refused to look. He'd begun avoiding even North Beach at night, confining his drinking to Sausalito and the no name bar. Even there, he half-expected to see Jaime come through the door.

Charlie parked in the Standard garage up the block from the Mark and walked to the hotel with his hands jammed in his front pockets. At least the thing would be out on the table, no longer beyond his control in New York. He'd pick up the manuscript, carry it home, read it in leisure, and then call Bill Ratto. If Jaime happened to show up, he'd have her read it too. If not, then not. Charlie was a big boy. He could handle it all by himself.

Ratto's room was a tiny cube down a long dark corridor. Charlie had assumed the Mark Hopkins was a luxury hotel, but it didn't look like one from the inside. Bill yelled "Come in!" and Charlie opened the door to find Bill on one of the twin beds, dressed in dark pants and a white shirt open at the throat. He was plump and round-faced, with a sharp little nose. He wore silver-rimmed glasses and had a small moustache. He had a manuscript in his hands and there others all over the room, as many as fifty of them, Charlie estimated, on the other bed, on the furniture, and on the rug.

"Just the man I wanted to see," he said, as if they hadn't had an appointment. Charlie closed the door and took a couple of boxes of manuscript off one of the chairs and sat down.

"Hello, Bill," he said, trying to calmly set the tone for the meeting.

"I want you to find me some pot," Bill said. "I thought it would be easy, but the bellhops here don't even seem to know what it is, and the writers I've been talking to either can't get it or won't. How about you?"

"I can't help you," Charlie lied. "But I'll ask around."

"Just a couple of joints. To remove the hotel flavor from my life."

"How's it going?" Charlie said, not eagerly, but calmly.

Bill sat up and put the manuscript down. "You ready to read a great book?" he said with a pursed smile. "Are you ready to die over a book?"

"Yeah," Charlie said, and grinned. He began to feel better. Bill rummaged around and came up with a big fat unrecognizable pile of pages, held together by thick rubber bands. "Is that mine?" he asked.

Bill handed it to him. "I took the liberty of having it typed. It was a mess, you know."

Charlie hefted it. Couldn't be more than five hundred pages. Out of at least fifteen hundred he'd sent in, all told. "How long you in town for?" he asked Bill. "I can read it and call you, or we can meet or something."

"Are you kidding?" Bill said. "I want you to read it here and now."

Charlie numbly sat down and began removing the rubber bands. He didn't want to sit here and read it. He'd read just a little, say something nice, then take the fucker home. "Nice title," he joked. The title was his own, *The End of the War*. The trouble wasn't the title, everybody loved the title. He started reading the first paragraph. The telephone rang and Bill answered it, not lowering his voice at all, making an appointment with somebody. Charlie kept reading, his face going numb. There was a knock at the door and Bill jumped up, mumbled with somebody at the door, and came back in with another hefty manuscript, this one all done up in wrapping paper and string. Charlie read on, his heart freezing. He recognized hardly anything but the character names and a few four-letter words. The rest had been so screwed around that he had a feeling of lightheadedness, as if he was about to faint. He read on while Bill talked on the phone, waiting to see if all the dramatic rewriting came to an end, maybe after the first chapter. No. It went on and on, page after page of stuff he simply did not recognize and intensely did not like. Gradually he lost his temper. His novel had been turned into a pile of shit. He stopped reading, the manuscript on his knees. He breathed deeply, trying to get control over himself.

"Well?" said Bill brightly. "How do you like it?"

Charlie thought carefully. He had nothing against Ratto. Bill had been trying to help. He'd worked hard trying to turn Charlie's manuscript into a publishable novel. Perhaps he had. It read smoothly enough. In fact, too smoothly. It had a nice slick tone. It might be pretty good commercial fiction now, instead of worthless words on paper.

"Well?" Bill's face was wide open for some praise.

Charlie sighed. "Haah." He carefully put the manuscript on the floor and stood up. "I can't do it, Bill." He grinned at the floor, embarrassed. "I'll give back what I've been paid. Of the advance. I'm sorry."

The surprise on Bill Ratto's face could not have been more complete.

PART FOUR

C Block

50.

Stan Winger's cell was seven feet long, five feet wide, and nine feet high. It was in the middle of the third tier and fairly quiet. Stan had a few books, but no other personal possessions. He swept the cell every morning and made up his bunk. Once a week he washed all the surfaces in the cell and rubbed them dry with an old tee shirt. He liked it as clean as he could get it, but he was not a clean freak. The men in C Block didn't go to jobs or eat in the big dining hall or leave their cells for any reason except hospitalization. They were better off than the men in the Rehabilitation Center who were in strip cells. In C Block you had a toilet, a bunk, and your clothes. You had a broom to sweep with, and all the personal junk you could cram in. But you couldn't leave, except to exercise once a day for an hour, or to shower twice a week.

C Block was for the inmates who needed, for one reason or another, to be off the main line. If a politician or a judge or a police officer was sent to prison he ended up here, among the snitches, the queens, the child molesters, and others, like Stan Winger, whose lives might be in danger. Stan was in here because the administration felt he would get into trouble on the main line for the creative arts program, which he had started.

Up in Oregon State pen there had been an arts program, and Stan had done quite a bit of painting. He liked to paint. More than writing, painting got you out of there. You could fall into the brush strokes, disappear, or you could get so turned on by the act of painting that your whole body felt a rosy sexual glow. Painting was great, and Stan meant to do some painting during his nickel bit. He complained and agitated and acted like a complete jerk by demanding that the administration get on with the business of rehabilitation. There had been a little gift shop in the visitor's center, but it had lapsed under changing conditions. The shop had sold hobby work made by the cons, the woodwork and metalwork, the rings and earrings made from toothbrush handles, etc., and Stan decided that the gift shop should open again, only now also showing prison art. Plenty of the men were talented. They could sell their stuff and become rehabilitated. So Stan argued.

The program had been a big success. They had their first big art show, with the public invited, and a couple of newspapers and television stations gave them coverage. The show brought in several thousand dollars, although Stan himself sold nothing. But he was generally credited with bringing the money into the joint, and word spread that he was a pretty good guy. They began having regular shows, the gift shop was reopened, and Stan Winger developed a reputation not just as a good guy but a guy to know. A minor celebrity on the big yard.

His fellow convicts reacted by trying to get him to use the art shows to smuggle goods into the place. The administration reacted by trying to turn him into a snitch. Eventually he ended up in C Block for his own good. The irony was that the fine arts program went on without him, and was spreading to other prisons. Another irony was that he gave up painting and instead devoted himself to finally getting published as a writer. It was cheaper to write than to paint. Stan liked to paint with fresh oils. He loved the smell of them, and liked to apply the paint with a long thin palette knife, and that was expensive. But he could read and he could write. The library queen came around with the book cart three days a week, and Stan began cutting out the blank pages that books had in the front or back, padding, he assumed, to make the books look bigger and thereby justify a higher price. Stan needed the paper to write on. He already had several pencils, each lifted as the opportunity arose.

With paper being so scarce, Stan decided he'd do his composing in his mind, only transferring the words to paper when he was sure of them. He wasn't just writing to pass the time. He had a plan. Fawcett Gold Medal Original Books. They were mysteries and suspense novels, usually hardboiled. An article in *Writer's Digest* had informed Stan that Fawcett paid twenty-five hundred dollars for a Gold Medal Original. It had to be from fifty to seventy thousand words. And it had to be like all the other Gold Medal Originals, Stan assumed. He'd write one himself, and then this time, when he got out of the joint, there would be some money waiting for him. He wouldn't have to turn right around and come back in.

Stan had only been on the bricks a total of eight days between prison terms, and he was determined that this should not happen again. The eight days had been very exciting, and a lot of fun, looking back, but insane. He and the two guys he met on the bus leaving Oregon State Prison teamed up for a bunch of robberies in Oregon, Nevada, and finally California. They were arrested after a high-speed chase through the Sacramento Valley, Stan and his two friends escaping in a CHP car and finally wrecking it just outside Manteca. Stan was knocked around a little by the police, but one of the guys, Tommy Sisk, was shot in the head and died that night. So Stan was ready, more than ready, to become a productive member of society. He'd do this by writing fast-paced pulp paperback novels. Once he learned the trick, he reasoned, he could turn them out like Toll House cookies.

It took him four months to write the first book. It was written in pencil on various sizes of paper in various conditions, a thick stash of messy-looking paper under his bunk. When the guards searched the cell they found it, of course, but they were kind-hearted and let him go on working. Technically, he had the right to write a book, but in actual fact he was at the mercy of the administration or any member of it, from the warden down to the lowest guard. But they kindly let him write his book, and for a while he was so deeply engrossed he actually forgot where he was and who. It all came back to him when he finished the thing and had to decide how to get it to the Fawcett Publishing Company in New York City. He was all but helpless. He had no way to get the thing typed, for one thing. Well, he'd skip the typing.

He only chance was to con one of the guards, convince him that by smuggling this mess of paper out and mailing it to Fawcett, he'd be cutting himself into a lot of money. He picked the dumbest of the guards available and sang his song. It took a week, but the guy finally went for, promising to package and mail Stan's manuscript to Fawcett in exchange for eight hundred dollars on the come. Now he had to hope the people at Fawcett would have the perception to read it.

After two months of waiting, Stan finally realized that the guard had not mailed the manuscript at all, just dumped it somewhere. He even got the guy to admit it. "You're a daydreamer," the guard said in defense of himself. Stan lay on his bunk for three days. It was the worst thing prison had ever done to him. It had killed his hope. He swore revenge.

51.

There was no point in writing anything down. He no longer trusted anyone. Stan had a good imagination and a good memory. He'd work on both, improve both, and write his fucking book in his head. The best part was that they would think they'd beaten him. That was all they really wanted. And for the first time since he'd been jailing, Stan decided to get in shape. He had no muscles, and laying around jail had made him soft and weak. He couldn't go out into the yard and pump iron, so he did what the militants did over in the Adjustment Center, he employed the techniques of "Dynamic Tension," and pitted his body against itself.

At first he could do only a few pushups. Of course the food was crap, but he decided to stop blaming the food, the administration, the world in general, and start thinking and working for himself. Push-ups, leg-ups, pulling the bars apart, pushing the bars together, grunting and groaning for at least two hours a day. He did not try to write in his head while he exercised. That was another part of his day, to be exhausted from exercise, and then to let his mind wander around in the outside world. Not just for the freedom, but to see details and try turning them into words. The first task Stan set for his literary imagination was to find the words to describe the thing that frightened him most when they brought him into Block C. Looking up at the five tiers of cells, he could see along each railing festoons of filthy matted human hair, like some insane bunting. It was that hair, not the noise or the dirtiness or the gloom or the cold, no, just those festoons of hair. Once every couple of weeks the inmates were issued buckets and mops and mopped out their cells onto the guardrail (or not, if they wanted to live in filth, fine), and this water always contained a few human hairs, along with other bits of stuff. Then the regular mop con would come down the tier swishing his mop back and forth, taking all the dirty water from the cells and sweeping it over the side, the water dripping down but the hairs catching on all the other hairs left from years and years of mopping. This created the festoons. He wouldn't have known to call them festoons, but for the guards, and it was a while before he found out where they got that name. It was from a limerick:

> There was an old whore from Azores
> Whose cunt was all covered with sores
> The dogs in the street
> Would not touch the green meat
> That hung in festoons from her drawers.

The former chief of police on Stan's left told him the limerick, and the old queen on his right told him festoons were festive decorations. "Like my testicles, darling."

Stan spent a long time trying to come up with a description of the hanging hair that didn't use the word festoons, but finally had to give up. Hemingway was right, words should be right on the money. Charlie Monel had introduced him to Hemingway, asking him to read "The Killers" and tell him if he thought it was authentic. It seemed full of clichés to Stan until Charlie explained that Hemingway had been stolen from so much that everything he wrote seemed trite. "But he did it first," Charlie had said. "Him and Dashiell Hammett." Then he and Charlie had gone down to Cameron's on SW Third, and Charlie had led him through the bookstore to a musty back room filled with stacks of old pulp magazines. They'd spent an hour choking on paper dust looking for old copies of *Mercury Mysteries* with stories by Dashiell Hammett, stories, Charlie pointed out, that had been published before Hemingway's first book, some of them as early as 1923. These stories had the same clipped realistic prose that Charlie loved. Stan, lying in his cell, tried to remember the Hammett stories he'd read so long ago up in Portland, sitting around Charlie and Jaime's on a rainy afternoon, everybody doing as they pleased, Jaime perhaps in the kitchen baking cookies, Kira running around squealing, Charlie stretched in front of the fireplace with his nose in a book, Stan doing the same. Maybe they'd be drinking beer, classical music or jazz might be playing, and the rain would hit the roof with a steady pleasant drumming sound. He tried to remember the smell of fresh beer in a glass, just as you tip the glass under your nose to drink the beer, the little bubbles popping in your nose, the sharp taste hitting your tongue.

Charlie and Jaime had been nice to him for no reason. There actually were such people in the world. Stan had to hang onto that, otherwise there would be no reason to write, to get out of here, to change his life. But they *were* out there. It was possible to live decently. The whole point of his revenge was to become an ordinary citizen, something the system did not expect and frankly probably didn't believe could happen. Well, fuck the system.

Even this honorable wrath died down after a while. It wasn't personal, they didn't want to hurt him, destroy his life. They did only what their limited imaginations allowed them. Stan, having more imagination, should rise above them, not go to war. Do his time. Write his novel in his head. Become the Buddhist angel of Kerouac's dream.

The novel, he decided, wouldn't have the same story or characters as the one he'd lost through his stupidity. He'd write a brand-new story, with a cop as the hero. Only this cop would also be a thief, a murderer, and finally, a dead man. He even had a great-sounding title, one that, in his estimation, would sell books. *Felony Fuzz.* It rang like a bell, and for a long time he lay on his bunk, pronouncing the title over and over in his mind, experiencing the joys of creation, the pleasures of the poet.

At other times he lost his sense of revenge and purpose and fell into despair. Reviewing his life, as he was compelled to do in this mood, he saw clearly that the fault was not his. He'd been given no chance. He'd not been given two good parents to raise him, in a house full of love, religion, school, happiness. He'd not even been given one parent who loved him enough to keep him. Instead, he'd been given professional parents, in it for the money. He couldn't blame them, sad stupid people incapable of love or tenderness. Not their fault, but not Stan's either. All he had to look forward to was an institutional life. He'd go from one facility to another, with days or hours of freedom in between, and finally he would die and be given one of those big government funerals you hear so much about, where they shovel you into a common grave. At times like this he could hardly breathe, much less write and memorize what he had written.

52.

They'd gone crayfish hunting, Charlie and Dick Dubonet and Marty Greenberg and himself, just the boys, you know, out for a day of sport. He tried to remember the name of the river, but couldn't. A little river, not like the Willamette or the Columbia, just a stream, really, fast-running in the middle, rocks sticking up out of the water and a lot of greenish yellow stuff growing in the shallows. That was where you caught the crayfish. Dick called them crawdads. The whole trip had been his idea. They'd been at one of those guitar and banjo parties, and Dick had been talking about the world falling apart, atomic bombs, crazy governments, it was time people learned how to hunt and gather. Ending up with the four of them out on the banks, drinking beer and waiting for the crawfish to crawl into their traps.

He tried to remember the traps. Like basketball hoops, he decided, big metal round rings with netting across the opening and a dragline. That was Dubonet's word, dragline. Dubonet had come up with the traps and taken Stan to the farmer's market downtown to beg some fishheads from one of the open-air butcher shops. Stan had been doubtful about the free fishheads, but the big red-faced butcher had just laughed and given them a bucketful. "Good hunting!" the guy yelled.

You tie fishheads to the netting and throw the hoop out onto some of that greenish yellow stuff, where it would just sit under water, the slow current taking the fish smell out into the stream. Stan had been surprised when he saw actual crayfish crawling toward the heads as advertised. They didn't get caught in the netting, they just sat there eating fishheads. Dick or Charlie would haul in on the dragline slowly, so as not to dislodge the crayfish. Then the tricky part, picking up the little guys without getting pinched, and throwing them into the live bucket.

Stan tried to remember all this in as much detail as he could, for a scene in his novel. His cop was going to be a bad guy on every level of his life. Bad cop, bad husband, bad father, bad companion, etc. For the crawfish scene he'd be out on a fishing trip with friends, other cops, honest decent guys who needed this holiday. Only Stan's guy screws up the trip. He gets too drunk, he gets verbally abusive, he makes fun of one young cop for being such a pussy, generally alienates the very people who are supposed to be on his side.

What's the matter with this guy? When Stan began forming the story in his mind the cop was bad just because he was bad, but as he kept thinking of things for him to do, a pattern emerged. The guy was a disappointed idealist. He starts out with the highest ideals, then the real world turns him into a cynic. Stan realized this explanation didn't cover why this guy took such pleasure out of cracking heads, out of sending the wrong guys up, and realized he wasn't only a disappointed idealist, he was a sadist. He got a sexual charge out of hurting people. No. The cop was just like Stan, only with more guts. He didn't really like hurting people, it was the other way around. He was hitting *back*, only of course he was hitting all the wrong people. He was taking his terrible life out on everybody around him, just as Stan might have done, if he hadn't been such a weak little punk.

The crawdad scene never made it in. A better scene occurred to Stan later, the same scene, only at a police picnic, with women and children, and his cop gets drunk and makes a pass at his best friend's wife. And gets his face busted. And later sends the other cop into a death trap. And then goes and tells the wife she's a widow, pretending to be terribly upset. What a bastard, Stan thought with pleasure. The more bastardly he is, the more fun to kill him at the end of the book. Stan hadn't yet decided how.

He knew if he was to sell it to Fawcett it had to be like the other Gold Medals, fast action, clear straight language, no bullshit. There couldn't be a lot of deep psychological stuff, as if Stan knew any anyway. But he felt he had to know the guy from the inside, to write about him with confidence. The important thing was the plot. Gold Medal books had ironclad plots, even if most of them fell apart sooner or later. He had to have a strong plot but it didn't have to be perfect. His would be solid, a real story that could really happen. Just to make it easier to memorize. And blunt dialogue for the same reason.

The plot became simplicity itself. We meet this cop getting a commendation, being promoted to lieutenant, big ceremony, flags, a band, cops sitting outside on folding chairs. His wife and kids are there in the front row. Proud as punch. Then the ceremony ends, but instead of going home with his family and friends, he goes to the house of his girlfriend, and when she bitches about missing the ceremony, he knocks her on her ass. Each chapter would cover about an hour, the whole book to cover the weekend, between the ceremony and his actually taking over as lieutenant of the burglary detail. Stan set himself the challenge of making each chapter show the cop in a worse and worse light, until the reader is mightily relieved to see him killed, probably by some poor asshole he stepped on or kicked out of the way. Now here was a book that was fun to write.

The memory part turned out to be easier than he'd expected. In fact, it was the easiest part. Every sentence was like a brick, added to a brick wall. Every sentence had to carry its own weight, and he would lie on his bunk tasting the sentence over and over, until his mind either memorized it, changed it, or dropped it. It was wonderful to wake up in the morning, get through the daily details, then settle back, always with a bit of nervous anxiety, to see if he could still remember what he'd done before. There were fuckups along the way, of course, but soon he had the trick of memorizing whole chapters by chapter title. He didn't know how it worked, but it worked.

Not the hard part, no. Nor was the construction of each scene. He wanted everything as visible as possible, because it made things easier to remember, and so he'd build each scene around some visible thing, a shoe, a window-pane, anything to keep the scene in focus. He did the same with characters. Every character had some visible characteristic so Stan could remember who he or she was, hair that sticks up in the back, a cigar smoker, a guy who pulls his left ear when he gets nervous. All stolen from real people Stan had known. Memorization was just trickery, he decided.

The hard part couldn't be dealt with by trickery. The hard part was that his sympathy for this outright bastard kept growing every day. The worse he made him, the more Stan found excuses for him. At first he left this out, angry at himself for having such sympathy for the devil. Fuck the devil, he'd write his revenge book without any cloying sentimentality. That's why he liked pulp fiction, none of that silly sentimentality. Yet he couldn't avoid the truth. The poor bastard had had no more chance than Stan himself. He was still a bastard, and Stan was still going to kill him in the end, but with regret rather than pure pleasure. One thing about this cop, God damn it, he had guts, in a world where having guts just got you shot down. He might have been a thief, he might have been a terrible man in every way you could think of, but somehow he had integrity. He was his own man, and he'd go down, but like a giant. Stan had his ending. Not the means of death, but the end of the book. "*Only his daughter cried for him. She was eight.*"

Only his daughter and Stan Winger.

53.

After he finished the book in his mind, he did his best to forget it. But of course it would not go away. The book was now called *Night Cop*, and his cop was named Jack Tesser, aka Jack the Bastard. A real person to Stan now, one Stan wished would go away. All the energy, all the feeling he had put into the book, was now backing up on him, making him crazy to get out of the joint. He woke every morning with nothing to do. Physical exercise could not cut it, even though he was up to six hours of grunting a day. No matter what he turned his mind to, it wouldn't work. Desperately he tried to think about nothing, but there was no escape left in him.

The joint eventually ironed him flat. He stopped the daily craze and settled into waiting out the beef. The one thing he did not do was daydream about the future, about when he'd be freed. He knew too many stories about guys who sat in the joint year after year, dreaming over the same jailhouse fantasies, until they were finally let go and blew out of the joint at 180 miles per hour into the nearest brick wall. Not for Stan. Getting out would have to take care of itself. He tried as well not to think about the past, because of course the past was over. Those he'd known on the street were no different people. The sole thing he kept near his heart was the way he'd been treated in Portland. Those were good memories, so long as he didn't expect be able to recapture any of that. He especially cherished Jaime Monel's trust. She'd known he was a thief, and yet trusted Stan to care for Kira, to be alone with her. Stan had never told Jaime how much that meant to him. He remembered Kira's large dark eyes and the way she'd stare at him, mouth open. She was so beautiful, her skin so pure. Stan searched himself many times to see if he had in him the seeds of a child molester, for even a speck of erotic allure in what he felt for Kira, and found none. He'd loved to pick her up, so light in his arms, and carry her around. He remembered carrying her down the slope to Latourette's pier on

Lake Oswego, how confident and strong he'd felt, protecting this child. She'd be eight years old now. She wouldn't remember him. That would be all right, he'd still love to see her. He was glad now he had no children of his own. Judging from how he felt about Kira, imagine how he'd feel locked up in the joint with a kid of his own running around with no father to protect her. He could cry just thinking of it. It didn't bother him to cry every once in a while. It let off the feelings.

Finally they let him out. They asked him where he was going to reside and he pointed vaguely south, so they assigned him a parole officer in San Francisco. They gave him a sweater, pants, shirt, shoes and socks, all jailhouse goods, and forty dollars. They put him on a bus for San Rafael with the other men being released. He sat by himself.

Stan's parole officer got him a job working for a non-union painting contractor. Stan had a suspicion that this wasn't entirely legal and that Morello was getting a kickback, but it was a good job, and the days he worked he spent rollering paint and drinking wine with the other guys, and on the days they didn't work he stayed in his room and tried to calm down. Getting out of the joint was very emotional for him. He found he'd lost a lot of common skills, such as being able to walk into a restaurant or a store without his face getting so red and congested he felt it would explode. Or getting on a bus. Or talking to a stranger. Very difficult. Feelings going crazy. For Stan it was just another beef to sit out.

Finally he bought a typewriter and brought it home to Capp Street. He was sure he'd forgotten his book by now, but there might still be other things he could write. The notion of writing a Gold Medal Original was still a good one, and the twenty-five hundred dollars would come in handy. Stan's room was on the second floor. He set up his typewriter and opened his ream of cheap bond paper. He remembered teaching himself to type in Portland, years ago. He wondered if it would be like riding a bicycle, and it was. Clackety-clack, he knew where all the letters were. No sooner had he started typing a few sentences just for exercise than the guy from downstairs came thundering up the stairs and beat on his door. "Hey, you can't type in here!"

Stan slid back his wooden kitchen chair and went to the door. He opened it and saw the angry face of his downstairs neighbor. A tall thin man with clenched fists and a red face.

"Fuck you," Stan said quietly, and shut the door. He sat back down and started typing again. He heard nothing more from his neighbor. His new used typewriter, a Royal Standard, was a good one. Stan like the feel of the keys. Then something stirred, down below his stomach somewhere. Anticipation of something dreadful or wonderful about to happen. He took the paper out of the machine and fed in another sheet. He typed night cop, centered at the top. Double space. Chapter One. He searched his mind for the key word to the first chapter. He typed "Ceremony," double-spaced, indented, and began to write.

An hour later he'd written the first chapter. He felt light, but not particularly tired, until he tried to stand up and walk down the hall to the bathroom, when his legs buckled slightly. He pissed, his mind empty, then came back to his room to read what he'd written. He wondered what the hell it would be. As he read it over the hairs on the back of his neck rose. Spooky. The first chapter read beautifully. It was as he remembered it.

The trick would be to make the rest of the chapters come out the same way. He wondered what part of his ritual was necessary, and what parts were not. Did it always have to be this time of day? Would he need his neighbor to come up and bitch at him? He didn't know. But every day when he wasn't called to paint, he wrote, and in a few weeks the book was done, on paper, only waiting for him to get up the guts to send it in. He read it over twice, making hand corrections as neatly as possible. Was he living in a dream? No, it seemed to him a good, fast-paced action yarn. The only possible problem being that it didn't have a hero, only an anti-hero. That was okay, the pulps did that sometimes. He would just have to take his chances.

He waited three more weeks before sending it in, just enough time to really learn to hate painting houses. He thought about sending it to Robert P. Mills, the agent who'd helped him, but no. He'd call Mills if and when his book was accepted. Fat chance. But he sent it anyway, and heard back with amazing speed, three weeks. He'd expected to wait at least a month, maybe more. But here was a letter from Knox Burger, editor of the Gold Medal Original series, saying they'd accepted his novel, they had a few changes they wanted to discuss, and please call. There was also a check for thirty-two hundred dollars and a four-page contract. With his neck hairs up he went down to the corner bar and made a toll call to New York.

"That's the best fucking manuscript I've read in years!" Burger yelled at him over the phone. "Why don't you come to New York? We could use a man like you on the staff."

"Uh, okay," Stan said.

54.

Of course he could not come to New York. He was a parolee. Morello told him he could not so much as raise up to fart without permission, and he wasn't giving his permission. In fact, Morello seemed irritated that Stan had sold a book and made so much money. When Stan said he was going to quit house painting and write full time, Morello snapped, "Writing isn't regular employment. You quit your job, you're very close to being violated right back into San Quentin." But Stan sensed that Morello was only being grumpy. He went ahead and quit painting and moved into a nicer apartment in the same building, one with its own toilet. Capp Street was close to Mission, shopping, bars, and best of all, lots of people walking around freely.

Stan didn't actually have to know people, or talk to them. It was enough to sit among them, or walk along unnoticed, relaxed, not prying, just listening to the way ordinary people talked. It was comforting, and helped him get used to being free. At home in his apartment, freedom wasn't going so well. Back in the joint he'd made some resolutions, one of which was that he not masturbate. The point wasn't moral. It was supposed to help him get into some kind of normal relationship with a woman. He reasoned that if he jacked off all the time or went to hookers he just put off the time when he'd enter the normal world. Now he found it very difficult to stick to this resolution. Since he'd been locked up, the kind of magazines they sold in stores had changed. You could go into a store and buy outright pornography, take it home and jack off to your heart's content. And hookers were everywhere. He'd never seen so many hookers. The temptation was great, but he managed to resist it. Maybe he was just too shy.

He poured his sexual energy into writing, or at least that's how he liked to think of it. Where the sexual energy actually went he didn't know. He wrote every day. His new book, another Gold Medal Original, he hoped, was about a couple of funny happy-go-lucky kids who go on a run after getting out of juvenile. They rob, steal, get drunk, get laid, crack jokes, steal a police car, etc., until at the end of the book the two buddies end up cellmates in prison. Another anti-hero story, but this time he tried to get into the state of mind when you go on a criminal run, that high, light, brilliant, carefree mood, nothing in your veins but pure adrenaline. He called his book *The Run*, and it took him six weeks to write. He thought about sending it to Bob Mills to see if they could get more money for it, but he knew Gold Medal paid a flat fee, so what was the point? He had a good relationship with Knox Burger, who insisted he call him collect anytime, and his first book was due out any day now. Stan mailed off the second one without calling Knox, and went into a state of nervous collapse the minute the damned thing was in the mail. He walked out of the Rincon Annex post office knowing he'd mailed off a dud, wishing he had the brains to go over the thing once more.

He knew why he'd thrown himself so convulsively into the new writing. His old bag was opening up right in front of him. He couldn't walk down the street without thinking the thoughts of a burglar, seeing signs of an empty house, feeling the tickle in his gut, the lightheaded desire to cut the civilized knot and penetrate some invitingly empty home. He was through with that, but he could still feel it. Someday he might get drunk or see a beautiful woman turn up her nose at him, then slide out of control back into the joint.

The letter from Knox Burger was too soon to be a reaction to his new manuscript. His heart sank as he ripped the envelope open. What the fuck could this be? But it was unbelievably good news. Fawcett had sold the film rights to *Night Cop* to Universal Pictures for forty-five thousand dollars. Of which ninety percent was Stan's. Knox had scrawled in pencil at the bottom of the note, "*Think maybe you cd afford a phone?*"

Morello looked angry, then defeated. Stan asked his permission to move to Los Angeles and Morello just shrugged and reached for a Form 24. Stan had no plan. He just wanted to be near Hollywood, in case anybody wanted him to work on the screenplay of his book. And to get away from Morello, who was too emotional about being a parole officer. Stan had an ambition to write for the movies. Even television. He hadn't allowed himself to think about this, it seemed so remote. Now, maybe it wasn't out of reach.

The best part was buying a car. Charlie Monel had taught him how to drive years ago in Portland, but now to get his license he went to a driving school out on Geary and let a pretty college girl teach him all over again, then take him down to the Department of Motor Vehicles for his license. Then, with his temporary license in his pocket, he went into his branch of the Bank of America and withdrew three thousand in cash. He knew the car he wanted to buy. A pale blue 1961 Cadillac convertible, with a cream-colored top and a tinted windshield. It was sitting in the front row of a used car lot on Mission, and the sign in the car's window said, "A steal at thirty-five hundred."

Stan walked the ten blocks to the lot. It was a nice sunny day, and he was wearing a white tee shirt and Levi's. He looked like a guy who might work in a gas station or car wash, an ordinary low-class guy, looking over the big expensive machines he obviously couldn't afford. He walked around the car of his choice, looking for tiny flaws. He tried the door. Locked. There were three salesmen standing near the white shack at the back of the lot. Stan waved at them but they neither waved back nor came over. They think I'm wasting their time, he thought with pleasure. He reached into his pocket and took out his huge wad of money, thirty hundred-dollar bills, fanned them as best he could, and held them up, waving them gently. That got their attention. The salesmen said something to each other, then one of them, a big Mexican-looking guy in a plaid suit, came over, a small smile on his face.

"Like what you see?" he asked.

"I'd like to get inside." The guy unlocked the door and Stan climbed behind the wheel. "I'll give you three for it right now," he said, after his test drive.

The Mexican-looking salesman said, "It's three and a half." He grinned at Stan. "You can afford it."

Stan smiled at the salesman, who was every salesman he had ever met in his life. "Three is my final offer," he said, and started to get out of the car.

"Three, did you say?" the salesman said with a smile.

Stan drove south on another sunny day, his top down, sunglasses protecting his eyes from the glare, everything he owned in the trunk. He drove down 101 because he wanted to see the countryside, and near the Monterey turnoff he picked up a girl hitchhiker. There were lots of hitchhikers on the road these days. The girl he stopped for couldn't have been over seventeen, washed-out blonde hair, a long dress made of some kind of velvet, an old army combat jacket, lots of wooden beads. The girl was stoned.

"Where to?" Stan asked her after they got rolling.

"I don't much care," she said.

After a while he said, "Are you running away from home or something?"

She turned toward him. Her eyes were bloodshot. "You wanna get loaded?" she asked. She pulled out a joint and lit it with the car lighter, sucked in a lot of smoke, and handed it to Stan. Up until now, he'd committed no criminal act. Not since he got out of the joint. Unless you counted jaywalking. He took the joint and sucked in a lungful.

"We could stop at a motel," she said after a while. "You got bread? We could eat takeout food. I'm really hungry."

"Me too," said Stan happily. The hippie girl spent the night with him. She ate like a wolf and then, when it was time for bed, said, "I think I have a disease, but I'll blow you."

"That's fine," Stan said. The next morning he fed her again, this time in the motel coffee shop. While they ate their eggs he told her he was going to Los Angeles. Her name was Serene. "You wanna come along, uh, Serene?"

They were in Santa Barbara. "I have friends in Goleta," she said. "I think I'll go hang out with them."

"I can take you. I'm in no hurry."

She smiled. She wasn't very pretty, but she had a nice smile. "You're sweet," she said. "But I can make it on my own, if you'll just loan me fifty dollars. I could really use the bread."

Driving on to Los Angeles, Stan figured he had already committed enough crimes on this little trip to net him about a hundred and fifty years in prison. But there you are.

55.

Three weeks later he was all set up with a rental house in San Fernando Valley, a block off Laurel Canyon Boulevard. The house was furnished and had a nice big fenced backyard with swimming pool, trees, a patch of lawn and some white-painted cast-iron garden furniture with a glass-topped table and a striped umbrella. The little house was cool and dark inside, too big for Stan with two bedrooms and two baths, but he couldn't resist. His first home. He had a lot of Hollywood money burning a hole in his pocket. The real estate lady made him feel like a cheapskate, babbling about all the high-priced properties she wanted to show him up in the hills. This place was just fine.

He'd been putting off calling Knox Burger until he was all settled, but now he could put it off no longer. He really had no faith in himself, he decided. He was afraid his second book wasn't quite as good as the first. It had been more fun to write, but that was partly what made him suspicious. Maybe he'd never make his living as a writer, had just had a lucky first sale, that was all. He called Burger, sitting straight up in his little breakfast nook in his sunny kitchen, looking out his window at the cool blue of his own pool, while some bird sang a long complicated song.

"Stan, where the hell are you?"

He told Burger his address and telephone number, and waited nervously for the axe to fall. But all he heard was good news. Five copies of *Night Cop* would be mailed to him that day, it looked good, maybe a little garish. Stan asked nervously how it was selling and was told those figures would not be made available. There was no royalty rate for a Gold Medal Original, so there would be no accounting. But the really good news was that the new book was accepted, and a check for thirty-four hundred dollars would be sent instantly.

"That's great," Stan said, feeling a little deflated. Would good news always depress him? Who knew? "What about movie rights?" he heard himself saying.

Burger chuckled. "You went Holly wood real fast, didn't you?"

"Why not?" Stan said, embarrassed.

"You said it!" Knox was enthusiastic, but he didn't handle film rights. In fact, he didn't seem to have any advice for Stan about getting the job of writing his own screenplay. "Just call the studio," he said. "Tell 'em who you are. See what happens."

"Okay." Stan's big move to Hollywood seemed stupid, another crazy criminal run. Sure, he was going to break into the movies. That's what they all thought, the poor saps who wrote books.

But he did call Universal. The telephone operator wanted to be helpful, but she was unable to tell him which of the dozens of producers on the lot had his project. He hadn't realized Universal was a collection of producers. He'd assumed they'd know what books they had bought, but no. He hung up irritated, feeling like the dupe of all time. He called Knox Burger back. Burger was out of the office. Stan was polite to the secretary and hung up the phone gently, then said "Shit," to his empty house.

It was the same with his swimming pool. He'd been looking forward to his first dip, and had included the pool in his exercise plans. He'd rise early every morning and step out his bedroom sliding doors to the pool, jump in, swim laps. Then emerge, dry himself on his big new beach towel, and have his breakfast right out here in the morning sunshine. A bigger contrast to C Block he could not imagine. Trouble was, on that first morning when he stepped out through the sliding doors, he suddenly felt cold and shy, his arms crossed over his naked chest, feet cold against the rough bricks of his patio. He looked around. His garden was completely fenced with grape stake, and thick shrubbery grew on both sides. Nobody wanted to watch him. He was alone under the light blue morning sky. The water looked cold. He'd always wanted a pool, but he hadn't realized they took so much maintenance. A heater, hidden behind some shrubs, a pool net on a long handle for fishing out leaves, and once a month the pool man would come and maintain things at a cost of fifteen dollars a month. Stan wanted to jump in, but his body wouldn't. It just stood there getting colder. The first time he'd jumped in a river it was the Columbia, at Rooster Rock, a million years ago. He'd been drunk, so when a bunch of guys jumped in he followed, and damn near drowned, the current sucking him downstream with astonishing strength. He had to fight to make it back to shore. Of course he hadn't said anything. People would have laughed at him, so naïve about rivers.

He walked back into the house, his face red. Fixing breakfast in his own kitchen cheered him up. He'd always eaten food prepared by others and now would begin cooking for himself, starting small with breakfast and lunch, but eventually graduating to making dinners, instead of eating alone somewhere in a restaurant. The first morning, he had fried eggs and toast. Both of which he fucked up. He kept his butter in the refrigerator, and when the toast popped up he whacked off a chunk of butter and tore the toast in half with it. "Shit," he said, and put the torn toast on a plate while he cooked the eggs. He used his Revere Ware frying pan with the copper bottom, and maybe too much butter, and the eggs fried hard around the edges but were still runny. Not the way he liked them. He ate his cold torn toast and sloppy eggs in his breakfast nook, instead of outside where the birds could laugh at him.

He finally got Knox late that afternoon. He called from a bar named the

Lion's Head, in a pretty good mood. "The guy to talk to at Universal is a chap named Fishkin. Bud Fishkin. He works for Andrei Kelos."

"Who's Andrei Kelos?"

"That's your director," Knox said. "I'm not sure of these facts, but give 'em a call."

Stan waited until eleven the next morning. This time he wasn't so hyped up. "Bud Fishkin please," he said.

"Bud Fishkin," the operator said, and put him through.

"Bud Fishkin," a woman's voice said.

"I'd like to speak to, uh, Mister Fishkin?"

"May I ask what in regard to?"

"Uh, *Night Cop?*"

There was a pause. "Are you acquainted with Mister Fishkin?"

Stan's ears started to heat up. "I wrote *Night Cop*," he said.

"Oh, the book," she said. "One moment."

Stan waited nearly five minutes, then heard a deep male voice, smooth, rich, a really nice voice.

"I'm so happy you called," said Bud Fishkin. "I think you're one of the finest young talents in America, and if we don't get together on this project, it would be a crying shame. What are you doing for lunch?"

"Nothing," Stan said.

56.

They met at a little health food restaurant in Studio City. Stan hadn't known what to wear so he showed up in Levi's and a blue work shirt, just about what he wore in the joint. Might as well be straightforward. He felt comfortable right away, because the woman with the menus was dressed in cutoff jeans and a Hawaiian shirt tied up showing her stomach. She gave him a dazzling smile and a menu.

"Uh, Mister Fishkin is expecting me," he said, and she took him to Fishkin sitting at a back table.

"I'm trying to lose a few pounds," Bud Fishkin said as Stan sat down. He was a handsome man with large dark eyes and dark hair, looking more like an Arab than a Jew, as far as Stan was concerned. Sleek rather than fat, he was dressed in a beautiful dark blue suit. "Let me order for you," Fishkin said, and ordered smoothies for both of them. "Don't ask what's in it," he said. "It's healthy."

"I've been doing my own cooking," Stan said. The lack of formality seemed bizarre, but this was Hollywood. "Not very well."

"My wife loves to cook," said Fishkin. "But we have a maid." He looked around the room. "These are all television people. Recognize anybody?"

Stan admitted he did not watch television.

"Where have you been, on the moon?" Fishkin smiled. "I don't watch much either. The idea of sweating and straining over a picture, and then having it show up on that tiny little screen, makes my bowels itch." He shrugged. "That's the fate of everything now. Television. Get used to it."

Their smoothies came, and Stan was surprised to see that it was like a milkshake. "It's got yeast and all kinds of healthy shit in it," Fishkin said, reading his expression. He sipped his own and made a little face. "Okay, pal, you want to know about your project. Do you know the work of Andrei Kelos? No? He's a director." Fishkin named three movies and seemed amazed that Stan hadn't seen any of them. "Don't you go to the movies either?"

"I've been in jail for a while," Stan admitted. Bud Fishkin dabbed at his mouth with his white napkin, clearly surprised.

"Jail?"

"Well, prison. San Quentin." He explained that he'd written *Night Cop* in the joint. Fishkin sat back with a look of theatrical amazement on his face.

"Andrei is going to love this." He immediately put a hand on Stan's. "Don't get me wrong. Listen, Andrei read your book flying to London, he's nuts about it. He wants to make it in black and white, fast, snap snap snap, no stars, almost a documentary. But he's gonna love it that you're an ex-con, please, don't get me wrong, but in this particular circumstance it's a positive."

Stan grinned at Fishkin. He liked this guy. "For me," he said with a little smile, "being out is the positive." They both laughed so loud people at other tables looked at them. Bud put a finger to his lips.

"People are taping us at this very moment," he said. "I'm joking, but you never know. Anyway, tell me about prison. No, I mean, if you want to talk about it."

"I don't." Stan didn't really mind, but he didn't want to seem boastful or arrogant. Better to pose as the strong silent type.

"Anyway, Andrei's going to love you." Fishkin waved for the waitress. "Would you like to come to the lot? We could talk in my office, between phone calls. I have a great idea. Who's your agent?"

"I don't have one yet."

"We'll get you one. Then we'll see if we can't get the studio to buy you as screenwriter." He smiled obscenely. "We'll tell 'em you're an ex-con."

"Is that a good idea?"

Fishkin patted his arm. "In this town? You bet!"

Out in the parking lot under the hot sun, Fishkin was giving Stan directions to follow him to Universal, when Stan belched. "It wasn't the smoothie," he apologized. "I couldn't get my eggs to cook right this morning."

"Eggs? What kind of stove do you have?"

Stan told him electric, and Fishkin held up a finger. "That explains it. What you need, my friend, is a gas stove." So instead of going over to Universal, Stan left his car baking in the sun outside the health food restaurant while he and Bud Fishkin drove through a maze of freeways to a place in Glendale, a storefront with brown paper on the windows and an old sign saying "Reopening Soon." All the way over Fishkin had talked about the Los Angeles Dodgers while Stan pretended he understood or cared. When they got to the storefront Fishkin said, "Let me do the talking, okay?" and took him into what Stan recognized as a hot merchandise drop. His first Hollywood contact had brought him directly to a fence. For the purpose of buying him a gas stove. Stan leaned against an old desk with his hands in his pockets as Fishkin talked to the two guys working the place. Both guys Stan recognized as a thief. They didn't give each other the office or anything, but the recognition was there. Maybe Hollywood wasn't going to be so hard to deal with after all.

Stan and Fishkin carried the stove out to Fishkin's Mercedes and got it into the trunk with the door open but tied down with some manila twine. Stan reached into his pocket to pay, but Fishkin just waved, his suit mussed, sweat on his face. "It's on me," he said. "Somehow, some day, I'll get the studio to pick it up."

And so off they went, back to the health food restaurant to get Stan's car, and then to Stan's house, to take out the old stove, put it in the garage, and hook up the new one. They had to call PG&E and by four in the afternoon the new stove was in. Fishkin looked happy in his shirtsleeves, dirty on his face and hands. "That was fun!"

He left Stan alone, but with an appointment to come in the next day and talk about the script. Stan gratefully stripped, showered, then walked naked through his house to the pool and fell in the water.

The next morning, just as he finished his breakfast of beautifully-fried eggs and properly-buttered toast, orange juice and coffee, the phone rang.

"My name is Evarts Ziegler," the voice said. "But people call me Ziggie." Ziggie was an agent, and perfectly willing to be present that morning at his meeting with Bud Fishkin. This wouldn't commit Stan to anything. Only serve to protect him. "They take no prisoners in this town," Ziggie said. After he hung up Stan wondered if Bud had told Ziggie he was an ex-convict. Of course he had. That was the selling point, wasn't it? Stan had to laugh. Anywhere but Hollywood, a black mark against his name. He'd certainly come to the right place.

57.

Stan saw his novel for the first time in Bud Fishkin's office, on his first visit to Universal, which turned out to be only a few blocks from where he lived. The guard who filled out his temporary pass and stuck it under his windshield was about his age, with red hair and freckles, his hair too long to look right with the police-style hat. Rather than saying "Get a haircut, man," Stan asked directions to Bud's bungalow. The guy wasn't a cop, he wouldn't know a thief if one came up and put his hand in his pocket. Stan followed the guard's directions to the bungalows, and parked in a space marked andrei kelos, as Bud had suggested. Kelos was still in London.

The bungalow was white with green shutters and dark shingles, surrounded by trees, shrubbery, and singing birds. Inside was a nice light airy waiting room with a secretary at her desk. She was a stocky woman of about fifty in a white satin blouse and red slacks.

"Stan Winger?" she asked with a smile. "Bud's on the phone. Can I get you a cup of coffee? The trades? He'll only be a minute."

Stan waited. The secretary answered the phone, which buzzed every few minutes. There was a shelf of books, and from where he sat Stan read the titles. Mostly books he'd never heard of, new-looking in their dust wrappers. Some were paperbacks, and among these he saw his own book. He got up and pulled it from the shelf. The cover was garish, but he liked it. A guy looking straight out at the reader, wearing a brown suit with his badge pinned on the lapel, a gun sticking out of one coat pocket and some money sticking out of the other. Instead of a face, just a blank, a white blank. *Night Cop*, by Stan Winger. A Gold Medal Original.

Stan sat down, feeling very strange, and started reading his own book.

"We just got those," the secretary said, her hand over the telephone mouthpiece.

"I've never seen it before," Stan said, reading on. He was finding a lot of stuff right on the first page that he hadn't written. His face got hot and his ears started ringing. Not important changes, just different word or phrase choices, more and more of them. He told himself furiously that he wouldn't have minded so much if the changes had improved the flow of the book or something, but they were just changes, for the sake of change, as far as he could tell, and ultimately *goddamn fucking ridiculous!*

"What's the matter?" the secretary asked.

"Nothing." Stan had to calm down. Of course it had been rewritten, and of course Knox Burger hadn't told him. They owned the book, they bought it outright, they could change it all they wanted. Still he felt angry, and a little betrayed.

At this moment a man came in. He smiled tired at the secretary and held out his hand to Stan. "I'm Ziggie." He was dressed in an immaculate blue suit with chalk stripes. He had thin blond-gray hair, pale blue bloodshot eyes, and a red face. His hand was warm and firm. Stan stood, and Bud came out of his offices in shirtsleeves, smiling.

"So you've met," he said. "Come into my domain."

The office seemed large, but Stan had nothing to compare it to. Movie posters on the walls, a lot of comfortable leather furniture and shelves of books. It could have been the office of a college professor, except for the movie posters. Stan hadn't seen any of the movies, but then he'd been away.

Instead of sitting behind his desk, Bud joined Stan and Ziggie around a little coffee table, over by double windows looking out at shrubbery and blue sky. "I see you have your book in hand," Bud said. To Ziggie he said, "Have you read it yet?"

Ziggie shook his head. Stan handed him the book. Ziggie frowned at it and put it on the coffee table. "I'm just here as a referee," he said.

"You're probably wondering why I'd have an agent present when I could have just run you over the bumps," said Bud. "The answer is, I want to work with you on a legitimate basis, no later recriminations, and you really need an agent on your side. Anyway, the studio's paying, so I'm not cutting off my own nose, just theirs." Bud smiled. "Do you understand what I'm saying?"

"Sure," Stan said. He grinned to indicate that he was completely in the dark.

"If I end up representing you," Ziggie said in his tired voice, "I negotiate with the studio, not with Andrei Kelos associates. We're all in this together against a common enemy."

"I get it," Stan said.

"Ziggie's not my agent," Bud said.

"I represent writers, a few directors."

"I wanted you to have the best," Bud said. "But I didn't bring you to my agency because I didn't want you to think I was running a number on you."

"I wouldn't have thought that."

"Maybe I should leave the room for a few minutes," Bud said, and went out the door. Stan felt like he was going to be asked to the prom. He waited.

"I need a drink," Ziggie said. "But I can't. I never drink during the week, it interferes with business. You know those lunches cost you whole afternoons. So I start drinking at around six on Friday and drink my way right through the weekend. My hangovers last around three days. You want to be my client? We won't sign anything. I'll represent you until you holler quit."

"Okay." Stan held out his hand. Bud came back into the room only seconds later.

"Do you have a deal?" he asked.

"I'm representing Mr. Winger, if that's what you mean." Ziggie hooked a finger at Stan. "Let's get out of here." Then he laughed and sat down. "Talk deal," he said to Bud.

It lasted twenty minutes. Stan realized he was going to have to learn a new language, if he wanted to stay in Hollywood. As he understood it, the great director Andrei Kelos was going to direct *Night Cop* as his next picture, starting in a year or so. A screenwriter hadn't been hired. Kelos usually relied on one or another of several favorite writers, most of them English. But now that Stan had arrived, it was Bud Fishkin's notion that Stan be tried on an experimental basis, to get the extra stuff they wouldn't from an English writer. The American underworld criminal stuff. Bud was morally certain he'd get the go-ahead to hire Stan. Stan would work every day with Bud and, if necessary, Bud would hire another screenwriter to help Stan learn the ropes. If Stan was interested, they'd call Andrei, and if Andrei went for it, they'd come up with some numbers and hit up the studio.

"You can't have him for a nickel under seventy-five thousand dollars," Ziggie said. Stan was shocked. Bud just grinned and said nothing, escorting them out to the front door. When Ziggie and Stan were outside, Ziggie said, "They want you pretty badly. I think we can get seventy-five."

"I thought the studio put up the money."

"Under pressure only. We have to strike while Andrei is in love. These big directors tend to run off in all directions. But don't worry. That's why you have me. Go home and write another book."

Stan found a package of five copies of *Night Cop* in his mailbox. He started reading again, losing his temper all over at some of the stupid changes. Finally, exploding with anger, he called Knox Burger. Burger answered the phone himself.

"I just got my copies. I'm a little pissed off about some of the changes."

"Oh, grow up," Burger said. "Did you expect to coast through on your own prose?"

It was Stan's turn to be embarrassed.

"We do that to all our books," Burger said. "They did it to Hammett, they did it to Chandler, and they'll do it to you. As I said, grow up. You're in Hollywood now. What we did to your prose is nothing compared to what they'll do to it. Capeesh?"

58.

When he didn't hear from either Evarts Ziegler or Bud Fishkin, Stan decided everything had fallen apart and it was his fault. He went over his meetings with both men to try to find out what he'd done wrong, but finally had to admit he just didn't know. Hollywood was mysterious. He didn't call them because what would he say? He didn't call Knox to find out how his book was doing in the marketplace, if Knox even knew. Gold Medal Originals didn't get reviewed. They were issued in huge numbers and gobbled up by eager readers like Stan himself, then vanished. According to Burger, there were Gold Medal writers who turned out five or six a year, under various pen names, a damned good living. Or so it seemed until you heard Evarts Ziegler talking lightly about seventy-five thousand for writing a screenplay. Stan had hoped to make a living. Not get rich, though once the possibility opened up, he couldn't help daydreaming. For now he turned to Ziggie's advice to write another book. But there was nothing there.

He adjusted to his day-to-day life in the Valley, waiting to hear from anybody. Since there was a television set in the living room he turned it on once in a while, more as a professional looking at the competition than as a viewer, or so he told himself. He recalled Fishkin's words, about television reducing everything to tiny pictures. There'd been television sets in C Block, but Stan hadn't had one. He could hear them, though, and hated the sound. He preferred his Zenith radio, a big portable job that drew stations all over the world. He liked to splash around the pool and then sit at one end, in the water up to his neck, with the radio playing music. He let his mind empty out and his body relax, with the pool water "warm as piss." He could afford it.

Driving around in his Cadillac convertible, he got acquainted with the varieties of Southern California, and loved it. Of course. A Portland kid, he half-expected it to rain every day. When instead it was hot and sweet he just naturally felt good, full of optimism and hope. He drove to the beach towns as far south as Long Beach and north well past Malibu, surprised by the dullness of the beaches themselves compared to the drama and beauty of those in Oregon. Maybe if he got really rich he'd move out here to Malibu, or maybe even up to the Oregon coast, with a huge beach house to entertain all his friends. What had happened to them, his Oregon friends? When he'd been arrested he'd thought of calling Charlie, asking for help, for bail or a lawyer, but was too embarrassed. Now too many years had passed.

He walked in Hollywood, Beverly Hills, Westwood, the only places that seemed worthwhile to stop and walk around. Hollywood, he discovered, was full of bookstores, and his little house began filling with books. He'd never before had so much money, so he bought stuff he only maybe planned to read, as well as a lot of used Erle Stanley Gardner, John D. MacDonald, Ross Macdonald, Chandler, Hammett, etc. He looked for any books by Charles Monel but couldn't find one. And nothing by Dick or Richard Dubonet, or by Jaime Monel, but one day he saw a picture of Jaime on the back of a book in a bin of remainders, out in front of a store on Hollywood Boulevard. She'd published under her maiden name, of course. He bought the copy of *Washington Street* and took it home, more excited than he could understand.

It was a hot day, so his first act was to strip and run out and fall into the pool. His scruples about swimming dirty had vanished under the pleasure of hitting that water all hot and sweaty, feeling the explosion of cold. Then, after a nice little swim, he got out, shook himself like a dog, sat down on his big white towel draped over his white wrought-iron chair, and read Jaime's book cover to cover. At first it was like science fiction, so remote was it from his own experience, but Jaime pulled him into her life and the life of her parents and neighbors. Not a thief in the lot, no killings, no chases, no cops, and yet exciting, even thrilling. Jesus, she could really write. Jaime in her Lake Grove kitchen, white tee shirt, jeans, standing at the stove smiling and cooking, her daughter in her high chair, old Charlie sitting there, a big warm smile on his face. Stan felt extraordinary. A gush of feeling like nothing he'd ever felt. Or could remember, anyhow. Was it just the book? No, it was love. He loved those people. They were the only people he loved. He thought of writing Jaime care of her publisher, explaining why he'd so suddenly disappeared six years earlier, and including the happy news of his book and movie possibilities. Everybody thought Charlie was going to be an important writer. Nobody thought about Jaime, although they'd certainly respected her for finishing her little book. Dick Dubonet had called it that, "her little book."

Were they all still in Portland? He was tempted to call and find out, just to see if they were in the phone book, but didn't. The past was over, remember?

He realized too that they'd not likely be reading his book. They didn't make a habit of reading drugstore pulps.

"Well, fuck 'em," Stan said to his pool. He felt good. He inventoried his well-kept yard, the shrubs and trees, the red-brown grape stake fence, the patch of lawn. Everything grew down here. He thought about going into gardening heavily, working in the sun. It would help him wait. He sighed. He thought he'd learned all there was to learn about waiting, but no. He looked at himself, naked in the sun. He'd gotten pretty tan in the few weeks he'd been here. He was in good shape, but it wouldn't hurt to buy some exercise equipment. He could afford it. He'd pump iron until somebody called.

In the middle of the night he woke sweating and terrified. What had her book done to him? He sat at his kitchen table in the midnight with a cup of instant coffee, the radio playing low, and tried to figure it. He didn't have to think long. It was obvious. Jaime's book had reminded him of how empty his life was. Because there was no woman. He was afraid of women. Afraid of losing control of himself. Sexual feelings and burglary. He had to face it. He was so scared he was afraid to jack off, much less get into bed with a real live woman. All the rest of this shit was a joke. What matter money and success and Hollywood without a woman? He knew the answer. It meant nothing. He wasn't really waiting for Hollywood to come through, he was waiting for himself to break out of himself.

He had to laugh, sitting there in the semi-darkness, planning the greatest jailbreak in history. Stan Winger finally breaks out of himself. Suddenly he remembered Linda McNeill. He'd blanked her from his mind. Another thing Jaime's book had done, recalled to him the one woman he could have loved. Now in his emptiness her face floated back to him. He wanted to put his head on the table and cry. Since there was nobody around to see him, that's what he did.

59.

This one would be about a man who kidnaps a woman. Linda. The man would not be Stan, but some poor sap who is egged into it by seeing beautiful women all day, and not getting to touch them or even talk to them, except to pass them in and out of the studio. The rent-a-cop at Universal. Only it wouldn't be Universal, it would be some out-at-the-ass broken-down hack studio where they make cheesy movies for the gutter trade. Red. Red the boob. Red the hungry. Red the dreamer. Red Reemer. One day poor ol' Red just snaps. Maybe it's one of those really hot L.A. days, *The Fifth Hot Day in a Row*, that would be his working title. Poor Red hasn't slept in days. He keeps tossing and turning, this one girl in his mind, the girl that comes in and out of the lot in Stan's Cadillac, or one just like it, a blonde, lots of wonderfully curly hair blowing in the wind, always a big smile and a friendly hello. As Red all but drools down her cleavage, in she comes, out she goes, he has no idea what she does, he assumes she's an actress in one of the sleazeball movies they turn out around here, so one day when the heat is cooking his brain, Red gets his ass chewed off by some fat executive with a cutie at his side, and as he is standing there after a long hard day in the melting heat, swallowing the executive's insults and remembering the little bimbo's nasty smile, here comes the blonde in the Caddy, and when she gives her big friendly smile, something snaps. He gets into the car beside her, pulls out his gun and points it at her. "Turn right and keep driving straight," he says to her surprised face.

Stan realized the girl in his story wasn't Linda at all, but somebody fresh, somebody he didn't know. A secretary, not an actress. Everything Red thought about her was untrue. So she would be a mystery. This was going to be fun.

He was happy to be back. Work gave focus to his day. He got up early, took his swim, made his breakfast, ate listening to the radio either outside or in his breakfast nook, and then, dressed only in jockey shorts, went into the bedroom he'd made over into his office. He wrote a chapter every day, each representing an hour in the story, the same as his first two novels. Only in this one he had not only Red and Sissie—the blonde—but Frank Greise, aka Greasy Frank, detective on the LAPD, who is assigned to the case of the missing secretary because nobody thinks it is important. Poor Frank is only a cop because he couldn't get on the fire department. All he wants to do is get through his day so he can start drinking. Frank has a rule, no drinking before sundown. That's because he tends to go nuts drunk. So every other chapter would be about poor hapless Greasy Frank, the last guy in the world you'd expect to solve a crime. Which of course he doesn't. He just falls into it. Although Stan didn't know exactly how he was going to get there, he knew what happened at the end of the story. Red would gradually convince himself that she loved him. She'd give him every reason to think this, and the reader must think it, too. Finally, near the end of the book, when through fumbling and stupidity Red has both the girl and the ransom money, and it looks like they'll flee together to Brazil, he hands her his gun while he zips his fly or something, and since this is actually the first opportunity she's had to shoot him, she does. Just as Greasy Frank arrives, drunk out of his mind. Another triumph for justice.

Finished with a day's work, he'd take another swim, make lunch for himself, or head out. He liked to drive all afternoon. It was creepy, in a way. There were lots of hitchhikers, and Stan had to admit to himself that he picked up girls and drove them places in the hope of getting laid. He was still too shy to hit on the girls, but if one of them should hit on him, that would be fine. None did. Some tried to con him by acting sexy and pretending they were interested, to get him to take them where they wanted, but then jumped out of the car. A lot of them were very young, and Stan was sort of ashamed of himself, and went out of his way to give the young ones lifts so that some other rotten pervert wouldn't pick them up. It was generous of him, but it didn't get him laid. A lot of them called him Pops or Dad or Old Man, and he was thirty.

Every two weeks he drove downtown to visit his parole officer. This one was named Bob Gomez, a man of about fifty who was enthusiastic about Stan's chances in the movie business. He seemed impressed by Stan's book sales and told Stan that if he ever did need a real job, Gomez would do his level best. "Lots of folks try the movie business," he said. He showed his gold tooth. "I'd try it myself if I didn't already have a good job."

Evenings were difficult. This was temptation time. Time to hit the bars. Stan wasn't specifically prohibited from drinking, only from drinking with thieves. But this thing about women was starting to get to him, and he could see himself getting nice and tight and hitting on the wrong lady, ending up back in the joint. He'd heard rumors about Hollywood all his life, so why didn't his Hollywood friends fix him up? They didn't even call. He wondered at their easy friendliness, their apparent honesty and openness. Why weren't they getting him dates with actresses? He laughed. He was turning into Red. Well, Red wasn't such a bad guy. Just a fuck-up. Red would have been hitting the bars, trying to get his pimply ass laid. Stan was smarter. He stayed home reading. When he did go out, he went to movies. Generally he was sleepy by around ten or so.

He finished *Heat Wave* in six weeks, two full drafts. He let it sit for a day, read it over, and liked it. He took the manuscript down to a typing service on Highland near Franklin, where it was typed and a copy sent to Knox Burger. He'd still not heard a word from either Bud Fishkin or Evarts Ziegler, so he took a copy to Ziegler's office on Sunset, and left it without asking to speak to his agent. He'd never been up there before. It seemed a lot like a doctor's waiting room. Or a dentist's. More like a dentist's, and he was glad to just leave the thing and go.

Ziggie called two days later. "I think I can sell this," he said. Stan hung up after a few minutes of pleasant conversation about his book, and wondered what to do with the rest of his day. He hadn't thought to ask about Fishkin, and Ziggie hadn't said anything. He had plenty of time and money. And freedom. He had to laugh. If he didn't find a girl to at least talk to, he was going to go crazy. It was really all his fault. It took some guts to pick up a girl.

His problem was that he lacked guts. He had to go into a bar, yes a bar, and sit down, drink some drinks, size up the single women in the place, single women were everywhere, then go up to one of them and saying something inviting. "Hi!" Or, "Oh my goodness, you are certainly attractive!" Or, "Say, baby, how's about it?"

The trouble with getting manners out of pulp novels is that they don't really supply you with any good pickup lines. Stan was sure he needed a good pickup line. The truth in this case wouldn't work. "Ahem, I'm a fairly well-to-do young writer, here in Hollywood to work in movies." Sure you are, Bozo. Like the last ten guys who tried that line.

With a sigh and rap on his kitchen table, Stan decided to just go ahead and try it. If his voice broke in the middle of his pitch, so what? What could they do? Stick him in the hole?

60.

Driving around L.A. he'd seen plenty of bars, but they were nothing like the friendly taverns of Portland. Most were really restaurants, the others full of men in suits and women dressed for office work. Just walking in made him walk out red-faced for no reason. He tried some of the bars on the Sunset Strip, but there was too much action, and on the weekends you couldn't even drive, there were so many hippies walking around. He tried mingling with some of these weekend crowds on Sunset, but had felt the presence among the hippies of a large number of both cops and criminals. Too much heat, again. And everybody so young. Guys his age were predators. He walked Sunset only a couple of nights and then gave it up.

Ziggie called one morning when he was going crazy trying to start a new book, and told him that Fawcett loved *Heat Wave*. But now that Ziggie was in the game, things would be different. Instead of paying a flat thirty-four hundred dollars and publishing as a Gold Medal Original, Fawcett was being asked, by Ziggie, to pay Stan fifty thousand for the paperback rights alone, farm the book out to a hardcover publisher for the initial publication, half that price going to Stan, and of course Stan would own his own film rights, TV rights, foreign rights, and so forth. "It's time to get you out of the slave pen," Ziggie said in his dry voice.

"Do you think they'll go for it?" Stan asked.

"If they don't, they're crazy."

"What's going on with Bud Fishkin?" Stan remembered to ask. He was amazed at how calmly he was taking all this.

"They still haven't heard from Andrei." So the long silence had been from the director. It occurred to Stan that his entire Hollywood career was based on one guy liking one of his books. If that one guy changed his mind, Stan was out in the cold. Why didn't this bother him? Maybe he was developing a little self-confidence. Meanwhile, there was the problem of starting a new book. He'd graduated from the Gold Medal Original type of story to the hardcover novel type, Ziggie's call proved that. But it was like draw poker, he had four to a straight flush, with one card to draw. Don't bet too hard until that last card, he told himself. He'd just let his mind wander, try to find something to write about that didn't have to be just one slam-bang action scene after another, something that didn't require that heavy suspense aspect.

What writers usually did at this point, he theorized, was write about their lives. Was it time for a long autobiographical novel? He sighed. His life. His poor little stupid life. Who'd give a shit? He wanted to write another book only because he was bored, but he didn't want to write another speedy little action story. Maybe he'd developed an ego.

Ziggie called him a little after six. "Do you know why I love this business?" He sounded tired. "Because I get to make calls like this one."

"Good news?" Stan was in his pool, up to his neck.

"We have a deal," Ziggie said. Fawcett's check for half the fifty thousand advance would be delivered to Ziggie's New York agency contact by close of business Friday. Stan hung up, a rich man in his pool. He lit a cigarette and blew a smoke ring at the sky. He celebrated by driving to an Italian restaurant he liked on Ventura, having a couple of beers before dinner, a nice bottle of wine with his lasagna, and then a leisurely drive over to Hollywood, where he walked on the Boulevard for a while, hands in pockets. Hollywood Boulevard was a tough street, with a lot of action. He liked it. He looked at stuff in the windows for a while, then on impulse went into the Warner Theater.

The movie was *Easy Rider* and the theater was full, only one place for Stan to sit. A woman sat alone in the aisle seat, a vacant seat next to her. Stan sat down, conscious of the woman, but not looking at her. The movie started, and Stan was immediately drawn into it. So was the rest of the audience, and Stan forgot about the girl next to him until one scene was so funny and exciting that he turned toward her to share the moment, and found himself looking into her eyes. A feeling passed through him like electricity through a wire. He turned back to the screen, three guys roaring down the road on two motorcycles. At the next big moment he looked over again and found her looking at him. He laughed and she laughed, and they went back to watching the movie. He knew to a moral certainty that when the picture was over, they would talk. He knew he wouldn't be shy. When the lights came up she was sniffling into her handkerchief.

"Those sons of bitches," Stan said to her.

"Yes," she said. She blew her nose. She was about his age, nice-looking, dark hair. "Excuse me," she said to Stan, and stood to let him by. The aisles were crowded.

"Let's wait," Stan said. "Or would you like to get a cup of coffee?"

"Sure," she said, after taking a second, harder look at him. They walked out of the theater onto Hollywood Boulevard. Normally Stan would have been full of the movie, but this was more interesting. She was as tall as he was, a nice figure, dressed in a flowered dress but not a hippie.

"My name is Stan." He held out his hand.

"I'm Carrie Gruber," she said, and shook his hand.

Stan had never felt so bold. "We already like each other," he said.

"Yes," she said.

"Where's a good place to go?" he asked her. "I'm kinda new to Los Angeles."

"We could go to my place," she said. She looked at him openly. "It's over in the Valley."

Stan followed her to her apartment building on Lankershim, a big dark building. She signaled for him to follow into the underground garage, then pointed with her arm where he could park. He tried not to think, and not to feel triumphant. After all, he didn't know what was coming. It could just be a cup of coffee and a nice conversation about movies. He was prepared for that, but in his heart he expected more.

She had a quiet apartment, bigger than she needed, very neat, no sign of a man. Stan relaxed even more. Instead of coffee they had bottles of beer, all very polite. They did talk about movies, and when Stan told her he was trying to write for them, he was unsurprised that she was unsurprised. "So many movie people in Los Angeles," she said nicely. She worked for a chain of Laundromats. The girl Friday, she did everything in the office. Her boss had been in television. Not a good actor, but he'd made enough to buy the Laundromat chain, and now he spent most of his time in Gardena playing poker. If she didn't keep the place running, her boss would go broke in a month. She didn't plan to be in the laundry business forever, however. She was saving her money to open a business of her own, what kind she didn't yet know. She'd been married and divorced, no children, and born and raised right here in the San Fernando Valley. "Some day I hope to live in the South Seas," she said.

When they'd come in, Stan chose a single overstuffed chair to sit in, rather than going right to the couch, which might have seemed forward. She sat on the couch, and when he finished his beer he wondered whether to move over to the couch and put his arm around her. A bad move. In fact, any move would be a bad move. He just sat and let her make all the moves. Which she did.

"Would you like another beer?"

"I guess I'd better leave," Stan said, without moving.

"Please stay," she said. She looked right at him. No urgency in her voice, no sign of mental illness. A perfectly decent, honest human being, asking him to stay.

"I'm pretty clumsy," he said.

"If you don't want to," she said, looking embarrassed. He saw that she thought he was rejecting her, so he got up and went over and kissed her on top of her head. She took hold of him and pulled him down into a real kiss, a very hungry kiss, on both sides.

61.

They couldn't get over the luck. He'd walked into the movie on impulse. Carrie had almost given up finding a parking place but had lucked into one at the last minute, then got her seat when a couple moved, leaving the empty seat for Stan. And they both admitted they were shy, but by some lucky accident they weren't shy with each other.

They made love that night twice in her perfumed bedroom. She was hesitant at first, her skin prickly with goosebumps, but Stan must have done something right because soon she relaxed, and in a few minutes was panting passionately. Stan couldn't get over how wonderful she smelled, or the incredible softness of her skin. It was like falling down a well of love. Only, they weren't exactly in love. Stan was careful not to tell her he loved her, but he did tell her how much he liked her, and how good she smelled and tasted and felt. Stan had never before done much talking while making love. Whores didn't encourage it. But with Carrie he talked. And moaned. Even yelled a little. So did she, yelping with surprise, it sounded to Stan, when they had their first long sweet orgasm together. After it was over Stan lay in her sweet-smelling bed in a self-congratulatory mood. He wanted to boast, but didn't. He did say, turning to her in the dim light, "You really make me feel wonderful."

"You too," she said shyly. They smoked the traditional cigarettes, and when Carrie got up to go to the bathroom, Stan was thrilled at the sight of her padding naked across the room. All the right things in the right places. No, more than that. It wasn't just getting laid. There was something more here.

They talked a while, then made love again, but afterward Stan couldn't get to sleep, and Carrie seemed restless.

"What's wrong?" he asked.

"I don't know." She sat up. "I think maybe you should go home now." She rubbed his shoulder. It felt good. But she was right.

"We'll all sleep better in our own little beds," he said lightly, and threw back the covers.

She loved his house, especially his swimming pool. They had a pool where she lived, but you couldn't swim naked and there were always people around. Carrie had a hard time relaxing around her own pool, but at Stan's house she could just sit there naked except for her white plastic sunglasses, oiling her body with Bain de Soleil, or reading magazines, just taking in the sun. She had a dark tan, like Stan's, and on weekends they spent most of their time in Stan's backyard or Stan's bed. It turned out they were both sex maniacs and sun freaks. She even liked to spend a little time pumping iron with Stan's equipment, which he kept in the backyard. He felt as if he'd finally, after all this time, become a normal person. It had taken a lot of doing, but he was glad to be free.

His work life was another story. Nothing had come to him by way of a next book. Not that his three pulp novels were all that original, but they'd come to him easily. The new one wasn't coming at all. As for the movies, Stan began to learn the ropes. He had to swallow his impatience. Ziggie was being strategic. He wasn't trying to market Stan's novels until he heard from Andrei. "Your price jumps if he hires you as a screenwriter," Stan was told, although he couldn't quite see the connection between his becoming a screenwriter and selling *The Run* or *Heat Wave*. Of course with *Heat Wave* Stan had already made an obscene amount of money, figures so dizzying and remote from reality that Stan had no real problem believing them. It just wasn't real. His huge savings account at the Bank of America? That wasn't real either. He told Carrie he felt like every time he walked into the bank he was going to rob the joint.

He told Carrie all about himself and gave her a copy of his novel. He left out the sexual part of being a burglar, but told the rest, and she seemed able to absorb it without a fainting spell. "My cousin was in prison," she said.

"Really? What for?"

She smiled. They were out by the pool, naked and oiled up. "All he ever wanted was to be a surfer," she said. It turned out her cousin robbed liquor stores all over the Valley to support his board, and ended up doing six years at Soledad. "He's out now, going to graduate school."

"You mean he's robbing banks?" Stan joked.

"He's studying criminology."

"Ah," said Stan. "Revenge." He was very hot now, his sweat mingling with the Bain de Soleil Carrie had lovingly rubbed all over him. It was time to cannonball.

Carrie took his novel home, but if she read it she said nothing. He decided she wasn't much of a reader. There were no books in her apartment, just magazines. At Stan's she read only magazines and the newspaper. Maybe a good thing. In fact, he was sure it was a good thing.

Then came the call he'd been waiting for.

"Andrei's coming to town," Ziggie said tiredly. "I'll try to arrange a meeting."

"Do I have to meet him?" Stan asked humorously. Ziggie didn't laugh.

"It would help."

Two days later Ziggie called to say that Stan had been invited to a party at Andrei's house in Bel Air. "Can I bring my girlfriend?" Stan asked.

"I wouldn't," Ziggie said.

"But I want to."

"All right, no problem. It's just that we'll be working."

"We've been invited to a Hollywood party," Stan said to Carrie on the telephone. He told her the details, then had to wait while she answered another line. When she came back she said, "I don't really want to go. Do you mind?"

"Why not?"

"I'd feel out of place. I have nothing to wear."

"I'll buy you something," he said. He was getting hot under the collar. Nobody wanted her to go except him, it seemed. She wouldn't accept his offer of a dress. Stan hung up mad, but Carrie called back an hour later and said she'd changed her mind.

"Good," she said. "We can go shopping together." Her call had made up his mind. It was time to buy some real clothes, a nice suit or two, some decent kicks, Florsheims, nice shirts, cuff links, ties, tie-tacks, the works. Carrie could help him shop.

Then, when they did drive over to Hollywood to the department stores, he decided in a flash to buy a new car, too. But when he wrote out a check for the entire amount, the salesman got suspicious. Stan had to say, as airily as he could, "Oh, fine, you cash the check and I'll be back Monday." Stan took Carrie's arm and they left the Cadillac agency and the skeptical salesman. On Monday Stan came back to claim his brand new Cadillac convertible, pale green with a cream-colored top. This time the salesman was his best friend. Stan drove out of the place thinking that maybe his new life had now actually begun. Now, maybe, a house in the hills. Not buy, of course, but rent. He daydreamed of taking Carrie to this new house in, let's see, Beverly Hills? No. Malibu. That was the place. He imagined the surprise and delight on her face. A simple person, just like Stan. She'd love Malibu, wealth, a dreamlife on the beach. She'd even quit working. Stan made plenty and would make plenty more. He could set her up in any business she wanted. They didn't love each other, but so what?

62.

What attracted Carrie so much was Stan's simplicity. Most of the men she dated were salesmen or office workers, men she ran into at work or at Credit Managers. They were usually married or had other complications in their lives, but not Stan. After only a couple of dates, she decided he was just what he said he was, a book writer trying to break into the movies. She tried to read the book he gave her, but it was a man's book and she couldn't get interested. It didn't matter. And it didn't matter that Stan wasn't handsome. He wasn't ugly, and his face had character, but he wasn't the kind of man you'd call good-looking. He had soft eyes and a firm sensitive mouth and was gentle with her. Most of the men she dated didn't know how to make love, or were too uptight. Stan was different. More like a little boy, she decided, eager about everything but polite, like a polite little boy sitting down to a big dish of ice cream. She understood after a while that it was probably because he'd spent all those years in prison away from women. He wanted to try everything. He didn't seem to know the difference between ordinary sex and crazy stuff, he wanted to try it all. And then of course everything he did to her, she felt she had permission to try on him. Very liberating.

Stan was not only great in bed and getting better, he was a man with lots of money. She didn't have an eye on his money, but more to the point, he didn't seem to have his eye on hers. So many men these days were just looking for a place to crash. Or wanted to assume control of her savings. Or tell her what business to go into and how to run it. Some, after getting to sleep with her, wanted to tell her how to run the laundry business. Stan not only had no opinions as to how she should run her life, he was always asking her how to run his. Once she realized he was completely sincere, she felt sympathy. He'd been brought up without manners or social skills, thrown into prison with animals, and yet wasn't bitter or mean. One day she planned to take him across the Valley to meet her family.

The Grubers weren't a small family. Carrie had five brothers and two sisters, all living in Southern California, and her parents still held the family home in San Fernando. Carrie and her siblings had been taught to be independent, to go out into the world, to make and save, become financially independent, which she had done. She didn't much like her family, but she was glad her papa had given her a good solid upbringing, exactly the kind Stan had been denied. She meant to teach him Gruber values.

But Stan was more than a piece of clay for her to mold. If his face was nothing to write home about, he still had a beautiful body, tanned and muscular, and he made good money in a glamorous business. Of course, she saw show business from a slightly different angle than most, working for Lyle Freed. Lyle had begun in high school as a cheerleader, then went into Special Services in the army, singing and dancing for the other men who had to fight. She'd heard the whole story a million times. His lucky break had come when a bunch of Hollywood people came to his army camp for a show. He was master of ceremonies and they liked his act, and an agent told him to call the day he got out of the service. The rest was history. A role in a series, the series a big hit. Lyle spent five years wearing the same clothes and saying the same dumb jokes until he wanted to kill himself, but he saved enough that when the show was canceled he could purchase the laundromats.

Lyle hated show business and everyone in it. Stan wasn't like that. He had nothing bad to say about the people who were keeping him dangling. He didn't even seem nervous. Lyle had told her so many times that nobody in show business was to be trusted, but Stan didn't care. Maybe his life in crime had made him immune to dishonesty, like a flu shot. All she knew was that Stan was the most decent and straightforward man in her life.

"He's an ex-convict, Papa, but he's going to be rich." She could hear her father saying, "Well, how rich?" Stan himself never talked about marriage or even love. He was careful not to say, "I love you," even when they were making love, and she was just as careful. But something made her think he did actually love her, in the same friendly way she loved him. They were friends, they were lovers, and they were compatible. What more to want? To show him her feelings, she went out and had her hair done blonde, just the way he liked it. Actually, she'd always wanted to be blonde. Stan loved it. "You're my Marilyn Monroe," he told her.

They didn't have to get married. Why rock the boat? They'd go into business together. Stan would put money into any business she chose. Part owner, silent partner, not taking over because he was a man, just investing in her because he believed in her. Naïvely he'd tell her he didn't know how to manage money and that she could do it for them both. "You can be my business manager," he'd said. She told him about business managers. Lyle was almost poetic in his hatred of business managers. All they did was take your hard-earned money and put it into fly-by-night ventures. When things went wrong they'd just hold their hands up in surrender, like Jack Benny. "Gee, we didn't know!" They never went broke, just their clients. Carrie was pretty sure Stan would soon be in the big money, and she looked forward to helping him invest it. Not in her business, but in stocks and bonds.

These days she daydreamed of a candy store. Good for her, because she didn't eat much candy. Candy was like show business. In hard times, business would be good. The worse things got, the more they needed little treats. She had an idea for a very special candy store, one featuring candies from all over the world, exotic candies, the favorites of people everywhere. As the owner, she'd travel the world, searching for good interesting candies, getting the recipes and test marketing them here. There would have to be a chain of stores. She'd start with one, then expand. A real possibility. She and Stan could travel, have a good time, and sample candies. Stan could make the store a favorite with his Hollywood buddies.

Stan had no objection. "We'll open the first store in Malibu," he said. "And live over it." He was open to travel. "I've never been anywhere," he told her, then tapped his head. "Except in here."

They had the top down on his Cadillac, and Stan was wearing the Hawaiian shirt she had bought for him, wearing it the way she'd shown him, unbuttoned with a white tee shirt underneath, and his red bathing trunks with the white stripe down the sides. She wore her black bathing suit and one of his dress shirts open down the front. They both had on their sunglasses and it was going to be a wonderful day. She'd taken the day off just so they could go to Malibu when the beach wouldn't be crowded with hundreds of thousands of people, a sunny Tuesday morning, and Stan had told her he had to run downtown for a minute to visit his parole officer.

They pulled into the parking lot next to the State building and Stan got out of the car, walking around to her side to give her a kiss, when another car pulled into the lot and this big fat Mexican man got out. He wore a light brown suit open in front, and his belly hung over his belt. He looked about fifty, and he stared at Stan angrily.

"Do you know that man?" she asked him. Stan turned and grinned. "That's my parole officer," he said, waving at the man, who walked toward them, his face hard.

"You're dirty," he said to Stan.

Stan looked very surprised. "Huh?"

The parole officer was taller than Stan, and looked down at him coldly. "You're violated."

Stan's face contorted, then he seemed to get control over himself. "I'm not dirty."

The officer looked at him in his open shirt and bathing suit, sunglasses, brand new Cadillac, his girlfriend with the big tits and the blonde hair, and said, "Bullshit. Up against the car."

"Stan, what's going on?" she asked. She was scared, but Stan looked at her as if he didn't know her. "Stan?" He didn't answer, as the big Mexican man handcuffed him.

"Stan!" she cried. "What about the car?" But neither of them answered as Stan was led into the building. She learned later that he hadn't been sent back to San Quentin, he wasn't going to be punished that hard. They were only sending him to Los Padres National Forest, to a road gang, where he would cut brush for two years.

PART FIVE

Freedom

63.

Charlie hadn't thought about his novel in a long time. He didn't even know where the damn thing was. He'd gotten three big packages of paper from Bill Ratto six or seven years ago, but wasn't sure what he'd done with them. It certainly wasn't in his home office, because he ransacked the office right after Bill called.

"Remember me?" came the fake Ivy League voice over the telephone.

"Are you calling from New York?" Charlie asked, just to seem provincial. But Bill Ratto had left publishing and was now a producer in Hollywood.

"No wonder your voice sounds so clear," Charlie joked.

"I was just sitting here thinking about you. Remember that novel you wrote, that brilliant Korean War novel?"

"Oh, the Korean *War* novel," Charlie said.

Bill Ratto had been thinking. Charlie had disliked the version of his novel that Bill came up with, and Bill had no problem with that, he even tended to agree. "I think I turned a silk purse into a sow's ear," he said. But never mind the past. Bill had the beginnings of an idea. "Why don't we make a movie?" He perfectly agreed with Charlie that it would be foolish of them to get back into the novel per se, but, now consider this, what about using the novel as the source material for a really serious big film about the Korean conflict. "Korea hasn't been done, you know. Not really, not the way we could do it."

"Everybody hates war," Charlie said dryly.

"That's just it!" Bill's voice was filled with enthusiasm. "Everybody hates war. Time has passed. These days everybody agrees with you. It could be one of the great pacifist movies of all time."

Charlie didn't know how to take it. He sat at his desk, killing the morning until he had to go to work. Looking out the window he could see a light haze over the bay. It was going to be a nice warm one. Another perfect day in paradise. "What the fuck are you talking about?" he asked abruptly. "I quit writing years ago."

"Charlie, that was a mistake. Quite possibly you didn't have the skills for writing the novel you set out to write, a very ambitious book. But this is a movie we're talking about here. Movies don't require the same skill level. Are you following me?"

Right into the sewer, Charlie thought, and then was ashamed. There was nothing wrong with movies. Charlie loved movies, especially bullshit movies. "So, what do you want of me?"

What Bill wanted was permission to think about making a movie out of Charlie's manuscript. But he didn't have a copy either of the original or the "modeled" version he'd so painstakingly put together. The version that was more Bill than Charlie.

"I don't know where that fucking thing is," Charlie said. "Maybe we threw it out. That was a long time ago, man."

"It doesn't matter," Bill said. "Could you hold a minute?" And he was gone. Charlie analyzed his feelings. He wasn't a writer, but it didn't hurt anyone. He'd never really been a writer. His literary ambitions, like all his ambitions, were not so much absurd as obsolete. Why bother? Yet what Bill was talking about did sort of interest him. To make a movie would be to get over all those nagging literary problems, and pull the thing straight down into plot and dialogue. As a kid dreaming about his giant war novel, he'd always imagined it would be turned into a giant epic movie, though at the time he was cynical and thought they'd wreck the book if they didn't hire him to write the screenplay, because Hollywood hacks were, well, hacks. No wonder he was being sarcastic. He didn't want to get his hopes up. Poor Little Charlie.

"Are you there?" Bill asked. "Here's what I had in mind. Find that book, read it over, think about it, and give me a ring."

Charlie hung up and looked at his watch. He was working the eleven to six shift at the no name bar. The bar opened at eleven thirty to accommodate the Sausalito alcoholics, but he still had an hour before he had to leave home. He could look for the manuscript. He felt calm, but there was a film of sweat on his brow that hadn't been there before. Maybe the call made him more nervous than he cared to admit. Was he still ambitious? His old novel had been ambitious, so ambitious, so full of shit. Also the center of his life for ten years, until he met Jaime. Like his first child. She, he, and Bill Ratto, a man he didn't quite like, go out into Potter's Field, dig up the little corpse, clean off the dirt, put makeup over the corruption, and sell the body to the American public? Hmm.

"What's in it for me?" Charlie asked the air. He had to laugh. The notion of making money, a great deal of money, appealed just fine. At least it would be a change. As a bartender he wasn't pulling in all that much, in fact, he couldn't have afforded to live where he lived on his income. Thank God for Jaime and goddamn books. Not that he hated her books. He didn't. He loved them. They kept him in Mill Valley. But they also seemed to keep Jaime out of Mill Valley. She'd come home for a week, two weeks, even a month, and then she'd be off again, either traveling or over in North Beach at the apartment, writing. She wrote there even though Charlie had often told her she could have his damned office at home. All Charlie used it for was to read or sleep on his couch. But if Jaime stayed home she stopped writing. Her absence might seem to offer him a wonderful freedom, but freedom to do what?

Charlie lit a joint, the first of the day. Good thing Bill hadn't called after he turned on, he would have talked his ear off and probably flown down to Hollywood that morning. Pot really made Charlie feel good, but it also made him talkative and easy to manipulate. Which is how he liked to be.

After looking in vain for the manuscript, he walked out through the French doors to the lawn. The haze was clearing and the sky was going to be pure blue. Charlie took his third hit and pinched out the roach, sticking it into his watch pocket. He'd take another couple of hits when he parked, so his stroll down Bridgeway to work would be enlightened by the dope. At work throughout the afternoon people would come in with a variety of things to give away, and being in the spotlight as the bartender meant he got a lot of free stuff from admirers—coke, hash, weed, acid, codeine, Percodan, bennies, amps, meth, barbs, seconal, a whole pharmacopoeia of friendly little helpers, which Charlie knew had to be taken in moderation or avoided entirely, since he didn't want to turn into an addict. He'd sample one one day, another another day, and the stuff that was passed to him routinely he'd pocket and then give away to friends. Neil Davis didn't know about it, or if he did he kept his mouth shut. For Charlie it was part of the new spirit of anti-government. The only hopeful sign anywhere.

Charlie walked around the house to the garage, where their battered old Porsche waited for him. Jaime didn't drive to the city anymore. She'd take the bus or let Charlie drive her, but they'd given up the garage as too expensive, and parking on the street was impossible. Charlie sold his old Volkswagen, practically the only valuable thing he owned, and they were a one-car family. The dusty black Porsche showed a rusty crease down the right side, where Jaime had drunkenly scraped something one night. Poor old thing needed a wash. Not Jaime, the car. He wanted to call her at the apartment, but this was her peak working time, and anyway Charlie had been smoking and she could tell it. Jaime was fierce about drugs around Kira. If they were caught with drugs in their house they could both be arrested and hauled off to jail, and then Kira would be stuck in a foster home, and how would he like that? He wouldn't. But it wouldn't happen. He didn't let Kira see him smoking dope because he didn't want to encourage her to use it. Charlie got into the car and started it up with a nice throaty roar. Driving stoned was fun. Every trip down the hill a ride on the marijuana rollercoaster. Halfway down the hill he remembered his call from Hollywood, and began to daydream about writing a movie, a big movie, a big war movie.

64.

After school or in the summer, Kira sometimes took the bus to Sausalito to spend the afternoon on Bridgeway. Charlie didn't mind, so long as she got her schoolwork done. Though he was never quite sure with Kira, who could be an extraordinarily adept liar. Bridgeway was a circus, the shops and sidewalks crowded with tourists, especially now in summer, so you couldn't drive through town in under an hour. Colorful hippies, leisure-suited Midwesterners, Japanese in their blue suits and white shirts, waterfront people, street people, anything you wanted. Kira and a lot of other kids hung out on the steps or bummed change from the tourists, which Charlie tried to forbid. Kira looked at him with her big dark eyes and said she wouldn't, but she was always spending money Charlie hadn't given her. She was tall for her age, and had been having her periods since she was ten, so Charlie also had to worry about Sausalito street philosophy, which suggested that if you were old enough to bleed, you were old enough to butcher. At twelve Kira was tall, skinny, and incredibly beautiful, at least from her father's point of view, and could pass for fourteen. Plenty of runaway hippies that age came through Sausalito, and might tempt his daughter into a life of empty leisure.

Exactly the life he led himself, if you stopped and considered it. Working behind the bar at the no name wasn't exactly leisure, unless you compared it to the life he should have been leading. Working as a bartender, Charlie didn't have to exert himself, didn't have to think, didn't have to face any hard conclusions. He stood on the plank and grinned and gave people what they wanted. He arbitrated disputes, gave advice to the lovelorn, guided destinies, and never had to take responsibility for the results. He was a bartender, what did you expect?

He often saw Kira afternoons. He hoped to today. To see her was to experience five minutes of relief, to know she was okay at least for the moment. Then she'd vanish. Jaime didn't worry about Kira nearly as much as Charlie, but then when Jaime was home Kira didn't come down to Bridgeway. She stayed home with her mother. They'd whisper together or go off in the car, and when Jaime was in residence there'd be kids over at the house, bunches of squealing girls, from whose activities Charlie was naturally excluded. His daughter was getting as normal a life as they could provide, given the circumstances. Kira did miss her mother, they both missed Jaime, but the advantage went to Kira, who spoke with Jaime on the telephone every day. And Jaime sometimes took Kira for a weekend in the city, and Charlie would be left alone. Not that he minded. Working afternoons took it out of him, and sometimes he'd just come home, wolf dinner, and go straight to bed. Of course usually by that time he'd be full of drugs, his head buzzing, his body in a pleasant state of nonexistence, or apparent nonexistence.

Kira's face appeared in the open window at the front of the bar. She rested her arms on the windowsill and her chin on her hands. "Hi, Dad."

"Hold on," Charlie said. The bar wasn't busy, so he wiped his hands and went outside, blinking into the brightness. Kira leaned against the building, her arms crossed. She wore jeans and her red blouse, and looked about eight to Charlie. "You okay?" he asked her.

"I'm fine. Can I have five dollars?"

"No."

"Okay," she said, which worried him.

"What do you want the money for?"

"It doesn't matter."

He reached into his pocket and gave her two dollars. "Make that do," he said.

She smiled, took the money, and turned and ran down Bridgeway, slipping in amongst the people. Charlie's heart nearly broke. So delicate, so beautiful, in a life that was so dangerous. He'd wanted to tell her about his call from Ratto, but she hadn't allowed him the opening. Both his daughter and his wife were smarter than he was, at least about practical matters. Well, fine, maybe Kira would take care of him in his old age. *Don't plan for the future*, his heart warned him. *Children die*. He returned to the bar.

When he got home that night Kira was there, sitting in the living room watching television. Mrs. Hawkins was in the kitchen making dinner, which smelled like pork chops. Mrs. Hawkins was only a few years older than Charlie, perhaps forty-five, and came over every day to clean and cook, going home to Marin if she wasn't needed after dinner, or staying on as baby-sitter until either Charlie or Jaime came home. She was from Lacoumbe, Louisiana. She had mahogany skin and a cheerful singsong voice. Kira loved her, and Charlie almost did. Mrs. Hawkins was their anchor. Charlie yelled hello and went into the bathroom. When he came out he sat on the couch behind Kira, who was on the rug.

"Have you talked to your mother?"

Kira turned and lay on the rug looking up. "Yes," she said.

"She still working?"

"I don't think so," Kira said. "She was pretty drunk." She rolled back over to watch the news.

Charlie laughed and said, "I'll give her a call." But there was no answer when he did. He wondered if she was down at Enrico's drinking. Or maybe at the corner store, talking to Old Rose, the Chinese woman who ran the place. Or she could be at the Caffe Sport, wining it up with the junior Mafia. Or just asleep, unable to answer the phone. Or in bed with somebody. He wished Kira didn't know Jaime was drunk so much of the time, but what hypocrisy to keep it hidden. Even if they could keep it hidden.

"I think I'll go into town," he said aloud, and Kira turned and faced him again. "I wanna go with you."

"I'm sorry, I won't be home until late."

Kira got up and sat beside him. Her warmth made him almost tearful. She was so fragile. She gave him her most innocent look and said, "Are you going to rescue Mother?"

He laughed and put his arm around her, pulling her warmth to him, as if he could keep her alive with his own life. Why was he worried about her mortality? He tried to remember what drugs he'd taken that day. None, unless you counted marijuana. "Kira," he said, reaching for his deepest, most confident voice. "Your mother is just fine."

"Then why are you so sad?"

No point trying to fool her. He gave her a big hug and kissed her on top of her head. The three ate at the dining room table, Mrs. Hawkins keeping her eyes to her plate as always. After dinner Charlie very deliberately showered and shaved, dressed in fresh jeans and a fresh blue work shirt. Mill Valley was warm tonight, but San Francisco might be foggy. He put on the old black leather jacket Jaime had given him. He looked at himself in their full length mirror. A big man, tall and thick, with a bushy dark red beard streaked with white. He looked into his own big brown eyes. Was anybody in there? He didn't know.

65.

Charlie walked through the evening crowds on Columbus, his hands in his jacket pockets, wondering which way to go. Jaime wasn't likely to be at City Lights or Vesuvio, it was too early for Tosca, and besides, they didn't like any of these places quite as much as in the past. More likely either Enrico's, sitting at the bar, or up at Gino and Carlo's. Or at any one of a hundred other bars. Or a party in Pacific Heights. A literary party.

He walked down to Enrico's. The outside tables were full but there were only a couple of people at the little bar. Charlie sat and waited for Ward the bartender to come over. Ward was a huge man, probably twenty pounds heavier than Charlie, but all muscle.

"Have you seen Jaime?" Charlie asked when Ward came over, just to get it out of the way.

"Who wants to know?" Ward growled. Then he smiled. "She's in the toilet." He went to the other end of the bar, picked up a half-finished glass of something and a napkin and brought them over. "I guess she'll be sitting with you," he said reluctantly. Because they were both so big, Charlie and Ward pretended to be antagonists.

"Yeah, well, I'll have what she's having," Charlie said, to cover his feelings of relief. When Jaime slipped onto the barstool next to him he was drinking his drink, gin and tonic, ugh.

"Hi, honey," she said, and leaned her cheek against his arm. She didn't seem too drunk. He put his arm around her and kissed her hair.

"Hi, sweetie," he said.

"You got here just in time," she said. She straightened up and drank some gin and tonic. "I was about to leave. Now we can have a drink together, and you can take me home." She put her hands in her jacket pockets. "I talked to Kira," she said. "I knew you were coming."

"How are you?" Charlie asked. "You okay enough to listen to something, or should I wait until morning?"

She smiled, looking into her drink. "How serious is it? If it's serious, let's wait."

"It's not serious." He told her about Bill Ratto's call. Her face hardened, and she held up a finger for Ward, who came over. She ordered two more drinks and then started going through her pockets again. She was in her green velour jacket with the puffy shoulders.

"Are you searching for a cigarette?" Charlie asked. "We quit, remember?"

"Just a habit," she said. They'd both quit smoking a couple of years ago, and had almost divorced over it. Now she smiled. "I've been waiting for Hollywood to call, and they call *you*," she said. "What's that shit about?"

Jaime's second book had been optioned for a television series, but nothing had happened except that she made a lot of option money over the years, and they finally let it lapse. Of course her first book had been bought outright by the late Joseph E. Levine and then let die. Jaime always claimed that she hated Hollywood but loved their money.

"I think it's a chance at some gold," he said.

"Gee, you aren't going to do it, are you?" she asked, and laughed.

"What the fuck else am I doing? Neil can take me off shift for a few weeks, I'll fly to Hollywood, gather a few pesos and fly right back home. Wanna come?"

She pretended incredulity. "Me?" Then her face changed. She was drunker than she looked. "I'm sorry," she said. "You're serious. And he did call. Of course, we'll go down there and beard the lion. We could also duck the fog for a while, no? Get a suite in a nice hotel and play movie star."

"I'll call the bastard tomorrow." Charlie waved at Ward. "Bring me a Wild Turkey, Ward, please?"

Jaime was deep in a long story she thought might actually turn out to be a novel, or a novelette, or novella, whatever the hell you call them. Short novel. She'd been writing short stories lately, a string of them, and getting them mostly printed in the *New Yorker*. She talked of her work for a while, while Charlie had his Wild Turkey.

Then he said to his wife of twelve years, "Okay, what do you want to do?" They both looked through the glass at the people sitting outside at the marble tables. High grade drunks, the cream of San Francisco bar society.

"I want to fuck that girl over there," Jaime said, pointing to a beautiful woman in a red evening dress, who sat at a table full of dressed-up people. The men looked like lawyers. Charlie, too, would have liked to screw the woman in the red dress, but he only smiled at Jaime.

"I mean us," he said. "Shall we hit another bar, or do you want to cross the river? We could stop at the no name for a night. Or not. Or I could take you up to the apartment. Entirely up to you."

"I'm sick of the apartment," she said, putting hope in his heart. She put her hand on his cheek, her eyes almost wet with tears. "But I gotta stay. The old bitch won't let me." Charlie knew she meant that the story was keeping her. She wouldn't come until it was done. Again he realized why she was a writer and he wasn't. She was mystical about the work. The work really did come first. For Charlie the work had come first only until he'd met her. Then her, and Kira. Something had somehow put Jaime out of reach of these feelings. He'd read her first novel, about her wonderful family life, and couldn't see anything there to make her this way. The only way she could love her family was to write about them.

Charlie smiled at her sadly. "Let's have one more," he said. "And I'll walk you home."

She smiled glassily. "I love you," she said, and giggled.

66.

Charlie was met at LAX by a driver holding up a sign with his name on it. Actually the best part of the trip was getting into the limousine, Charlie's first. He hoped his fellow passengers on the commuter flight could see him now. Him in his Levi's, boots, garbage shirt, and black leather jacket. Them in their commuter suits. He knew he looked like a dope dealer or a rock musician, and they'd put him through the mill at SFO, making him put his hands against the wall while the little airport cops searched his bags and patted him down. They missed the baggie of marijuana he carried in his hip pocket under his dirty handkerchief.

"I'm Charles Monel," he said to the driver, who was a young guy, thin, with very dark glasses and pale skin. The driver pulled open the back door and Charlie grinned at him. "Thanks," he said, and bumped his head getting in. Bill Ratto's sweet-voiced secretary had sent Charlie tickets and asked which hotel he'd prefer. Charlie didn't know anything about L.A. hotels, so the secretary put him into the Beverly Wilshire. All the way there, driving mostly on backstreets and avoiding freeways, the driver talked about his own Hollywood ambitions.

"I'm not like most of the drivers," he said. "They're all writers or actors. I'm gonna produce." He explained that in Hollywood only the man who controlled the purse strings had any creative power. "Everybody else has to suck his ass," the driver said. His eyes met Charlie's in the mirror. "Can I give you some advice?" he asked Charlie.

"Sure."

"Don't rub your eyes. It just makes it worse."

Charlie stopped. "What the hell is it?"

"Particulate matter," the driver said.

Charlie's room at the Wilshire was nice, nothing special. He'd somehow been expecting luxury. There was a little red blinking light on his telephone. The message was from Bill, asking him to call at once.

"Charlie! How do you like Southern California?" Charlie couldn't think of an answer and Bill didn't wait for one. "I need to do a couple of things around here, then we can have lunch right downstairs in your hotel."

Charlie found the restaurant, El Padilla, in the back of the hotel. He gave his name to the uniformed waiter, who took him to a banquette. The room was about three-quarters full, and buzzing. Charlie felt a kind of nervous excitement that had nothing to do with his meeting. What if a star walked in? Instead Bill Ratto slid in next to him and told the hovering waiter to bring them menus and a telephone. So every cliché was to be played out. Bill was wearing a suit and tie and had tucked his sunglasses into his lapel pocket, one temple bar hanging out raffishly. His shirt was white, his tie was silk, but still he looked Hollywood. The tan, maybe. Bill's plump face had thinned, and his hair receded. He no longer looked like an owl, more like a hawk. A cartoon hawk.

He turned to Charlie and stuck out his hand. "We're meeting my partner," he said. "Meanwhile, how are you? You look great, a little heavy, but good. How's your wife?"

"Jaime is fine," Charlie said. She hadn't come because her story had turned into something longer. "Don't let them fix you up with any actresses," she said, and kissed him wetly. Kira wanted a tee shirt from Hollywood.

The waiter plugged in the telephone, and with an apologetic smile Bill picked up the instrument and talked quietly into it. Charlie picked up the menu, trying not to listen. When he put down the menu another man was coming toward them, smiling brilliantly. He was very good-looking in a Hollywood way, with dark hair, and dressed in jeans and a collarless blue work shirt. He reached for Charlie's hand.

"You have to be Charles Monel," he said. "I'm Bud Fishkin." Fishkin's handshake was firm and dry. Fishkin slid into the booth and asked for a menu and a telephone. Now Charlie was surrounded by producers with telephones, murmuring into the instruments while Charlie tried not to be embarrassed. But of course no one was looking at them and no one was laughing. Without being obvious, Charlie started listening to the conversations. Ratto was talking to his secretary, going through the phone calls that had come in since he left his office. Fishkin was talking to his agent. Charlie felt like calling the waiter over and getting his own instrument, so he could call Jaime and tell her she was missing a pretty funny lunch.

"Bill tells me you were in Korea," Bud Fishkin said in a warm voice after he hung up. "I must say, you look the part."

Ratto said, "We have an idea for your picture, but first I'd like to explain a few things. Remember your book?"

Charlie smiled. "Yes."

"Well, not exactly like that, but the spirit of that. Novels are thick. Movies are flat. We want to flatten your novel, but retain the same intensity, the same flavor. That's why we'd like you to work with us on the script. If you'd like to. If it wouldn't piss you off too much."

"Novels get raped and murdered in Hollywood," Fishkin said with a warm smile. "Lots of times the book writer is too protective. We felt you might not be this way since your book was never published. So you've got nothing to live down, nothing to defend."

"I see," said Charlie. "You want me to help with the raping and killing."

Fishkin laughed. "You can be first." Both Charlie and Ratto laughed.

"What's in it for me?" Charlie asked, dabbing at his eyes with a big, red napkin.

"Wait a minute, wait a minute, I take that question seriously," said Fishkin. "What's in it for you is, first, your novel will now see the light of day, although in somewhat different form. This should be or could be of great creative satisfaction, and all that shit. Then there's the money. There can be a hell of a lot of money in a movie, money you don't even think about, residual rights, foreign sales, television series, electronic rights, it goes on and on. And if you make a name for yourself as a screenwriter, you can get pretty rich. And you can acquire greater control."

"That's important," Ratto said. "Because with this first script you won't have much control. That has to be earned."

"You have to learn the ropes," said Fishkin with a smile.

"What's the plot of my movie?" Charlie asked. The waiter came up, and Charlie noticed that neither of the other men ordered anything to drink except coffee. Charlie did the same. He wasn't going to get blasted and let them take advantage.

After the waiter left, Fishkin and Ratto exchanged a look, as if to say, You or me? Then Ratto said, "Let me. The movie's about you, Charlie. A war hero who gets captured by the Chinese, then has to survive the prison camp, even though he has tuberculosis. It's about survival."

"It's about winning over evil," said Fishkin.

"I doesn't sound much like my book," Charlie said. Fishkin raised an eyebrow.

"Really? Describe your novel in one sentence. The sentence you'd see later in *TV Guide.*"

Charlie thought a moment, then said thoughtfully, "A bunch of assholes get caught in a war."

"I love it!" said Fishkin.

67.

Jaime loved North Beach in the mornings. It was like a Mediterranean village on a hill, bright clean blue sky, empty streets and narrow alleyways. Jaime liked to get up with the sun, shower, dress, and walk down the hill to the Caffe Trieste for an espresso with chocolate sprinkled on it, perhaps a brioche if she didn't have too bad a hangover. The place at that hour was always busy, people standing at the little counter arguing in Sicilian or Italian with the people behind the counter, scavengers out on the street in front, having their espressos after a hard morning picking up San Francisco's garbage. Jaime loved these people. They knew her, at least by sight, and nearly every morning the young men out front would say things about her in Italian and laugh. It had taken years for her to be served promptly inside. She was never sure whether this was because she wasn't Italian or wasn't male. But now they'd start her espresso right away, singing out, "Jaime! Brioche today?" while others waited impatiently. Then she'd sit with her back to the window and read whatever paper was lying around, smelling the hot chocolate, the Italian cigar smoke, hearing the hissing of the espresso machines and the loud conversations all around her. It was her daily moment of humanity before returning to isolation and work.

With Charlie in Hollywood Jaime had to interrupt her routine and go home to Mill Valley to be with her daughter. Jaime couldn't write at home with Charlie there, which broke her heart. Charlie would be so considerate of her privacy and her need for a smooth quiet routine, always offering his own office, but all that self-sacrifice on his part made her too sad to work. How could she explain this to Charlie without hurting him? "I can't work here because you're a failure." She assumed Charlie understood, but it was a little catch between them, one more thing they couldn't be open about. They mounted up, these silent catches.

When Charlie flew to L.A. Jaime had two choices, go home to work, or bring Kira to the city. She feared leaving Kira to wander around North Beach while she wrote. Kira was not only too tall for her age, she was too smart, too curious, to self-reliant. So Jaime went home. It was supposed to be for the one night, but Charlie called up and said he'd been invited out to Malibu for the weekend. "To talk shop," he said, without a trace of humor, so she was stuck for three days. She brought her manuscript and her Hermes portable, but Kira seemed to have decided that she wouldn't let her mother work. On Friday they drove to Stinson Beach and walked along the wet sand looking for sea shells. Kira seemed to know the names of all the shells, green rock oysters, purple-hinged scallops, sand dollars, turban snails, etc. and etc., always running ahead of her mother and picking up whatever glittered, discarding the imperfect shells and putting the others into her pants pockets. There were dogs on the beach, and Kira ran and played with the dogs, although she claimed she didn't want a dog of her own. She'd been told she'd have to take care of any pets, so she'd said, typical Kira, "Then I don't want any." Yet her room was full of dead butterflies, dragonflies, dried mushrooms, pictures of wolves and hawks, as well as the usual stuffed animals and children's books.

Jaime had never been happy with Charlie's quitting writing. She understood his terrible pain when he had to reject publication of a butchered version, Bill Ratto's vain attempt to play Maxwell Perkins, but she expected after a year or so of working as a bartender Charlie would come to his senses and get back to his desk. But no. After all these years he seemed perfectly content to tend bar and support her writing, as if he were secondary in their marriage. She knew better. This Hollywood thing really worried her, Ratto again, not letting Charlie get on with his life. Another battering for Charlie, coming up.

But when she met him at the airport Charlie was explosively cheerful. "Jesus H. Christ, it's good to be back in San Francisco!" he said. "You can't imagine what that fucking place is like. You can't even rub your eyes." But the energy bubbling up out of him had a different source, she was certain. That night, lying in the darkness after making love, he talked quietly about his visit, about what these producers had in mind and how he felt about it.

"I think I can beat these guys. They're not dumb or anything, but it's so obvious what they want."

"What?" she asked.

"They want to win." He put his hand on her stomach and rubbed her gently. "I love your stomach," he said.

"And I love yours," she said. "How do you beat them? If they're so set on winning?"

"By helping them win," Charlie said. He chuckled as if he had discovered a great secret.

He really wanted to try Hollywood. Her own bad experiences made her hate the business, though she'd made money. Never again would she sell a book outright. Her first and possibly her best, certainly the most widely read of her books, was now buried under the corpse of Joseph E. Levine, late of Embassy Pictures, then Avco-Embassy, and now God knows what corporate monstrosity. And she'd been so thoroughly rolled by the television people who'd optioned *Judy Bell* that she automatically wanted to vomit when she heard the words, "I have great news!"

When they met, Charlie had seem relaxed about political ideas. "I got my Marxism from a different nipple," he said, laughing at those who hoped to save the world. Then Vietnam came rudely in everyone's lives, and she and Charlie stood outdoors with ten thousand people at a Berkeley soccer field listening to Dick Gregory and Norman Mailer exhorting them all to defiance. They'd cheered that day with the rest, but after a while Charlie got disenchanted with the anti-war movement. "They're attacking troop trains," he told her. "Fuck 'em."

"But those soldiers—" she started.

"Those soldiers have no choice," he said.

They were in the Coffee Gallery, drinking ale. "They could choose civil disobedience," Jaime insisted. She'd read Thoreau, knew what she was talking about.

"Civil disobedience is something you do alone," he said mysteriously.

He was against the war and against the war-resisters. No man's land for Charlie. He'd never killed anybody, but he'd tried. She feared what might be going on under the surface, though he was nearly always his old cheery helpful self. You can't spend ten years of your life writing a novel without leaving a lot of yourself in it. Each book is like a child, not just in a metaphor but in your heart, and a bad fate for your child hurts terribly. Charlie was very badly wounded, and Jaime wasn't at all sure what effect Hollywood might have on her damaged hero.

68.

Jaime called her friend Susan Beskie at the Zeigler-Ross Agency, who handled her for dramatic rights, and asked her to look into Charlie's possible deal with Ratto. Jaime had never actually met Susan and imagined her as tall and thin, with steel-rimmed glasses and short straight hair. Her voice was high and thin, more reassuring to Jaime than a sensual voice might have been. And she was an enthusiastic agent, wanting to help Jaime finally get rich from her writing.

"My husband wrote a novel a long time ago," Jaime began. She told her about *The End of the War* and Bill Ratto's interest in making it into a movie. "Do you know Bill Ratto?" she asked.

"Oh yes," Susan said. She said she'd look into it and get back to Jaime, but it was Evarts Ziegler who called at a little after six. He sounded tired. He asked for Charlie, and when Jaime said he wasn't home, Ziegler said, "Ask him to call me. I think we can work something out."

Charlie made the call the next morning, impatient for ten o'clock, when the agencies opened. He couldn't eat his breakfast, and went into the yard to walk up and down with his hands behind his back. He's combative, Jaime thought. He really wants to get into this. She wasn't sure this made her happy. Anything, sure, to get him out of bartending, but Hollywood was the virtual center of broken dreams. Maybe that was what drew him.

"You could call it 'Private Lazarus'," she said at lunch. She and Charlie and Kira were having a rare lunch together, in honor of Ziegler's agreement to "look into" Charlie's deal. They were on the deck of the Trident, watching the sailboats on the bay.

"'Sergeant Lazarus,'" he corrected with a smile.

"I'm getting jealous," she said.

"What about?" Kira asked. She was eating a gigantic hamburger.

"Daddy's going to Hollywood," Mommy said.

"I'm not kidding myself," Charlie said to Jaime. "I know what they want. A nice big splashy war movie, with an anti-war message."

"Isn't that what you want?" Jaime asked.

A man of about thirty with long greasy dark hair and an American flag shirt came grinning up to them, especially at Kira. "Charlie," the guy said, "Where'd you get this one?"

Kira looked up at the man briefly and then back down at her hamburger. Charlie smiled, though Jaime could tell he was angry. "This is my daughter," he said.

"Hey, great," the guy said, his eyes still on Kira. Then the message seemed to get through, and he backed away. "Oh," he said.

Charlie watched him leave the deck. "Probably a little stoned," he said, irritated. "I want to make the movie right," he said. "And it can still be a big splashy war movie and make a fortune. Only no John Wayne."

Jaime was surprised. "They want John Wayne?"

Charlie laughed. "His people probably won't even call back. You know, they didn't say a word to me about an agent."

"Don't get paranoid."

Charlie smiled at her, but there was something wrong with his face. "You know that Buddhist line about desiring causing suffering?" She nodded. "I really did put my novel away. I was finished with it. I stopped desiring, I really did. You know, like the fucking TB. You lay there spitting up blood like Old Faithful, and you tell yourself it will either end or you'll die first. It's the will to live that fucks you up. You have to give up on that, and I did. The reason I made it was because I didn't care. You know what I mean?"

"I do," Kira said.

"I'm sorry, honey," Charlie said to his daughter. "I didn't mean to talk like this in front of you."

Kira gave Jaime a look that said *Men.*

So they'd brought his desire back to life, Jaime understood. Charlie had been in suspended animation, because the only thing he really wanted had been denied him. And now it was again being offered, by what kind of under-the-rock Hollywood scum she didn't know. She couldn't protect Charlie. She couldn't even protect herself. Not from this stuff.

The call came the next morning at eight-twenty, so Evarts Ziegler got to the office early when he needed to. Charlie took the call in his office and came out with sweat on his forehead.

"What's up?" she asked.

Charlie sat at the dining room table with Jaime and tapped his finger on the tablecloth in a very irritating manner. He sighed and Jaime waited. "Well," he said finally, "I'm guess maybe I'm gonna go down there for a while."

Jaime was surprised. "You mean move to Hollywood?"

He raised his eyebrows defensively. "What should I do?" Ratto and Fishkin had offered Charlie fifteen hundred per week for six weeks, renewable to twelve, to come south and work with them on a script. "What is that?" he asked her.

"It's either nine or eighteen grand," she said. "And you won't have to give it back."

"We could use the money."

"We sure could."

"Why do I feel so stupid?" Charlie asked her. Kira came into the room at that moment, dressed in her blue and black bathing suit, which was too loose around the leg holes, giving her a raffish look. She was getting so tall. She heard Charlie's last remark and waited for Jaime's answer. But Jaime didn't have one.

They drove Charlie to the airport, Kira scrunched up in the back seat. Jaime was upset, but Kira was really upset. On the way back to Marin County Kira announced that she, too, wished to move to Los Angeles.

"I hate Marin," she said. "Everyone's so perfect. I was thinking about moving to San Francisco with you and going to school there. But this is better. I can live with Daddy and go to Hollywood High."

"I doubt you'd like Los Angeles," Jaime said like a true parent.

"It's not Los Angeles so much," Kira said.

"What do you mean?"

Kira explained that she preferred her father to her mother. "If you ever split up," she said. "I want to go with him."

69.

Kenny Goss was having problems.

He'd become Charlie's friend, hanging out at the no name bar when his ship was in port. Kenny had worked aboard the *Breckenridge* for nearly five years, steadily writing the whole time, but getting nowhere. At first he'd tried short stories, but no one would buy them or even comment on them except to send him printed rejection slips. He had no idea what he was doing wrong, or even if he *was* doing wrong. Maybe he was doing right, and *they* were wrong. He couldn't know. After a while he put his heart in his mouth and showed a story to Charlie, handing it to him right across the bar. "See what you think," was all he could say. The respect Charlie showed was at least encouraging. "I'll put these with my coat," he said, and carefully carried the manuscript into the back room. He said he'd read the story that night.

"What do you want to hear?" he asked.

Kenny was surprised. "What you think," he said. "Not praise," he added, and Charlie nodded.

"Good," he said.

Kenny went home across the bridge, to his little apartment at Jackson and Larkin, over the Chinese laundry. Usually he wrote at night, but with Charlie reading his story he couldn't. By 4:00 a.m. he was certain Charlie would tell him to stop writing. He didn't really know why Charlie's opinion mattered to him. Charlie had never published anything. But he had a good mind. Kenny'd never met a bartender with a better mind.

Charlie smiled and said, "I can see what's wrong right away." He handed Kenny his pages, and Kenny automatically rolled them in his hands.

"Bad stuff," Kenny said, nodding.

"No, you asshole. Your work is beautiful. But it's too intricate."

"Intricate?" He'd never thought of his work as intricate.

"I don't mean too intricate," Charlie said. "I mean too intricate for the people you're showing it to. *Playboy* isn't going to buy a story about a guy who's obsessed with the sound of his own blood. They probably wouldn't even know what you're talking about."

Writing is really strange, Kenny thought. You can write and write and never know what the hell you're doing. He hadn't written a story about a guy who was obsessed with the sound of his own blood. He'd written about how *fascinating* it is to listen to your own blood.

"Why don't you write for children?" Charlie asked, and changed Kenny's life. It was as if his whole life had been just a little off-register until now, when Charlie touched it into place. Children. Of course. They were the only ones he trusted. They were the ones he would write for. He and Charlie stared at each other over the bar. Kenny searched his mind for words.

"Aren't I too intricate for children?" he asked.

"Oh, hell no," Charlie said easily, and moved off to fix a drink for somebody.

Later Charlie introduced Kenny to his wife and, as they sat in front of the bar drinking beer on a Sunday afternoon, they discovered a common thread between them. Kenny had helped Jaime's mother, long ago, when her father died and her mother had to sell all her stuff. She would have been ripped off if it hadn't been for Kenny, and he was proud of what he'd done.

"My mother told me somebody helped her," Jaime said, and touched him on the wrist. "That some marvelous person had come out of nowhere to save her from the vultures." She gave him a beautiful smile. "My mother will be so happy to know I've met you," she said. She explained that her mother had married and was living in a place called Troutdale, east of Portland. After that, any time Kenny saw Jaime in Sausalito or North Beach they would get together like old buddies. Karma, Kenny thought. I did a good thing and now I'm getting it back. Because he loved Jaime. She could *really* write.

And she confirmed Charlie's opinion on his work. "You're great!" she said, and immediately begged Kenny to let her send something of his to a children's book editor at Harper & Row, just to show the kind of writer he was. The editor wrote back enthusiastically, and launched Kenny into his first deliberate children's book. But once he'd made clear to himself who his audience was, the writing became more difficult. He liked children. They didn't bullshit you. Not the little ones. So there was this terrible obligation not to bullshit *them*. For Kenny it was a credo: No Bullshit.

Another change came into his life when he decided he finally couldn't stomach another week out on the sandbar. Working aboard the dredge wasn't just boring, it was maddening, and though the money and hours were excellent, better than he could do elsewhere, Kenny finally quit. Now he had a future. But in order to live without plundering his savings, he looked for and got a job in the book business, this time working for a rare bookstore specializing in Western Americana. Instead of going around looking for books in Goodwills and people's houses, Kenny spent his days looking through warehouses and estate sales, not so much looking for sleepers as cataloging, examining for condition, and pricing.

Just as bad a job as dredging sand, except for one thing. His boss, Calvin Whipple, who'd been doing the same kind of work all his life, first for his grandfather and then for his father and now for himself, kept a large fishbowl brandy glass on his desk about half full of white pills. Kenny was welcome to take as many as he wanted. The pills kept you alert, and at first naïve Kenny had thought they were NoDoz or some other caffeine stuff. They certainly helped with the work, but then he had trouble writing nights unless he took a pill first, and then he found that instead of getting four or five hours of sleep at night, he got none. He'd work all day, go home and write all night, then shower, eat some white sugar or something, and head up for work again. On his days off he'd drive over to Sausalito in his old white Chevy pickup and try to relax, drinking beer and looking out the window at the tourists. He told himself he was looking for girls, but since the advent of the little white pills he'd not been horny, and all he was really trying to do was drink enough beer to make him sleepy.

Every once in a while he'd drink with Jaime, and they'd talk about writing. He wanted to tell her about the amphetamines, but couldn't. She might lose respect for him if she knew. And then one night he found himself wandering the streets of North Beach with the overwhelming sense that the world was about to come apart. All the people he was seeing were already dead, just walking around, like himself, dead but unable to stop. He felt a great welling love for humanity in the hour of its death, and saw everyone in a shimmering halo of light. And then he found himself face-to-face with Jaime. She was staring at him. It was at night, they were on the street.

"Help me," he heard himself saying from a long distance away.

"Of course," she said. They drove over to the University of California hospital in her Porsche and waited in the big waiting room. A girl there, with her mother, suffered a headache, and Kenny wanted to die in sympathy. When the doctor saw Kenny he told him he couldn't help him. The doctor was younger than Kenny and his face wore an expression of dislike. They left the hospital and Jaime said she'd take him home to Mill Valley, but Kenny said no. She drove him to Jackson and Larkin.

"I'm just fucked up on drugs," he finally admitted. They parked in front of the laundry. It was six in the morning.

"Come over to our house," she said. "Charlie's in Los Angeles. You can sleep in his office. Just until you get off the drugs."

Kenny had to say, "I don't want to." He must have been painful to look at, because Jaime turned away. When she turned back there was a beautiful compassion on her face. "Okay," she said. She touched his cheek.

Kenny got out of the car and watched it drive off. Beautiful car, he thought, and went into his building and up the stairs, being as quiet as he could. Once inside he washed down a couple of pills and lay down to sleep. But he did not sleep.

70.

The first surprising thing about Hollywood was how much he liked it. Ratto's secretary had gotten him "a suite of rooms" at the Tropicana Motel on Santa Monica, which turned out to be a dinky smelly pair of rooms with a noisy little refrigerator, stove, a red linoleum countertop that looked as if somebody had been chopping things on it, and a dirty old green shag carpet throughout. The smell was complex. He could identify piss, shit, vomit, stale wine, perfume, and tobacco smoke, but there were other, more elusive flavors. The bed was too hard and the Mexican maid came into the room any time she wanted. There was a little restaurant downstairs that was famous for its breakfasts, but the place was always jammed with the rock musicians who seemed to be the motel's only other clientele. Charlie loved the place immediately. He felt right at home. The rockers were friendly and always laughed when he said he was a writer. "Writer, huh?"

He'd hoped to make it through without a car, but that was impossible. He rented a Volkswagen bug from Dollar-A-Day, which cost him six dollars a day, and drove to the studio each morning just like a regular office worker. Fishkin-Ratto was at 20th Century Fox, about two miles from the motel, and Charlie would show up for work at around ten. The day would be spent sitting in either Ratto's or Fishkin's office. The boys, as he began to call them in his mind, had several projects other than Charlie's, but while he was in town they tried to concentrate on his. The first day they sat in Bill's office with the door shut and talked about war and war movies in general. Ethyl the secretary was instructed to hold all calls, and they put in a full day. At around five thirty Bill pulled a bottle of Jim Beam from his desk drawer and buzzed Ethyl to bring in the setups. They had a couple of drinks, an evening ritual, and talked about casting. Charlie was amazed at the range of actors mentioned to play the character based on him, but after a couple of days he understood not to take seriously anything that was talked about over the evening drinks. By this point phone-call prohibition was breached and somebody was on the phone all the time. Sometimes Charlie had to go out and sit in the secretary's office. He learned patience from Ethyl, a woman of about forty who'd been a Hollywood secretary all her life. Between phone calls or errands she knitted. "I get a lot done here," she told Charlie. Fishkin's secretary shared the office and herself did crocheting.

Every day they talked about the story. After a while Charlie could see some trends. Fishkin saw it as a hard-hitting anti-war movie, gritty, black-and-white maybe, no stars, just the true-life events of Charlie's career. "Damned near a documentary," he would say. "People are ready for this." Ratto on the other hand seemed more ambitious. He wanted the picture seen by a lot of people. "We need to reach people with this story," he insisted. "What we have to say is worth their time, but they need to be sucked in." He wanted John Wayne. Or somebody else of great stature whose name would drag people into the theater.

"How about somebody under fifty?" Charlie suggested without a trace of irony.

"Of course, of course," Ratto would say.

Charlie saw his major task as listening. Ethyl had already told him not to worry about the screenplay format. "I do all that," she said.

"Good," he said. "Because I don't know the first thing about it."

She smiled. Fishkin and Ratto were each in their offices, taking calls. "You should see some of the stuff we get," she said. "I have to spend hours deciphering."

"I'd like to see some stuff," he said, and she sent him home with a pile of screenplays, some made into movies and some not. Charlie lay on his hard bed listening to loud music through his walls and reading. At first he was shocked at how stupid they seemed, how flat, how boring and trite. How unliterary. The grammar stunk, the word choices were uniformly bad, etc. This was no place for an English teacher. But after reading a dozen, Charlie had a better idea of the job. Maybe this was going to work out. No room for all the massive bullshit Charlie always seemed to get stuck in, lists of equipment, descriptions, stuff like that. In a screenplay all that stuff is to one side. The writer isn't troubled by detail, but must stick to raw story and dialogue.

There was something wonderful about it, once he got over his shock. No wonder all his favorite war novels had been made into such shitty movies. Even the much-touted *From Here to Eternity* was really a bullshit movie if you looked at it closely. All that realism in the name of some bullshit truth. It was Charlie's secret wish that his movie not be bullshit. That the realism be in the name of realism. He didn't want to bullshit, and as for the truth, he didn't claim to know the truth. Unless, of course, the truth was bullshit. Tricky.

He soon decided that Fishkin, not Ratto, was closer to his viewpoint. In fact, Bud Fishkin was a nicer person. Pure Hollywood, sure, but that didn't seem to mean what Charlie had at first assumed. Bud Fishkin was well-read, civilized, a jazz fan, a husband and father of two wonderful girls, whom Charlie had met at the beach. He had a nice little beach house, nothing ornate, but certainly not tacky, and his wife, although an actress by profession, was a great cook and a wonderful conversationalist, somebody Jaime would like immediately. On the other hand, Bill Ratto lived in a luxurious apartment by himself, right down the beach from Fishkin, and seemed to have hardly unpacked from New York. How long had he been here? Five, six years? Still unpacked, his collection of posters, paintings, and drawings leaning against the living room wall next to the fireplace that burned gas. Fishkin at home seemed comfortable and human, Ratto at home was a dog in an animal shelter, friendly but nervous.

Subtly it became two against one, Ratto acknowledging that his ideas were "a little grandiose." But he insisted that to set out to make a depressing black-and-white picture wasn't going to inspire the money people. "This is not an automatic sell," he said once, objecting to Fishkin's idea that they use untried boys as actors.

Fishkin turned to Charlie. "You want to see those same old fat extras in your starvation camp?" A simple point, easily won. They'd have to go with young kids, drama students, to get the right look. Which dictated in turn the ages of the stars. Nobody over thirty, that would be the rule.

"I hope the bankers like it," Ratto said. Fishkin and Charlie exchanged looks. Ratto was really acting like a studio pimp. Then Charlie would get home to the motel, or be sitting in his new favorite bar down the street, the Troubadour, and realize they might be playing him hard cop soft cop. Only he couldn't figure out why. They all wanted the same thing, didn't they? They all wanted to win. Charlie knew after only a couple of weeks that he was really on his own. Without waiting to be asked, he began his script, sitting in his smelly apartment, using long yellow legal pads and writing in pencil, as he'd begun so many years ago.

71.

When Fishkin and Ratto found out he was already writing they were happy to let him go back to Mill Valley. "Go home, write, send us a thousand pages," Fishkin said in his deep rich voice. Ziggie the agent explained that Charlie's weekly paychecks would begin even though the deal wasn't signed yet, and not to sweat the details. "You're a new boy," Ziggie said. "I can't do much for you. But if you turn in the right script, this town will open up like a diseased asshole." Charlie was mildly shocked to hear such words coming from the mouth of such a distinguished-looking gentleman. But he flew home with every intention of doing just what Ziggie said.

Charlie was amazed to see what had been done to his fifteen hundred per week, which by the time a check reached him, amounted to a little less than half. Still, it beat bartender wages, and Charlie didn't have to dress to go to work. Jaime moved her typewriter and manuscript out of his office, but didn't move to San Francisco. She set up in their bedroom, at her vanity table, moving a lot of bottles and jars, and Charlie couldn't figure out how she could sit and write with the mirror to look into. But she did.

Another little hitch was that either Fishkin or Ratto would call him nearly every day and ask how he was doing, which made him nervous. He didn't like talking about what he was writing. The phone might ring at ten in the morning or ten at night and without any preliminaries Bud Fishkin would say, "I've been thinking about the Montana scenes. You know, it would really be great if there was a girl he was saying good-bye to, you know? A sort of symbol of what he's leaving behind."

"You want me to turn the father into a girlfriend?"

"No no no no no," Fishkin would say warmly. "I think we should *add* a girl. That makes the leaving poignant, touching, you know?"

"So he gets kicked out of high school, has an argument with his father, kisses this girl, and gets on the bus." All for a scene they'd planned to go under the titles. And there had been no girl, of course. The girls of Wain and the surrounding countryside hadn't appealed to young Charlie. That was half of why he left. But he'd learned better than to argue over the telephone with his producers. They always won, using their knowledge of moviemaking to beat him over the head. Nonetheless, most of their ideas were terrible, and so Charlie had to be a diplomat on the telephone and then just go ahead and write his script.

Which was a lot of fun, once you got over being scared. Just set the scene, put the folks into it, and let them go. Charlie found he'd spent so much of his life thinking about his military career that he knew the scenes by heart even before he wrote them down. He wrote on his typewriter now, because it was easier to see the scenes in print, and found himself turning out ten or twelve pages a day. It was liberating not having to put in all those petty details he'd once thought so important, or the nuances of character. Nobody in a movie is subtle, he was told, and from the scripts he'd read and the movies he was seeing, he was told correctly. He learned to show things instead of having people say them. He began to learn a little about dramatic structure, enough so that twice he threw out all his pages and started again, determined to turn in a first draft they could shoot.

The calls kept coming. Were his producers even right for his movie? They seemed to have no idea what he was trying to do. They kept coming up with stock characters they wanted to throw into the picture, "to help tell the story." The girl in Montana, another girl in Korea, a good Chinese and a bad Chinese, a good guard and a bad guard, a nurse he falls for, a foreign correspondent he falls for. Finally Charlie had to call Ziggie and ask what he could do about the incessant calls.

Ziggie laughed. "They're paying you for a draft, and they want to get ten drafts for their money. Ignore them. Unless they say something you can use."

At the end of his six weeks Charlie was halfway through the story, and the script was already a hundred pages long. "Keep writing," Fishkin told him, and the checks kept coming. Charlie finished his first draft at the end of ten weeks, looked at himself in the full-length mirror, and discovered to his amazement that the writing had cost him forty-six pounds. Otherwise he looked healthy, except for his eyes, which were bloodshot from marijuana. Of course he didn't smoke while working, only afterward, before he showered. He wasn't drinking, it made him muzzy in the morning. How could Jaime still go out and get roaring drunk and then get up at six the next morning and start writing? Charlie was getting old. Maybe Jaime wasn't.

He sent the script down to be professionally typed at Barbara's Place, a typing service they told him to use, and when the copies came back in covers he was surprised to see that the count was two hundred and forty-five pages. Barbara's Place had sent copies to Fishkin-Ratto and Zeigler-Ross, and Charlie set himself to hear the bad news. Far too long. Too many gloomy characters. Too much profanity. Not enough women. No sex. No good guys. Gunfire without resolution (Fishkin had told him that gunfire had to resolve something or it was exploitative). Ziggie told him to relax, that this often took a couple of weeks, but Charlie wasn't ready to relax. He'd tossed a hand grenade and he wanted to hear it explode.

Kenny Goss was getting to be a problem. Jaime told Charlie about going looking for Kenny and finding him quite crazy, wandering North Beach muttering about angels. Kenny had wiped himself out on speed. Charlie remembered when speed had first run through North Beach in the late fifties, turning hipsters into murderous punks. Charlie hated speed. It made you think you were smarter and faster, but when you reach for your dick, you can't find it. He preferred cocaine, a cleaner, clearer high, and also natural. Speed, he'd heard, was something thought up by Hermann Göering and his Luftwaffe scientists, because Göering was afraid the war would cut off supplies of cocaine from South America. Charlie didn't care. The shit was wrecking Kenny Goss.

Kenny seemed to have developed a crush on Jaime. He thought she had the answers. Famous, successful, a really fine writer, and yet nothing had spoiled her. She was still a fine human being. These were all Kenny's words. Kenny reminded him, sadly, of the young thief who wrote pulp stories and then vanished. Charlie couldn't believe he wasn't able to summon the name. The thief, too, had come around Jaime wanting to find love. He too had been quiet and secretive. Thinking of him made Charlie recall Linda McNeill and his only act of adultery. Wherever Linda was, he imagined her tanned and beautiful, hauling in sail somewhere out in the deep Pacific. He hoped.

Many afternoons Charlie would emerge from his office to see Kenny's white pickup out in the gravel drive, and find Kenny in the kitchen or out in back, talking to Jaime or Kira, or even Mrs. Hawkins. Charlie had to explain to Kira why Kenny was sometimes so strange.

"He's taking medicine that's bad for him," Charlie said. Kira knew what speed was, and said so. "Well, that's what he's taking," Charlie admitted. "And it makes him crazy." He didn't add that he preferred Kira not taking drugs, but she said, "Daddy, all your friends take drugs," which kind of ruined his moral position in advance. So far as he could tell Kira didn't even drink. Charlie had started drinking at ten or eleven. Everybody knew he had.

"How's your book coming?" he asked Kenny one day, right after he'd turned in his script. They were both at the no name bar in Sausalito, drinking beer on the patio, in the dappled light from the overhead greenery. Kenny smirked down at the table, then said, "I can't do it anymore."

Charlie let that sit. There wasn't anything to say. Here was a fine young mind blown to pieces by amphetamines. Was there anything encouraging to say? He drank his beer.

"What's it like, being married?" Kenny asked him.

Charlie was surprised. "Why do you want to know?"

Kenny smiled at him. He was a handsome man, with pale blue eyes. He'd have no trouble attracting women. But Charlie had never seen Kenny with a woman, except talking to them in bars. He wondered if Kenny Goss was homosexual. No, he couldn't be, he was in love with Jaime. Charlie said, "You looking for a wife? Maybe that's a good idea. To answer your question, being married is good. For me, necessary. Without Jaime I'd be dead meat." In saying it he realized it was true.

"I'm dead meat," Kenny said. He drained his beer.

"No, you aren't," Charlie lied. "You're a good man and a good writer. But you need to get off that shit."

Kenny smiled sadly and stood. "I need to do something," he said. Charlie watched him leave the patio and walk through the dark of the bar.

He saw Kenny again just after getting the call from Hollywood. "Come on down," said Ratto cheerfully. "We have to pitch this thing." Kenny wasn't so cheerful, but he too had good news. He showed up at their house at night, nearly ten o'clock, and had a woman with him. She was thin and freckled, a nice-looking person, maybe twenty-five. She and Kenny stayed next to each other throughout the fairly uncomfortable fifteen minutes of the visit. Her name was Brenda Feeney, and they were to be married. They'd met in a bar in the city and fallen in love in three days. Now they were driving down to Modesto to meet her parents and get hitched. Brenda was a student. After they left, full of good wishes from the Monels, Charlie asked Jaime, "What do you think?"

Jaime shrugged. "Maybe a little nookie will do him good."

Charlie had to laugh. Women were something.

72.

Charlie's weekly pay had come from Fishkin-Ratto's own bank account. Now the job was to take the gigantic mess Charlie had written and turn it into a "selling document." Something to show the bankers. Something that would excite their greed. "What we need is a treatment," Bud Fishkin said. Charlie sat in one of the red leather chairs opposite Fishkin. In the other, a fake Thompson machine gun, a prop from Fishkin's last movie. Charlie wondered at the symbolism of the machine gun resting barrel-up in Bill Ratto's chair. Bill was in New York. "We don't need him for this, do we?" Fishkin asked Charlie slyly.

"What's a treatment?" Charlie asked. "I mean, technically."

Fishkin shrugged. "Whatever we want it to be," he said. "The point is, we want something on paper we can leave with them, that they can read over in our absence. But make no mistake, *we* have to sell the story." Charlie understood that he and Fishkin were eventually going to have to walk down the corridor of the third floor to the office of the head of the studio and pitch their movie.

"But first, there's somebody I want you to meet, another writer. If you guys get along, maybe you can work together on pulling this script together." Charlie must have made a face. Fishkin smiled. "I know, you'd rather work alone. You're a novelist. But in the movies nobody works alone."

"I don't mind," Charlie said. "I can use all the help I can get."

Fishkin looked at his watch. "He should be here soon. You'll probably get along. This guy's an ex-con." Fishkin gave Charlie a deep look. "But he's also a writer with three books, very tough pulp stuff."

"What's his name?"

"Stan Winger," Fishkin said. "Have you read any of his stuff?"

How strange. Charlie had so recently been trying to summon that name. He grinned happily. "Yes, I have."

Even so Charlie didn't recognize him when he came into the room. Charlie remembered Stan as a twenty-four-year-old with an unformed face and a body without definition. The man who entered the room was lithe and muscular, darkly tanned, with a face both hard and humorous. He wore a faded blue workshirt and faded jeans, and suddenly Charlie knew where Fishkin got his taste in clothes.

Charlie stood. It was obvious Stan didn't recognize him. Of course Charlie was older too, and bearded now, and even slimmed down was heavier than he'd been in Portland. He held out his hand and saw the polite expression on Stan's face, felt his hard grip. "Stan Winger," Stan said.

"Charlie Monel," Charlie said.

"I'll be a son of a bitch," Stan said. He hugged Charlie.

"You crazy asshole," Charlie said. They looked at each other, still holding onto each other's shoulders.

"Charlie," Stan said, his eyes glistening.

"Ex-con, huh?"

"Sorry I didn't write."

Fishkin came up to them, smiling. "You know each other?"

"This guy was my creative writing teacher in Portland," Stan said.

"And this guy was my best student."

"Well look at this," Fishkin said. "I must be a genius."

Once they'd finished with Fishkin they walked down the third floor corridor to the stairwell, Charlie with his arm over Stan's shoulder, like he didn't want to let him go again. The meeting had fallen apart, of course, and they agreed to come back and try tomorrow. All Charlie wanted to do was sit with Stan and talk. Once outside, they crossed the wide, sunbaked lot to their cars.

"How's Jaime?" Stan asked. "How's Kira?"

"They're fine. How about you? Married?"

Stan smiled at the ground and said, "Well, sort of," and Charlie shut up about that. Stan had published three books and Charlie hadn't even heard of them, but Stan knew all about Jaime's career. Nothing had to be said about Charlie's. At his rental Volkswagen, parked in the shade of one of the big sound studios, Stan said, "Let's go in my car." A brand new Cadillac, Charlie noted, a black convertible, whose top automatically folded back when Stan pushed a button on the dashboard. They drove out through the gate and Stan said he knew a bar.

"I'm new to Los Angeles," Charlie said. "You can take me anywhere you want."

They got roaring drunk at a little neighborhood bar out in the middle somewhere, not in Hollywood or Westwood or any of the places Charlie knew. After they were drunk, Stan whispered to him that it was a thieves bar, and everybody in it except he and Charlie were thieves. Charlie looked around. They looked ordinary to him. "Sometimes I just have to be among thieves," Stan said.

As they drove back to the lot for his car, Charlie was reminded of their project. His former book. "Can we do this thing?" he asked Stan.

"They didn't tell me anything except that they had this new writer who needed help," Stan said. He told Charlie that Fishkin-Ratto wanted to produce his new book, which was due out in a year.

"What's it about?" They pulled up next to Charlie's Volkswagen.

"Some guy in prison," Stan said, almost shyly. They agreed to meet in twenty minutes at the Troubadour. Charlie felt wonderful, drunk as he was, and waved cheerfully at the cop as he went out the gate. The Troubadour wasn't open yet, and Stan stood arguing with some guy at the door. Charlie parked.

"He won't let us come in and sit down," Stan said.

"We're not open for twenty minutes," the guy said. A tall thin hippie with a leather hat and greasy yellow curls.

"Can't we just come in and sit down?" Stan asked. "We won't make any trouble."

"Yeah," said Charlie.

"The place is closed," the guy said.

"Fucking Hollywood," Stan said. "Let's go to Dan Tana's. More high class."

"Aren't we too drunk?" Charlie asked. "We could go to my motel. Two fucking blocks away. Pick up a sixpack, drink beer, and talk over old times."

"Fuck that noise," Stan said. He'd certainly changed a lot, good old Stan Winger. They got into Stan's car and drove to Dan Tana's, which turned out to be an Italian Restaurant where a lot of Hollywood people drank and even sometimes ate. Seated at the bar, they began putting away Wild Turkeys. "Let's get really drunk," said Stan. "I'm not on parole anymore. I can do any fucking thing I want."

"Okay," said Charlie happily. "We have to call Jaime." The place was noisy as hell, and he had to cover his free ear to use the payphone. Kira answered, and Jaime wasn't home. "Guess who I met in Hollywood?" he said.

"I don't know." Obviously Kira didn't care.

"Stan Winger," he told her anyway. "An old friend, from when you were a baby."

"Oh, I remember him."

"You couldn't possibly," Charlie said. He told her to wait and brought Stan to the telephone. "Here, it's my daughter, she says she remembers you."

Stan took the phone, looking at Charlie. "Hello?" he said. He listened for a while, and then a smile appeared on his face. "My God," he said softly. "You do remember." When he handed the instrument back to Charlie there were tears running down his face. At the bar they ordered fresh shots. "She remembers me carrying her down the hill, over at Latourette's. Jesus Christ." He turned to Charlie. "I thought about you people, when I was in the joint."

Charlie drank his shot, enjoying the burn down his throat.

"You saved my life," Stan said. "I would have gone crazy without some real people to think about."

"You're perfectly welcome," Charlie said. "Any fucking time."

73.

As they sat, nursing drinks at Dan Tana's until closing time, it struck Charlie that Stan's story would make a great movie. He'd matured into a smart cool guy, quietly competent, but still the same nice kid, somehow, that Charlie had known in Portland. Smiling without irony he told Charlie about his life in Hollywood before he'd been violated. He described how Carrie Gruber, a sweet blonde Valley girl, had watched in horror as the parole officer, crazed by envy, had put Stan back into the system. "She did everything," he said. "She took care of my Caddie, she hired a lawyer, she moved into my house, took care of my business, wrote me every week . . ."

"Jesus," Charlie said.

Stan gave a wry smile and rubbed at a wet spot on the black vinyl bar top with his finger. "Yeah."

"What's she like?"

"Actually, she's really smart," Stan said. Carrie had tried every way to get Stan out of the system. When nothing worked she went ahead with her plans, to start her own business. She wrote Stan asking if she could borrow from his savings. Stan sent her a power of attorney, giving her virtually unlimited use of his money. "What the fuck," he said to Charlie. "If she was going to rip me off, this was the time to find out." She didn't. She was a methodical person, and she continued looking for the right business to go into. Carrie didn't want to set the world on fire, she just wanted a little blaze for herself. Not the laundry business. Too boring. Something she could put her heart into. She settled on candy.

"Candy?" Charlie asked. "I would have thought liquor."

Stan laughed. "For that you need a license." He explained that Carrie wanted to travel the world, sampling exotic candy. She'd reasoned that rich people love treats, and that even in the worst of times people ate candy. It was a cheap high and made you feel rich. She wanted her stores in the rich neighborhoods because why fuck around? The rich had all the money. So being the matter-of-fact person she was, she took a job in a candy factory in Torrance, rolling chocolates for three dollars an hour. Working among Mexican women she improved her rudimentary Spanish. She also learned a lot about candy making. She read the industry magazine, *Great West Candymaker,* and she ate, slept, dreamed, and lived candy for six months. She sent Stan boxes of chocolates she'd rolled herself, and looked around for a perfect location for her first shop. Meanwhile Stan cut brush and lived in a barracks. Carrie sent him detailed accounts of how she spent his money, but he didn't care. He trusted her.

She'd always loved Malibu, even just the name, and against her better judgment she began looking for a location along the Pacific Coast Highway. The building she found was just south of the actual Malibu, well, considerably south, but it was on the PCH and included an apartment upstairs where she and Stan could live if they chose to. The location was expensive, but the dream of Malibu turned out to be stronger than the dream of world travel, so Carrie decided her shop's specialty wouldn't be candies from around the globe, but expensive chocolates, rich people chocolates. She rented the location, bought four thousand dollars worth of used candymaking equipment, hired a couple of her Mexican friends from the Torrance factory, and went to work.

"By the time she picked me up in Los Padres she had a going business," Stan said. In fact, Malibu Candy had been an immediate hit with the beach crowd. "We're paying the rent, paying off the equipment, and cutting a little profit."

"We?"

Stan smiled. "We got married five days after I got loose. We live over the store. The beach is a block away."

"Well," Charlie said drunkenly. "You fell into a tub of shit and came out smelling like a rose."

"Well put," Stan said. "So let's get out of this Hollywood dump and head for the beach. You'll stay in the guest room. If there's a God in heaven Carrie and I will repay some of the hospitality you showed me years ago."

"You've certainly learned to talk like a gentleman," Charlie said as they stood to go.

"You fuckin' aye."

But they didn't drive to the beach. They were too drunk. Stan stayed on the couch in Charlie's suite. Drunk as he was, Charlie couldn't sleep, and lay listening to Stan snoring in the next room. Running into Stan was hard to absorb. Stan's life was hard to absorb. Charlie's own hell had lasted only three years, counting the time on the TB ward. The rest of his life had been soft and smooth. Stan's horror show had gone on for years and years. That terrible moment, on the way to the beach with his girl, suddenly slammed back into prison. Stan hadn't said much, but it must have been horrible, far worse than anything that had happened to Charlie. He imagined Stan out in the hot sun, bent over hacking at brush with a cutter, his naked back red and wet with sweat, his face closed, his mind closed, his heart cold. Stan sitting in solitary confinement all those years, memorizing his novel. Yet here he was, married, owner of a candy store, and Hollywood's hot new young writer. Or words to that effect. And a published novelist. Charlie's former pupil had passed him by. The tortoise and the hare, but no, that was ungenerous. He was no tortoise, and Stan no rabbit. Charlie only hoped he wouldn't be jealous, and could enjoy Stan's books.

74.

Stan offered, practically insisted, that Charlie come live at the beach. If not in Stan's spare room, then a rental. "What do you pay at that hotel?" he asked Charlie.

"Twenty-five a day, but I don't pay it," Charlie said. "Fishkin-Ratto pays." He liked Stan's place, and he probably would have enjoyed riding in to work with Stan every morning, like a commuter. But he wanted to keep his hotel suite. In his first place, he liked living in a hotel, even one with no real room service and an unheated pool. The other reason was Carrie.

Her smile had been warm, but her eyes and hand cold. Charlie understood. Keep off. Private Property. Trespassers Will Be Violated. She wasn't that beautiful, more like handsome, with strong clear-cut features, a real peasant face. The blonde hair was short and straight, the figure shapely and sturdy. Here was a woman who could fuck all night and then spring up in the morning to do a day's work. Carrie Gruber was that. She looked like a Gruber. He liked her.

The apartment over the candy store made Charlie reflect on Stan's life in prison. The place was all windows and light, filled with plants in windowboxes and hanging from the ceiling, ferns and begonias and orchids, African violets on tables and avocado plants luxuriating out of terra cotta pots. The furniture was simple, mostly Danish modern, a big Mexican carved mahogany sideboard in the dining room, a glass-topped coffee table in the living room, several prints on the walls, all landscapes without human figures. The spare bedroom was also Stan's office at home, with a wall of books, mostly paperbacks, an IBM Selectric typewriter and a single bed, covered with magazines. There was also a small portrait of a black man on a piece of red cloth, tacked to the wall next to Stan's typewriter.

"Who's that?" Charlie asked.

"Malcolm X," Stan said.

"Friend of yours?" Charlie joked, but Stan just laughed and said nothing more. Back out in the living room they sat down to coffee and cakes, which Carrie brought them on a tray. On the coffee table, beside three copies of the *New Yorker*, was a .45 automatic, just sitting there. It looked like an army Colt, but Charlie couldn't be sure. He wanted to ask about it, but didn't, and Stan said nothing. It might as well have been a sculpture, an art object. That whole first weekend nobody mentioned the pistol on the coffee table, and after a while Charlie decided that the gun was a symbol. Stan wasn't a gun guy. It said, "I'm free. I'm not on parole. Fuck you." Charlie bet it was loaded, too.

While Carrie ran her store downstairs, Charlie and Stan were on their own to take walks on the wide sandy beach or down to the Venice Pier. Their immediate favorite place was a little beer bar on the pier with a couple of pool tables and a really loud jukebox. Despite the sawdust on the floor, the longhaired scraggly-bearded pool players often played while on roller skates. Nearly everybody in the joint wore skimpy bathing suits and was years younger than Charlie or Stan, who sat unbothered at the bar, drinking beer, and marveling at their surroundings.

"It's like Portland, only insane," Stan said.

"Here's to Portland." Charlie raised his beer glass. "Don't you wish this beer was Blitz-Weinhard?"

By Sunday night Charlie and Carrie had come to a peaceful settlement, entirely without words. Charlie made it clear he wouldn't be an unsettling influence, and Carrie that she'd protect Stan no matter what. They were on the same side, but Charlie wondered how Stan liked being the object of such an intense protectiveness. It was like having a big mean loyal pit bull. At the weekend's end Charlie was glad to be winding his way across to the Valley, to his home away from home.

At Fox things settled into a routine. Fishkin and Ratto were developing at least five pictures that Charlie knew about, so he didn't see much of them. Ratto's secretary, Ethyl, brought him coffee or tea in his bare little office and otherwise left him alone. Stan worked on his own project down the hall, and although Ratto had said Stan would be working with Charlie, that never actually happened.

"I get it," Stan said. "When they found out we knew each other, they decided I'd probably help you without being paid to."

"Counting on you to be a good guy."

"Exactly," Stan said. And Fishkin-Ratto won their bet. Stan showed up every day at twelve thirty and took Charlie to the commissary. At lunch they talked over Charlie's project. After lunch Charlie would go back to work and Stan would leave the lot.

"Aren't we supposed to work all day?" Charlie asked.

"Where does it say that?"

Since nobody was checking up on him, Charlie could have left too, but he had nowhere to go. Easier to stay in the little office and try to write. It didn't come as easily as everyone said it would. It had been one thing to generate what he now understood was a loose, novelistic two-hundred-and-fifty-page draft, but he had a harder time reducing his ideas to the kind of clichés, the recognizable gestures, that screenplays seemed to be made of. Still, he plugged away, listened to Stan, and turned in his pages at the end of the day. What he got out of Ratto, when he finally spent some time with him, was unsatisfying. The meeting was for five thirty, and as he walked into Bill's office, Ethyl came in with a bottle of whiskey, two glasses, and a bucket of ice.

"Casting time," Bill said, and they sat sipping whiskey and trying to decide which actor could best play Charlie.

"Brando, of course," Bill said, staring at his glass. "But I think he's gone crazy or something. What do you think about Paul Newman?"

Finally Charlie asked how Bill liked his pages.

"Just keep plugging away," Bill said. "If you have any questions, ask Ethyl or Stan Winger." He shrugged and grimaced, the light bouncing off his glass. "Wanna smoke a joint?"

When Charlie got back to the hotel in the evening he would call home. Jaime worked at home now, in his old office, and her book was coming along. Kira talked about moving to Hollywood, living in the hotel with Charlie. "What would you do?" Charlie asked her. "I'm away at work all day, just like anybody else."

"What do I do here?" she asked. Her voice was getting deep, he thought. "I'm sick of this, daddy," she said one night. "When are we going to have a real family life?"

Never, Charlie thought, and changed the subject, knowing he hadn't gotten away with anything. After one of these calls he'd have a drink or smoke a joint, then go for a walk on the Sunset Strip. During the week Sunset wasn't so crowded, and it was pleasant to stroll along, thinking about nothing more pressing than where he should have dinner. There were several restaurants he'd come to like, especially the Imperial Gardens, an ornate three-story Japanese restaurant where the waitresses were all Japanese girls right off the boat, most unable to speak English. Charlie liked trying out his rusty Japanese on them. If he didn't feel like Japanese food there was Schwab's Drugstore, across the street, where he could have a hamburger or a salmon steak. His evenings were otherwise intensely lonely, spent reading in his room. He read Stan's published novels and was amazed at their quality, though they sometimes lacked in any basic reality. The action was good, the dialogue great, and Stan's sense of irony was delicious. Stan was a much better writer than he'd ever be. He knew what Charlie had never learned, how to slam those words down on paper. Charlie felt an outrageous twist of envy at Stan's ability to capture the commonplace, while Charlie himself was hung up on high ideas that never came out right. Or maybe Stan was writing pop trash, and Charlie was after so much more. Literature, High Art. Move over Leo. Step aside, Herman.

At the end of six more weeks Charlie hadn't solved the draft, as Bill Ratto put it.

"Am I fired?" Charlie asked.

"Oh hell no," Bill said without smiling.

75.

They'd have a meeting with Bud Fishkin as soon as he got back from Paris. Meanwhile, Charlie flew home to San Francisco full of dread, as if he were coming home from school with a bad report card. Not that Jaime was his mother. Anyhow, he'd never brought home a report card to his mother, only his father, who'd burble on for an hour about responsibility and then pass out dead drunk. Sitting on PSA Flight 17 Commuter to San Francisco, thinking of his old dad, he felt even worse. Chuckmo, his friends called him. Ol Chuckmo from the lumber yard. He'll load your truck, but don't ask him to add the figures, because he'll take half the morning and then get it wrong, his forehead furrowing, his grimy stubby fingers clutching the pencil. Poor old dad. Charlie never wrote him, never even wanted to go back to Montana. His father always had such great plans, he was such an optimist, and he was so stupid. There was no other word for it. It had been such a shock to Charlie to find out that what was the matter with his dad was stupidity. Not ignorance. Not just bullheadedness, although he was bullheaded. Stupidity. A man full of stupid daydreams.

He was exactly like his father, whether he liked it or not. He too had unreasonable dreams. He too was unbearably stupid, though with a hell of a fine vocabulary. Charlie's dream, if he looked at it closely, was to be king of the world. It wouldn't be enough to write and be published. If that, why be fucking around with Hollywood? Hollywood had nothing to do with writing well. To the contrary, he was learning how to write less well. How to convince, to persuade, to bully people into belief. Suspension of disbelief. Unfortunately, Charlie had suspended his own disbelief, and now, flying back to reality, he saw he'd gotten nothing out of this trip, apart from the money in his bank account. Well, one other thing. A growing sense of cheapness.

Seeing Jaime automatically sweetened his stomach and his disposition. She was late and didn't meet him at the gate, but as he walked up the ramp into the airport proper he saw her small figure approaching. Her hair had gotten longer while he was gone, shoulder length, blonde almost white. And of course there was a guy trailing her, Charlie could see the guy's mouth working as he tried to hustle Jaime. Big guy, jean jacket, long greasy black hair. Perfect.

"Jaime!" Charlie roared, and started toward her, his arms out. She saw him and threw her arms up into the air, her face brightening, the guy behind her grinning stupidly while Jaime and Charlie embraced.

"Oh God, Charlie," Jaime said. They kissed hungrily and Charlie's mind went blank. By the time he could think again they were walking arm-in-arm up the ramp and the stranger had disappeared. Too bad. Charlie had hoped the guy would start something, so Charlie could vent his frustrations on the convenient target.

On the long drive up Bayshore Jaime apologized for not coming to Los Angeles to visit him. "I'm sorry," she said. "I just freeze up thinking about Los Angeles."

"Oh, it's a great place," Charlie said. "You'll love it. Let's move down there. We can buy a little house in Laurel Canyon. Kira can go to Hollywood High, which is about as high as you can get. We'll spend our time with the Fishkins and the Rattos and the Newmans and all them . . ."

"Oh, stop," she said. "I'm so glad to have you home."

They stopped in North Beach and had lunch at Enrico's, sitting outside in the sweet San Francisco air, listening to the roar of the trucks going past on Broadway. An old married couple. No need to rush off to bed. With Charlie's pockets full of Hollywood gold, there were drinks to buy, friends to brag to. They didn't get home to Mill Valley until well after ten, and, incredibly drunk, they were lucky not to be picked up by the cops. All the way home Charlie told Jaime the things he was going to do to her, and she told him how much she wanted him to. But when they burst into the house Kira was up and waiting, a tall thin shape sitting alone at the dining room table.

"Where the *hell* have you been?" she asked, in an eerie imitation of her mother. Charlie tried to gather her in his arms but she struggled out of his grasp, cursing and fuming in her young voice while Charlie laughed. "I'm home, God damn it!" he yelled.

"You're drunk!" his daughter said scornfully.

"Oh, shut up and have a drink," Jaime said, chuckling at her daughter.

"I'll never drink." Kira slammed into her room. Charlie and Jaime looked at each other. Over the roaring in Charlie's head he heard himself say, "What are we doing?"

"We're drunk," said Jaime. "We have to go to bed now."

"This isn't the homecoming I'd planned," Charlie said seriously, but Jaime took him by the arm and led him into their bedroom. They undressed each other.

"I want a shower," Jaime said. "You stink." She giggled, naked, and walked into their bathroom. Charlie followed, and they ended up making love wet on the bathroom tiles.

The next morning the place was quiet. He lay in his own bed, a slight headache from the night's drinking, but nothing unusual. Outside, linnets, a scrub jay, the whistling sounds of swallows. Home again. He got up and went out into the house. The door to the office was shut, Jaime surely in there working. Kira was off to school, probably humiliated by her drunken parents. Charlie sighed, and went into the kitchen to make himself a cup of tea. While the water boiled he went out onto the lawn. The sun softened the haze over the East Bay, the scattering of boats. Fun, if he could, to go sailing today, and forget everything. He went back into the house, thinking, I have to get organized.

He was still sitting there in his jockey shorts when Jaime came out of the office with her coffee mug. "You're awake," she said, and went into the kitchen. When she came out she sat down. "How does it feel to be home?"

He grinned at her painfully. "It feels just like a hangover," he said. "I think we're getting old."

"I think we should get a divorce," Jaime said, looking him in the eye. Steam rose from her coffee mug.

Charlie waited for the punch line. After a few moments he realized he was expected to speak. "Really?" he said.

"You don't really love us anymore," she said calmly.

"I called every night," Charlie heard himself saying. "What the hell are you talking about? Divorce? Why?"

"You don't love us anymore. It doesn't matter how many times you called. It wasn't every night, by the way. The truth is, I don't think I love you anymore, either."

"Who is it?" Charlie asked coldly.

"It isn't anybody," Jaime said too quickly. She picked up her coffee mug in both hands. Her hands were trembling. So it was real. Charlie's face went cold, then hot. Some bastard.

"I'll kill him," he said to Jaime, as evenly as he could. "What's his name?"

Jaime went back into the kitchen. Charlie sat wondering why, when his life was collapsing, he felt this tiny flicker of joy.

76.

The house belonged to Jaime. All Charlie had to do was sign some papers. They didn't bother with an immediate divorce, since neither had any marriage plans. Plenty of time to get a no-fault for twenty-five bucks, saving a lot of lawyer fees. They both hated lawyers. Jaime would sell the house and move with Kira back to San Francisco, and Charlie could keep the apartment on Telegraph Hill, which is where he moved the day Jaime told him she didn't love him. Or, of course, he could go fuck himself. Move to L.A. He was a free man. Possibly for the first time in his life. Up in Wain he'd been terribly constricted by small town life, fled to the army, felt terribly constricted by army life, got shipped to Korea, where the Chinese grabbed him and threw him in prison. Then Operation Big Switch, Tokyo and the TB ward, where he put the noose around his own neck by becoming obsessed with literature. Then he trapped himself into the institution of marriage, where he'd languished for thirteen years. Now, at last, free. He felt terrible.

Why not just walk down Telegraph Hill, that first night, get as drunk as he could, pick up some girl, and start his life over? He hadn't counted on being depressed. Descending the Kearny steps he remembered the night he and Jaime had climbed them together for the first time. She like a little chamois, jumping, Charlie huffing and puffing. His lungs, you know. By the time he got to Broadway tears streamed down his face and into his beard. Poor fucking Charlie, he thought. There wasn't a bar he could go into that wouldn't have memories of her. Not Tosca's, nor certainly Enrico's, Jesus Christ. Nor Vesuvio or Twelve Adler or the Jazz Workshop, where they'd held hands and stomped their feet to Dizzy Gillespie. Thank God Mike's Pool Hall was gone, because he couldn't have gone in there either, or up to the Yank Sing where they'd eaten dim sum together. He walked into City Lights and found himself looking into the eyes of Shig Murao behind the counter, Shig who'd always flirted outrageously with Jaime when they came in. Charlie felt his eyes wet and without saying anything walked back out. On Columbus there was a topless bar catering to Filipinos, and Charlie went in. Here, over a badly watered gin and tonic, he realized North Beach was hers. San Francisco, in fact, was hers. He'd have to move to Los Angeles whether he wanted to or not.

So, a career in the movies? Well, he certainly hadn't made it writing fiction. A beautiful young Chinese woman danced nakedly on the bar, and Charlie sat looking into his drink. How had he fooled himself all these years? Not just about writing, but about everything. The great realist was not only truthfully a romantic, but ridiculous. The Chinese girl wasn't completely naked. Charlie watched her shiny red-heeled shoes, not wanting to look any higher. All cunts look alike, he told himself, then was immediately ashamed. Jaime wasn't a cunt. And this Chinese girl was just making a living. Charlie got up and left and the cold foggy air felt good against his face. He walked slowly back up the hill to his apartment.

He couldn't sleep. Jaime was all over the apartment, of course. And his daughter. Who'd returned from school to find her life destroyed. Kira had burst into tears and run to her father. Charlie explained carefully that it was nobody's fault, but Kira glared at Jaime through her tears and said, "God damn you, Mother," then run into her room.

Forget sleep. Remember Kim Song, where "Fuck Everybody!" was the rule of the day. Save yourself, asshole. Charlie got up and dressed. It wasn't even midnight. He considered the apartment. There wasn't anything he wanted to keep. When he'd moved into this place in '57 or '58, he had only his typewriter, his sleeping bag, a few books, a few changes of clothes. Now it was full of Jaime's things. A few books were his. Mostly school books, nothing worth keeping. His important books were at the house, Kerouac, Hemingway, Steinbeck, Faulkner, O'Hara, Jones, Melville, Tolstoy, Joyce, the heavyweights, the contenders. He could go to Mill Valley in the morning for the books, just his, none they'd bought together. But no. How childish. The books are for Kira. With that, he knew there was nothing, absolutely nothing, to keep him from going out, getting into the little Porsche, and driving south. Jaime could rent a car. Jaime could close the apartment, deal with the realtors and lawyers, and he'd sign whatever she asked him to. So be a perfect Buddhist about it. Possessions, faugh. Heartbroken, he recalled their long conversations about Buddhism. He didn't want to see her again. Cowardice, of course. If they met to exchange stuff and he broke into tears she'd wonder what it was she ever saw in him.

She'd done it not because of another man, but because he'd not lived up to his promise. When they met he'd been the hotshot, scholarship, Saxon Award, a monster manuscript everybody thought was going to be the next big war book. The next big war book had been *Catch-22*, which Charlie read with grudging admiration the first time, and then unabashed love the second and third times. And then the next big war book was *The Thin Red Line*. Jaime had married a fraud. When he'd gone Hollywood, the last straw. She'd stood being married to a failure, an honorable failure, even a bartender, but not a prostitute.

So, Hollywood had sucked him down into its vortex. Fair enough, he'd blame Hollywood. Charlie was just a country boy, he didn't know any better. He'd done his best, trying to write a work of art, but they wouldn't let him. He packed the few personal items he could find. He'd go down to Hollywood and leave all his literary baggage behind him. Be a movie writer. Coldly. Efficiently. Writing crap for money. Stan could help him. Stan knew the ropes. God knows how he learned them in prison all those years, but he did, and Charlie meant to study him. In the back of his mind somewhere was the thought that if he made enough of that Hollywood gold, he'd win her back.

"You're pathetic," he said aloud to himself. He put down his cardboard box to lock the door for the last time. When he first opened this door he'd known exactly who he was and what his life was going to be. Now, all blown to hell.

77.

Stan worried. His old friend came back from Northern California looking as if someone had killed his dog. Charlie refused to say anything, however, just grunted that everything was fine. Stan wouldn't pry. It was great to have Charlie around. Life at home wasn't all that good, and Stan needed a drinking buddy. In truth, he was having a terrible time adjusting to married life. Not that Carrie lacked anything, just the opposite. Carrie ran her business, kept the books, cleaned the apartment thoroughly, cooked dinner, was nearly always ready to make love, and tactful enough to know when Stan didn't want to. What was the matter with her? Nothing.

So why did Stan feel so trapped? It was as if he'd been, upon parole, issued a life. Life, 1 ea., w/ blonde wife. Arguing against himself, he wondered if he hadn't sold out for a pair of big tits and some shiny blonde hair. Despicable thoughts, but he had them. When he'd first been cut loose he loved her. She'd done everything for him. It was all so new, having someone who cared for him, so he sat back and let it happen, devoting his energies to the business of writing. Which was what was so great about Hollywood, where writing was indeed a business. But his string of good luck gave him a sticky feeling. Sure, he'd had a long string of bad luck, so maybe this was just some kind of balance. But no. There was no balance anywhere else in life, he'd observed, so why should there be any in his? Something else was working, something he didn't like. The con factor. How much of his good luck was because he was an ex-convict? Usually it worked against you, but Hollywood wasn't like any other place, and here, for Stan, it seemed to be working quite well. Both Fishkin and Ratto were happy to hang out with an ex-con. Stan could be certain of this because when somebody came into the office or they went to lunch together it would always manage to come out in the conversation. Fishkin and Ratto had been bragging.

At first Stan enjoyed it, but after he'd been violated back into the system he had a lot of time to think, out under the hot sun, bent over hacking at the manzanita. Meanwhile his big book deal fell through and nobody from New York or Hollywood came around, called, wrote, or even admitted he existed. His whole life on the outside boiled down to one person, Carrie. When he came out, there she was, sturdy, beautiful, waiting to take up their lives together. Of course when they heard he was out, when he called Ziggie and said, "Sorry it took me so long to get back to you," his Hollywood friends flocked around again happily. The deal for *The Fifth Hot Day in a Row*, as they were calling it again, had been dropped only until he got out, and would now be revived.

"You can't promote your book from prison," Fishkin explained. "And the book, the paperback, foreign sales, and the movie are all tied in together." Sensible enough, but Stan wasn't far removed from the many hours he'd spent lying on his bunk at night, musing on the collapse of his life and the loss of his new friends.

He tried explaining all this to Charlie, as they sat in the bar at the Troubadour, drinking beer. "I like Bud Fishkin," he said. "But after I got violated he just vanished. The picture we were working on, from my first book, got turned around, the director went off to do something else, and I guess Fishkin went with him. When I got out and he came back around, I guess I was a little bit cynical." Charlie stared down into his glass of beer. "You all right?" Stan asked.

Charlie didn't even look at him. "Yeah," he said.

Surely it was Jaime. Charlie wouldn't admit that there was trouble in paradise. With the so-called perfect marriage, Charlie was ashamed. Oddly, sitting there while loud rock boomed out of the showroom on the other side of the wall, Stan wondered if they'd married the wrong women. Stan had always loved Jaime, in a worshipful way. Now she was a successful novelist, and would make a perfect mate for Stan if he made it in Hollywood. He was right on the edge, if he said so himself. They'd make a great pair. Which would leave Charlie with Carrie. They got along well, cracked wise back and forth, and Carrie was the kind of pioneer woman Charlie needed to support either his desire to write great literature or to loaf around all the time. It was clear enough that Charlie wouldn't be happy with the movie, if they actually made a movie. Carrie could support him. Stan didn't need a supporting woman. Not anymore.

Was it possible Stan didn't know how to love? He'd been reading up on the subject. He'd be willing to accept the verdict: no love had been put into him, and so none was going to come out. A simple psychological fact. But he didn't really believe it. He'd loved Linda McNeill, maybe just puppy love, but it felt real enough. He'd known plenty of psychopaths, and no matter what the books told him, he wasn't one. It wasn't that he couldn't love, but that he didn't. And so long as he was married to Carrie, he was in no position to go looking. He was incapable of being disloyal to Carrie.

"I'm worried about Carrie," he said to Charlie, who only snorted and drank off half his beer. Stan doggedly went on. "She's great, but at night we just sit there. We don't have a hell of a lot to say to each other, you know? If she's working over the accounts and I'm reading a book, we're comfortable. Across dinner, we've got nothing to say. It's sort of ugly."

With all that priming, Stan kept it in. Maybe he was only brooding over his script. The first draft had been awful, Stan had read it because Fishkin was concerned. "Can this guy write?" he'd asked Stan. Looking over the draft, the thick blocks of exposition and five-page dialogues, Stan would have said no. But he knew Charlie, hell, he'd studied creative writing under him. Charlie could do better than this.

"Well?" Fishkin asked.

"You want my opinion?" Stan grinned at Fishkin. "Hire me and find out. I'd be glad to help." Still, he relented for Charlie's sake and sat in on some of their meetings for free, just so Charlie would have an advocate. The five of them, sitting around Fishkin's office, which was barely larger than Ratto's, Bud's secretary Jane taking notes and the rest just throwing ideas into the middle of the room. Stan found it bizarre that so much time and effort were spent this way, but he couldn't complain. As for Charlie's movie, Stan held out little hope. Fishkin-Ratto and Charlie were on a collision course. Charlie obviously wanted to make the movie about his own experiences. Fishkin-Ratto wanted something more universal, with more jeopardy.

"I want this movie to be about all wars, especially Vietnam," Fishkin said, his eyes lighting up. "We've gotta make an *anti*-war movie!"

"Sure," Charlie said. He sat low in Fishkin's red leather chair, his long legs under the coffee table. "But we can't make Korea Vietnam. They just ain't the same."

"But the principle—" Fishkin insisted.

"Not the same," Charlie said stubbornly.

"Look," Stan said to him, when they were alone in Charlie's cubicle. "You don't have to fight these guys. Just listen to what they have to say and then come back here and write what you please." Charlie couldn't grasp that the story conferences had nothing to do with the script. "They're just talking ideas," Stan said. "You take what you take, you leave what you leave."

"Well, they've got *your* ass tied to a tree," Charlie said meanly. He was frightened, Stan understood. Hollywood can be frightening. At last one night as they were out getting drunk again, Charlie broke down and admitted that Jaime had thrown him out.

"Oh Jesus," Stan said. As they got drunker and drunker, Charlie fell apart, pouring out his loud testimony that he was untalented, unlovable, and miserable. Stan confessed the same. A horrible evening. Stan had to drive Charlie to his hotel, and it felt good, the little driving the big guy home, but he was so drunk himself that he had to stay the night.

78.

Carrie Winger was glad Stan had a real friend. Her husband was a complex man and it had broken her heart that she couldn't love him. She'd tried, but you can't get blood from a turnip. Dazzled by the glamor of the man, when they finally got married she'd expected to find herself deeper in love, but no. This wasn't the man she wanted to have children with. Their marriage settled into politeness and lust. There were no fights, no arguments, Stan trusting her absolutely and letting her run the money end of things. Apart from the Hollywood money. She'd tried to get along with Evarts Ziegler and the others, but it made her angry just to talk to them. They were all Jews, of course, or if not actually Jews, just like them. Carrie had nothing against Jews, in spite of her father's dinner table rantings about Jews and communists and fairies, which just made her laugh. But something about these Hollywood people made her extremely nervous, and she was always glad to hang up the phone, feeling the sweat under her arms.

More and more the candy store occupied her mind and heart. She'd dreamed it up, she'd done all the work and all the sleepless worrying, and the thing was hers. Stan hardly ever came into the place. "I'm not much of a candy man," he told her with a little smile. "Aren't you glad?"

She was. She'd half-expected that when he got out he'd automatically try to take over the store, being a man. Her old boss had foolishly laughed at her when she told him she was opening a business of her own. But the joke was on him, and for months after she left him he'd called day and night trying to keep from going under. "I can't get good help," he'd complain desperately over the phone.

"Tough shit," she didn't say. She was properly sympathetic and advised him as much as she could, but eventually she'd had to make it clear that she was gone and he'd have to get along without her.

Eventually, so would Stan. Once she found a way for them to separate without hurting him too much. Stan was quite sensitive, though he tried not to let it show. He harbored grave doubts, as to whether he was a good person, a good writer, a good lover, a good husband. He was all those things, and she told him so. Yet she didn't love him.

Charlie was a great help. A wonderful man, big but graceful, handsome and at the same time common-looking, with a big wide grin and warm brown eyes. According to Stan, Charlie was really just a big baby in Hollywood matters, one needing all the help Stan could give him. The two spent a lot of time together, Stan often spending the night at Charlie's place, some hotel. Carrie never worried about Stan stepping out. If he did, she was certain she'd be able to tell right away. Stan was enigmatic to others, but not to her.

The money kept them together. Stan made criminal sums working for the movies. If she was going to open a new store she'd need plenty of money. The new store ought to be in Hollywood or Westwood, she wasn't sure yet, but knew she needed to hunt out the best location. Location was everything. She had to laugh at her dumb luck locating Malibu Candy where she had, between the wealthy customers from Venice and Washington Boulevard. She hadn't known about the junkies when she moved into the area, but they were her first customers, and over time her best, lining up for box after box of exotic chocolates. She'd worked hard and enjoyed dumb luck, and hoped for both again when she opened the second store. If it was a hit, she'd franchise, sell the rights to open Malibu Candy stores anywhere, using her recipes and methods of operation. She couldn't do this without Stan, and she couldn't keep Stan without a little hypocrisy.

On this particular Sunday morning Stan was in town, doing she did not know what. She'd imagined he was with Charlie, but Charlie came trudging up the outside stairs and knocked on the back door.

"Hello, Charlie," she said, opening the door.

"Is Stan home?" He wore a white tee shirt and jeans, his hands jammed into the back pockets.

"No, but come on in." Alarm bells went off in her head. Was Charlie here to make a pass at her? She offered him a cup of coffee and the two sat at the breakfast table, sunshine pouring in through the windows. Charlie looked hurt. "Are you all right?" she asked.

"Oh, sure," he said, and grinned painfully. "I thought Stan would be here."

"I think he's in town."

"Gee," Charlie said.

She wanted to make Charlie smile. "Maybe he's got a girlfriend."

"Oh, no," Charlie said. Looking alarmed, he stood. "I shouldn't even be here."

"Oh, sit down. I was just joking." That got a half-smile, but Charlie's face relapsed into pain. "Let me fix you some bacon and eggs," she said.

He said nothing, just sat with his hands folded, staring at his coffee. She got up, cooked some lengths of bacon and scrambled a few eggs. When she put the plates on the table Charlie looked at his and said, "I can't eat."

Carrie put ketchup on her eggs. "Love trouble," she said.

Charlie laughed and sighed and then it all poured out. His wife had left him. He was in terrible pain. He'd had no idea how much he loved her until now. He'd neglected her. Taken her for granted. Let love die. And now he was dying of pain. He couldn't believe the pain.

"I understand," she said, and touched his hand. He had known Stan wouldn't be here. He needed the sympathy of a woman. He probably didn't even realize it. He'd just gotten into his car and driven blindly, ending up here.

"Sit here a minute," she said. "Try to eat your breakfast. I'll be right back." She went down to the candy store. Maria was behind the counter. Since it was Sunday nobody was in the back rolling chocolates. There were a couple of customers chewing free samples and looking over the display. She could count on Maria to keep things clean, no chocolate bits on the counter, the floor swept. All looked fine. She went back upstairs. Charlie sat with the breakfast a cold ruin in front of him. He needed to lose a little weight. She pictured taking him for a run on the beach. She liked to run in the early morning. If Charlie moved to the beach, he could run with her. It would ease his pain.

"Charlie," she heard herself saying. He turned to look at her, his big sad eyes tugging at her heart. She held out her hand and he took it. "Come on," she said softly, and led him into the bedroom.

PART SIX

The Literary Life

79.

Consider the unborn Buddha spirit. Unborn, because when your Buddha spirit is born, you become enlightened. Jaime was at the moment unmistakably *pre*-enlightened, a perfect open loving creature, sensitive to everything and naïve about everything, the dupe of the senses. Right now Jaime was so sensitive she couldn't open her eyes, for fear of what she'd see. Easier to lie there with her eyes shut, the unfamiliar pillow under her head, the unfamiliar covers over her body. A hotel room? She hoped she was alone. Her unborn Buddha spirit always did better alone. Jaime had become a Buddhist in self-defense. Nothing else seemed to work, and if Buddhism itself seemed to have no working parts, that was fine with her. After life, nothing. Fine. Maybe by telling herself she was a Buddhist she was really saying, I am not a Christian, I am not a Jew, I am certainly not a Muslim, yet I believe in something. The universe? No. Bigger. More loving. Something. The Buddha looks like a nice guy. Blame it on him.

She stirred. There was too much light in the room, wherever it was. She tightened her lids and tried to reconstruct the night before. It wasn't a shock anymore to awaken to a blank memory, but it did stir up old sensations of dread, the Monday morning school feeling. Let's see. Go back as far as lunch yesterday. Lunch at Enrico's. Was that yesterday, or the day before? She had lunch at Enrico's every Friday, or nearly every Friday. So, today would be Saturday. Kira wouldn't be in school. And then, remembering, her skin went cold. She felt sweat prickling on her body. Kira was missing. Jaime opened her eyes. Big windows behind dark green silk-looking drapes. A man's bedroom, and from the look of things, the man had money. She turned and saw Brighton Forester smiling at her from the doorway, his white hair tousled, his handsome red face tilted in sympathy.

"You're awake," he said. My God, she must have slept with him. Brighton Forester, someone she'd known or known about for years. Not one of her heroes. A member of the San Francisco establishment, a rich man, a novelist with one good book out. And, as she well knew, a married person.

"Where's your wife?" Jaime asked. Humorously, she hoped. That son of a bitch. He'd been after her for years, and now she was in his bed. They probably fucked in the night, and she couldn't even remember. She blinked painfully, her fingers clutching the edge of the quilt.

"She's in the mountains," Brighton said. He wore a terrycloth bathrobe. "Why do you ask?" Apparently these society people went around fucking whomever they pleased. Of course they'd be hypocrites about it. Mum's the word and all that. Jaime's eyes hurt. She remembered Kira. Kira was missing.

"What happened last night?" she asked. Brighton came into the room, his eyes warm and sympathetic, and sat on the edge of the bed. Jaime sat up and pinched her nose to make the pain stop. It didn't.

He explained that they'd run into each other at a party, gone off with a handful of people, and ended up here in bed. He smiled fondly. He obviously liked her, aside from anything else. She liked him, for what it was worth. A nice man, tall, well-built, civilized, Princeton educated, and so on. But she needed to think about Kira. She needed to remember yesterday, in detail. How did Jaime know Kira was missing? Had the school called?

"I have to get up," she said to Brighton. "My daughter is missing."

Downstairs in the breakfast room Brighton told Jaime over coffee that she'd already solved the problem. "That's all you would talk about last night," he said. "How your daughter had run off to Los Angeles."

"Los Angeles?" She wanted to bite her tongue. She was horribly ashamed of her loss of memory. But Brighton was calm, encouraging. Kira had taken a bus to Los Angeles, he explained. To be with her father. The bus was likely pulling in about now.

Jaime sipped her coffee, trying to absorb the information. Reassuring, at first, to know Kira had made good on her threats. Then the dreadful feeling came back. "How do you know this?" she asked Brighton.

He smiled. "You told me. Remember? You stopped on Van Ness to telephone."

"Who did I telephone?"

"I don't know."

He was no fucking help at all. Jaime got out of there as quickly as she could, turning down Brighton's offer to drive her home. "I can take the bus," she said, gave him a kiss meant to indicate only friendship, and went out his big front door to find herself on Cherry Street, in Pacific Heights. She walked down to California Street. It was a sweet blue morning, but she couldn't enjoy it. She took the bus out to Eighteenth Avenue and walked north to Lake Street. Her flat was Seventeenth at Lake, one door in from the dead end. The *Chronicle* lay on the reddish brown doormat, just as if everything were normal. She picked up the paper, keyed open the front door and went up the short flight of stairs to her flat. "Kira," she said without hope. No one answered. Tuffy the cat was curled up on Jaime's bed. He looked up at her, then went back to sleep. Jaime undressed and took a shower, still waiting for her mind to clear. It didn't, not much. She checked her answering machine. Several messages, but none from Kira or Charlie. She wondered if they were together, and if so, how Charlie was dealing with it. Being responsible for a fifteen-year-old girl in Hollywood. Kira in particular, with a mind of her own, to put it mildly, and taller than her mother by six inches already, and still growing. The body of a woman, also mildly put, thank you, and the mind to match. Jaime had initiated a talk about sex once, but all Kira said was, "Oh, shit, Mother," and walked out. To big, too smart, too pretty. Now, well, Jaime didn't want to use the word runaway, but she couldn't think of another. Like half the children in America, Jaime thought, then felt contempt for herself. Sure, that's the excuse. Everybody's doing it. Jaime didn't want her daughter to be the last hippie runaway.

She dialed Charlie's hotel. Charlie wasn't in or wasn't answering. When the desk clerk came back on the line, Jaime asked, "Have you seen my daughter? His daughter? Is she registered?"

"No, she's not," the clerk answered in a distant polite voice, and she hung up, her face flushing with guilt. Where the fuck is Kira? She thought to call the school, but it was Saturday. Wasn't it? She looked at the newspaper. Yes, Saturday, April 12, 1975. Then she remembered. Friday, yesterday, she'd finished writing, had showered and was headed down to Enrico's for lunch with friends, her regular lunch crowd. The school called. Kira had left at midday without permission. Would she look into it? They loved Jaime at Drew, and would do anything for one of their most famous graduates. But they couldn't help with this. Now she remembered vowing, in a heat of anger at Kira, not to wait for her daughter to come home. She'd instead gone ahead to Enrico's. Later she could bawl Kira out for cutting school. But Jaime had never gone home. Instead she and Kenny Goss and Richard Brautigan sat around getting drunk, Jaime jumping up every few drinks to call home. Kira never answered. Jaime must have decided, in some cleverly drunken way, that Kira had run off to Los Angeles. When in fact she could be anywhere, including some pretty bad places. Jaime blocked herself from further speculations.

She looked into her daughter's bedroom, half-hoping to see her in her own bed. No. Jaime tried to identify which clothes were missing, but she didn't recognize half the stuff she found in the closet or on chairs or on the bed. Kids traded clothes all the time. Some of this stuff was pretty weird, blue leather hotpants she was certain she'd never seen before, a leather jacket which must have cost a fortune. Jaime realized she knew almost nothing about Kira. After the breakup that had brought them into the same home, she'd learned less about her daughter, not more. Kira, blaming her mother, had closed herself off. Charlie, though not a bad man, had become sanctified in Kira's mind. Writers should never marry anyway, Jaime told herself. We're too selfish.

With that thought she began to relax. Kira understood her pretty well. Her daughter would hurt her, surgically, using every weakness she sensed in her mother, then come home. There was no need to call the police or do anything else dramatic, just wait for her daughter to come home. Jaime started crying, but even that was just the fucking hangover. Kira was fine. It was Jaime who was suffering.

80.

It had seemed like such a good simple idea, an exercise almost, to write a short story about a girl Jaime had known only slightly, but whose tragedy had terribly upset her. In real life the girl's name had been Mary Bergendaal. Jaime kept the Mary for the overtone of the virginal, and made her last name Rosendaal. Rose, doll, and Scandinavian. The real Mary had been a French horn player with the Portland Symphony, who'd killed herself at the age of twenty-four. Charlie, coming home one night, had told her about the suicide, because she and Charlie had met the girl one afternoon downtown, with Marty Greenberg. Jaime recalled a soft little blonde girl, hanging onto Marty's arm and not saying anything, her eyes unfocused.

"Is that Marty's girlfriend?" she asked Charlie afterward. He just laughed. A month later she killed herself, blowing her brains out with a shotgun. Charlie had felt terrible, especially about laughing. "Oh, God, the things we all said about her."

Jaime had begun her story at second remove, with the main characters reacting to her suicide, then threw away what she'd written and started over with Mary at the center. If she could write about Mary from the inside, maybe Jaime could animate the enormous sympathy she felt for her, and find out by the end of the story why she'd killed herself. Of course the obvious was the obvious. She'd killed herself because she was angry. It was a revenge killing. She was the *blow* queen, she gave everybody *head*, now she would show them what it really meant.

The story had grown as she'd submerged herself in Portland memories. She had enough material, really, for a good short novel. A story about Portland, centering on Mary but not restricted to her. Fifty-six pages in, she could imagine it would run to almost two hundred. Her instinct for the stories' proportion was good by now. Today her head hurt and her stomach fluttered, but this wouldn't stop her. Writing with a hangover, pecking out the words one painful letter at a time, pausing and staring without comprehension at the words, often produced her best material. She didn't know why. Kira's mysterious absence made her sweat with anxiety, but there was nothing to do but blot out everything and write. If you ever gave in, stayed in bed, let your anxiety win, you'd end up hugging your knees in terminal terror. "I can't work! I'm going to die!" Instead she plugged away blindly, letting the words come without thought.

At some point she sat, panting, wondering what the next sentence would be, then realized she was done for the day. A light sweat covered her body. She picked up the pages she'd written. Four of them, just enough. She stood, wobbling slightly, and went into the bathroom, and there stripped off her tee shirt and underpants and got into the hot shower. Her mind was almost empty. She was shampooing her hair when she thought of Kira. Oh, shit. All the good feeling from work ran down the drain. She stood helpless under the spray, the worst mother in America. No wonder her daughter ran off, no wonder she couldn't attract a decent man. She was just an old whore without a brain.

She was dressed in her favorite blue tee shirt and jeans, sitting at her desk correcting and editing the morning pages, when Kira came in through the back door. "Hi Mom," she said, and opened the refrigerator door. Jaime's face flushed. She sat with her arms at her sides, relief and anger flooding her. Kira had obviously only been upstairs. She hadn't run away. She'd been visiting the neighbors, a couple of craftspeople, nice people, friends. If Jaime had been home, not drunk out in North Beach, she'd have known. As if to emphasize the point, her headache returned in full force. "Oh," she groaned, as Kira came into her office wearing clothes Jaime had never seen before.

"Where the hell have you been?" Jaime asked, in a gnawing, whiny voice.

"Where the hell have *you* been?" Kira asked in an unkind imitation.

"Where did you get those clothes?"

Kira posed, her arms out like a model. "You like?" She wore pale pink crushed velvet bellbottoms and an emerald green silk blouse with long puffed sleeves. "Borrowed," she said.

"You weren't here when I got home," Jaime said, and immediately regretted it.

Kira grinned at her. "When *did* you get home, Mom?" she asked.

Jaime smiled, and the episode was over. She'd failed to bawl Kira out for cutting school. Kira changed clothes and headed out the back door.

"Where are you going?" Jaime asked, though she knew.

"Back upstairs."

"You aren't bothering them, are you?" Jaime asked, as a formality. The couple upstairs liked having Kira visit.

"I'm learning how to carve," she said. Jaime listened as Kira went up the wooden staircase. What a fucking relief. Now if only the hangover would go away, her life would be back in the groove. The telephone rang. Charlie.

"What's going on?" he asked, sounding tired. Charlie was making a movie, at least he hoped he was. He'd started so many, but none had actually gotten made. "Where's Kira?"

Jaime had forgotten calling the hotel. "Oh, it's nothing," she said.

There was a pause, some crackling on the line, then Charlie said, "The desk clerk told me you asked if she was here."

"I thought she'd run off." It was hard to force words out of her mouth. Talking to Charlie put her on the defensive. She explained what she could, but Charlie hardly sounded satisfied.

"There must be something going on, if you thought she'd come down here," he said.

"Why don't you just take her?" Jaime said dryly. "How's the movie coming?"

"Fine," Charlie said with some sarcasm in his voice. "How's the book coming?"

"Fine," she said in imitation.

Charlie chuckled. "Lemme talk to Kira."

"She upstairs learning to be a craftsperson." Charlie knew and liked the second-floor neighbors.

"How are you?" Charlie said after some silence.

"Fine. Hung over."

"Did you write this morning?"

"Yeah. Did you?"

"Yeah. Well, Stan's coming over, we're gonna go out by the pool and pick up starlets."

"Give him my best."

"Tell Kira I love her."

"I will."

"G'bye."

"Bye, Charlie." She hung up. Another shower would be necessary. She held her forehead. It seemed hot. She should have known, the leather jacket was a dead giveaway. Kira wouldn't run away without taking it. Jaime decided she was losing her mind. Not dramatically, just dribbling it away.

"Brain drain," she said to no one.

81.

Kenny Goss knew Jaime's upstairs neighbors too, and spent a lot of time around their back room, smoking dope and listening to rock 'n roll. They dealt some of the best marijuana in San Francisco. At the moment they were dispensing purple sensemilla from Santa Barbara, at twenty dollars an ounce, worth every cent so far as Kenny was concerned. He'd tried importing marijuana himself but the whole deal had gone terribly bad, and Kenny had found himself, at three in the morning, lying face up on the San Bernardino

Freeway as traffic whizzed past. His car was somewhere nearby, upside down, after a brush with a truckful of people. Kenny lay waiting to be crushed. He was alert, and knew he'd die any second now. He'd given up on religion long ago, yet the Virgin Mary seemed to hang above him in midair, about ten feet above him if he was any judge. She just hung there, parallel to the ground, wearing a white robe, with a blue shawl edged in gold over her head and shoulders.

"Get up," she said to him. Cars whizzed past. "Get up and walk to the side of the road," she said in a clear calm voice.

"I don't believe in you," Kenny said.

"Get up and walk to the side of the road," she said, and vanished. Kenny stood up and walked to the side of the road. There was a lot of traffic for this time of the morning. Here was his car, upside down, steam rising from the engine. And here came red lights flashing. Kenny walked down off the roadway and hid in the bushes. He wasn't hurt, just bruised and a little dazed. When the cops started looking for him with flashlights he moved off, and finally found his way to a truck stop. It took him most of the day to find the CHP garage, where his car had been towed. He identified himself to the guy on duty and said he wanted to get his stuff out of the car. This took a little nerve, and Kenny was jangly as he went to his car, which was a total wreck. But he'd stored under the fenders two socks full of marijuana, about a pound. If the cops had found the stuff, he was walking into a trap. But he had every dime he owned tied up in the goddamned stuff, and he meant to have it. By some miracle it was still where he'd hidden it. Without glancing around, he pulled out the two fat socks and put them into the paper bag with his dirty underwear. Carrying his stuff he nodded and said thanks to the guy who held the big cyclone fence open for him. After walking two blocks with his heart in his mouth, he relaxed. They weren't coming after him. It was while sitting on the bus for San Francisco, possessions on his lap, that he remembered seeing the Virgin Mary. A visual hallucination?

"Thanks anyway," he said to no one in particular, and decided to get out of the dope business. Except, of course, as a consumer. Which led to the upstairs flat on Seventeenth Street. It was an amazing coincidence to find Jaime and Kira living downstairs, amazing and delightful. Their lives kept weaving together. Maybe it meant something.

Kenny's own marriage had not worked out. Not Brenda's fault. She'd apparently been waiting all her life for some man to come along, marry her, impregnate her every year or so, and beat the hell out of her to keep her in line. Otherwise nothing worked. Brenda would be cool and calm, the perfect housewife, and then she'd go crazy. Kenny worked at home, both his writing and his small rare book business, so he was around all the time, except when scouting books. Their apartment had been on Pine Street, between Leavenworth and Jones. Not a great neighborhood, but the place was cozy, three floors up, and Kenny felt comfortable. He had four children's books out and they all brought in nice regular money, not a lot, but enough for Kenny to able to relax and let his wife stay home. This was fine with Brenda, but after she'd done all the cleaning and washing and vacuuming she felt the time heavy on her hands, and so would start drinking beer. Ninety percent of the time even this was fine. Kenny would be in his little cubbyhole writing or dealing with his books and she'd be in the kitchen, sitting at the table with the radio on, drinking beer and reading the paper. But sometimes she got lonely or something, and would come and talk to him. Not just talk, but talk and talk and talk, the words tumbling out like a mountain stream over granite boulders, or so he ironically told himself as he endured the torrent. Not just words, hard words. Brenda Feeney Goss was a Catholic girl, and she wanted her babies. "Listen, if it's not my fault it's your fault, and if it's not your fault I don't know whose fault it is, but somebody's got to be at fault," and on and on until he wanted to slap her silly, no, what he really wanted was to ball his fist and smash her face, breaking teeth, hearing her nose snap, seeing the blood gush. Oh boy. What a horrible soul. If there was such a horrible thing. Immortal soul. Stuck with the same personality forever. Thanks a lot, God.

Stupidly, Kenny had told Brenda all about his experience with the Virgin Mary. He was talking of the power of childhood, how the things we believe as children never really go away. She took it as a genuine miracle, and held his own faithlessness over his head. "Eternal hell, my friend," she said to him. "And you're taking me with you."

"Oh, batshit." But he had an uncomfortable feeling she was right.

"You notice the Virgin didn't say anything about the grass," she said another time, apropos of nothing. They'd both quit drinking and depended on their marijuana. But stoned she could be even worse, gliding into his cubbyhole like some gigantic cobra, hissing at him about anything she could think of. Never anything important. Kenny told her every which way he could that he was an easy-going guy, but you just had to leave him alone when he was trying to work.

"Work? You call that work?" All real work was done with a pick and a shovel, as far as she was concerned. "You can call it work if you want, but it ain't work." Contemptuous laughter bubbled out of her.

"Then how come they pay me for it?"

"Because you're a criminal!" she yelled. Marijuana was supposed to cool you out, but apparently it had the opposite effect on Brenda.

He could have put up with the interruptions if she'd loved him. She didn't. Once they were married she made it clear she found sex disgusting, except as a means of reproducing. They only real fun they had sexually had been while drunk or stoned. Then afterward she'd be relentlessly guilty. She wasn't a good Catholic, either. She never went to Mass. Quite an irony for Kenny, because when Brenda finally did leave him, she ran away with a priest.

For months Kenny was depressed, though not so depressed he couldn't write. When he sold his fourth book he moved to a flat on Arguello, a nice big one with two bedrooms, just in case he found a woman he could really love. He decorated the place himself, spending careful weeks going through the stock over on Clement Street and down at Busvan on the Embarcadero, picking out old wooden pieces and some very nice Oriental rugs pretty cheap. He kept the new place immaculate, nothing like his bachelor pads in the past. With Brenda gone he felt like he could safely go back to drinking beer, and did.

Upstairs over Jaime's was a good place to meet women, but not the marrying kind, or even the dating kind. The unapproachable kind. The rich and beautiful kind. The Pogozis catered to the high rollers, rich young rock 'n rollers, rich young craftspeople, with nothing to do but try on jewelry and smoke dope. Karla Pogozi made jewelry out of 24-karat gold, heavy necklaces and earrings, while her husband, Vili, carved small animals and hash pipes out of ivory and rare woods. At any time of the day or night there were bound to be people up there, sitting around the back room. A great place to hang out, and Kenny did so a lot, even when he had dope at home. The company was always pleasant, the dope wonderful, the music hot. And the women who came through were delicious, in their leathers and silks. Too bad they were all taken. And too bad Kenny didn't make enough money to afford them. But he had to be optimistic. He was a good-looking guy. Maybe one would adopt him.

82.

The trouble with writing about Portland was that Jaime had been happier then, as she remembered it. No matter that her life now was carefully arranged the way she wanted it. In Portland they'd been young and full of their own power, with their raffish old house in Lake Grove, their bright young friends, the painters and writers and dreamers of Portland. And Kira had been a baby. It had all seemed so easy.

She found herself losing track of why she'd chosen to write about this time and these people. Not to show how wonderful everything had been, but to show how the wonderfulness must have looked to someone excluded from it. Someone who wasn't invited to the hootenannies or dancing parties, but only to blowjob dates in cars or in the back stairwells of the Portland Auditorium. Someone who learns that talent, perseverance, and desire would not be enough. You had to be beautiful or charming as well, you had to be *likable*. Jaime had always been likable, and to get inside Mary's character she had to shed her likable skin, her beauty and charm. After a while it was easy to do, and then of course the trick was to change back into herself at the end of the writing day. If she failed, she'd find herself going around all day as a mousy little girl with no confidence, waves of music passing through her mind, blocking out rational thought. The music was part of the process. Jaime always liked to have music playing softly in the background as she wrote, to block other sounds and sweeten her mood. Usually jazz, coming over the radio from KJAZ, but writing Mary's story she played only classical music, Bach, Haydn, and Mozart. Mary was a little snob, Jaime decided affectionately. She had her integrity. She found Beethoven a little blowsy and romantic. Haydn was her ideal.

The routine was simple. No matter what time she got home the night before, get up at six or six thirty. Slip into her gray sweatsuit and sneakers, awaken Kira, then walk across Park Presidio to the hidden entrance to Mountain Lake Park, through to its Fifth Avenue exit, then down Fifth to Clement, west on Clement to Seventeenth, and back to her flat. A two-mile walk, begun in sullen mindlessness and ending in cheerful anticipation of the workday. To avoid losing the cheer she'd take the paper inside unopened, leaving it for her post-work pleasure. If Kira wasn't up yet she'd rouse her and make tea. Other times Kira already had the water boiling. They spoke little at this hour, Kira groggy with sleep and Jaime already turning into Mary Rosendaal. Kira never asked what she was writing. So far as Jaime knew, her daughter had never read any of her work. Though it would have been in character for Kira to read the stuff secretly and say nothing. Normal enough, but Jaime wanted Kira to admire her. To tell Jaime she loved her writing, that she knew her work was important and understood why her mother was so strange. Apparently they weren't close enough for this kind of talk, and Jaime wouldn't force it on her. Bad enough that she'd wrecked their family life.

Kira at fifteen looked more like eighteen or nineteen, ripe and ready to plunder, one of the reasons Jaime didn't bring men home. Her daughter was beautiful, but not the kind of beauty that translates into modeling jobs or wealthy marriages, more the beauty of youth. The kind which as she grew older would turn into handsomeness and character. Jaime hoped. She hardly wanted her daughter to be a model or actress. She most particularly didn't want her daughter to be casually seduced by one of her literary friends. Or God forbid marry one of the bastards. So she saw people not at home but at Enrico's or Tosca, though who even knew if Kira was still a virgin? Or had herpes. Or clap.

This got into *The French Horn Player*. The character became Jaime's second daughter, someone Jaime had known since birth, someone she'd protect with her life. Jaime often cried as she wrote, knowing that no matter what she did, no matter how well she loved her soft little Mary, she'd also have to kill her. At times she sat desperately wishing for a way out for Mary Rosendaal. But there could be no way out. The book was begun to show a certain hard truth, and she couldn't back out now, just because it was breaking her heart. Poor fucking Mary Rosendaal, moving slowly toward death.

She had another task in managing the difference between the real Marty Greenberg and the character she required for her story. The real Marty Greenberg had reappeared a while before, while she was still married to Charlie. She'd run into him at Tosca's, and they sat drinking cappuccinos and talking about the I–Thou philosophy of Martin Buber, one of Marty's heroes. Their final parting came when Marty put his hand on Jaime's exposed knee and gave it a meaningful squeeze. "We should make love," he said, smiling sincerely into her eyes.

She pushed his hand away. "Really? Why?"

"Everyone should make love with everyone. That is the true I–Thou."

She learned later Marty had tried this I–Thou shit on most of the women he knew, and some of the men. Kenny Goss had been scandalized by it. His former shipmate from the *Breckenridge* had made a pass at him. "Get the clouds out of your mind," Marty had said to Kenny. "Love is love."

Marty then moved to Berkeley, and Jaime hadn't seen him since. She fought not to wreck the character with her personal feelings. The book required that she show Marty as a nice person, a good person, bright, friendly, everything he ought to be except compassionate. More and more her book was about coldness. And the meaning of words. Words like "blow job."

So Marty the philosopher must turn into Marty the pimp, without at the same time losing any of his charm. An intricate literary problem. She hoped her unconscious would solve it.

83.

She might not bring one home, but Jaime was looking for another man. She hadn't given up on herself. She wasn't necessarily after a husband, just some guy to hang onto, talk to, think about, have. She was thirty-five, and lonely too much. There were plenty of males around but very few men. On the worst days, writing *The French Horn Player* and drinking heavily, she'd stay home with the television on, wrapped in a bathrobe with a towel around her head, no point in dressing since she wasn't fooling anyone, just trying to decide whether or not to kill herself, she'd fantasize about deliberately finding some rich guy to marry. Some sucker who loved her for her work.

> *Dear Miss Froward,*
> *I am writing to tell you how much I enjoy your writing, especially* Washington Street, *although I have read and enjoyed all your books. Please keep up the good work! I work here in K.C. for Hallmark, the greeting card company. I write some of those little verses you see in greeting cards, so we are fellow professionals in a way, although of course I do not think of myself as a creative writer. I come to S.F. from time to time and would like to invite you for lunch at some future time. If this is an imposition I apologize, but if not please let me know. Thank you,*
> *Sincerely,*
> *Charles Drakeman*

Unfortunately, Charles didn't include a photograph and a copy of his D & B report. She wrote a nice polite little note thanking him but making no mention of the lunch proposal. There really was no legitimate way to meet men. Her parents had met at a meeting of the Youth Labor Brigade in Berkeley, back when the communists were trying to recruit high school kids by throwing beer busts. A socialist in dirty spectacles and wool pullover? No, not for Jaime. Not after Charlie. Charlie had been a wonderful husband in many ways, even if he'd failed to deliver. Really, he'd never represented himself as more than he was, she'd just seen him that way, a beautiful youthful giant, full of promise. Who'd turned into a clown before her eyes.

She thought about marrying another writer, or an artist, but they were worse than socialists. At literary parties the single ones kept their distance, while it was the married writers who made passes at her. Or would respond when she made a pass. Strange? Maybe not. Maybe the single writers were single for a reason. Either they were gay or they didn't know what they were. Honest straightforward single heterosexuals were rare.

It was at the book parties at Minerva's Owl Bookstore on Union that society and literature came together. If you were a local author and you weren't asked to have a signing party there you might as well kill yourself. Jaime was invited no matter who the author was. She liked the informal gatherings in the narrow little shop, and especially liked it when one or another of the local society hostesses would quietly circulate through the crowd whispering of another party elsewhere, for the select. These later parties, usually at somebody's house in Pacific Heights, were fun because you were mingling with the rich, who were, you had to admit, charming and pleasant people. Parties led to parties and the next thing you knew your name was in the society column of the *Chronicle*. Yet nobody was fooled. These people knew who was society and who wasn't. She told herself she went only to meet men. Perhaps some rich developer or scion of the gold-fields would take her out of this misery and put her into a house on the hill. Jaime kept hoping for that rich fool who was also big and handsome. God damn Charlie anyway.

It was at the tail end of a party at Minerva's Owl that she met Torry. Actually, she'd missed the party. It was one of those rainswept nights, and Jaime had had the usual hard time finding a parking place. She parked so far away she had to stop at Perry's up the block to dry off, go to the toilet, and have three drinks. By the time she was coming in the door of Minerva's Owl Torvald Hetter was coming out. He'd published on novel a few years ago, a brilliant small novel about three fishermen lost in the Sierra. A book without women, and hailed as some kind of macho masterpiece. Jaime had hated it immediately without reading it. Then one day at a friend's house she saw a paperback copy lying on the floor and picked it up, read a couple of sentences, and was immediately lost in admiration. She borrowed the book and took it home, planning to find its weaknesses and be properly scornful of this one-book author who'd become famous so fast. But the book was a poem. Every word mattered. Jaime always corrected books as she read them, but there was nothing here to correct, and Jaime found herself profoundly moved by the fate of these three very ordinary men. She still hated the author for being so famous and so good, but when she found herself face-to-face with him, she grinned in his face like an idiot and said, drunkenly, "Hey, you're Torry Hetter."

"I am?" He smiled down at her with both recognition and lust. He wasn't as tall as Charlie, but his narrow face was classically handsome, big eyes, heavy lids, a long straight nose and lips neither full nor thin, but just right. She watched his beautiful mouth say, "Let's get out of here," and turned right around, feeling his hand on her elbow as they walked out into the rain and down Union, side-by-side, not speaking.

Jaime wasn't quite drunk, but she wanted to be. She'd already made up her mind to sleep with Torry if he made a pass. At her house, if necessary. Jaime's bedroom was in the front of the apartment, and Kira's in the back. They'd whisper, and Kira wouldn't have to hear a thing.

"You want to stop in here?" he asked. They stood in front of Perry's. The place was packed and noisy, the entryway packed, drinkers standing out on the sidewalk, even in the rain.

"No." She looked at him inquiringly. If he was a real man he'd know that she was his for the asking, no drink, no chatter, just jump right into bed. His eyebrows raised slightly, his face asking her if it was really true, and without moving a muscle Jaime's face said yes, it is true, and he touched her hand. Next thing they were in his car fucking. His book had not been a lie. He was a real man. He drove her to her car and let her out.

"I could follow you home," he said through the window, as the rain hit his face, and she knew he had somebody else.

"Not now," she said, completely sober. She told him her telephone number and he nodded as if he'd memorized it. But he didn't tell her his.

"I'll call you," he said, and drove off. His car was an old wreck, a Chevy or something. The inside had smelled like old socks and stale lunches. It reminded her of the smell of school lockers. So he had no money. And only one book out. She'd heard he was unable to write, but elsewhere that he'd written a huge second novel all about life somewhere, but had it rejected. She didn't care. The lovemaking had been intense. She told herself she hadn't fallen in love, thank God, but knew she wanted more of the sex. She knew she'd call him, but before she did she wanted to know more. Who did he live with? Was he merely afraid to bring Jaime home to a dump, or was he just making sure things were on his terms?

At home she tried to find a copy of his novel, but couldn't. It was eleven thirty. She drank a glass of wine to calm her nerves, and was about to go to bed when the telephone rang. She knew it was Torry.

"What took you so long?" she purred into the telephone. His answering chuckle was thrilling.

"Can I come over?"

"Wait a minute," she said. She went down the hall and opened Kira's door. Kira sat up in bed carving a piece of wood with a knife. Curled bits of wood were scattered all over the quilt. Kira looked up from her work. "Hello," she said.

"I thought you were asleep," Jaime said.

"Are we having company?"

"It's late, go to sleep." Jaime closed the door. Over the telephone she said, "Not tonight."

84.

Torry couldn't get enough of her. But after that first time, only in the afternoon. Jaime knew he lived with somebody, that was obvious, though Torry said nothing about it. She didn't care. She told herself she was in love with him because of his beautiful body and because he didn't like to talk much. A perfect combination. She daydreamed about him, about making love to him, about the way the light struck his skin. They couldn't meet at Jaime's because of Kira, and they couldn't meet at his place, and so they got in the habit of checking into the Pacific Manor motel on Broadway, a few steps west of Grant and Columbus, and conveniently close to Yank Sing, where they'd meet to drink tea and eat plate after plate of dim sum.

Torry loved to eat, yet his body was slim and muscular. She loved it as she'd loved Charlie's body before he got soft and fat. Well, not that fat, just too fat for Jaime. Torry could drink beer all day, eat three or four big meals, and still look like a racing dog. Would his metabolism some day make a little shift and boom, he'd be two hundred and fifty pounds? Probably not. Sometimes Mother Nature was deliberately unfair. Torry was one of those men who always looked hungry, and women would always want to feed him a bowl of soup or take him to bed.

After a few weeks of keeping her ears open, Jaime knew Torry was a kept man. The woman who kept him was herself married, to a gay husband who had young men running in and out of their Presidio Heights mansion, while all of high society pretended it wasn't happening. She gathered that in spite of his macho image, Torry feared his society woman learning about Jaime and throwing him out, forcing him to fend for himself in a cruel world. Torry's book had done well, was never out of print, and had been translated into a dozen languages. The Japanese edition was used in Japanese schools to teach English, which made Jaime squirm with envy. Brautigan told her, at Enrico's one night. "Every time I go to Japan people ask me about Torry-san," he said. Richard himself sold well in Japan, and he'd go out only with Japanese women these days. "I tell them Torry-san is working well."

He wasn't. This fact, among so many others about Torry-san, should have made Jaime draw back, but instead drew her closer. Poor fucking Torry. He got up every morning in his mystery apartment in the Mission, sat down at his desk, and wrote his heart out. Eleanor Plinckerd, his society woman, was his remorseless editor. Torry turned out page after page in his tiny precise handwriting, using a fountain pen, and then Eleanor would read the work quietly, her fingernail tapping the paper, her lips pursed, her brow furrowed. "She's the best editor I ever met," he said one afternoon. "She won't let me get away with anything." Eleanor had high standards, at least so far as literature was concerned. Her father had inherited a love of literature from his own father, as well as a gigantic wad of money, and Eleanor was keeping up the tradition. Her father had met James Joyce and had a signed copy of *Ulysses*.

"Oh, what's his writing like?" Jaime asked. "Drunken scrawl?"

"I've never seen it," Torry said with an ironic smile. "I've never been in their house."

She'd been sexually fascinated, right up to the instant it became obvious he needed her more than she needed him. "What a bitch I am," she thought often. Now it was his hunger for her that drove the relationship, and now he spoke freely of Eleanor. Who'd gone to Radcliffe, which was practically Harvard, spoke French and Italian, and had at one time been quite good-looking, or so Jaime had heard. Looking at her picture in the *Chronicle* Jaime would have guessed she was at least fifty, but these women often had face-lifts and tucks and touch-ups, so you couldn't really tell their age. Until one day they quietly collapse into a pile of dust. That she must have been years older than Torry gave Jaime some satisfaction, though not much. Eleanor wasn't her rival, she reminded herself. Jaime simply had to consider herself the mistress of the kept man of the rich lady whose husband was a queen. *At last I am part of society,* she told herself.

Society wasn't getting her anyplace. She wrote nothing that lasted more than a page and a half, then to be torn up in anger or slipped into the wastebasket with a sigh. Torry's work, if you could call it that, consisted these days of getting up in the morning, drinking cup after cup of coffee, then falling into a gloom. He brightened only when he saw Jaime, who was beginning to feel like the Salvation Army. Then one day he didn't show up.

Jaime wasn't permitted to call, in case you-know-who was there. She had always to wait for him to call and apologize, beg her to see him. Not this time. Jaime finally learned from the *Chronicle* that Torvald Hetter was in Cannes for the film festival. In the same day's society column she read that Mr. and Mrs. E. Stanton Plinckerd were in Cannes for the film festival. Little surprise there. But she hadn't expected to feel so bad. She spent about three days in a deep depression until, standing at the refrigerator opening a container of kefir, her story about Mary Bergendaal flooded back into her, and the pain slowly went away. Mary was a lot more interesting than Torry anyway. At least Mary didn't whine.

Jaime half-expected to see Torry at Enrico's this particular Friday. The Cannes festival was over. Torry didn't hang out at Enrico's but he knew Jaime made a religion of Fridays, and would calculate this as a good public place to run into her. Jaime dreaded it, but she'd hardly forego her lunch with friends just because that weakling coward sniveling hungry-looking wretch might appear to beg her forgiveness. She was right, intuition had served her well. Torry sat at the bar, over by the cigarette machine, looking through the glass at the people seated outside. The place was crowded, the day sunny, and Jaime almost walked right past Charlie, who sat at an outside table grinning and squinting up at her.

"Hi, baby," he said.

85.

"Just a sec," Jaime said, her mind suddenly empty. "I'll get a drink at the bar and be right back." Charlie was sitting with people she didn't even look at. She walked into the bar and faced Torry. She meant to say hello and sit down, but instead said, "Where the hell have you been?" and all but put her hands on her hips like an angry housewife. Torry looked mildly shocked. People sat near, obviously listening. Bob the bartender leaned over the bar, listening. "I'll have a kir," she said to Bob.

"I had a sudden emergency," Torry said with his crooked smile. He'd try to use irony to get out of it. The truth was, his pretense of being in love with her, being obsessed with her, was in ruins over a free trip to Cannes. "You little whore," she couldn't keep from saying. Maybe Charlie gave her the courage, who knew? Torry's face went out of control for a moment, but only a moment. Then he managed a smile.

"Okay," he said. "Say what you want."

"I have to go sit with my husband," she said, and went outside. She felt in a fury of clarity. There were no chairs. The sidewalk was full of well-dressed people yapping and eating. Jaime signaled to Kenny the waiter, who rushed inside and rushed back out with a chair for her. She sat beside Charlie, her back to the bar. "Thank you, Kenny," she said. She smiled at Charlie and the three men sitting with him. One of them was Kenny Goss, she realized with a little shock. "Oh, hi, Kenny," she said, and laughed. "Too many Kennys around here." She smiled at the other two men, waiting for Charlie to introduce her. They were both smiling, but one of them was smiling more than politely. "Good God," she said.

"Hi, Jaime," Stan Winger said. His eyes were shining. He reached across the table for her hand. They'd said hello a couple of times on the telephone, but this was the first she'd laid eyes on him since Oregon. He looked remarkably different, tanned, gray hair at his temples, a massive gold watch on his wrist. His hand was warm and dry. His eyes strong. All traces of the sad unformed kid she'd known were gone.

"Prison seems to have done you good," she said with a small smile. Stan laughed, and after a second, so did the others.

"Yes, prison makes a man of you," Stan said. "If it doesn't make a woman of you first." Everybody laughed, including people at nearby tables. Or maybe they were laughing at jokes of their own. She casually turned her head, still laughing, and saw Torry glaring out through the glass.

"Jaime, this is Bud Fishkin," Charlie said, and she turned to face the man sitting on her left. He was darkly handsome, with big dark eyes and an easy smile.

"I love your work." He took her hand and gave a gentle but firm squeeze.

She knew from her agent that Fishkin-Ratto had turned down everything of hers they'd seen. She smiled at Fishkin without sincerity. But there was Stan grinning at her, and she had to grin back. "You look great," she said.

"You too."

"We're up here pitching our movie," Charlie said proudly. He put his big hand on her shoulder familiarly, and she felt the old Charlie electricity pass through her. He still had his touch, she thought, and suddenly felt very good. This was not only the best possible revenge on Torry, here was Stan Winger, somebody she really did like.

They chatted and opened their menus. "On Fishkin-Ratto, eat expensive," said Fishkin. As they sat discussing what to order, Torry came out and walked past Jaime, touching her on the shoulder as he moved out onto the sidewalk and out of sight.

"Who was that?" Charlie asked. Jaime had a sudden image of Charlie knocking the shit out of Torry. "Torvald Hetter," she said. "He wrote *Lost in Heaven?*"

"Jesus Christ," Stan said. "My favorite book." He looked at Jaime and laughed. "By a man."

"That book's been turned around three times," Fishkin said. "Every time there's a new head of Universal. Five or six screenplays, including two by Torry. Nobody can solve the damn thing."

"It's too simple," Stan said.

Jaime knew Torry had been driven crazy by Hollywood. They romanced him, flew him places to talk to famous directors or stars who wanted to play his macho men, and of course there'd been plenty of option money. But never a movie, never Big Casino.

"What's the big problem?" Kenny asked, as usual the quietest at the table. He'd addressed Stan, but Bud Fishkin answered.

"No girls in the picture," he said.

"And no guns," Stan said.

"And nobody dies," Bud said.

"Yet the book keeps on selling, all over the world," Fishkin said. "I was in Paris the other day, in a bookstore, and there it was, a big stack of 'em."

"It must break Hollywood's heart, not being able to cash in on it," Charlie said seriously, but there was a twinkle in his eye.

"It breaks *my* heart," Fishkin said honestly, and Jaime decided she liked him. She'd been hearing about this slick bastard for years, but now found him charming. Maybe that was how he did it. Now that Torry had stamped out in a rage, this was going to be a nice Friday.

The movie they were trying to get financed hadn't actually been written yet. Just a twenty-nine-page treatment, written by Stan and Charlie one marathon weekend. Stan had a house in the Hollywood Hills with a swimming pool, and the two of them sat around the pool drinking Dos Equis, eating McDonald's double cheeseburgers, and throwing ideas around. They thought they had a hot story, about a couple of Toledo, Ohio, working-class brothers who get drunk, rob a bank, and run for Las Vegas, where they win big only to have the hookers strip them of all the money in a single night. Then they go back to Toledo and their old lives. The working title was *The Big Runaround*, but nobody liked it. All the majors had passed, so they were up here talking to upstart producers like Fantasy and Zoetrope. They'd had their morning meeting with Fred Roos of Zoetrope, and were headed to Fantasy that afternoon, and would be on the plane back to Hollywood that night.

"I hoped you'd be here," Charlie said to Jaime.

"Why didn't you call me?" she asked. He just grinned and shrugged.

"When are you gonna come to Los Angeles?" Stan asked her.

"It would take a million dollars," she said, and smiled at Fishkin.

He laughed and said, "If I have anything to do with it," and let it go at that. Lunch broke up at two thirty. They had to be over in Berkeley at Fantasy at four. As they stood and said confused good-byes, Charlie looked down at her and said, "Can I see you tonight?"

Seeing Charlie upset her, though it shouldn't have. "I thought you were flying back," she said.

"I'd rather stay." He took her hands. Stan and Fishkin stood nearby. Was he doing this for show?

"No," she said, and immediately felt bad. His face creased and aged as she watched. Charlie was losing some hair, but it made him handsomer, she thought. His beard was shot with gray and suddenly she noticed the shine of contact lenses on his eyes. Charlie was getting old.

"Okay," he said quietly, and let go of her hands.

Stan was less gentle. He grabbed her in a big hug and said into her ear, "You saved my life. Up in Oregon. I'll never forget that." He pulled back and looked at her, his face suffused with love. "Thank you," he said.

"Stan," she said, and tears came to her eyes.

"I'm really glad to have met you," Bud Fishkin said with a warm grasp of her hand. "I'm gonna look into a few things. Who's your agent?"

"Ziegler-Ross," she said. She wanted to add, "Don't forget," but didn't. Not a bad guy. And then they were gone. She went into the bar and sat next to the cigarette machine. The place was almost empty, just a couple of drunks at the other end of the bar and some other drunks at tables, too drunk to go back to work, she supposed. She very badly wanted a Lemon Hart and orange, but ordered a kir instead. One Lemon Hart would be the equivalent of five kirs. So she had a lot of drinking to do.

The End

Finishing Carpenter: An Afterword

Part of my job as a clerk at Berkeley's great used bookstore Moe's, in the early 1990s, was to scour the massive wall of fiction and confront the books that weren't selling. Out of all the staff I claimed this task because it interested me the most, and because it suited my vanity to be able to claim that "I run the lit section." Codes, written in pencil and discretely tucked into the corner opposite the asking price, revealed when a given title had hit the shelf. After six or eight months you reduced the price. Once it had been knocked down a couple of times, two options remained: chuck the book into the pile of discards under the staircase or take it home and read it. *A Couple of Comedians*, with its great title and Norman Mailer blurb, got me to flip it open. When right there in the stacks I was met with Don Carpenter's punchy prose, and with his grabby, wry, and humane outlook, I took the book home. I read it. I loved it. I looked downstairs, in our pocket-size paperback stacks, and found a copy of *Hard Rain Falling*, Carpenter's first novel, repackaged with a Tom of Finland–style painting and corresponding jacket copy to sell as "gay lit" ("The hard-hitting novel of a young street tough and his inevitable journey toward prison—and self-knowledge . . ."). I read *Hard Rain Falling* and thought it made two masterpieces in a row. The suggestion given by the dust jackets of the two books—and the move from the Northern California bildungsroman of *Hard Rain Falling* to the entertainment industry hijinks of comedians, was of a writer who, failing to sustain a literary career, had migrated to Hollywood and was, all too typically, never heard from again.

My next move—a compulsive one, for me, when I discovered an out-of-print writer—was to go to Peter Howard's Serendipity Books, a legendary Borges-like physical compendium of seemingly every book ever published, which happened to be just down the street from my house. You could call my visit the equivalent, nowadays, of "googling." At Serendipity, sure enough, I found a run of all of Carpenter's early books, including an autographed copy of *Blade of Light* I purchased and still own. I also found the three late-1980s books published by Jack Shoemaker's North Point Press. Carpenter, from the evidence, had not only survived Hollywood, but was alive and writing and living nearby. After I'd read a few more of the books, I flirted with the idea of finding my way up to Marin and presenting myself to Carpenter as his "biggest fan" ("and I run the lit section!"). It appeared that finding him might not require more than puttering around Mill Valley's central square for a few hours and poking my head into a coffee shop or two. I didn't manage this, whether for the better or worse I'm spared knowing. In 1995 came word that the sixty-four-year-old Carpenter, who'd been suffering a host of illnesses that severely restricted his ability to work, had killed himself.

Though I wasn't actually alone in my admiration, it took a while for Carpenter's scattered constituency to discover one another. For years he was "in print" only in as the protagonist of a few anecdotes in—and as the dedicatee of—Annie Lamott's talismanic writer's handbook, *Bird by Bird*. George Pelecanos and I each advocated for *Hard Rain Falling* to Edwin Frank at the *New York Review of Books*, and when it was published in their reprint series, with a Pelecanos introduction, it gave occasion for tributes from fans like Ken Tucker and Charles Taylor and Sarah Weinman, readers familiar with Carpenter's other books, and with his great screenplay, *Payday*. For all of us, Carpenter, though difficult to categorize and never famous in his own day, was a writer who mattered, one who not only wouldn't go away, but grew more significant in memory. This in turn encouraged those who were caretakers of a substantial unpublished manuscript—Shoemaker, and Carpenter's daughter

Bonnie—to reexamine the case for publication, after a nearly forty-year time-out. That's where this more specific story of *Fridays at Enrico's* begins.

When asked by Shoemaker if I'd weigh in on the "unfinished" manuscript that had been supplied him by the estate, I felt exhilarated and trepidatious. Even a single additional paragraph of Carpenter felt like a gift, but what if the book wasn't good, or wasn't good enough? Plenty of writers slide toward the end, and though I was grateful for the existence of Carpenter's last few books, they weren't exactly the ones I was prone to obsessively rereading, or recommending to others. Then again, who would I be, to presume to recommend against publication? I'm a fan of scraps, fragments, letters, any trace of a writer I admire; I like *The Castle* and *The Crack-Up* and *Edwin Drood*. Still, it might be perverse to follow the rediscovery of *Hard Rain Falling* with something marginal. Not while the terrific Hollywood novels, and others that Carpenter had deemed ready, and which had been embraced by readers, if too few, remained out of print.

My concerns were misplaced. I'll leave it for others to rate *Fridays at Enrico's* amid Carpenter's best—I'm too far inside this book now to play the role of its evaluator as well—but from page one the manuscript cast me as an appreciative reader, not a triage nurse. The voice was in place, the architecture solid, Carpenter's wily purposes well-enacted throughout. It had a fine ending, too. Knowing the book existed, that Carpenter had pulled it off, whether destined to be published or not, made the world a slightly but crucially bigger place. I told Shoemaker I thought he should publish, and that I'd do what was necessary. The chance to flatter myself by coming in like Mariano Rivera in the ninth was irresistible.

I retyped the whole book, wanting to get Carpenter's syntax into my body, to trust myself with anything I changed. More than anything, I took stuff out. Carpenter's unedited draft restated certain motifs, making preliminary gestures in an early chapter for effects he'd carried through in later pages, so I deleted the preliminary gestures. He used the word "but" too much, and his characters "grinned" or were "grinning" far too often—they still probably grin too often, but I did what I could. Some things I took out only to put back in: an apparently irrelevant bit of business with a parking attendant, for instance, turned out to set up a writer's inspiration for a story a few pages later. Carpenter was subtle. Among his subtleties was a restriction of the book's vocabulary, which, despite seeming repetitive at times, gave the novel a certain humble integrity, bringing the voice into the range of the characters and their world. I'd only wreck it if I tried to impose variations. Four or five chapters I needed to turn inside out—they'd begun on the wrong foot, but the right foot was waiting, a page or two in, for me to bring forward. Against what I removed I added just a few passages, covering some missing transitions, the odd inexplicable lapse or two. There might be five or eight pages of my writing in this book, but I'd like to think you'd never guess which, should you bother even to care. Mostly, to be truthful, this was a job of data entry: the book proved itself right by the way it *refused* to be altered, moving through my fingers, as a house might prove itself sound by being lived in awhile.

Fridays at Enrico's is a book about writers, lots of them. But it never feels insular, because none of the characters, even those who publish, effectively inject themselves into any "literary" milieu. They remain outsiders and strivers, defined by their struggles even to believe they can lay claim to this calling, let alone turn it into some kind of career. In their estrangement simultaneously from the lives of common working folk yet also from any exalted or precious notions of living the life of an "artist"—and in the way they mediate their estrangement through drinking—Carpenter's characters recall those of Richard Yates. This may partly be a matter of simple realism in the depiction of certain lives that were being lived in the 1950s and 1960s, but as a final statement this book reminds me specifically of Yates's own, the underrated *Young Hearts Crying* (admittedly a book cursed with one of the worst titles going). Of course there were twisty little ironies attendant in rewriting a manuscript that concerned not only writers writing manuscripts, but writers being rewritten by editors and feeling bitterly betrayed by the results. The task even had the power to make me self-conscious of my typing habits, so keenly does Carpenter attend to this now-retro feature of his characters' avocation (there's also an important learning-to-type scene in Carpenter's second novel, *A Blade of Light*). I hadn't retyped an entire manuscript since one of my own in the early 1990s. It's a good habit, one I may have to resurrect.

Of course, this book's writers, like Carpenter himself, were estranged from the literary establishment in a way Richard Yates could never have conceived: by three thousand miles of incomprehension. In a tender and revealing reminiscence of his close friend Richard Brautigan, called "My Brautigan: A Portrait from Memory," Carpenter wrote, "Over the years (our) walks and talks got to be more and more about what Richard called the East Coast Literary Mafia. Richard's work was known and respected all over the world, in many languages, but somehow he could seldom get a good review in America. He made the whole thing into an East vs. West issue, which maybe it was and maybe it wasn't." The tone is typical Carpenter, compassionate, and worldly without being cynical. The West Coast traditionally celebrated in American letters is an allegorical one, encoding Manifest Destiny, presenting the place as an existential testing ground for notions of utopia and self-reinvention, even if only to expose the bankruptcy of those prospects. Raymond Chandler, Nathanael West, Ken Kesey, the Beats, even Brautigan himself can be understood on these terms (ironically, it's a fundamentally *Eastern* view of the West). The California in Don Carpenter's books, whether Northern or Southern, and the settings in Portland, Oregon, reveal something simpler but in some ways stranger to consider. Carpenter writes as someone who knows the West as a real geography, with a culture of its own, a place to live out the usual quandaries of existence, rather than a petri dish for American Destiny. For that reason, too, his view of the writer-in-Hollywood is free of the clichés that plague the genre.

Speaking of Brautigan, the suggestion has clung to *Fridays at Enrico's* that the project began for Carpenter as an attempt at a memoir of their friendship, or even a biography. I can't really see how this explains the resulting book, except that novelists frequently begin with one thing and end up with something else. Carpenter was plainly a true native of the realm of the novel, so that any portraiture or self-portraiture here—and surely there's both—has been distributed among several characters, then subsumed in the other kind of truthfulness that a novel, by its form, demands. For what it's worth, the character of Stan Winger—my favorite in the book—seems directly influenced by the life story of Malcolm Braly, the much-incarcerated author of *On the Yard*, in my opinion the other best prison novel in U.S. literature—besides *Hard Rain Falling*, that is.

Yet I have no evidence that Carpenter knew Braly personally, not that I've done much digging. I still know barely more about Carpenter's actual life story than you can learn from the dust jackets of the books, from the interstices of William Hjortsberg's encyclopedic biography of Brautigan, and from the lovely volunteer website (www.doncarpenterpage.com) maintained by the estimable and modest "Chris." It was there at the website that I discovered, in the scanned pages of a priceless 1975 interview, that Don Carpenter only ever spent a single night behind bars: "Seaside Oregon. Carrying six cans of beer down the street. Moping with an intent to gawk. That's the most jail time I've done." How, then, did Carpenter attain his extraordinarily sympathetic portraits, in *Hard Rain, Blade of Light,* and now in *Enrico's*, of the prisoner's life? The usual way: with his ear, with his curiosity, with his vulnerabilities, with his talent. In the same interview, discussing *Blade of Light*, Carpenter makes clear he sees incarceration as a baseline condition, that of selves stuck in bodies, and bodies stuck in fates: "He's inside there, and he knows he's trapped in there, just as you know you're trapped in here, see? . . . I mean, you know, we're all caught in this thing. We all wake up at three o'clock in the morning saying 'How am I gonna get out of here? . . . Can I start over? Can I do anything to be someone else?'" Consider that those were the words, in 1975, of a man who had yet to lose his health, and much of his eyesight. By the time of *Fridays at Enrico's*, it's hard not to see his portrayal of Stan Winger, locked in solitary confinement and working to set in language a vivid description of the fresh taste of a the first sip of a glass of beer, as a self-portrait of a writer in a failing body reconstituting a world of sensory pleasures from which he's increasingly barred. Similarly, near the end of *Enrico's* the female novelist Jaime Froward reflects on her apprentice days in the woods outside Portland, learning to write while caring for a new baby, days fiercely lonely and embattled as she lived through them, yet in recollection the finest she'd ever known. In the breadth of human experience imparted by this book, we're taken as near to memoir as we'd ever require from Don Carpenter, who said, "If I was able to express my views of the universe without writing fiction, I would do so." Lucky for us he couldn't.